"*The Juliet Code* has _____ ___ from one of Pepper Basham's books. Witty banter, literary references, swoony romance, and in true Grace and Freddie fashion, a delightful madcap adventure that kept me guessing. In *The Juliet Code*, Pepper has crafted a nail-biting mystery that never takes itself too seriously. She deftly weaves laugh-out-loud moments with danger, sprinkles intrigue with grace, and tosses toe-curling kisses around with abandon. *The Juliet Code* is a delight for the mind and the spirit that you don't want to miss!"

–Lynn H. Blackburn, bestselling, award-winning author of the Defend and Protect series (and the one who made her write this. Blame accepted.)

"Enchanting, witty, clever, and dare I say, positively brilliant! I had the best time sleuthing with Freddie and Grace in this entertaining mystery and uncovering the twists and turns in a plot thick with delightfully suspicious characters. I loved every second of it!"

–Natalie Walters, award-winning author of *Blind Trust*

"*The Juliet Code* is a fun mystery that takes the reader on a romp through Venice with delightful characters I won't forget. Basham's unique voice kept me smiling and riveted to the page. Don't miss this one with its splash of married romance and strong sense of place!"

–Colleen Coble, author of the Annie Peterson series

"Romantic mystery filled with my favorites: Italy, art, and Freddie and Grace. She's also won me over to kissing books. It's a mystery that would make Agatha Christie proud. I highly recommend it."

–Cara Putman, author of *Flight Risk*

A Freddie & Grace Mystery
(Book 3)

The JULIET CODE

PEPPER BASHAM

BARBOUR
PUBLISHING

A FREDDIE & GRACE MYSTERY
BOOK 1 - THE MISTLETOE COUNTESS
BOOK 2 - THE CAIRO CURSE

The Juliet Code ©2023 by Pepper Basham

Print ISBN 978–1–63609–694-0
Adobe Digital Edition (.epub) 978–1–63609–695-7

All scripture quotations, unless otherwise noted, are taken from the King James Version of the Bible.

This book is a work of fiction. Names, characters, places, and incidents are either products of the author's imagination or used fictitiously. Any similarity to actual people, organizations, and/or events is purely coincidental.

Cover Model: © Elena Alferova/Trevillion Images
Image Background: © Des Panteva/Trevillion Images

Published by Barbour Publishing, Inc., 1810 Barbour Drive, Uhrichsville, Ohio 44683, www.barbourbooks.com

Our mission is to inspire the world with the life-changing message of the Bible.

 Member of the
Evangelical Christian
Publishers Association

Printed in the United States of America.

Dedicated to Lynn Huggins Blackburn
She made me do it.
If it's a flop, blame her.

Acknowledgements

There's a lot to be said about the company we keep, and in the case of Freddie and Grace, the company is delightful and challenging all at once. I never set out to write a mystery series, and especially one where the main characters stay the same, but in *The Mistletoe Countess* the "bigness' of Grace's personality paired with the way she matched Freddie forged me into this new and exciting fictional world. I've LOVED traveling along with them and their adventures, but I've also had to push myself to learn how to write a series of books where the main characters stay the same.

As in life, our most meaningful character growth usually happens through trials and suffering, and many times the trials we face are caused by the brokenness of others impacting us. That's the case with several of the characters in this story, our darling Grace not excluded. Christians are not immune to suffering. We live in a broken world where broken things happen. But perspective changes how we see those trials, either through the lens of a helpless victim at the whims of "chance" or through the understanding that the King is on his throne and is working all things for our good and His glory. It may not feel good, seem good, or look good, but we have a very small vision in the span of eternity. The true definition of ultimate goodness can only be defined by the one being who IS goodness and sees the bigger story not just the chapter or page of our lives. We are not strong enough or faithful enough to grasp this on our own, but praise be to God, He has given us His love and His assurance that His plans for our lives will be completed, and we will find all we need and more in Him, whatever the danger…or adventure.

As with any adventure (fictional or otherwise), I am humbled and grateful to have so many wonderful people along with me on this journey. Thanks to author Lynn Huggins Blackburn who encouraged me to keep growing my skills in writing mystery and gave a strong nudge in writing this story. I sent her a possible synopsis and she was like "Okay, you HAVE to do this", so…along came *The Juliet Code*.

As usual, my little team of reader-encouragers like Joy Tiffany and Beth Erin helped keep me moving forward, despite how tough this story was to finish. Andrette Herron, Michelle Lunsford, and Deanna Peterson also joined the early reader encouragement list this time around and I'm so thankful to have them and their wonderful perspectives.

A special shoutout to authors Amanda Dykes and Natalie Walter for just being the encourager extraordinaires that they are! I am continually humbled and awed by the wonderful Christian bookish community that we have!

As with so many of my more recent books, I am grateful for my agent, Rachel McMillan, for championing these stories…and me. In return for all her hard work, she says I "pay her phone bill". :)

And, as always, I am ever grateful for my wonderful houseful of adventurers. Most of my family members may not read my books, but, boy oh boy, do they encourage my writing journey. I am so grateful to have them in my life!

And, finally, to the Master Storyteller, who works every letter in every sentence of every paragraph on every page of the story of our lives together for our good and His glory. We are in good hands in the grip of a loving Father's grace. There is peace, strength, hope, and joy in that knowledge. Have courage, dear heart, and rest in Him.

Chapter 1

Grace Percy had always dreamed of being part of a dashing pursuit of some villain; she'd just never imagined doing so in a gondola with a complete stranger.

Her darling husband, Lord Frederick Astley, had just paid the gondolier for his services to take them to the famous St. Mark's Square in Venice, when a rather unkempt man rushed past them, snatched Grace's purse, and dashed down the canal-lined street into the late afternoon crowds. Without hesitation, Frederick took off in pursuit, leaving Grace to stare for a second at the bewildered gondolier as if he knew exactly what to suggest next.

"It was the purse I recently purchased in Florence, you see?" But the older man only nodded without one ounce of recollection in his expression.

Just as Grace started to follow Frederick, a shout shook her to a stop.

"That thief stole my watch!" The call came from a towheaded man running toward them, his white jacket flapping behind him. "And he won't get away with it. Not on my watch."

A faint twinkle lit his eyes as the man slid to a stop in front of Grace, whether from his pun or some other mischief, Grace had no idea. Nor did she have time to consider. For not only did the man have an American accent, which distracted her already, but he made a rather impressive vault from the pier onto *her* gondola. Truthfully, he had beautiful athleticism, and she would have said so if the stranger hadn't begun untying the gondola with what appeared to be an intent of stealing the vehicle she and Frederick had just hired.

"A minute, sir," she called, stumbling forward onto the shifting little boat. "My husband and I already paid for this gondola, and I will not have you—"

"Take the next one," interrupted the stranger, and with a little jerk, the gondola moved away from the pier.

Heat rose into Grace's face as she reached for the single oar in the man's hand. Athletic or not, she would not condone another thievery. "Release your hold on this gondola or I shall have this very fine gondolier expel you himself."

The astonished gondolier unleashed some exclamation in Italian at the same time the American tugged the oar from Grace's grip. With a huff, she snatched it back, only to have the little tug-of-war result in the oar rising skyward, efficiently knocking her hat from her head before giving the poor gondolier a wallop hard enough to send him, with very little athleticism, over the side of the boat into the canal.

Grace reached out toward the man to no avail. The gondolier made a small splash and then surfaced, sputtering unintelligible Italian—or she supposed that was what he sputtered, but since she spoke very little Italian, she had no idea.

She frowned. And she'd been so looking forward to being serenaded by a gondolier.

"*Mi dispiace*," she apologized to the man floating away. It was one of the few phrases she knew well enough to say, likely due to the fact of having to use it so often.

Her attention shifted to the stranger at the oar. He wasn't

very old. Probably nearer Frederick's age than hers, and he rocked forward and back while moving the oar, as if he knew exactly what he was doing. She'd observed a few gondoliers and wondered how a single oar on one side of a boat could make it glide so effortlessly and quickly through the canals. It appeared to have something to do with the rocking motion of the driver and the boat's shape.

The sound of commotion pulled her attention upward toward the land. She searched the crowded street running along the canal, her gaze barely catching sight of her dashing husband as he pursued the dastardly thief on foot. Centuries' old, pale brick buildings, stone columns, and classic domes towering just beyond recognition sped by, taunting her curiosity.

"Oh," she cried, as a sudden bump of the boat sent her into a seated position.

The craft picked up more speed, closing in on Frederick's chase.

What to do?

She focused back on the stranger.

Observation was a vital characteristic of a good detective. Or at least that's what Detective Jack Miracle's book stated, and Grace had read it cover to cover three times.

However, the stranger didn't look villainous. But of course, she could reference several novels where very non-villainous-looking people turned out to be quite villainous indeed. Mr. Wickham to start. She shivered. Or Dr. Jekyll.

The stranger's hair lay much longer than most gentlemen she knew, and if the wind hadn't been blowing the soft brown curls, they'd likely make it to his shoulders. Perhaps he was a buccaneer. Or an artist. Weren't they known for having long hair?

He was clean-cut with dainty but strong-looking hands. His shoes were scuffed on the sides, but other than that, she couldn't figure out anything else worth noting. Her frown deepened. Detective Jack would be so disappointed in her.

Before she could muster up a good Sherlockian question, the man sent her a glance, the tiny hint of a grin poised at the corners of his lips. "I don't usually have such lovely accomplices on my adventures. Especially ones who dispatch innocent gondoliers with such efficiency."

Grace's bottom lip dropped at his accusation, and she sent a look back behind her. Thankfully, the poor gondolier was climbing to safety out of the canal. She couldn't say the same for her hat.

"I believe we both were at fault with the gondolier," she answered, sending another look to the crowd. They were closing in on Frederick. And the thief.

"You're an American?" He sent her a more pointed look from shoes to her hatless head. "Well"—he made a quick motion of the oar and doffed his hat—"we'll have to be properly introduced later." Then, before the gondola hit the canal wall, the man leaped from the boat and dashed into the crowd as swiftly and gracefully as an antelope.

Grace stared in awe in the direction the man had disappeared before rallying her wits, standing from the gondola, and, after a few attempts and the assistance of a passing Italian, climbing onto the street side. She'd never witnessed a man move with such agility before, except once, but that involved heated tongs and an angry cook.

Hitching up her skirt, she dashed in the direction of the stranger. The small crowd seemed to sense her pursuit because they slowly parted as she ran. It was fortunate the stranger was rather tall. He proved an easy target to follow.

A cry rang out just as Grace came to a clearing in the middle of a small, stone-paved courtyard. At the center lay the thief, with Frederick on top of him and the American stranger looming over both, his expression more confused than. . .well, whatever he should have been feeling about having his watch stolen. With a slight struggle, Frederick stood, bringing the man up with him and tugging Grace's purse from the thief's hand.

Frederick's gaze found hers on the edge of the crowd, noting her presence with a dip of his chin. Her smile quivered wide. She loved how he did that. Found her. Even when he was in the middle of wrangling a thief. It was a tremendously romantic thing to do.

"Let's find the authorities." Frederick pulled the man forward, but the American stranger rushed ahead, blocking Frederick's path.

"I'll take it from here, sir." He grabbed the thief by the arm, giving his head a sharp shake. "After all, there's no real harm done."

"No harm?" Frederick drew back and Grace moved to his side. "He's a thief."

"But not a very good one, if you ask me," the stranger said with a sigh and turned toward the thief, whose hair was much shorter and darker than the stranger's. "Why on earth did you steal the lady's purse, Paul? That wasn't a part of the game."

Frederick loosened his hold on the man and caught Grace's gaze, his expression reflecting the same surprise she felt.

The stranger knew the thief by name? Was he some popular thief like Fagin from *Oliver Twist*? Ruthless and rascally and hard-hearted. Or worse, like Sikes! She grimaced and shook her head, examining the man with his ready smile. Surely not. And then he tossed her a wink.

She narrowed her eyes.

Well, maybe a little rascally.

The thief shrugged the shoulder of his well-cut suit jacket. There was another mark in his favor for not being similar to Oliver Twist. A stylish jacket with not a patch in sight.

"Old habits and all of that," came the thief's response. Another American? "I would have returned the purse on my own."

The thief dusted off his sleeves before reaching his hand into his jacket.

Frederick stepped forward, creating a barrier between the thief and Grace, only to find that the thief removed not a weapon but. . .a stopwatch? He clicked the button at the top of the watch and sent a grin up to the American stranger. "He beat your last time."

The first stranger looked over at Frederick, his eyes wide. "*He* beat my time?"

"By three minutes." The thief turned the stopwatch for the American to see. "I think you're losing your touch, Danny boy."

An indefinable noise came from her husband as he stepped forward.

"What is going on here?" Frederick moved toward the American. "A game?" He waved toward Grace, his body growing taller and broader as he growled out the accusation. "Where someone puts the well-being of a woman in danger?"

A thrill moved through Grace. Protective was incredibly heroic.

The "Danny boy" American had the decency to don a guilty frown. The thief named Paul bent his head like a little boy in trouble.

"We meant no harm, sir." The "Danny boy" American offered his hand to Frederick. "Just a silly competition me and my friend engage in once in a while, and usually"—he shot the thief a narrow-eyed look—"it is *only* between us."

"Perhaps you should be more particular about which friends you choose," came Frederick's reply as he offered Grace his arm.

Danny boy's laugh burst out. The thief's frown deepened.

"Paul's usually the best of friends, sir," Danny said with another laugh. "When he's not pinching a fine lady's purse." Danny removed his hat and took a low bow before Grace. "I'd be happy to try and make it up to the both of you."

So all along they'd been playing some game? Was the man named Paul acting as a thief and Danny attempting to catch him? A game of cat and mouse through the streets of Venice? It sounded like the mischief two young boys might engage in, but two men? No wonder Europeans held such varying views on Americans!

"I've heard enough." Frederick tugged Grace forward. "We're finished here."

"There really was no harm done," Danny shouted as Frederick brought Grace to his side and moved away from the crowd. "And I'll make things right with the gondolier, madam."

Grace looked back over her shoulder to find Danny dusting off the thief. . .er. . .Paul's jacket. A much more friendly action than villainous. What a strange pair! They must be very bored, indeed, to engage in such dangerous activities. Perhaps they weren't readers.

Grace's gaze moved to her husband, whose clipped pace and stiff jaw refused to relax despite the distance they'd created between them and the two men. With a little squeeze to his arm, she pulled his attention.

"It wasn't so bad, Frederick." She smiled up to him. "No one was hurt."

"Fortunate for them and us." His brows drew closer together. "How did you reach us so quickly?"

"The gondola. It's a much faster way to travel than I imagined. Nothing like grandfather's motorboat, of course, but very efficient, nonetheless."

"Your grandfather had a—" Frederick shook his head, the tension in his face relaxing a little. "Of course he did."

"I was rather good at steering it, as long as there weren't too many birds to distract me." She smiled up at him. "Who would have thought this day would start with such an adventure, and it's not even noon."

The tension in his shoulders lessened a little more, and the faintest smile softened his features. "It seems adventures follow you aplenty, Lady Astley."

"Who's to say they're not following you, my lord?" Her grin responded to his. "After all, your dear home of Havensbrooke had its many secrets long before I ever arrived. And if you'll remember, our little adventure in Egypt involved *your* family." One of her brows tipped ever so slightly.

He narrowed his eyes in a mock glare.

Her smile twitched as she continued her teasing. "And if I'm not mistaken, you've increased your mystery reading selections lately, which would make one think that perhaps adventures might be growing on you just a little."

"Or I'm attempting to become better prepared for life with you." The light in his dark eyes inspired her smile.

"Very good strategy, my lord. Who's to say reading fiction doesn't help in very real-life situations."

He chuckled. "I would prefer adventures of the less life-threatening sort than our last few, if I could choose them." His gaze roamed over her face. "But I suppose I do have the best sleuthing partner should adventures await."

She nearly breached the distance between them and kissed him directly on the mouth, but since they were in the middle of the street, she made do by just offering a dreamy sigh. Partners in every way, but sleuthing? Oh yes! Given a few more chances, he had the makings of an excellent sleuth. He only wanted more experience. And perhaps a few more excellent novels.

Adventures left such wonderful stories to write in her journal. . .and recount later with an extra dash of excitement sprinkled in here and there for posterity. Though she really hadn't had to embellish as much as she'd used to. Her healthy dose of fictional adventures had taken on a very real-life expansion since marrying her wonderful earl. What with two murder attempts, a solid man-napping, and a partially successful tomb robbery, it seemed too much to expect anything more, especially in the luxurious beauty of Italy.

She sighed up at the cerulean sky. No wonder people enjoyed traveling so much!

This warm and wonderful world of Italy bloomed with tranquility and delight.

Except for the fake purse thieving, of course.

Egypt had boasted the rust-colored desert, breathtaking pyramids, art etched into tombs, cities of tent merchants with the scents of hookah pipe smoke and jasmine in the air.

But Italy gleamed with white columns and aqua water, ancient houses painted with varying colors and embellished stone. Though the sun had shone every day in Egypt, as it had done for Frederick and Grace while in Italy, this country's reprieve from the heat came in the form of an almost constant cool breeze. And on that breeze ushered the scents of freshly baked bread mingled with wisteria and magnolia, both in abundant bloom on every street.

Without another hitch in the day, Frederick and Grace strolled the streets, enjoyed lunch, and took in a few of the most visited sites in Venice, all neatly tucked around the famous St. Mark's Square. Without her hat, she made do with the shade of a fashionable new parasol, which brought her number of parasols up to three. The few articles she'd read on using the handy device as a weapon only fueled a certain interest in collecting more.

She felt the same way about knives but kept that particular interest to herself for fear it might interrupt what little peace of mind Frederick still had after marrying her.

As they wandered from the newly reconstructed, red-brick Campanile rising high into the Venetian skyline to the magnificent St. Mark's Basilica, they took their time—with Frederick, the ever-patient one, allowing Grace moments to make quick sketches of the sites. . .and question the locals, using Frederick as interpreter.

St. Marco's Square truly was a remarkable representation of Venice's history and beautiful architecture. Pale stone paved the square, and glorious structures framed each side. The grand and ornate dome-shaped St. Mark's Basilica held features similar to the

Cairo Citadel, but with added adornment related to a cathedral. The Doge's Palace on another side rose like a beautiful three-tiered rectangular cake, with the bottom consisting of an arched loggia, the middle an open veranda, and the enclosed top third boasting a line of pointed windows. Her guidebook stated that the palace style was "Gothic," perhaps due to the small, spire-like designs lining the top of it like spindles, but Grace had the hardest time matching *Gothic* to the beautiful pale structure. *Gothic* brought visions of Dracula's Castle or Misselthwaite Manor or Thornfield Hall. Nothing as bright and hope-inspiring as this.

As the afternoon waned, the fading sunlight took on a lovely golden sheen, glistening down on the palace, the sun's glow turning its cream exterior into molten hues. Massive statues of the Roman gods Mars and Jupiter stood on either side of an equally grand staircase. But Grace's favorite sight thus far, and the one in which Frederick's patience required the most practice, was the grand, fifteenth-century clock tower. Something about its unique beauty captured Grace, mostly because of the large and ornate astronomical clock in the center of the tower, its azure and gold decorations reflecting the colors of the sky above.

A statue of the Virgin Mary holding baby Jesus perched just above the clock, with mother peering down at the square below. Grace wondered if this was to give some consolation to all the people historically executed in this square with their backs to the water and their faces toward the clock. . .or Mary and the Christ child. But of course there was the pinnacle of the tower—the dark bronze statues that rang in the hour. From a distance, their situation at the top gave off the look of a crown, but as Frederick and Grace drew closer, the "crown" took the shape of two bronze men striking a massive bronze bell in rhythm to create the wonderful chimes.

The view of Venice from the clock tower's pinnacle proved breathtaking and encompassed not only a view to their hotel and beyond but also the branch-like canals braiding in and out of the city to spill into what was called the lagoon, a beautiful bay of the Adriatic Sea. With all the many waterways, more numerous than streets, no wonder Venice was known as the Floating City.

Frederick was finishing up a conversation with a guide in the square about the workings of the clock, while Grace tried to complete her sketch, when a strange sort of awareness tingled up her exposed neck. She paused her pencil's scratching movements against the paper and straightened, casting a look behind her. The benign passing of tourists and natives met her gaze—nothing out of the ordinary. She looked back at Frederick, but his focus steadied on the guide, whose arms moved in exaggerated ways.

The people in Italy certainly lived up to their reputation of being highly expressive when they spoke. Many times Grace had no idea what they were saying, but they said it with such conviction, she found herself nodding along anyway.

She returned to her sketching, but the odd feeling resurrected, moving down her neck and across her shoulders. Was someone watching her? She scanned the area again, but the only eyes pointed in her direction were the ones from nearby statues. Tucking her sketch pad beneath her arm and holding the pencil between her teeth, she reached into her rescued purse and drew out a small mirror. She'd only started carrying one after reading Jack Miracle's book on being a detective. He highly praised the value of a mirror and gave a few thorough examples of why. Carefully, she raised the mirror with the hopes of looking behind her without being conspicuous, but the mirror caught the sun's reflection.

She squinted and nearly stumbled back, blinking. Clearly, she hadn't practiced spying through a hand mirror enough to be proficient. With a shake of her head, she turned her body a little and made a second attempt. This time, it worked. She skimmed her gaze along the courtyard, past Frederick and the guide, and then stopped. In the shadows of a columned building behind her she saw a tall figure. His position cloaked any recognition, but his size and stature confirmed he was a man. Oh, if she only had their trusted valet, Elliott, or their newly adopted daughter, Zahra, along as another set of eyes, but they'd sent their beloved valet off to seek his possible romantic fortunes with a thief, and little Zahra wasn't allowed to leave Egypt until certain paperwork had been completed. So. . .until Elliott returned or Inspector Randolph delivered Zahra to them, she had to rely on her eyes alone, which, after her near-blinding, were seeing spots. She pressed her eyes closed to clear them, and when she reopened them, the man was gone. Turning, she blinked through the spots and surveyed the area again. Nothing.

Not a trace.

And now Frederick was walking toward her.

Should she tell him about the man? She frowned. Well, it wasn't as if she had any *real* evidence, and they'd been having such a lovely time after the fake robbery, she hated to sully the afternoon with another concern. Besides, she wasn't too proud to admit that sometimes her imagination did gallop off into all sorts of assumptions.

At times it was fiction's fault.

But not always.

"Fascinating. All of it." Frederick grinned and gestured back toward the tower. "To think of the ingenuity of centuries ago."

"Truly. And I'm still in awe that only a few weeks ago we witnessed the pyramids, which are over four millennia old," Grace added. "It's all the more proof that God loves creativity."

"Indeed, and imagination. To conjure up these designs? These inventions?" He offered her his arm. "I'm afraid my mind runs more toward practical than fantastical."

"That's why we are so well suited, don't you think?" She slid her arm through his. "My fantastical brain is in desperate need of your practicality, though I must say you are incredibly inventive when you want to be."

"Am I?"

The slightest hitch in one of his brows paired with a rather intense look completely distracted her from any shadowy figures. She hadn't meant for her compliment to run in a rather rascally direction, but once he'd placed the thought in her mind, she didn't see any reason for dismissing it. Her smile took a slow curl. Her darling sleuthing partner happily filled her days with historical and artistic adventures and her nights with deliciously roguish ones. Heat made a wonderfully ridiculous climb up her neck and into her cheeks. Why did she ever think marriage would be dull and boring?

"Well, I meant in more ways than the romantic sorts, but you are incredibly clever and talented in the romantic sort as well." She raised her own brow and practiced some of the teasing looks he'd been so deliciously using on her for months. Or she hoped. Despite practicing in the mirror on occasion, she still wasn't certain if she looked inviting or. . .angry. "In fact, I feel you deserve a very thorough reward for such a valiant rescue of my purse."

His gaze dropped to her lips. Ah, the practice must have worked. "What did you have in mind?"

Her grin slipped wide, and she rocked up on tiptoe while tugging his jacket closer. She whispered a detailed description of his thorough reward, which resulted in her darling hero releasing a low growl.

"To the hotel, then." He cleared his throat and leaned close, his voice low. "Your imagination is one of my favorite things about you."

She laughed as he tugged her arm through his and began a rather quick walk toward one of the canals where water taxis waited to glide them to their destination.

"It's a marvel anyone's imagination could be stifled in such a place as this." She shook her head with a sigh. "And those enormous bathtubs really are conducive for all sorts of creativity."

His steps increased another pace.

A giggle burst out. Oh how she loved loving him—and being loved by him. It really was one of the most delightful reciprocities she'd ever known. And she had the sneaky suspicion he was warming up to the whole sleuthing idea. Which somehow made him even more dashing than he already was.

Then she felt it again. The tingle of someone watching her. Her steps faltered a moment, the break in the pattern alerting her to another sound. Steps behind them in pace with theirs.

She refused to turn around. A careless move would alert the possible assailant of her awareness. Frederick stopped and turned, his gaze searching hers.

The footsteps stopped as well.

"Are you ready to return to the hotel, darling?"

She examined him. They'd already come to that quite delicious conclusion, she thought. Especially when it involved bathtubs. "Yes."

He nodded and resumed their walk, but she continued to study his profile. What was he doing? The steps started again in time with theirs.

Frederick's body tensed, and he brought them to another halt. "And there are no other sites you'd like to see today?"

Late afternoon light faded to twilight all around them. Apart from an evening gondola ride, she wasn't sure what else they could do. And then she froze. He knew. He was pausing their movements to gauge whether the person following them stopped too.

"You hear it, don't you?"

Frederick's head dipped at her statement.

"Someone is following us."

He nodded and resumed their walk, his pace a bit slower. "The footfall sounds like a man. Clipped. Heavy shoes, not boots."

Grace's bottom lip dropped the teeniest bit. Perhaps her dear husband was more prepared for this sleuthing business than even *he* realized. "What do you suggest we do?"

"Stay close." He tightened his hold on her arm. "And follow my lead."

A wonderful thrill ran from the back of her scalp all the way down her spine, and she nearly vaulted into his arms to claim his frowning lips. But thankfully, common sense prevailed, and she merely stared at his lips for so long she almost stumbled.

"When we turn up ahead, stay behind me. Do you understand?"

"Yes."

"And keep an eye out for anyone else."

She nodded, gripping the handle of her parasol, and envisioned a sword fight worthy of *The Three Musketeers* or *The Scarlet Pimpernel*.

If only she'd brought her pistol!

Chapter 2

Frederick huffed, a groan waiting in his throat.

Was asking for a simple, unimpeded day too much? Especially with such an inducement as being alone with his wife?

He released a long sigh. Traveling came with its own rewards as well as struggles, he supposed, but in all of his life, he'd never experienced drama in such quick succession, not even while working in his military post. Surely Grace's fictional world couldn't bleed into the real world, could it? Or did an obsession for fictional suspense work as a magnet in the everyday? Lord, help him. He hoped not.

Though, as strange as it seemed, he was beginning to anticipate possible disaster on a regular basis. Military training only prepared one for so much. . .and certainly not the unexpectedness of Lady Astley.

Frederick took a tighter hold of Grace's arm, increasing his pace. But he'd nearly lost his wife, and the memory of pulling her from the Egyptian tomb's sandpit, lifeless, still haunted him. His pulse pumped in his head, his jaw set. Apart from locking her in a tower, he'd do about anything to keep her safe. He frowned. Why did he have the inclination that his daring wife would even find a way out of that? He rolled his gaze heavenward. Surely God knew exactly what He'd been doing when He bound Frederick to this darling woman in marriage, didn't He? Was it some sort of cosmic trust exercise?

He almost grinned. But wasn't God always working in the world to increase His children's trust?

Up ahead the building turned, and a small gap between it and the next afforded a perfect spot to tuck Grace while he addressed the situation of the man following them. With a fluid movement, he swept Grace into the protection of the makeshift cleft and spun around to ready himself. The steps neared, and just as the person turned the corner of the building, Frederick grabbed him and pinned him to the wall, pressing his face into the stone.

"Who are you?" Frederick tightened his hold on the man's arm, which he'd twisted up behind the stranger's back.

"Excellent form in defense against a pursuer, my lord," came the strained response. "Perchance, have you been reading my book?"

Frederick looked over at Grace to ascertain whether she had heard the same sentence. She blinked wide eyes at him and lowered her parasol from what he presumed was its attack position.

Frederick spun the man around and stared at the unmistakable face of Detective Jack Miracle. "Jack?"

"Yes, and if you'd be so kind as to loosen the grip you have against my arm, good man, I will be happy to explain." Jack gave a nod of his golden head down to Frederick's fingers digging into the man's shoulder. "I would be much more focused on my eloquent speech than the pain in my arm."

"I thought I recognized that jawline." Grace rushed forward, helping dust off the man's jacket. "I'm so pleased to discover you are not a scoundrel, Jack."

"Don't forgo that description, my lady." Jack's grin flared crooked as he dipped his head to Grace. "It does depend on the day."

Frederick dropped his hold, still staring at the man. "What

are you doing in Venice?"

"Do you mean a lowly detective like myself is not permitted an exotic holiday now and then, my lord?"

"Lowly." Frederick's lip pinched, and he placed his hands on his hips, hoping this look proved as credulous as the tone of his voice. "The son of a viscount?"

"Former viscount, if you recall." Jack reordered his fedora to his preferred tilt. "Father not only lost his estate to the debtors but his title due to his prison sentence, so I can truly forgo all pretense of peerage now."

"Ah, but you are a gentleman to the core, despite your protests." Frederick's smile slid wide, and he placed his palm on the man's shoulder. "And as I recall, your father left you anything but penniless."

Jack's pale brow rose ever so slightly. "Comfortable and disgraced," he clarified.

A calm fell over Frederick. He wasn't certain why the idea of Jack being nearby took the edge off his senses, but it did. A friend. Especially with Elliott back in England for the foreseeable future and life being somewhat. . .unpredictable when Grace was involved.

"So you're on holiday? In Venice?"

"Holiday?" Jack's pale eyes took on an added twinkle. "Doesn't my work always feel a bit like a holiday? Especially your sort of holiday, I hear?" He raised a brow, his reference to their recent Egyptian adventure loosening Frederick's jaw.

"You're solving a mystery, aren't you?" Grace shot Frederick an excited grin. "Right here in Venice?"

Jack's eyes twinkled in such a way that Frederick's stomach tightened. Was he the only sensible person among them? They'd barely survived the previous "adventure"; the last thing they needed was another in quick succession.

He sighed. It felt very much like God had placed Frederick

on earth to keep Grace Percy alive. Though in all honesty, she'd brought life back to him, so perhaps it was a fair trade.

"Maybe I am." Jack's smile spread. "I was particularly requested to investigate this case. All expenses paid." He shrugged. "How could I refuse?"

Grace squeezed her fingers together in front of her, ready to jump right into another venture as if they hadn't experienced enough thrills for one day. Her energy was endless.

"Is it some historical mystery etched into the very fabric of Venetian history?"

Jack chuckled. "Venetian history is a part, but I believe we may be dealing more with canvas than fabric."

"Canvas?" Grace pulled her notebook from her bag. "As in paintings, you mean? Oh, Jack! How exciting. And incredibly fortunate that we're here in case you need an extra set of eyes or two."

"How did you know about Egypt?" At least Frederick could attempt to distract his wife from thrusting herself into another mystery. Especially since there was a quite capable detective on the job already.

"You're British aristocracy in a foreign country with a family scandal on your hands, my lord." He tagged on a wink. "Everyone keeps an eye out for you."

"Is it something about stolen paintings?" Grace continued, undeterred, jotting a note into her journal. "I read about an Italian patriot who stole the famed *Mona Lisa* from the Louvre in Paris only a few years ago. If he hadn't attempted to sell the painting, he may not have been caught at all."

"Ah, you read some nonfiction in with all of the fiction you consume, my lady?" Jack sent Frederick a grin. "Are you broadening your sleuthing interests, then?"

"Not enough to brag, I assure you." Grace shook her head. "But sometimes when Father left the paper out, if the headline was particularly gripping, I'd feel compelled to read it. It's rather remarkable how sometimes real life proves even more tantalizing than fiction." She looked at Frederick and flashed one of her dazzling smiles. "It certainly has been for me."

"I feel this particular conglomeration of mysterious ridiculousness is something you would find fascinating, my lady." Jack's countenance sobered. "And an extra set of eyes? Well, that may not be such a bad idea."

"Jack?" The sudden change in his friend's tone brought Frederick to full alert. Could Jack *need* their help with his mystery? Frederick blinked. No, of course not! What was Frederick thinking? No, Frederick wanted to enjoy a rather delightful and perhaps even decadent honeymoon with his wife—not stumble around in the middle of who knows what with Detective Jack Miracle!

The man's smile resurfaced, but he failed to meet Frederick's eyes. "Oh, nothing to worry about; it's just a bit tricky, is all." He turned to Grace. "But since it is getting later in the day, perhaps we could discuss it over tea tomorrow?"

"Very well." Grace's grin resurfaced in full bloom. "I do love anticipation. It's one of the many delights of well-written fiction."

"To keep you sufficiently entranced, Lady Astley, I shall add that the mystery involves stolen artwork across three countries." Jack's lips slanted, and without moving his attention from Grace, Jack handed Frederick a card with a hotel's name printed on it. "And a possible secret message from the grave."

"How marvelous!" Grace gasped.

"A bit dramatic, are we?"

Frederick's droll response merely incited Jack's grin all the more. "Only playing to my audience, your lordship. After all, you're the only couple I know who solves mysteries together."

"Solve mysteries togeth—"

"We do!" Grace exclaimed into his bewildered response,

wrapping her arm through Frederick's and bathing him with a look of unadulterated adoration. He almost lost himself in the renewed awareness of how heroic she saw him, how. . .brave and strong. "We have already solved quite a few, and that should put us into a very elite category. There aren't very many husband-and-wife sleuths in the world, are there?"

Frederick pinched his eyes closed. Sleuths? Heaven, help him. Surely he wasn't made to be a sleuth.

"And this mystery shouldn't be nearly as life-threatening as your previous adventures." Jack raised a brow to Frederick, his expression taking on a consolatory look. "It's merely a case of stolen art, my lord. How dangerous can that really be?"

Something in Frederick's chest twitched, like the pinch of doubt, and underneath the twitch paired with something utterly and completely shocking.

Curiosity.

A thrill.

The memory of the rush of adventure, of dashing into the unknown. The possibility of rising to heroic stature once again. He *had* engaged somewhat successfully with a few mysteries since Grace came into his life, hadn't he? And the thought of bringing escapades from the fiction he loved into the real world held a certain magnetic appeal. He glanced down at his wife, heat seeping from his face.

What was her influence doing to his pragmatism?

He pushed away the unnerving thoughts.

But as Grace's gaze met his, he wondered if she felt his shock too, because her lovely eyes sparkled all the more.

Frederick cleared his throat and turned his attention back to the lesser of two influences, inserting clear logic to combat the fascinating draw of intrigue. "Jack, you know as well as I that when you're dealing with unpredictable people, anything can take a dangerous turn."

"Exactly," Grace agreed with a nod. "Which is why you can rest assured, dear Jack, that we are at your service, should you need us. In fact, we're sublimely intrigued by the possibility." Grace looked up at her husband, her eyes bright. "Aren't we, Frederick?"

His definition of sublime and his wife's were two very different things.

His gaze locked with Jack's, and a sudden disquiet lodged like a knot in Frederick's throat. He drew in a breath and tightened his jaw with his smile. "Of course."

Forcing a singular thought to the front of his mind, Frederick stared hard at Jack and hoped the thought breached the space between them to ensure his friend of one very clear unspoken understanding.

Frederick Percy was an earl, and a second-hand one at that! *Not* a sleuth.

Frederick welcomed the lifestyle Grace's dowry afforded them but still attempted to keep their travel expenses on the more practical side of extravagant. He took care to provide for his wife's conveniences, of course, but the finest hotels? There was no need for opulence when elegant would do just as well and save them money in the long run.

However, Detective Jack Miracle's hotel glittered with magnificence. With views of the Grand Canal behind them, they ascended the steps into an ornate and grand foyer, complete with embossed trim, dark wood highlights, a parquet floor, and dramatic red wallpaper.

A chandelier dropped from the equally ornate ceiling and lit the room with electric lights.

"Is it a palace?" Grace whispered as the concierge led them up a grand stairway and through an archway into a smaller room of white cloth–covered tables and myriad artwork at every turn. They bypassed one of the four white stone columns in the room.

"I believe it may have been once. Or owned by someone of similar importance."

They stepped out onto a veranda lined with tables similar to those inside, except these featured umbrellas. At the far end of the veranda sat the infamous detective, as smartly dressed as ever in a beige suit and open-collared, white button-up. Jack stood as they approached, his ready smile offering his greeting before he extended his hand.

"Keeping the accommodations subtle, aren't we, Jack?"

Jack's laugh burst out at Frederick's friendly jab. "Now, now, your lordship, you know if it were up to me, I'd manage quite well in an inn on the outskirts of town, but my current client would have nothing but the very best for me."

"How you must struggle with the sheer luxury of it all."

"Abominably." He took his seat along with them and raised his glass to them. "Torture of the acutest kind."

"I'm so glad I've caught on to sarcasm between the two of you." Grace donned a rather matriarchal look toward two unruly schoolboys. "Otherwise, one would think you didn't enjoy the beauty and wonder of it at all, but I am quite aware, Detective Jack, that you are almost as much a lover of fiction as I, so you would certainly appreciate a bit of magic to any place."

"I don't believe anyone can measure up to your fictional prowess, my lady; however, I can assure you I am enjoying the splendor with appropriate devotion. And the location of the hotel has afforded me an excellent starting point from which to do some investigating."

"Oh, please elaborate." Grace squeezed her hands together and leaned forward in the chair as the server left sandwiches and pastries for them. "I've read your book at least three times and am always curious about your cases." She sent Frederick a look. "We both are."

To which Jack glanced over at Frederick and then, as if covering a smile, ran a hand over his pinched lips.

"To temper your expectations, Jack, I've only read your book once."

"Thank you, my lord, I was concerned my pride might prove uncontrolled at the idea of your adoration for my investigative prowess reaching the heights of your wife's."

Frederick's chuckle burst free, and Grace laughed.

"The two of you are like the dearest of friends in the best of books. Did you know that? The witty conversation? The familiarity." She sat taller. "The best stories should always include faithful friends." She placed her serviette over her lap. "I haven't yet met a peer for me, but I know there must be one written somewhere in my story. Aunt Lavenia is a start, of course, but she's more mentor than peer, I think."

"I believe your aunt Lavenia may be more protector." Jack gave a slight shiver to his shoulders before placing a palm to his chest. "She glared at me once, and I felt it to my heart."

"Ah, perfect," Frederick interjected. "You are duly intimidated and can imagine your fate should anything unhappy befall us in light of your investigation."

"Do tell us about your mysterious case, Jack," Grace added, placing at least eight strawberries on her plate.

Jack's lips tipped ever so slightly as he turned to Grace. The right people always seemed to appreciate Grace's unusual combination of naivete, joy, and ready intelligence. Jack didn't underestimate her, and for that, Frederick knew he'd grow into an even better friend for the both of them.

"Actually, the case is widely known in Venice and stretches all the way to jolly old England in its mystery." The detective gently poured the tea for Frederick and Grace with effortless precision, a skill surprisingly untrained in upper-class gentlemen, which proved a testament to how much Jack's life had changed in the past few years. From future viscount to famous detective. "My client has made no attempt to keep the investigation private, so having a few extra heads in the know and ears available for listening may bring this spot of trouble to a close sooner rather than later."

"What sort of artwork is missing?" Frederick asked, raising the teacup to his lips.

"Several different sorts, but the most valued by my client are related to a collection of nine paintings known as *The Juliets*."

"As in Shakespeare's Juliet?"

Jack nodded to Grace. "Exactly the one. Evidently, the paintings were created by a famous Venetian artist of the mid- to late 1800s who once lived on his own island off the coast of Venice."

"His own island?" Grace lowered her teacup with a little clink. "Oh, I'm not sure how I feel about him now. There is only one of two ways the story can turn out if one owns an island. Dreadful and terrifying like Dr. Moreau or adventurous and dangerous like Robert Louis Stevenson's classic."

"What about extravagant and mysterious?" Jack added, taking a sandwich from the salver. "Or that is what I've learned from my research so far. My client owns the island now."

Grace's eyes widened, and she turned to Frederick, who, despite all attempts to remain unmoved and disinterested, asked, "Your client owns an island?"

Jack nodded. "Which is why he's entrenched in the mystery, I suppose. Since he purchased the island six months ago, he's become rather fond of various art pieces related to Italy. His grandfather possessed one of the famed *Juliets*, and my client had added two more to his collection. A few weeks ago, one of his portraits was stolen en route from his home."

"Only one?" Frederick asked.

"The only one being transported to a local gallery for display. This fact brings with it its own curiosities and possibilities." Jack took another sip of tea. "Despite my client's best attempts, he's not been able to locate the thief. To add insult to injury, two weeks ago, a private local art gallery that houses two more of *The Juliets* was vandalized. Several art pieces were stolen, and among them were—"

"*The Juliets,*" Grace announced. There was no doubt his bride was mentally cataloging every word. "Are all the others missing? Besides the two your client still has?"

"I'm still gathering information, and since I've only been in Venice for a few days, I have a great deal to learn about the entire affair. But it appears no one knows exactly where most of the other *Juliets* are." He took up his cup, his eyes alight with the joy of the mystery. "I am expecting a wire any day to provide more information on that score, since two of the other pieces were last seen in England."

"And you're to find the other stolen art pieces too, along with your client's?"

Jack gave a shrug at Grace's question. "I've only been hired to find *The Juliets.*"

"So your job is to locate the thief?" Even as Frederick asked, he felt there was much more to this story than Jack had expressed so far. What about these paintings made them so special that a private investigator from England would be enlisted to track them down instead of the local police? Jack wasn't telling everything.

"My client cares less for the thief and more for the paintings." Jack folded his hands together and leaned forward, his attention shifting from Frederick to Grace, and something akin to an elf's grin curled the man's lips. "According to local legend"—he wiggled his brows—"a secret message within the paintings leads to a hidden treasure on the private island."

"What?" Grace nearly shouted. "A hidden treasure?"

Frederick sat up. "If you're spinning this tale for Grace's benefit, then I'd advise you to get to the true nature of the case, Jack."

"I'm not exaggerating." The man took another drink of his tea. "The fact that it fits into one of Lady Astley's beloved novels is merely a boon and more support for bringing along the two of you in this adventure."

Frederick gave his head a small shake. Was this his life? Truly? From murderous mistresses to tomb raiders to. . .treasure hunting? He wanted to deny the flicker of interest slowly growing to flame in his chest, but he couldn't. After all, Jack was his friend and had clearly asked for their help.

How could he refuse it?

"It's all very fascinating and novel-like, for certain. I can see why my particular brand of knowledge would be helpful to your investigation." Grace sighed back in her chair and looked over at Frederick, the shadow from her hat doing nothing to hide the pure pleasure in her expression. "And since we are here for at least another week or two, I think we could certainly be of assistance. Don't you agree, Frederick?"

If Frederick wanted to shower his wife with the types of presents she loved best on this honeymoon, the answer came clear and evident. No expensive jewelry or extravagant gifts for her.

But near-death experiences and daring adventures? His shoulders dropped for a moment. Well, at least he didn't have to try and wrap them. "If you need us, Jack, we're at your service."

"Perfect." Jack's hands came together as his grin grew. "Then I'll only need to ask my client if the two of you can join us at his home tomorrow."

"Join you?" Frederick barely had the question out when a shadow fell over their table. "At his island home?"

"Ah, perfect timing." Jack stood, his attention focusing on a spot just over Frederick's head. "Let me introduce my client."

Grace looked just over Frederick's shoulder, and her bottom lip dropped before she turned those wide eyes to Frederick. A sudden dread pushed through him as he stood and turned. Standing before him was one of the "thieves" from yesterday. The one who had ridden in the gondola with Grace. The mastermind behind the entire "game."

"Lord and Lady Astley, I'd like you to meet Mr. Daniel Laraby."

Chapter 3

A rush of warning shot through Frederick, sending him shifting closer to Grace. And now? To learn the same "thief" from yesterday proved to be Jack Miracle's newest client? Frederick had already agreed to assist Jack in his investigation, but to help with such a man?

He turned his attention to Grace and stifled a groan. Why did hindsight always have to prove so humbling?

But his lovely bride only scanned the man from head to toe. If he didn't know her so well, he might have felt a sting of jealousy from her rather obvious perusal, but if he'd learned anything about her at all, she was likely taking inventory as the amateur sleuth she was.

"What a surprise." The man, Daniel Laraby, blinked as his attention shifted from Frederick to Grace and back. "I had hoped to see you again and give a proper apology, but to learn you are acquainted with my detective? That's awfully convenient."

"You've met?" This from Detective Miracle, who'd walked around the table to stand nearer Mr. Laraby.

"Not formally." Laraby's grin resurfaced too quickly for any true remorse.

"And not in a way I wish to replicate," came Frederick's quick response. He turned to Jack. "Do you realize your client is a charlatan?"

"Now, now, Lord Astley, charlatan may be a bit extreme." Laraby tugged at the lapels of his jacket, his smile hitched wide. "You see here before you a reformed swindler."

"You're not helping your case, Laraby." Jack shook his head and looked over at Frederick. "Daniel Laraby is a former circus man, but since coming into his inheritance a year ago, he's become not only ridiculously wealthy but quite the philanthropist and art connoisseur."

"You were in the circus?" Grace stood from her place. "In America?"

"Indeed I was, your ladyship." He took a dramatic bow. "Nearly my whole life."

"Oh, were you on the trapeze or a fire breather?"

"Perhaps a clown?" Frederick's grin tensed as he stared at the man.

"Perhaps a bit of all." Laraby wiggled his brows in true showman fashion. "But my particular specialty *was* trapeze, though I had to do a bit of everything."

"Might I suggest we continue this conversation at the table to prevent further travesty at Laraby's initiation?" Jack gestured toward the table and sent Frederick a wink. "Our tea is getting cold."

Grace grinned, her attention on the charlatan. "Since moving to England in December, Mr. Laraby, I've learned that there is nothing quite as disastrous to an English constitution as cold tea." Grace's eyes widened with a twinkle. "Except, perhaps, leaving the house without an umbrella."

A burst of laughter shot from Laraby, and Frederick rolled his eyes.

How many times had his darling wife gently teased him about some of the trite "disasters" of English life. His smile almost bent.

Of course, he teased right back about her American idiosyncrasies. The shared banter created the most delightful connectedness to her. He'd never imagined it could be so in a marriage, but her teasing the swindler didn't hold quite the same pleasantness.

"Circus antics or no, I offer yet another apology about yesterday. Paul and I engage in the silliest of adventures when we're in town to pass the time," Laraby offered again, once seated. "It really was just a lark."

"What on earth did you do?" The humor in Jack's voice was undeniable. . .and incredibly unhelpful to Frederick's suspicion.

"I made a bad first impression, I'm afraid, Jack." Mr. Laraby offered an apologetic grimace. "Paul and I were having a bit of fun yesterday, and your friends came upon us in the middle of it all."

"A bit of fun?" Frederick barely controlled his volume. "You stole my wife's purse, then our gondola."

"And you knocked the poor gondolier into the canal," Grace added.

"I believe that was a team effort, my lady." Mr. Laraby grinned at Grace in a way that did nothing to assist Frederick in controlling his volume. . .or suspicions.

Grace's cheeks darkened as she raised a hand to her hat, but she lifted her chin and held Mr. Laraby's gaze. "Which would never have happened if someone hadn't stolen our gondola, if you recall, Mr. Laraby."

At this, Frederick couldn't tame the faintest smile pushing at the edges of his mouth. Likely, his beloved wife feared her current hat was on the heels of being lost to the same fate as the last—which proved a rather consistent pattern—but he loved her ready wit and her willingness to rally to a challenge. Well, most of the time. When it wasn't at odds with his desire to keep her alive.

"Guilty." Laraby dipped his chin. "But I assure you, no one has ever gotten harmed in our little games. The people of Venice have great senses of humor, and I made sure to compensate the gondolier handsomely for his trouble."

Frederick's shoulders relaxed a little. Perhaps the man was more smoke than fire. But what was he to think of a former circus performer turned rich gentleman who planned faux pursuits through the streets of Venice?

A quote from Jack's book came to mind. *When given opportunity to observe instead of engage, take thorough inventory of even the most minute elements. You never know what may be of future significance.*

Not that Frederick had read Jack's book enough to memorize anything, but perhaps he'd reviewed certain parts of it more times than once.

"Are these the very same Lord and Lady Astley you've spoken about before, Detective?" Mr. Laraby's expression shifted from his faux-sullen state. "The ones who have joined you in your previous investigations?"

Assisted in Jack's previous investigations? Was he referring to the murders at Havensbrooke?

"You didn't tell me they'd be here to assist you in my little trouble too. That's excellent."

Frederick's attention moved back to Jack. Had Jack taken the case knowing they'd be honeymooning here? As if in answer, Jack offered a good-natured shrug. "It never hurts to have an extra pair of eyes or two when dealing with a case of such history and mystery, especially when hidden treasure is involved."

"You mentioned the treasure before." Grace lowered her tea from her lips, her eyes growing wide. "I'd love for you to elaborate."

Mr. Laraby had a deep scar above his right eye and appeared to have a rough go on shoes. Or at least the one Frederick noted nearest him. Despite their expense and relative newness, the scuffs etched deep into the sides. From lack of care? Rough terrain?

The cobblestone streets of Venice would not have led to such grooves, so what might have caused them? Scaling walls to infiltrate an art gallery?

"Evidently, there's a hidden message in the paintings, as I understand it." Jack gestured toward Laraby, encouraging him to continue the story.

Laraby tossed a grin to his audience, donning the showman's persona once again.

There was an easiness to his nature, an almost boyishness, but also the real sense of an actor who had learned the art of playing to his crowd. How deep his playacting went, Frederick did not know, but if he and Grace joined the—he frowned—case, then his guard would remain alert to any underhanded possibilities. Unpredictability never boded well. Either this case proved as ridiculous as yesterday's lark, or something much darker waited beneath the surface of Mr. Laraby's ready smile. . .and they were all players on the stage of his next performance.

"I suppose I ought to give you a bit of biography so you'll understand my connection with *The Juliets*." Laraby took a drink of his tea before continuing. "As Jack mentioned, I was in the circus in America. Raised there until I was sixteen, when my parents died in a trapeze accident." He paused, his lips pinching closed.

"Oh, how horrible," Grace whispered, her fist pressed to her chest. "I'm so sorry."

"Thank you," Laraby nodded. "It *was* horrible."

A little of Frederick's disquiet about the man abated. What a loss for a child to witness.

Laraby drew in a breath before continuing. "There had been an estrangement between my father and my grandfather all my life. I only heard rumors that it was about Father's financial choices, but I had never worked out any of the details and accepted that I'd never know my grandfather, but a few years after I was left orphaned, he came for me."

"Was he riddled with regret about his interminable estrangement?" Grace asked, leaning forward in her chair. "Did he long to amend the past?"

Mr. Laraby's lips twitched. "I would like to think that was part of it, Lady Astley, but I believe the greater worry for him was lack of an heir to his considerable fortune. And he wanted to ensure his successor took appropriate care of his money."

"And despite the estrangement, you agreed to his terms?" Frederick asked.

"While he lived. Which was a good six years after taking me on."

The chronology would place Laraby in his midtwenties. A young man inheriting a fortune without the weight of the work and history that goes with it is a curious thing—especially as to how he might handle his instant extravagance.

"After his death, I did exactly as I liked." The man's eyes flared a moment before complying with a smile. "There was no love lost in the relationship. But I must admit, the old man did right by my two closest friends. When I told him I would not come to live with him unless they joined me, he agreed without hesitation. Both were orphans like me. Paul, whom you met yesterday, had been a foundling who ran away from his orphanage to join the circus when he was about twelve, and Lydia was fatherless when her mother first joined the circus. We grew up as siblings, and now Paul serves as my"—Mr. Laraby waved a hand in the air as if searching for the word—"companion of sorts. And Lydia, as the cleverest of us all, endeared herself to Grandfather, who enlisted her as his secretary, and so she has continued on as mine. I trust her implicitly, though I likely do not treat her as she deserves." He chuckled and rendered a helpless shrug. "But what man really does?"

He sent Frederick a knowing look. Laraby's ready disclosure of elements of his life edged on uncomfortable, but Frederick had learned from marriage to Grace that this may be more of an

American trait than a character flaw.

"I'm glad to say my man is the exception then," Grace offered, sending Frederick a smile. "He treats me better than I deserve, at least if measured in peace of mind."

A somewhat choked sound erupted from Jack, who then cleared his throat and focused his attention back on Mr. Laraby. "Though you did not gain your business sense from your grandfather, you did inherit a bit of his passion for *The Juliets*. Is that so? Enough to inspire you to collect two more and purchase the island of their origin."

"Jack is not only trying to keep me from rambling but baiting you all as well, I see." Laraby chuckled.

"Lady Astley is a ravenous reader of all sorts of stories, Mr. Laraby, so I am inclined to rally my inner novelist to ensure she feels the full delights of your mystery."

"I'm already completely enthralled." Grace placed her hand on Jack's arm. "So far we have a former circus performer turned wealthy island owner who possesses a mystery involving stolen paintings that somehow lead to a hidden treasure. How can I not feel that every fictional delight has suddenly come into real life?"

This very thought had been thrust upon Frederick repeatedly ever since marrying Grace. Fiction and reality intersected on a regular basis whenever she was involved. Perhaps his tug toward sleuthing was providential. It may prove a life-saving interest.

"You're going to add some fun to this whole adventure, aren't you?" Mr. Laraby allowed his attention to linger on Grace for a bit too long.

"I suppose you purchased the island for sentiment?" Frederick did nothing to hide the sarcasm in his tone. "Unless you're a treasure seeker as well?"

"A little of both," Laraby responded in kind. "I am sentimentally interested in finding a treasure."

Frederick held the man's gaze until he looked away.

"Have you been able to make any headway on locating the treasure?" Grace asked, apparently oblivious to Frederick's somewhat primal and definitely nonverbal warning signs to Mr. Laraby.

"None at all." He shook his head. "You see, of the nine paintings, three are supposed to hold some sort of message that leads to the very spot of the treasure, but no one knows which three. I have photographs of most of *The Juliets*, along with possessing three of them." His face fell. "Well, two now that one has been stolen. But if there is some sort of message within the paintings, I've not been able to work it out."

"The only way to really get an idea is to see the paintings Laraby currently has and to review the photographs." Jack waved toward Mr. Laraby. "Your fiancée has a photograph of one of *The Juliets* that hung in the Romano Art Gallery, doesn't she?"

Fiancée? Frederick liked Mr. Laraby a bit better.

"Yes. Jasmine, or Miss Benetti, is a curator at the gallery and was deeply distressed by the recent robbery. In fact, most of the photographs I *do* possess I received from her. She's a scholar of the era and style, as well as being a native of Venice, so she's spent years collecting any information she can about the painter and his works."

"Are your current paintings secure?" Frederick asked.

"I feel as though the ones on the island are. I've not even shown Jasmine where my favorite *Juliet* is, but I do have a photograph of that one as well." Laraby relaxed back in his chair. "If I display them at all, it is a rare event and only on special occasions."

"Not even your fiancée has sorted out anything related to the secret messages?" Grace leaned forward, her mind whirling from the look in those eyes. "Since she is a curator and familiar with the paintings."

"She's very clever, but she's at a loss to any hidden message either, if there really is one at all."

"Oh, I wonder if it's anything like Sherlock's Dancing Men cipher," Grace announced, tapping her long, slender fingers against her lips. "It was rather tricky, so it took a great deal of deliberation to sort it out—even for the grand detective himself—but what a clever invention of a message. Symbols instead of words."

"Dancing Men Cipher?" Laraby looked to Frederick as if for clarity.

"Sir Arthur Conan Doyle's work," Frederick explained, curbing the sudden urge to chuckle. Leave it to Grace to make some literary reference that may very well end in some actual clue. "Sherlock Holmes?"

"Ah, the fictional detective. Yes." Mr. Laraby's expression shone with recognition. "I'm not much of a reader, but I've heard of him at least."

Grace blinked a few times at Daniel's declaration as if she didn't fully comprehend, and Frederick could almost hear her brain attempting to process the fact that Mr. Laraby wasn't much of a reader.

"So that leaves us with two original paintings and a few photographs," Frederick stated, sorting the information in his mind. "An island where a mysterious treasure is purportedly hidden."

"And a thief who somehow broke into the gallery yet hasn't attempted to steal anything from your island home," Grace added, her attention shifting from Frederick to Jack. "How far away is your island?" Then she laughed. "It's very strange to think of someone owning an island in real life, though I do hope yours will prove to be much less disconcerting than Dr. Moreau's. Any exotic man-beasts hidden among the stones and shrubbery?"

"Not to my knowledge, Lady Astley, though I am still fairly new to the island. However, I have collected quite the menagerie of exotic plants." Laraby's smile resurfaced, and he glanced around the table. "Well, I feel *The Juliets* will be in very good hands with the three of you."

And with that, Frederick and Grace joined the "case." Frederick released a sigh of resignation even as the inexplicable thrill tempted to resurface in his chest.

"It is very exciting." Grace's grin reappeared, and she trembled from sheer delight. "Our first official investigation. And"—Grace raised a finger in unison with her brow—"I have a magnifying glass should we need one."

Laraby chuckled. "Most women of my acquaintance wouldn't view an art heist as a delight at all."

"Oh, I can assure, Laraby," Jack offered, "whatever expectations you have for *most* women will likely not pertain to Lady Astley."

"Which the detective means in the best possible way, you understand, Mr. Laraby." Frederick raised a brow to Jack as if to nudge him to clarify.

"Of course. I've not met a woman more inclined toward sleuthing in my whole career." He tapped the table. "Which is why I trust the pair so implicitly. And I wager that once we set our eyes on the paintings, with Lady Astley's quick wit and her husband's keen observation skills, we may very well unearth some answers."

A man in a serving suit appeared at the table. "Pardon me, Mr. Laraby, but your man is here to see you in the lobby."

"Ah yes." Laraby stood and sent a sweeping look to the table. "It's likely last-minute questions about the house party. If you will excuse me for a moment."

As soon as Laraby disappeared from view, Jack leaned forward, drawing Frederick and Grace closer. "Now that you've been officially inducted into detective work, I'll share the plan I was making while Laraby told his tale."

"You've made a plan where we're involved? It's almost as if you were expecting us to help you all along." Grace's ready enthusiasm inspired Jack's grin. . .until he looked over at Frederick.

And then Jack donned some faux innocent expression that deceived no one.

From the small hints Jack had given to the two of them as he'd helped solve the case of the murder of Frederick's brother, Frederick knew the man was looking for friendships. Colleagues and friendships only sweetened the deal for the lonely detective. And the convenience of Jack arriving in Venice for a case just as Frederick and Grace took their honeymoon in the same city? Well, the poor man left no illusion at all. He'd taken this case knowing full well Frederick and Grace would be here. . .and most likely had meant to include them all along.

Frederick's desire to remain out of another mystery had failed from the start. With friends like these. . .

If Frederick hadn't liked Jack so much and found the idea of a real investigation the slightest bit interesting, he would have told Jack in no uncertain terms exactly what he thought of the man's plans to upend a very delightful honeymoon.

"Since you both were here already, it seemed selfish not to include you."

"How very thoughtful of you, Jack." Grace flashed Frederick a broad smile. "An Egyptian adventure, a delicious tour of Italy with my wonderful husband, and now our very own investigation involving robbery, treasure, and a mysterious island? Oh, Frederick, this must be the very best honeymoon ever invented."

Frederick wasn't even certain how he should respond and was rather glad that Jack intervened.

"No doubt, your dear husband thought of everything." Jack's grin edged on a laugh.

"I must admit, the camels were a surprise."

Jack's laugh burst free at Frederick's dry response, and then he sobered. "Now to the plan." He glanced back toward the doorway where Daniel Laraby had disappeared and continued. "Laraby is taking me to his island home tomorrow. He means to have a small house party for an author friend who, ironically, writes mysteries."

"An author?" Grace exclaimed. "Here?"

"Yes, Dolores Reynolds, if I recall correctly."

"Dolores Reynolds." Grace's grin wavered slightly. "I've not heard of her."

"She's been around a decade or so, from what I understand. Apparently, she is researching the history of the artist and his family. There appears to have been some tragedy in the past. I'm meeting with the local authorities this afternoon to learn more about it. From what Laraby said, however, Mrs. Reynolds hopes to set her upcoming novel on Laraby's island." Jack shook his head. "Laraby intends to offer some sort of faux mystery to enlist in Mrs. Reynolds' inspiration and in turn woo her to choose his home and island for the novel's location. Evidently, placing a small party on a remote island and having a murder occur brings about a great deal of inspiration for mystery authors. Though I believe the real reason for the house party's unique drama is for Laraby to influence Mrs. Reynolds' brother, Harry Finch, since Mr. Finch is a budding film producer."

"And Mr. Laraby wants Mr. Finch to use his home in a moving picture?"

Frederick grinned at Grace's question but added his own conjecture. "Or Laraby wants a bit of recognition and fame of his own?"

"My guess is yes to both answers." Jack looked between the two of them. "Now, since I've only been here a few days and am meeting with the authorities this afternoon, I've had little time to investigate the art gallery where the second robbery took place." His eyes took on an additional gleam. "So I hoped perhaps the two of you could do a little poking about?"

"You think the two robberies are connected." Frederick lowered his voice and noticed Grace's gaze fastened on him from his periphery.

He raised his brow, and she sighed. "It's incredibly dashing when you speak in sleuth."

A burst of air came from Jack. "I say, my lord, if we were to find you an eyeglass and trench coat, you might be nigh irresistible."

Frederick sent a powerless glare to his friend, and Jack raised a palm in defense. "I mean no offense. I only wish a few simple sleuthing questions garnered such adoration for me, but usually I end up gagged in a damp hole or chased by men with guns."

Grace's laugh bubbled up. "Perhaps you haven't met the right woman just yet, Jack."

The glint in his eyes dimmed ever so slightly. Jack had shared his history with Frederick once. Only small pieces, but enough to hint to Jack being desperately in love—and when Jack's father lost his title, his wife seemed to lose her love for him. How long ago had that been? Three years?

"I'm afraid I haven't, my lady, but your very existence gives me faith that there is hope for the right sort. I'm rather inept when it comes to the fairer sex, I'm afraid, so I hope she'll have more knowledge about the whole affair than me, and perhaps she can sweep *me* off my feet." He cleared his throat and braided his hands in front of him on the table. "Now, as to the robberies, the details I've been able to gather thus far are interesting. Despite someone trying to make the robberies seem unconnected, I'm certain they are."

"How did they try to throw you off their trail?" Grace leaned forward.

"The thieves stole other art pieces as well, no doubt in order to make it seem like a more generalized robbery." He raised a finger. "But most of the other pieces were items of much less value than *The Juliets*, proving our thief entered the gallery with one specific purpose in mind. *The Juliets* are not widely known, so they must have been the thief's primary object."

"So the thief wasn't stealing art in order to resell it to collectors and make money." Grace shook her head. "Like with our most recent case related to Egyptian antiquities."

Case? Had Grace just used the word *case* to describe their trip to Egypt? Frederick stifled the urge to pinch his eyes closed. Not only was she referring to them as sleuths, but now she recounted the beginning of their honeymoon in investigative language. The strongest urge to laugh tightened his stomach. There was no use fighting it anymore. He might as well just give in full-heartedly to the tug. . .or trap of it all.

"Exactly." Jack nodded. "By all accounts, the thief broke in through one of the back service doors and made his way through the gallery rather quickly during the night watchman's break."

"So whoever it was knew the schedule of the gallery."

"Precisely." Jack nodded to Frederick. "And likely someone familiar with the layout of the pieces to be able to take what they did so quickly and without notice until morning."

"So you need us to visit the site, look for clues, and question the staff, don't you?" Grace reached to her side and drew out her notebook and fountain pen, frantically jotting down information. "Look for inconsistencies in stories or little hints to suspicious figures."

"Ah, excellent, someone who takes notes." Jack grinned. "I'm forever misplacing my pen, but yes, that's exactly what I'd hoped the two of you might do."

"Who are your top suspects so far?"

Grace gave a little gasp at Frederick's question, and he turned his attention to her. A somewhat happy daze donned her face. He replayed his question in his mind, and the answer emerged. He'd used the word *suspects*.

Jack's attention shifted from Grace back to Frederick, and the man fought a losing battle with his grin. "I do believe this may be my favorite case of recent history."

"Jack." The warning in Frederick's voice did nothing to still the man's grin.

"Yes, well, the information is still new, and we don't have all the details yet, but"—he cleared his throat, his eyes still alight—"the known possible *suspects. . .*could be anyone interested in *The Juliets.*"

"So art collectors, historians?" Grace offered.

"Or someone with a more personal design," Frederick added, the admission sobering him a little. If the case turned personal, it became more dangerous.

He rolled his gaze heavenward. He'd just used the word *case* too.

"Exactly." Jack nodded, taking another drink of tea. "The only people I've met in the whole ordeal so far are Daniel Laraby and his friend Paul"—Jack waved toward Frederick and Grace—"both of whom you've met, if somewhat inadvertently. I've had a passing conversation with Signore Capello, the owner of the art gallery, but that is all."

"And of them, any ideas?"

Surely there had to be something to go on so far.

"Laraby has a high interest in *The Juliets* as a collector, but I don't sense he is the cunning sort."

"The man literally faked pinching Grace's purse as a joke, Jack. What if the art gallery is just another lark to fill the time of a leisurely millionaire?"

"I've thought of that, but I can't quite see it as of yet." He drew in a breath and gathered up a pastry from his plate. "His altercation with you yesterday hints to being more of a prankster and performer than someone with a true malicious streak."

"And what about Miss Benetti?" Grace asked. "As an art curator with a deep connection to Venice, would she have designs on the paintings?"

"Possibly, but she has an alibi for the night of the robbery." Jack raised a brow. "She was on Laraby's island with him."

"Oh," Grace said rather nonchalantly, and then her expression slowly transformed, her eyes growing wider and her cheeks darkening. "Oh, you mean *with* Laraby on his island."

Humor resurfaced in Jack's eyes, and he raised his palms as if helpless to answer. "All I can say, my lady, is that Laraby and Paul both confirmed her presence for the duration of the night and said the others on the island villa could do the same."

"Laraby's friend Paul?" Frederick asked, internally shaking his head at the idea. As a dependent on Laraby's kindness and wealth, it isn't likely Paul would risk a real crime, is it?

"I know little of him, but he doesn't seem the sort."

"Those may be the very ones to keep an eye on, Jack," Grace offered. "Not only is it a common occurrence in well-written mysteries, but even in your book, you caution against overlooking any possible suspect no matter how unlikely."

"You are very right, my lady." Jack's grin grew wide, and he tapped the table. "All the more reason I need the two of you on the case with me. I'll be happy to have you put some of those smart deductions into practice with a little look around the gallery."

Grace beamed over at Frederick as if Jack had just given her the moon. No, his wife didn't seem the sort who'd want the moon. His shoulders slumped. More shooting lessons, perhaps? A new throwing knife? He shook the thoughts from his mind and grappled onto something less unnerving. The latest Conan Doyle book?

Laraby emerged from the hallway, his grin as broad as it had been when he left. "So sorry about that interruption, but I'm afraid I must be off to attend to the last-minute details of our party. I have high hopes of making it exciting for all." He waved toward the doorway as if that explained the problem and then turned to Frederick. "And I'd like to extend the invitation to you,

Lord Astley, and your lovely wife, to join Detective Miracle at my home tomorrow. It will be an honor to have you there, and you can assist more fully with the investigation. Besides, since Lady Astley is such an admirer of fiction, she may enjoy meeting my friend Mrs. Dolores Reynolds." He brought his palms together and shifted his attention from Frederick to Grace. "What do you say?"

Frederick looked to Jack for guidance. After all, if they went with Laraby to his island, it gave less time to visit the gallery.

"Well," Jack said, giving a shrug, "I am a huge proponent of making plans, but I always expect a change in them." He chuckled, sending Frederick and Grace a knowing look before turning to a confused Laraby. "If the Astleys are amenable to it, I think they would make excellent additions to your party, Mr. Laraby."

The glint in his wife's eyes told Frederick two things:

One, she was certainly amenable.

And two, he knew exactly where they would be visiting after morning tea.

Chapter 4

Observe.

Listen.

Don't be obvious.

Grace grimaced. That last one may be the most difficult detective rule to follow. She had a hard enough time trying to act coy with her darling husband in very comfortable surroundings. How on earth was she supposed to convincingly pretend to be disinterested or unimpressed when in a very real mystery?

In fact, *everything* seemed interesting.

She considered imitating the clever Lady Molly of Scotland Yard, but since Lady Molly always seemed to solve mysteries by using some magical woman's intuition related to domestic clues that men knew very little about, Grace was at a complete loss. She wasn't exactly certain if her woman's intuition worked at all, and her domestic knowledge was severely lacking. The few times she'd attempted to sew resulted in a shirtwaist with the second armhole sewn together and a blouse with crooked buttons.

However, if this case required the use of a rope, knife throwing, lock picking, tree climbing, swimming, or her newest achievement, riding a camel, she felt fairly adequate for the task. She excelled in book reading and puzzles too, so perhaps that bit of information would be helpful as well. And she knew about the plants of Derbyshire, but she couldn't sort out how that knowledge would help her in Venice. . .or with paintings.

Grace had made sure to read a few chapters in Detective Miracle's book before she and Frederick made their way to the Gallery Romano. But Frederick hadn't seemed surprised at all at her suggestion to visit before they went to the island in the morning. How did he seem to guess her thoughts sometimes, while at others he appeared completely shocked?

Perhaps the latter moments were those times when Grace surprised even herself.

"Did you know the gallery is housed within a former palace?" Grace squeezed close to Frederick, her arm entwined through his, as they walked the stone pavement of the narrow street. "So many of the palaces are used for other businesses now, since Venice is no longer in its golden era. Some of the ceilings and wall murals in these buildings are works of art in their own right and worth preserving. It's a good use of well-built places so that the history doesn't disappear."

Frederick nodded. "I have hopes that our village back home will continue to reinvent ways to use their existing buildings to keep the history and the village alive and well, even as the world changes."

The love for his home and legacy pearled through her dear husband, and the longer they were married, the more Grace appreciated how much the people in the countryside adjacent to their estate of Havensbrooke benefitted from and relied on Frederick's ingenuity and support.

Well, Grace supposed they relied on her now too, an idea she was still trying to fully grasp since, as an American heiress, she didn't fully understand the centuries-old heritage inherent within British aristocracy. In fact, she didn't understand a great many things about the aristocracy, particularly how to address certain people.

That's why being in places like Egypt and Italy had given her a much needed reprieve from sorting out dowager-lady-duchess-lord-sir greetings. Solving mysteries of the non-titled kind proved much easier. . .and more interesting.

"The Gallery Romano." Frederick gestured with his chin toward a three-story building of coral facade with the embossed name adorning the front.

"Do you think we should go right through the front door?" She lowered her voice as they neared the impressive-looking building, the slap of water along the canal edge just to their left. "Or should we have a look outside first?"

Frederick's lips quirked the tiniest bit before he turned those dark eyes of his on her with a thoughtful look. "I suppose you happened to ask Jack about where the thieves made their entry?"

She tipped her head, her parasol shading her from the warm sun. "It seemed an important bit of information."

"Indeed." He directed their walk to the right of the building as if to—

She gasped. "You asked Jack the same, didn't you?"

"It seemed an important bit of information." He tossed her own words back at her, the twinkle in his eyes the only indication of his teasing.

Her smile burst wide. "I knew bombarding you with sleuthing books would eventually winkle the mystery love into you."

"Perhaps so." He dipped his chin, watching her from his periphery with that little smile still tucked at the corner of his very kissable mouth. "But I believe my close relationship with my sleuthing partner may be more to blame."

"Sleuthing partner?" She sighed at the lovely way he said it with his beautiful deep English accent. "You're begging for another thorough reward, aren't you, my dear Lord Astley?"

"Your particular rewards are my favorites, my lady." His

focused attention and knowing raise of his brow heated her cheeks. "However, I believe that if I'm going to spend the rest of my life with you, I'd better become more acclimated to the ongoing danger that seems to find you more regularly than most."

"You keep blaming that on me and my imagination." Her laugh burst out, and she squeezed his arm with her hand as they entered the narrow alley between Gallery Romano and a neighboring building. "But I must admit, our married life has been nothing at all like I feared. I haven't knitted at all and have not felt the urge to run away from you once."

He coughed.

"Very well." She frowned. "Once I actually ran away *from you*, but not with any intention of it being permanent and only to make a point about our argument. All of the other times I ran away, they weren't *from* you but in the hopes of helping rescue someone." She raised a finger. "And I've promised to leave a note for any of the other times I run off."

He wrestled with his smile as they turned to the back of the building. A narrow black door stood at the center of a long, windowless wall, the only entrance to the gallery from the back. Jack had mentioned this as the entry point for the thieves. Well, Grace presumed it to be more than one person. Some of the paintings she'd seen before looked much too large for one person to carry—especially if they took more than one.

Frederick bent by the door, his hands moving over the broken wood by the door handle.

"Well, that's fairly obvious evidence of tampering," Grace said, kneeling down beside him.

He didn't respond but continued his perusal, then stood, bringing her with him. With a gentle tug, the door opened without resistance. "Odd."

Her attention followed his, and she leaned close to the door, examining where the latch fitted into place. The wood was cracked around the latch, but she didn't notice anything else unusual.

"The dead lock is not broken or even damaged." He frowned. "The door looks as though it's been vandalized but. . ." He turned a lever on the inside of the door, and the bolt lock shot out, completely intact. "It has every capacity to lock back in place."

Her gaze moved from the door to Frederick. "But wouldn't the thieves have broken the lock when they made their way into the"—she gasped—"Frederick, do you mean to say this door wasn't broken into?"

"I'm not certain." He stood, looking into the dark space within the building. It appeared to be a storage room with another door separating them from what she supposed was the inside of the art gallery. "Perhaps the gallery owner has already had the lock repaired?"

The doubt on her husband's face fueled her own. She slid past him into the storage room and kneeled to examine the internal door. If the thieves used the street-side door, they would have to enter through this one as well. The door's edge held the same superficial scratches but intact lock.

"Could they replace the locks without replacing the whole door?" She stood, looking over at Frederick. "Is that a possibility?"

"It is, but unlikely with the types of damage externally." He rested his palms at his waist, studying the internal door like the detective he was bound to become.

Grace pulled her mind from those distractingly exuberant thoughts and back to the matter at hand. "But then, if they didn't have to break the locks, it would mean that someone left the door unlocked?"

"Or someone had a key." His gaze fastened on hers.

Her bottom lip dropped open. Either way, if these locks had not been replaced, it meant that the robbery could very well have been by an employee of the gallery.

Grace was just about to speak her thoughts when the internal door swung open to reveal a tall, dark-haired man with the most impressive mustache she'd ever seen. It twirled into exquisite curls on either side. She couldn't quite take her eyes off it. How on earth did he make his mustache curl so symmetrically? Was there a brush for such a thing?

The man boomed forward, a long sentence in Italian erupting as expressively as his hand gestures.

Frederick tugged Grace back from the man and stood as a buffer between them. "Please excuse us, sir," he said and then responded in Italian.

Grace never tired of hearing him practice other languages, especially Italian. It sounded so lovely from his very kissable lips. "We are working with Detective Jack Miracle."

The man spouted out Detective Miracle's name in exasperation and sighed, appearing to compose himself, his impressive nose upraised. "The detective did not mention others."

"We only arrived a few days ago to assist him," Grace added, stepping to Frederick's side and attempting a subdued smile. She'd once read that bright smiles gave off the impression of someone either being too young, insincere, or mad. And even if she did devour gothic novels at times, Frederick never gave off any hint he thought her mad, which garnered a great deal of affirmation that she probably wasn't.

The man studied both of them, his doubtful gaze lingering on Grace.

"My name is Frederick Percy, Earl of Astley." Frederick gestured toward Grace. "And this is my wife." Her husband produced a card with his information, which appeared to calm the man a little.

"I am Signore Ettore Capello." His mustache offered the smallest shake with his sniff. "Owner of the Galleria de Romano."

"It is a pleasure to meet you, Signore." Frederick tipped his head. "I am sorry our presence came as such a surprise, but we thought to investigate the entry point of your thieves before coming inside."

Signore Capello moved his attention from Frederick to the open back door.

Frederick's diplomatic introduction calmed a bit of Grace's excitement, and she felt much more certain that her next smile was demure.

"These doors are lovely." Grace moved to touch the thick wooden back door. "Are they original to the building?"

"Si." Signore Capello nodded, the tightness in his face softening a bit. "I have attempted to keep the heart and bones of the original palazzo in excellent condition. Doors, walls, windows." He made a flourish with his hand as if to encompass the whole gallery. "It is one of the best gallerias in the city."

"Would we have the opportunity for a tour?"

Grace's question caused the man's face to relax even more. Ah, all those years of detouring conversations with her father to get her out of trouble worked on other people too. Of course, if distraction worked on her, it may very well be of use on other people.

"Si, I shall arrange it."

"Signore, one question." Frederick walked to the back door and slid a hand over the edge of the door near the bolt. "Have you had the chance to replace the locks since the robbery? The...*rapina*?"

"No, there has been no time." He turned toward the inner door and touched a slide lock at the top of the door. "I had this one placed the day after the rapina, but the...um...*il fabbro ferraio*..."

"The locksmith?" Frederick offered.

"Si, the locksmith could not come to repair the entire door until next week."

Frederick slid her a glance before following Signore Capello through the inner door into a hallway. With the introductions out of the way and explanations made, Signore Capello's stance and tone reflected much more welcome.

"And what did the police determine from their findings?"

"*Polizia?*" Signore Capello's dark brows rose then crashed, his hand slicing in front of him. "No, no police. I will keep this little investigation private so it will not impact my reputation. This is why I joined with Signore Laraby to pay for the detective."

So why had the thieves left the appearance of a break-in? To confuse the investigation? Slow the process?

"A very good idea for anyone who wishes to keep an unfortunate event quiet among his patrons." Frederick nodded, his affirmation loosening Signore Capello's words even more.

Exactly as Frederick wished, Grace guessed.

She smiled. What a clever husband!

"I should have listened to my colleagues who warned me about purchasing any of *The Juliets*, but it was all *ridicolo*! We are modern people. We do not believe in a *maledizione*."

"Maledizione? You mean a curse?"

The words escaped Frederick's lips almost like a whimper, but why, Grace had no idea. The very idea that something peculiar revolved around the paintings made the whole mystery even more appealing.

Like Egypt.

A shiver of delight trembled over her and ended with a very certain tingle to her scalp.

Oh, this was going to be an excellent adventure.

Frederick replayed the word in his head.

Maledizione?

He drew in a deep breath. He'd already borne the brunt of two curses. The Astley curse and the mummy's tomb, and both ended in life-threatening escapades. This! This was supposed to be a simple case of an art heist.

"Whatever do you mean by curse, Signore?" Grace scanned the room, her expression shining with much more interest than an impending "tragedy" ought to entice.

Finding some pleasure in the intrigue of a mystery was one thing. A curious hobby or pastime. But delight? Perhaps he should encourage his bride to read a few more romances than mysteries. Perhaps even some solid nonfiction.

"Si. A curse." He spat out the word. "When I purchased *The Juliets*, one of my curators warned me of the history of these paintings, but the beauty, the colors." He breathed a sigh. "Accardi painted with such passion, such richness. And I celebrate our local artists here, unlike some of my competitors." He waved a hand. "A curse? Who believes in such foolishness?" His frown deepened to such an extent, his brows touched. "But the Galleria de Romano had never been robbed. *Mai!* And then I buy *The Juliets* and. . .bah!" He raised his hand and murmured something in Italian. *"Impossibile!"*

The fascination on Grace's face as she watched the man's passionate monologue nearly distracted Frederick, but the word *curse* won out. "What did you learn about this curse, Signore?" Frederick hoped weeding through some of the dramatic drivel would negate any such thoughts of real danger.

"I do not want to speak of it." He drew up to his height and gave his head a shake. "No, but Jasmine will explain." Then, as if the man had gotten over his frustration, he smiled. "Come, this. . .keeping room is no place for a lord and lady. Let me introduce you to my lovely galleria."

Jasmine? Laraby's fiancée? Her connection to the paintings would be worthy of exploration, indeed.

Frederick offered Grace his arm, and they followed Signore

Capello through the inner doors up a narrow hall. Grace leaned close. "Do you realize how many mysteries there are where someone from the inside is the very thief?"

Ah, her thoughts had turned in the same direction as his.

"I'm certain you can give me a detailed overview of each one." He attempted to cloak his smile with his hand.

"I don't know why you try to hide your smile when you're amused," she whispered back. "That's the very reason a lovely smile is supposed to be used." She stood a little taller as they followed Signore Capello. "Though I am particularly glad that I'm the reason you try to hide your smile so often. Perhaps my encouraging your ready humor will counteract some of the unfortunate perils I incite."

His smile flared full at that, especially considering his previous thoughts about the whole curse debacle. "Heart and humor, darling. You provide both and an ample supply."

"Ah, but peace of mind was clearly absent from your list." She looked up at him with the smallest tip to her lips.

"Two out of three are not bad odds, are they?"

Her smile spread, and she squeezed his arm. "Better than one out of three."

Suddenly, the shadowed hallway flooded with light as Signore Capello opened a set of double doors and led them into a vast room of sunshine with glossy floors of earth-toned marble. Flanking them on either side stood white marble statues of various people in heroic Roman forms. All the walls boasted gilded-framed paintings, mostly oils, and a few of the more contemporary style. It was magnificent. Frederick had always been drawn to artwork ever since his grandfather first took him to the National Gallery in London.

"You like paintings?" Grace's remark pulled his attention. "I can see it in your eyes."

"I do enjoy and have been drawn to art most of my life." He

smiled down at her, heat climbing up his neck. He'd rarely shared such an intimate and hidden interest. "Even attempted to paint rather poorly in the past."

"You? A painter?" Her smile spread wide, encouraging him to continue.

His brother had always scoffed at his attempts. His father deemed it a waste of time, but not his dear wife. Somehow she seemed to have insurmountable faith in him. Perhaps when they returned to England, he could pick up the hobby again.

"At the Galleria de Romano we celebrate our Venetian heritage with Bellini, Giordano, Ricci, and Guardi." Signore Capello's voice broke into their conversation. "But also masters from across the world, like Van Gogh, Cezanne, and Monet."

"Do you still have some of your own paintings?" Grace whispered, ignoring Signore Capello's continued praise for his gallery.

He didn't answer immediately. In fact, he wasn't certain what to say. *Did* he still have any of his own art pieces?

"Is that why there are so many lovely works on display in your office?" she continued. "Did you choose those yourself?"

Clever woman.

Indeed he had.

"You will notice even some more modern artists of the contemporary style there." Signore Capello pointed toward a corner of the vast room, his gaze expecting their attention.

"And interestingly, none of those famous ones were touched by your thieves," Grace continued, further confirming Jack's suspicions.

The thieves were after *The Juliets*.

"It is a truly remarkable collection," Frederick offered in response to Signore Capello's pointed look.

"Si."

"And how fortunate more of your valued works were not disturbed."

"It is by design." Signore Capello nodded and waved toward various rooms on either side of the main atrium. "Paintings are kept in separate rooms to deter a thief from taking too many of the classics before getting caught. We have guards all night."

"And *The Juliets*? Where were they kept?" This from Grace, with notepad at the ready.

Signore Capello sighed as if reminded of his loss. "I will show you." They turned to the left into another hallway that had a set of rooms on either side. A short yet sturdy man in uniform stood near the only closed door of the set.

"This is Agente Ricci, the guard who discovered that *The Juliets* were missing." Signore Capello nodded back to Frederick and Grace. "Ricci, I present Lord and Lady Astley. They are working with the *Britannico* detective, Miracle."

The way Signore Capello said *Britannico*, or British, was not flattering or confidence-bolstering.

"*Salve.*" Ricci dipped his head in response and then released a sentence in Italian.

Signore Capello interpreted, though Frederick caught the gist of the man's statement. "Agente Ricci says he will be happy to answer any questions."

"*Grazie,*" Frederick thanked Signore Capello and then turned to Grace, who was clearly attempting to comprehend. Instead of butchering his Italian, he decided to allow Signore Capello to translate. "Agente Ricci, would you tell us how you discovered the missing paintings?"

"And if there was anything unusual you noticed once you did discover them missing?" Grace added.

Ricci answered and Signore Capello turned to them. "He said he and the other agente met, as they usually did, in the front office of the galleria to exchange information before the previous agente retired for the evening and Ricci began his turn. Nothing looked abnormal when he emerged from the office, and Ricci heard nothing of concern."

Ricci offered another sentence, and Signore Capello nodded. "He says it was not until he had been on guard for an hour before he entered the room housing *The Juliets*. That is when he noticed the theft."

"And you checked the doors for a place of entry immediately?"

"Subito." Ricci nodded as Signore Capello translated Frederick's question.

"As you have seen from the doors," Signore Capello added, "the intruders broke into the back."

Frederick refused to look in Grace's direction and only hoped his wife kept her expression as neutral as she possibly could.

"Do you have any thoughts as to who would steal *The Juliets*?" Grace asked, her tone calm, measured.

Frederick curbed his grin, a tiny bit of pride rising through him at her effort.

"A madman impassioned by his love for the arts," Signore Capello answered, his hands becoming animated again. "Or expert thieves hired by some jealous collector who wishes to embarrass me."

"Is there such a collector, Signore?"

"There are many." Signore Capello's chin raised at Grace's follow-up question, and he sniffed, upsetting his mustache. "I make many jealous with my collection, especially with my Impressionists. No one values Impressionist paintings like I do, and Jasmine is fantastic at locating ones for me to purchase with her many connections."

"How long ago was it you purchased *The Juliets*, Signore?" Had Jack told them? Frederick didn't recall.

"One was six months ago from a Frenchman." Signore Capello shook his head, his frown deepening. "And it was a good thing I did, for the man's house burned to the ground only two days after I retrieved the painting from him. If I had not purchased it when I did, the painting would have been destroyed like the rest of his belongings."

What a horrible coincidence! A thought filtered in from Jack's book: *Remain suspicious of coincidences. They are rarely as common as people think.*

"And the other purchase?" This from Grace.

"Jasmine located it during one of her trips to England about. . .um. . ." He looked toward the ceiling and tapped his mustache as he murmured in Italian. "Five months ago? I had hoped to display one of Signore Laraby's *Juliets* with the two from my gallery to have a trio, but, alas, the curse attacked both Laraby and myself."

Signore Capello turned away from Officer Ricci and pulled out a key to unlock the closed door near them, but Grace approached the agente.

"And you didn't notice anything else unusual, Agente?" Her production of the word proved she had an ear for languages. Perhaps Frederick could turn her interests in that direction for a few months to detour one dangerous mystery after another.

Frederick translated to the man, and Ricci shook his head.

"I will show you the room of devastation." Signore Capello led them over the threshold into the locked room. As a corner room on the far side of the building, this particular location was rather out of the way, proving all the more that the thieves had a specific target in mind.

Some paintings still hung on the walls of the room, with a few blank spots where, presumably, the stolen items once hung.

The thieves had to pass myriad other works to obtain *The Juliets*.

Some works more expensive than *The Juliets*, as Signore Capello explained. "So I do not understand it at all."

"Signore, who can gain access to the gallery after closing

hours?" Frederick shrugged to attempt to ease the seriousness of his question. "Staff? Of course the night guards?"

"Si." Signore Capello pulled his attention from one of the empty walls, one dark brow rising. "The guards, the cleaning manager, our curators, but they are all trusted people. Many I have known for years."

The room was not well lit or particularly large, but each wall except for one still held paintings. A few sculptures dotted the center of the room as well.

"And who are your newest people?" Grace asked.

"Only three, but they have all been here for six months at the least. The cleaner, Marietta, is married to Ricci. But Ricci has been with me for ten years. Lorenzo, who assists with the accounts, and Jasmine Benetti." Laraby's fiancée. "We hired her as a curator when she had just finished university, and she has been *eccellente*."

"Did I hear my name?"

Poised in the doorway was a woman of beauty almost as impeccable as the statues lining the atrium. Dark hair swooped into a bun and complemented a pair of equally dark eyes. Her burgundy suit enhanced the color of her lips, which appeared too dark to be natural.

She smiled her welcome, a subdued look.

"Lord and Lady Astley wish to hear about the Juliet curse."

"Do they?" Her dark gaze flipped from Frederick to Grace. "It is a unique interest for most people outside of Italy, particularly Venice."

"Si," Signore Capello continued. "But they are working along with your fiancé's detective."

"Are they?" Both her dark brows rose, and she entered farther into the room. "I believe Laraby may have mentioned it to me as he escorted me here." She dipped her head in greeting, her dark gaze scanning over them with careful deliberation. "It appears he created quite the first impression, no?"

"I'm hoping he will improve upon further acquaintance," Frederick answered.

"He is a mischievous boy sometimes, is he not?" Her smile spread. "It is not good for him to become bored, but I am hopeful he will remain distracted with his dinner party for the next week so that he will not engage in such games as you witnessed yesterday, Signore."

Frederick dipped his head in acknowledgment of her understanding.

"What can you tell us about this curse, Miss Benetti?" Grace shifted forward, sending Frederick a frown before turning her attention back to the woman. "Signore Capello mentioned you warned him before purchasing *The Juliets*."

"It is likely nothing more than a sad coincidence, Signora." She shook her head, her smile apologetic. "These stories rarely mean anything more than ghost tales, but in my studies I was drawn to the early Impressionist works, which became my focus. Venetian artist Luca Accardi was one of those masters."

"Accardi is the painter of *The Juliets*?" Grace asked.

"Yes, but he is not widely recognized since *The Juliets* are his only known works."

"But those works are excellent examples of early Impressionism," Signore Capello added. "Of the same style as Renoir or Monet, except there is something all his own in them, which makes them special."

"Indeed they are, and from a Venetian," Miss Benetti responded with a smile. "Thus the reason I became a student of them. They fit my interest and my love for my home."

"And the curse?"

Her attention turned to Frederick. "Rumors really, but I thought Signore Capello should at least be aware of them." She trailed a finger along the frame of a nearby landscape before turning back to them. "With Accardi's sad history, it is no wonder people would place a curse upon his work. There is much, um—what is the word?—*mystery* surrounding these paintings. Not only because of what happened to Accardi and his family but also the misfortunes that seem to follow those who own the paintings."

Frederick's attention sharpened. *Like the man whose house burned?*

"Misfortunes?" Grace's question pierced the sudden silence. "What types of misfortunes?"

"The sort that collects the attention of thieves," Signore Capello answered with a dramatic wave of his hand toward the empty wall. "Thieves and art collectors."

"And these misfortunes led to the belief that the paintings are cursed?" Frederick asked, knowing full well the power of superstition.

"Yes."

"That sort of history does fuel all kind of imaginings," Grace added. "As well as interest, I would think."

"Unfortunately, the interest is not where it should be, in the beauty of the artwork itself." Miss Benetti's jaw tensed, her expression hardening. "The paintings should be here, among Accardi's native people, those who truly appreciate his work."

Ah, the passion of art lovers. "Detective Miracle informed us that the thieves were strategic in their entry and timeline." Frederick turned from Miss Benetti to Signore Capello. "Between the exchange of guards."

"Si," came her simple reply.

"Which means whoever stole the paintings was familiar with the gallery as well as with the changing of the guards," Grace added, her intelligent eyes shifting back to Miss Benetti.

"You think it was one of us?" Miss Benetti stood taller, her dark eyes narrowing. "One of the people who are committed to protecting these treasures?"

"We're merely attempting to consider all possibilities, Miss Benetti," Frederick answered. "Your treasures are certainly worth our thorough investigation."

"Be careful, Lord Astley, that you do not look for wolves among the shepherds instead of the sheep." One of her dark brows tipped. "Those who understand Accardi's work wish for it to be exactly where it belongs, curse or no."

With that, she raised her chin and exited the room, leaving the scent of citrus and an unsettling feeling behind her.

Chapter 5

"I don't know if I've seen a more beautiful woman." Grace slipped next to Frederick as they walked down the pavement toward their hotel. "No wonder she caught Mr. Laraby's attention in such a short time. Didn't he say they'd only known one another three months?"

"Since Laraby has only been in Venice for six months, I suppose it must be less than that."

"And already engaged? That is very efficient." She studied his face. Did he think Miss Benetti was beautiful? Something squeezed in Grace's chest.

"Not as quick as us, if you remember." His lips crooked. "Two weeks, was it?"

"Ours was very different, as you well know. Arranged marriages usually are." She nibbled on her bottom lip and gave in to her thoughts. "We'd better keep an eye on her. Beautiful women are notorious for being dangerous."

He cast her a look. "Are they?" Something in his gaze snagged at her attention. A glimmer?

"Of course." She pulled him to a stop in the middle of the street. Surely he'd read enough gothic romances or mysteries to figure that out. Not to mention his very own real-life experiences. "The most beautiful women in fiction are usually the most dangerous.

Just think of Sherlock's Isadora Klein or Kitty Winter."

"You're right." He studied her, his expression giving little away. "Beautiful women are dangerous."

Well, at least if he agreed Miss Benetti was beautiful, he'd also be on his guard. She frowned. That was something. Though she wasn't quite certain she liked that something.

"I think *you're* beautiful, and you're incredibly dangerous to my heart."

The tightened feeling in her chest unraveled and a little whimper crept up her throat. "You think I'm beautiful?" She blinked, trying to take in the sentiment, especially from her darling hero. "I've never thought of myself as beautiful, and certainly not *dangerously* beautiful. And it's not uncommon for men as dashing as you to be drawn in by exotic beauties like Miss Benetti."

"Grace, wise men recognize the treasures they already possess and do not go in search of more." He placed his hand over hers. "You have only continued to grow more beautiful the longer I've known you, and I have no interest in having any other dangerous women in my heart but you."

A sweet thrill erupted through her at his declaration. Dangerous and beautiful in the same sentence! Her dear Frederick had just turned a lifelong dream of hers into a reality. She ushered them back into a walk, a satisfied sigh on her lips. "Just so you know, Frederick, I plan to take very good care of your heart. If you recall, it's your peace of mind that I have trouble keeping in amiable order."

His chuckle surfaced, and she stared over at him. He always looked handsome, but now with a bit of sleuthing skills beneath him, he seemed to grow even more so. It seemed such an excellent combination for a budding detective. Attractive, smart, kind, and a little bit roguish. Surely Sir Arthur Conan Doyle couldn't have invented someone so perfect for Grace's own kind of life story.

"You were very good at looking for clues back at the gallery."

Grace nodded as she spoke. "If this is to be our first legitimate bit of detective work, you certainly handled yourself like a true professional. I knew Detective Miracle's book would come in handy."

His grin tipped in the way that told her he wanted to laugh.

"I admit I find the idea of solving a mystery interesting." His brow rose. "As long as it doesn't turn into a life-threatening feat."

"But an art heist suits you for our first real detective job, doesn't it?" She nodded. "Yes, I think it's an excellent start. No mysterious murders or men who appear to be very congenial but in the end plan to trap you in a tomb."

His smile fell, and she frowned. Oh, she'd reminded him of their near demise. She'd better change the subject. "I think you will be a much more congenial detective than Sherlock Holmes."

"Is that so?"

"Oh yes!" She could envision it now. The two of them solving mysteries across the world. Finding treasure. Dodging gunfire. Spending evenings in each other's arms. It sounded positively exhilarating. But she'd best not mention the dodging gunfire part to Frederick, especially after the recent tomb reference. "I think you'd prove more friendly and agreeable, like Morrison's Martin Hewitt. He was just as smart as Sherlock but was much less offensive."

"I appreciate your faith in me, darling." He grinned. "But clever Sherlock didn't have a lovely sleuthing partner to assist him, and I feel that makes all the difference."

A thrill of warmth splashed over her at his use of Sherlock and reference to her as his sleuthing partner. Paired with the fact that he was actually acknowledging their current adventure as an investigation, she felt certain her life was nearly perfect. There was something to be said for a man who cared more about a woman's ability to solve crimes than her knowledge about hats and which gown to wear in summer.

"I wouldn't mind the detective mind of Loveday Brooke, but even I can do better with fashion sense. Who would wish to wear a black dress all the time!" The old buildings framed their walk across the cobbled streets, the air tinged with pastries. She adored these simple conversations together among friends. Wonderfully married friends. "Did you know sometimes it's easier for a woman to investigate certain places because she is less likely to garner suspicion?"

His lips pinched as he helped her navigate around a group of tourists who were boarding a gondola. "I would assume so, and women often ask different questions or see things from a different point of view than men."

"Exactly." Grace nodded, but then, how had she noticed different things than Frederick? He picked up on the locks of the doors much more quickly than she. And he'd known Italian, which was not only convenient but also incredibly attractive. "There is no doubt about it now. The people who broke into the gallery were truly only interested in *The Juliets*. And whoever they were, they must have someone helping them on the inside."

"Or have visited the museum enough times to know the route well enough to evade the night guards."

"Of course, the person who was supposed to lock up on the night in question could have left the doors unlocked on purpose." She tapped the ground with her closed parasol.

"The possible accomplice, you mean?" He looked ahead, his expression thoughtful. "Yes, there had to have been at least two people to complete the robbery so quickly. From the spaces left behind on the wall, the paintings were not small."

"And certainly someone with access to the inner workings of the gallery." Her attention shifted back to him. "I wonder if Miss Benetti has an alibi for the night of the robbery?" Oh goodness! She sounded exactly as a detective ought. Even using the word *alibi.* She had the sudden urge to tilt her own hat a little farther over her forehead and purchase a new notepad to list clues.

"Jack mentioned she did."

Grace looked over at him and found the misplaced memory...and then her cheeks flushed hot. Oh yes, she'd been at Laraby's island villa all night long. She shook the thought away. "It's curious Jack didn't mention the doors, Frederick." She frowned. "Do you think he knew about them?"

"He's not seen the gallery, so I'd imagine not." A sparkle came to his eyes as he looked down at her, and she wondered if a little of the creative, imaginative boy who once took up residence in his heart was beginning to resurface. Wouldn't that be wonderful? That after all of the hurt and rejection, he finally felt comfortable and loved enough to dream again? "Which narrows down our *accomplices*"—he exaggerated the word, likely for her sleuthing benefit—"quite a bit, doesn't it?"

"You produced that word as if you liked saying it." She laughed, perhaps more from her dear husband's exuberance than his use of the word *accomplices*. "I think it's becoming abundantly clear that Detective Jack needs us." She wiggled her brows. "And perhaps *you* need a little more adventure."

Almost as if her sentence proved prophetic, a call rang out toward them from down the lane. They were near one of the larger canals, not too far from their hotel, and the sunset shone gold against the water and the buildings that lined it. The gorgeous scene of haloed stone and glimmering water stole her attention, but from the center, running down the lane, came the silhouetted figure of a man.

"Lord Astley," called the voice, his pace slowing, shoulders dropping as if in relief.

Jack?

Frederick picked up his step, with Grace at his side, both

meeting Jack on the cobblestone lane.

"What is it?" Frederick placed his hand on the man's arm. "Are you all right?"

Jack shook his head and leaned over to place his palms on his legs, catching his breath. "I thought I'd sent you to the wolves, and that's a fact." He straightened, a little color coming back into his face as he looked between the two. "You'll think me going barmy on you, but I couldn't shake the thought." He drew in a breath, lips tipping back into his ready smile, the previous concern washing off his expression. "Come, I'll fill you in over dinner. I'm afraid we've stepped into it." He sobered for a moment, a flash of fire lighting his pale eyes. "Much more than I thought."

Grace sent Frederick a look before following their friend to a nearby restaurant. Musicians played on one end of the room. A few couples danced in the center, with tables framing the dance floor. Jack dodged the tables, his steps determined, and led them to a back corner where Mr. Laraby sat. The man looked rather subdued, even sullen.

"Tell them." Jack waved toward Grace and Frederick, his attention on Laraby as he took a seat. "Tell them what's really going on behind this little game of yours, Mr. Laraby."

"What part?" Laraby barked back, a snarl on his lips. "It's not as if I misled anyone."

"No? You just failed to give full information, which changes the course of this investigation, and if you truly wish to get your painting back or not end up as another victim to the pattern of these paintings' history, then I advise you to keep the games out of it. You are no longer in the circus, and this is much more than a simple robbery."

More than a simple robbery? What did Jack mean?

Jack turned back to Frederick and Grace, gesturing for them to sit, his jaw set. "Mr. Laraby"—he voiced the name with a sneer—"hasn't been completely transparent about the entire situation with his past or *The Juliets*. Here I'd brought the two of you on, thinking you'd enjoy this simple and relatively harmless investigation of mine, but no, it's not simple." He shot a glare to Laraby. "Or harmless."

"What do you mean?" Frederick pulled a chair out for Grace and then took his own.

Jack cleared his throat and rubbed a hand over his chin, frown deepening before he braided his fingers together on the table and leaned forward. An intensity animated his eyes, bringing out a small tingle on her scalp. *Danger!*

"It appears that most of the people associated with *The Juliets* end up dead."

Grace sat up a little straighter at his direct pronouncement, her attention shifting to a still-sullen Laraby.

Jack placed a few envelopes on the table before them and ran an agitated hand through his blond hair, setting the locks on edge.

"I wired my contacts in London to see if they'd unearthed any more information to help in my investigation, and these missives arrived this afternoon." He waved toward them. "Of the six previous paintings, minus Laraby's, four of the last owners of *The Juliets* died under questionable circumstances. And one ended in—"

"Having his house burned to the ground," Grace finished.

Jack's attention zeroed in on her. "How did you know?"

"It's one of the paintings Signore Capello acquired," Frederick answered. "He boasted of nearly losing the painting by a day or two due to the fire." Frederick shook his head and leaned closer. "And the police were not alerted to this connection?"

"The police didn't have any reason to *suspect* a connection." Jack returned the papers to his jacket pocket. "*The Juliets* had been scattered throughout Europe, and other, less valuable items were often stolen along with them. Almost in every instance."

"So they looked like random robberies." This from her observant husband.

"Exactly." Jack nodded. "It would take someone specifically looking for *The Juliets* to truly notice a link."

"Did your contacts communicate how those individuals died?" Grace leaned even closer, lowering her voice. "Did they mention murder?"

"Only one was an out-and-out murder investigation." He sent another glare to Laraby before turning his attention back to Frederick and Grace. "The rest were all listed as 'sudden' deaths. One elderly woman fell down a flight of stairs. Another collector died of a heart attack at a surprisingly young age. A businessman who was transporting his *Juliet* to a new home was attacked en route and left for dead with no culprit or painting ever found. And then there's Mr. Laraby."

If possible, Mr. Laraby looked as if he wanted to become one with his chair, so far had he pushed himself into it. He finally released a long sigh and rolled his eyes, pulling himself straighter in his seat.

"Mr. Laraby?" Jack did nothing to hide the sarcasm in his voice. "Do share with us."

Laraby groaned. "I was tried for the murder of my grandfather, if you must know." His harsh whisper sliced into the silence. He cast a look over his shoulder as if any of the people nearby might be listening. "I didn't murder him—and the truth came out in the end—but I was brought on trial all the same. The old man was poisoned and, with my indifference toward him and my standing as the heir, of course I was thought of as the prime suspect."

"Yet the real murderer was never found, I'd wager," Frederick stated.

"I told the police it was the new cook Grandfather had hired. She'd only been in the house for three days. I'd seen her once, but she's the only one who had access to his food when he dined alone. Besides his valet. But his valet had been with me on an errand when the incident occurred."

"And the cook? What happened to her?" This from Grace, and the expression on Jack's face told all. "She disappeared."

Jack nodded. "And a description of her wouldn't help the police because evidently she'd been in disguise."

"In disguise?" Frederick echoed, his brows high as if the idea of a disguise seemed quite out of the ordinary.

Luckily for him, Grace had imagined many disguises and even attempted a few in her younger days, much to the dismay of her father, sister, servants, and the poor gardener, who nearly had a stroke at the vision of her pulling off a fake mustache.

"A blond wig was found in her room along with some of those ridiculous wedges that go in the shoes to change a person's height. And who's to know what other ways she altered her appearance," Laraby grumbled. "A little trick played back at me, is what I say, after all the tricks I'd caused on others."

"Yes, yes, we'll get to that later." Jack folded his arms across his chest and raised both brows in expectation. "But now, why not really introduce yourself, Mr. Laraby, because I believe it will provide a bit more clarity."

Chapter 6

Introduce himself?

Frederick's thoughts were already spinning with this new information. Possible murders. False accusations. Disguises.

He looked over at Grace, only to find his dear wife in rapt attention, those bright eyes taking it all in as if Jack and Laraby were recounting the most fascinating tale for her fiction-loving heart. He frowned. It *wasn't* fiction. It took on the same hue as the dangers they'd recently escaped in Egypt. People were not who they seemed to be.

And neither was Laraby?

Were they all living up to one of Venice's other names—the City of Masks?

"Come now, Mr. Laraby." Jack's voice twisted into mock comfort. "Or did you fail to count the cost of hiring a detective who actually does his research?"

Laraby's frown deepened, and he looked away. "John Walker." He bit out the name. "My name is John Walker."

"And?" Jack urged, his smile tight.

"My grandfather was Ebenezer Walker."

"The train tycoon?" Grace gasped, her pink lips opened in surprise. "I read about the murder trial in the paper." She glanced up at Frederick. "Of course, I usually prefer fiction, but the headline was much too gripping to ignore."

"When I made it through the trial and finally received my inheritance, I had to get away from all the blasted suspicion and talk," Laraby. . .er. . .Mr. Walker continued. "I left America with Paul and Lydia and started over. New name, new home, new life. *The Juliets* were my inspiration."

"And they led you to Italy a little over six months ago," Jack added.

"Do you think those who were after Mr. Walker's *Juliets* have tracked Laraby"—Frederick frowned—"Pardon me, tracked Mr. Walker here?"

Jack's expression harbored no doubt.

"And Mr. Walker isn't a name that is used here, Lord Astley," Laraby corrected. "He's dead for all I care."

"Well, we hope to keep you, whoever you wish to be, alive." Jack stared at Laraby. "But that is up to how much you're willing to listen to me and quit your games."

"Should the house party continue as planned, then—with possible murderers in pursuit of Laraby's *Juliets*?" Grace tried very hard not to reveal her disappointment, Frederick noted.

"You can't be serious." Laraby nearly shot up from his chair. "I have been planning this party for renowned mystery writer Mrs. Dolores Reynolds since I arrived in Italy. She is going to use my home in her next novel, and her brother may very well use it in one of those moving pictures of his. We are not going to—"

"There's no need to lose your head, Laraby." Jack raised a palm. "You Americans and your emotions can be regularly demonstrative, can't you?" Jack's subtle grin was aimed at Grace, who raised a playful brow at the detective.

Though she proved demonstrative in her emotions, Frederick was glad to note his darling wife's logic and wit balanced out the emotions on a continual basis, for the most part. A fact for which he regularly thanked God.

"The last *Juliets* are the ones in your possession on your island." Jack folded his hands together in front of him on the table and leaned forward. "Therefore, your island is where we must be. As long as you give me your word to be honest from this point on, I see no reason to alter your plans at present."

Laraby gave a stiff nod in appreciation.

"However, if things begin to become dangerously unruly, you must heed my advice. Do you understand?"

"Yes, yes." He blew out an exasperated breath and made to stand. "Are we finished here, Detective? I have arrangements to put into order before the party begins tomorrow."

Jack studied him, quiet building to such a degree Laraby squirmed. "Take care, Mr. Laraby, that you don't treat this situation like a game, because I can assure you, the people who desire your *Juliets* have proven they won't play nicely."

"Nor according to *your* rules, I should think," Frederick added.

Laraby tugged at his jacket and raised his chin. The arrogance pouring off the man dimmed only a little at Jack's warning, and as Laraby left, Frederick met Jack's knowing look.

"I've really held no previous conviction about circus folk one way or the other. In truth, I've had no acquaintance with anyone from such a life." Jack leaned back in his chair. "But if Mr. Laraby is a sampling of the lot, I'm not certain I wish future familiarity."

"Perhaps the money has a little to do with it, Jack," Frederick offered. "There's no knowing what someone who has lived without for so long might become with such sudden wealth."

"Hmm" was Jack's only response.

"I wonder, if seven of the nine paintings have presumably been stolen by the same people"—Grace drew out her notebook and quickly jotted down a few lines as she spoke—"do we have any idea at all where the paintings went?"

"That *is* the question I have some of my colleagues working on even now. I only know a hint of where two of the paintings went, but they're not helpful answers. For the elderly woman, a widow by the name of Lady Chambers, her *Juliet* was left to her maid, a woman by the name of Jane Smith."

"Which is a very unspecific name," Grace added. "And I would guess not her real one."

"My thoughts exactly, especially since no one has been able to locate this Jane Smith after the young woman left with the painting a year ago." Jack shook his head. "And it's all the more unfortunate because I actually was an acquaintance of Lady Chambers. She was the nearest neighbor to my father. As a child and young man, I would regularly cut through her garden on my way home to the nearby village, upsetting the delicate balance of her pug, if I remember correctly."

"How curious to have it be someone you actually knew." Grace patted Jack's hand. "I'm so sorry."

He smiled in a gently amused way at Grace. "I hadn't had contact with her since Father lost his title and lands over a year ago, but she'd always seemed the pleasant sort. Indulging to my bit of mischief, except for the anxiety my actions caused for her pug, of course."

"And the other case? What happened with the painting there?"

Jack looked to Frederick. "The painting went to a Monsieur Laurent's footman, with the unassuming name of—"

"John Smith," Grace guessed, her smile expectant.

"Very near the mark, my lady." Jack grinned. "John Miller."

"How far apart were these two incidences, Jack?"

Jack's attention turned back to Frederick. "Very astute question and something I asked my contacts. If my hunch is correct, I'd say it was a very short time between the two. Lady Chambers' death was not a year ago. In fact, I offered to investigate the fall down the stairs, but no one seemed remotely interested in a further look into her death."

"I still don't understand where the curse originated. If the related deaths are just now being connected to the paintings, then why a curse?" Grace muttered, marking something down in her notebook. "I'd always thought curses pertained to old things or places, like when we were in Egypt with the ancient tombs. But Accardi painted these in the middle to end of the last century. That doesn't seem old enough for a curse, does it?"

"Curse?" Jack's gaze sharpened. "Who told you about the curse?"

"Signore Capello," Grace answered.

"He associated the robbery with the curse, so to speak," Frederick added. "But it was something that had been shared with him, not an original idea."

"A curse is a perfect way to instill fear and to distract." Jack rubbed a palm over his chin.

"Are you suggesting one of the murderers may have started the idea of the curse?" Grace stopped writing in her notebook. "A clever way to keep others from collecting the art."

"Yes." Jack's response came slowly, almost absently, and then his attention sharpened back on them. "Perhaps the two of you should step back from this investigation now." Jack ran a hand over his face and gave his head another shake. "The plot of this particular story is taking darker turns than I'd anticipated."

Frederick felt Grace's gaze on him as he studied Jack. "What do you mean?"

"Disappearances and deaths have a tendency to encourage ideas of curses and the like." His frown deepened, an uncommon expression for their friend's face. "The past few days, I've been going over previous news articles related to Accardi, the painter, and his family. You see, I had hoped the robberies were merely that, simple thieves taking something of value for their own benefit. But after what you've told me and my own discoveries, I'm afraid it goes much deeper. Accardi's own history points to unrest and mystery. His son-in-law murdered Accardi's daughter and wife, and after the funerals, Accardi went after the rascal, ending in a murder-suicide by the son-in-law. From those origins, we have the possibility of something much darker than I'd thought." He sighed. "Now is the time to back out. Once we arrive on the island, you may be too much in the thick of it to turn back."

Frederick searched Grace's face, already aware of her answer, but Jack didn't give him time to answer.

"Take the evening to decide." He stood and smashed his hat on his head. "If I don't see you at the ferry in the morning, I'll know your answer." He gave a slight bow of his head. "Good night, dear friends."

He exited without another word, and Frederick's thoughts warred between two dissenting decisions. On one hand, the idea of helping his friend and benefiting from the—should he even admit it to himself—thrill of an investigation seemed the right choice for him and for his mystery-loving wife. But his thoughts turned to Grace—nearly losing her in Egypt had struck such a fear in his heart. The idea of putting her in danger again fought against any desire for mystery.

"You have a worried brow, my dear Lord Astley." Grace slid closer to him and placed her palm over his hand on the table. "But if you're concerned about my thoughts on the matter, let me put you at ease. I believe we should help our friend."

"I can't bear the idea of putting you in harm's way, Grace. Not again."

"I'm afraid you don't really have the power of keeping me from harm's way, Frederick." She tipped her head, her nose wrinkling with her frown. "Danger can be anywhere."

"But running headfirst into it is a certain way to find it."

"We are here for a reason, and Jack needs us." Grace squeezed his hand. "I know you want to keep me safe, as I want to keep you, but we also have lives to live in this very real moment. Who knows how God might use us to keep our dear friend and others safe?"

He stared at her, the vision of her wounded and coughing against him after he'd pulled her from a sand trap stiffened his resolve to let Jack do what he'd been doing on his own for years.

"Frederick," she whispered, drawing his thoughts back to her very alive and beautiful face. "I trust you to make whatever decision you think is best, but I say we've been given this opportunity to help, and we should take it. Together. As we should always be."

"You must promise me to do as I ask you, even if you don't completely understand." He tightened his hold on her hand. "And tell me where you are going, if you should need to leave."

"I promise." Her smile flashed wide with excitement. "And I'll be certain to leave a note if I can't tell you in person."

"And"—his frown softened a little—"we must find a way for you to mask some of your expressions, or anyone, good or bad, will read every emotion you're feeling. In this type of danger, that may be a detriment to you."

Her eyes widened. "Oh, so that's how you know what I'm thinking sometimes." She looked away, slowly shaking her head before returning her attention to him. "No wonder no one ever believed me when I tried to lie." She shrugged. "Not that I lied a great deal, but I was always caught."

"I don't want you to lie." He rubbed a thumb across her knuckles. "But perhaps putting your very good brain to use in practicing how to keep your expressions more neutral might be a good exercise if we're to embark on investigations."

"Oh yes, I will practice." She nodded and gave his hand another squeeze. "And I'm so glad you've already committed to the idea of future investigations before we've even really started this one. We were meant for adventure together, Frederick, and all the clues were there from the very beginning."

His eyes drew closed with his sigh before he looked back at her. "What do you mean?"

"Well, the way we ended up married started as a bit of a mystery." One thin auburn brow tilted. "Someone was trying to kill you before we even met and nearly drowned us in the river on our inaugural ride to Havensbrooke as man and wife. Then your former lover almost killed us after poisoning a few people."

Each sentence felt like a barb to his well-thought-out plans of keeping her safe.

"Then it was an adventure with your side of the family that caused all the delicious excitement in Egypt. Not to mention a smattering of ghost hunts and man-nappings."

His throat began to tighten. He'd thought all this time that Grace's insatiable love for fiction had somehow brought all the danger into their lives, but the truth was. . .he'd been the one to bring the danger into their lives from the beginning.

"So it only seems right that if so many adventures and mysteries find you on a regular basis, we may as well give in to the apparent tug and run headlong into them instead of finding ourselves surprised." Her bright smile and confident eyes contradicted the wild increase of his pulse. "Just think about how much better prepared we'll be."

How could he argue with her logic, as disturbing as it was? So he acquiesced to it all.

The mystery, the danger, and the fact that the life he'd imagined was not the one he would live in reality.

Something deep in his heart responded. . .

Perhaps reality would be even better.

Chapter 7

People often underestimated the wisdom of bookshop owners. With a little prodding, Grace had convinced Frederick to leave her at a lovely old bookshop while he went ahead to the hotel to initiate their packing for the trip to Laraby's island.

In truth, she'd wanted to find a few mysteries to take with her, and no matter which town they'd visited, there always seemed to be at least a few English copies of books in these little out-of-the-way places. But she'd also hoped to do a bit more investigating at the local level. Maybe. It couldn't hurt to try.

She rummaged through the narrow rows, bookshelves towering on either side, the smell of dust and old books mingled in with the smell of new. As a child, she'd always felt as if these sorts of places led to other worlds. Not just through the stories they held, but an actual realm hidden down a narrow stairway or behind a bookshelf. She'd longed for real-life adventures, but she hadn't needed a secret stairway or a magical potion.

She'd only needed to marry Frederick.

That scenario for adventure never seemed to make its way into the books she read. She sighed. Perhaps she should write one. Marriage was a very exciting, romantic, and sometimes life-threatening adventure that seemed highly underrepresented within the fictional world.

"*Posso aiutarla*, Signora?"

Grace looked up from the bookshelf of a few English titles to find an older woman, gray-and-white hair spun back into a bun. The woman wore a beautifully colored shawl around her simple brown dress, and her weathered face crinkled into a welcome smile.

"Ciao," Grace offered, trying out her little bit of Italian.

The woman smiled and pointed to the books on the shelf in front of Grace. "Do you need help finding something?"

Grace internally sighed with gratitude at the woman's quick awareness of Grace's lack of Italian. Did that show on her face too? "Yes, thank you. I was searching for a book on Venice's folklore or history."

"Si." The woman moved to a nearby shelf and brought back a few offerings, all in English.

"Thank you." Grace gladly chose the one with some illustrations; then her mind wandered a bit to her previous conversation with Jack. "I was wondering, would you have any books about an artist named Luca Accardi?"

"Luca Accardi?" The woman's brows rose and her smile faded. "Of *The Juliets*?"

"Yes, I know he was a native of Venice, and I try to learn about someone from the areas I visit when I travel." Which wasn't a lie. She'd attempted research on lots of different people while traveling. It just so happened her interest in this particular artist came with a mystery attached.

"No books, but. . .how do you say? La *giornale*?" She walked to a desk nearby and, after a few minutes of rummaging about through various shelves, brought back a few items.

"A newspaper?" Grace pointed to the folded pages in the woman's hands. "Yes, that would be wonderful. Are they for sale?"

The woman shook her head. "You can read them while here?"

Grace frowned. She couldn't read Italian, but perhaps Frederick could read them when he returned to collect her.

"Thank you, but I can't read Italian. My husband can, so if I may hold on to these until he returns, then he'll interpret them for me."

"Si." The woman nodded, her deep brown eyes searching Grace's face in a rather intense sort of way.

"I knew Luca Accardi," she offered, gesturing toward the paper in Grace's hand. "I help you? Answer questions?"

"You're willing to answer my questions?" Grace's smile broadened, and she slipped her hand into her bag, her fingers wrapping around her notebook. "Oh, that would be marvelous."

When Frederick arrived an hour later, Grace had filled out five pages of notes and even joined the lady, Signora Barese, for tea and had shared some of the khak cookies she'd brought with her from Egypt.

Frederick engaged in a few conversations with her in Italian, and even though Grace wasn't certain what they were saying, she just enjoyed hearing him speak the language with his deep, comforting voice. Perhaps she could get him to whisper romantic endearments in Italian when they were back in their hotel room.

She smiled heavenward. Mystery tingles were almost as delightful as the romantic ones.

Almost.

"Did the newspaper article mention the murder?" Grace asked as soon as they were on their walk back to their room.

"It did."

"Well, who can blame the man for seeking vengeance?" She frowned at the very dilemma. "If I'd walked into my house and found out that my jealous son-in-law had killed my wife and daughter, I'd likely respond irrationally too."

"Some could argue his response was quite rational." Frederick's voice brewed low, even deeper than usual.

Thankfully, she'd never been on the wrong side of Frederick's fury. True, they'd had a tiff here and there, but nothing horrible. The way his brow darkened and his voice deepened, she could only imagine how terrifying and powerful his fury would be. She tried very hard not to smile. Why on earth was the image so attractive? Her smile dropped. Well, as long as his fury turned in a direction away from her.

"I suppose he must have been somewhat rational," Grace continued. "Before he went off after his son-in-law, he must have stashed away the treasure and made arrangements for someone to look after his two grandchildren."

Frederick shook his head. "One of the articles stated that after Accardi's death, his property was turned over to the authorities. I can only presume to hold until the grandchildren came of age, but it doesn't appear that intention came to fruition."

Signora Barese hadn't mentioned that part. She'd only shared her concern for the two grandchildren left without mother, father, or grandparents. But to lose a home and financial stability too?

"What happened to the children?"

Frederick slowed his pace and turned toward her. "The children?"

"Yes, the grandchildren of Accardi. Did the article say anything about them?"

He resumed the walk, his profile pensive. "Nothing except the fact that they were the only survivors."

"But what happened to them?" The idea gnawed an ache in her stomach. Childhood brokenness lasted a long time. She still carried ridiculous fears about her mother's tragic death, but she'd had a father and grandfather who'd taken care of her. How much worse it must have been for those two children to have lost everyone!

Everything. "Signora Barese mentioned something about their governess taking them out of the country. Perhaps to England or America or France, but no one knows."

"The governess?" Frederick looked away, his pace slowing. "Was she Italian too? A young woman?"

"I asked those questions." Grace nodded, quite delighted that she and her darling husband were of one mind. "She was a young French woman who seemed to disappear from Venice as quickly as she'd come."

"With the two children?" Frederick escorted her through the doors of their hotel and up to their room.

"That is the understanding." Grace removed her gloves and placed them on the table. "If the murders happened fifteen years ago, then the children would surely be adults by now."

"They would." His gaze met hers.

"And how badly do they want their history and inheritance?"

"Or the governess learned of the treasure, and she's been biding her time to find *The Juliets*." Frederick removed his jacket and slid into a nearby chair.

"Oh yes! That is an option." Grace removed her hat and sat next to him, turning to face him. "Perhaps she's enlisted the help of her lover, and they've been slowly collecting all of the paintings and dispatching anyone who got in their way."

He looked over at her, his palm coming up to rest on her neck. "The way your eyes light up when you talk about people being dispatched is rather frightening."

"It's only the spark to my imagination." She leaned into his palm. "I don't really care to dispatch anyone."

His thumb trailed against her neck as he stared down at her, his brow creasing in thought. "Or it's someone as simple as an unassociated pair of art collectors or treasure hunters who'd learned of the Accardi treasure and have made designs to find it."

"Well, if Jack's information is correct with the mysterious footman and maid, then we're certainly dealing with a man and woman, whatever the case may be." Grace rested her head on his shoulder. "Maybe the French governess is the mastermind, and she's enlisted the assistance of two young people to go undercover in service for anyone who has a *Juliet*."

Frederick stared into the distance for a second. She imagined Sherlock Holmes having pensive moments where he mentally calculated all the clues and evidence in his mind, piecing it together like a puzzle until the picture emerged. If she stared hard enough at him, would she be able to guess some of his deductions?

Nothing came to mind.

But perhaps they still needed more time together before her clairvoyance rose to his level. She took her time admiring his pensive profile, the sharp angle of his chin, the dark chocolate hue of his eyes. Oh, he was such a handsome man, though she was certain he'd only grown more handsome because he loved her so well.

And perhaps the sleuthing helped matters too.

Her gaze fell to his strong hands, and a memory popped to mind. "Frederick, I have a small request."

His attention came to her, expression softening in that endearing look he always bestowed on her.

Well, when he wasn't staring at her as if she'd grown feathers from her head.

Or as if he was going to lose her forever.

Or as if he was bracing himself for some horrible revelation.

And then there was merely the confused look.

Hmm. What an odd assortment of expressions.

"Yes?"

"I was speaking with Jack yesterday about something in his book." She squeezed her hands together on her lap, and suddenly her husband's endearing look took a confused turn. Now, what on earth could have caused such a change?

"There's a chapter on self-defense that references cane fighting."

His expression dipped into the "horrible revelation" category. She'd better just rush on ahead to put him at ease. "And I thought that a parasol could be nearly as effective as a cane and wondered if you minded if I asked Jack to teach me how to cane fight."

His expression moved through various other looks, starting with the feathers growing from her head and ending with him pinching the bridge of his nose and releasing a long sigh.

Ah, she'd forgotten about that one. She called it the "God, help me" look.

"As you'll recall, my parasol has come in handy quite regularly, and I think that if I just knew a few techniques, I could disarm an assailant from close range and protect myself and others with my refined skills."

"Cane fighting?" The words scratched from her husband's throat. His eyes narrowed. "You want Jack to teach you cane fighting?"

"If he put it in the detective book, there must be a good reason for it." She sat up straighter, feeling more confident in her request now that Frederick was actually responding with words. "And I feel certain he'd be more than willing to show me a few counter moves and perhaps a jab or two." She moved her hands to simulate some of the illustrations she'd seen in the book.

Both of Frederick's eyebrows jutted northward, and he blinked a few times in quick succession.

"And if someone grabs me from behind, there were a few moves to free myself."

Something flickered in his eyes. Humor? Interest? And then he shook his head. "I don't think it would be appropriate for Jack to teach you something like cane fighting. There is a great deal of physical contact involved."

"Oh." She nodded, attempting to understand but not fully succeeding. "Well, I suppose I could try to read up on it myself."

"I'll teach you."

Her gaze connected to his. "What?"

He swallowed, taking his time, and then nodded again, his lips pinching and releasing as if he were trying to work up the words. "I know how to cane fight. In my younger days, I took some training for sport."

Her bottom lip loosened until her mouth opened, and then her imagination took over. Frederick teaching her cane fighting. Close proximity. Some parrying. Maybe a faux attack or two. Her smile began a slow uptilt. Oh, she couldn't think of anything quite so. . .invigorating? Heat climbed up her neck.

He seemed to use his clairvoyance to know exactly where her thoughts went, because he slipped his palm to her waist and drew her close. "Perhaps I've been going at this sleuthing and wife training all wrong."

His low voice murmured close to her ear before he kissed a wonderfully sensitive spot below her ear.

"What. . .what do you mean?" Her palms slid around his neck, fingers stretched up into his thick, soft hair.

"Instead of fighting against the mysteries." His kiss slid up her neck. "And the knife throwing." To her jaw. "The pistol shooting." Then her chin. "And cane fighting." He hovered close, his lips almost touching hers. "I think it's time to forge ahead, arm in arm."

"I do believe that acceptance will be a much better decision for your peace of mind." Her palm came to his cheek, smile quivering to release. "And I think we should seal your clever idea with lips to lips. What do you say?"

Words weren't necessary for a very long time after his thorough affirmation.

Grace's throat closed around a scream. She dared not take a breath. If she inhaled, the sand would fill her lungs. But she had to breathe. She pushed against the weight of the sand, attempting to fight for the surface, but her palms met an impenetrable wall.

"Grace," came a voice from somewhere far away.

She tried to listen as it came again. Familiar. Dear. Safe.

Frederick! Would he rescue her in time? She needed to breathe. She beat against the wall.

"Grace, darling. Wake up."

Wake up? She opened her eyes, her fists pressed not against a wall of sand but against the very sturdy chest of her husband. She raised her gaze to his, his angled features pinched as he searched her face.

She drew in a shuddering breath. "It. . .it was another nightmare?"

"Yes." He pushed her hair back from her face, his palms cradling her cheeks. "Only a nightmare."

"I'm sorry to have awakened you again."

He gave his head a shake. "Darling, you nearly died in an Egyptian sand trap." He breathed out a sigh and pulled her against his warm body. "It's no wonder you would have some side effects from such an ordeal."

She frowned and buried her nose into his neck. "But I've been trapped before and didn't have nightmares afterward."

He drew back, looking down at her. "You've been trapped before?"

She sniffled and nodded, sliding her palms across the planes of his chest in an almost comforting motion. He was so strong. Warm. Being in his arms was one of the most deliciously safe and comforting places in the world.

"When I was ten, I accidentally locked myself inside an old

trunk for several hours. It was rather cozy, and I just imagined I'd become a stowaway on a pirate ship until someone finally found me." She frowned. "It was usually one of the many governesses."

His jaw twitched. "Locking oneself in a. . .trunk isn't the same as nearly dying in a tomb, darling."

"Maybe not, but when I was twelve, I fell into an old well. I was there until nightfall and felt certain I may end up becoming a fairy if no one came to rescue me by the time the moon hit me." She nodded. "That's when I first thought about how important ropes were."

His brows pinched together, and he captured her hand with his against his chest, stilling her movements. "Your father and those governesses had a tremendous capacity to lose you."

"Which makes one wonder if the problem wasn't so much the governesses or my father." She sighed, a sudden flutter of fear rising into her chest. "If I keep having these nightmares, do you think I'll go mad? I've read about women going mad from lack of sleep or an overindulgence of nightmares."

"Grace, I don't believe these nightmares will lead to—"

"And if I become a mad wife, will you lock me in your attic?" Her gaze wandered over his beloved face, though his jaw stood a bit slack at the moment. "I can't recall what Havensbrooke's attic looks like, but I feel certain it would be very gothic and possibly romantic for any madwoman."

"Darling—"

She cupped his dear face with her hands, attempting to memorize it. Oh, even his confused expressions looked so wonderfully dear. "If you did lock me in your attic, at least I would still be near you, because I'm certain I would be a lot less frightened if I were near you and less mad than if I were away from you and mad."

"Grace." He drew her hands away from his face, rubbing his fingers over her knuckles and bringing her focus back to those eyes. His lips twitched ever so slightly. "You are not going mad, but rest assured, should you ever, I would keep you as near to me as possible."

She closed her eyes with a sigh. "I feel certain that would put any madwoman's heart at ease."

"However, darling, when I was in the military, there were times when the men would face a near-death experience or tragedy. Something that inspired a sudden and acute fear. It wasn't uncommon for them to experience successive nightmares or even panics afterward."

"Forever?" The word trembled out, but then she drew in a breath. At least if she knew she wasn't alone in her reaction, she could handle forever, couldn't she? Especially after Frederick's rather endearing and calm response about her possible impending madness.

"In many cases, the episodes and nightmares subsided with time." He offered her a tender smile. "Even now, you've not had them *every* night."

"It just feels rather cowardly to wake up in tears over a nightmare. And I do so want to be brave." She searched his serene eyes. "You don't need a coward for a wife, and panicky women rarely make excellent sleuths. I think it's because of the constant weeping."

He brought her knuckles to his lips and looked up at her. Was there a faint hint of humor in his expression? Then he sobered. "Being afraid doesn't mean you're not brave, darling." He tugged her back toward him, his warm skin transferring to her chilled body. "It's what you do when you *are* afraid that proves your bravery. And you usually choose brave things to do."

"Usually?" She nestled into him, her lips finding the spot at the base of his neck. "It is an encouraging thought that bravery is what we do instead of how we feel. I like it. Though I'm certain part of my bravery has something to do with my faith in fiction, I feel certain living through murderous plots and tomb robbers can't have been solely based on my books."

"I think a great deal of it has to do with who you trust to your life and soul, Grace."

His words rumbled deep in his chest, so much so they seemed to transfer over to her heart like the sweetest of heavenly reminders. Yes, she did garner her courage from her faith in God's loving hand holding her life. She'd always drawn such security from the idea of God having all her days very specifically written in His book. When she first discovered that verse in the Bible, it encouraged her even more that God loved books, since He had at least one where He wrote about His children's days. Then she'd drawn even more encouragement from the fact that God had written out adventures just for her in His book, which for a young girl who'd always dreamed of adventures, she found quite helpful on dull days in particular.

But as she sat snuggled comfortably against her dashing husband's chest, her pulse slowed from the frantic thrumming of only a moment ago. It was quite delightful to think of herself as a character in God's book instead of just a wandering character without an author or book at all. In fact, if He wrote her days and she was trying to love Him and others well, then she had all the reason in the world to live bravely, didn't she?

"I'm so glad God wrote you into the story of my life," she whispered, placing another kiss against his neck. "I'm sure I would have fumbled finding a hero on my own. I much prefer an author who knows what He's doing to make the story work best."

Silence greeted her, so she looked up from her cozy position. Dim light flickered in from the gaslights outside, creating a flickering gold sheen across his face. His lips crooked the slightest bit, almost at the same tilt as his head. "Characters, are we?" He pressed a gentle kiss to her lips. "If that's the case, I feel certain that you were written into my story for a very particular reason."

"Yes?"

He smoothed a palm against her cheek. "God knew my lonely, sad world was in desperate need of the right heroine's love and light."

Her smile spread, and she slipped her palms up his chest to wrap around his neck. "That is an incredibly romantic thing to say, my dear Lord Astley."

"I feel certain you've heard it before." He leaned close, his lips barely brushing hers.

Her entire body warmed at the way his words pulsed low, closer. The power of his voice to move her emotions still surprised her, even after over three months of marriage. Perhaps it was the way his English accent curled the vowels so deliciously or the depth of his bass tones warming the consonants, but maybe, even more so, it was the way he spoke to *her*. So intimately. Tenderly. In a way no one had ever spoken to her, and the timbre lit her pulse with a very different sort of quickening.

"But you know how I love words, and I should never tire of hearing those certain ones from your excellent lips." She drew his head down to breach the small space between them, and he obeyed with enough vigor to let her know his interests lay in the same direction as her own. It was a good thing neither had taken the time to dress before falling asleep after their previous amorous escapade. Buttons and ribbons proved rather cumbersome and time-consuming, especially when things ran in an amatory direction.

Maybe a nightmare now and again wasn't so bad.

Especially if her reward for surviving them ended up as a rather dreamy opportunity.

Chapter 8

Frederick moved through the crowd toward her as Grace waited to board the *vaporetto*, or small ferry, that would lead them down the Grand Canal to the lagoon. Evidently, Laraby's island sat on the edge of the lagoon in the Adriatic Sea, a fair distance from the mainland.

Her attention followed the trail of the glistening waterway to where it opened into a broader sea. Somewhere within the massive lagoon dotted with dozens of small islands—hemmed in by a patch of land on one side and Italy on the other—waited Laraby's own.

His own island. Rather mysterious—and quite appropriate for the rest of all the mysteriousness going on around them. And wouldn't an island with a lone villa be the perfect spot for dastardliness?

Much like Baskerville Hall in its lonely seclusion with a fiendish hound on the loose, which almost had the illustrious Sherlock doubting his senses. Of course, Venice was nothing remotely close to dark or desolate moor country. Oh no, light enveloped everything. Even the buildings seemed designed to reflect sunshine on the glimmering canal waterways.

But a shining city held humans, and humans had a tendency to misbehave much too frequently. *No wonder we needed a Savior so badly.*

She sighed and stared out into the waves, squinting to make out a few of the land masses in the distance.

What sort of villa would Laraby have on his island? Had Jack mentioned the island's name at some point yesterday? Yes. Something lovely.

Isola de Sogni. Island of Dreams.

Grace couldn't wait to question Laraby further on the history and the choice of the name, especially with Grace's current struggle with dreams. Not daydreaming. She'd never struggled with that particular form of dreaming, but the current nightmares? How curious that, during her very real difficulty, they'd find themselves on the way to an island of dreams.

Fascinating. She sent a glance heavenward just to let God know she knew He was likely up to something.

Then she grinned at her own ridiculousness. Well, of course, He was always up to something, and not just in the literal sense either.

Frederick made it to her side just as Laraby began ushering them aboard the boat. Jack had referred to it as a water taxi, which made sense in a way. Unlike a gondola, this boat was larger and longer, open in the first two-thirds with a railing framing the whole part and a dome-shaped roof overhead. The enclosed back third appeared to be for the captain.

"I have a missive you've been waiting to see." Frederick grinned, showing her the envelope in his hands. "Inspector Randolph hopes to leave for Italy within the week with Zahra in tow."

Grace brought her hands together to keep from wrapping Frederick in a hug. Oh how protocol curbed so many shows of affection. The glimmer in his eyes told her he was delighted too.

"He said not to expect them until late next week, but all the paperwork is finalized, and Zahra is to be ours very soon."

Theirs! Grace wrapped her arm through his and squeezed him close. After the little girl's unpredictable life from orphanage to street child and back, to give her a home with them? Truly? Oh, what would she think of England in exchange for Egypt?

"I'm so glad." She squeezed his arm again. "And even happier that it makes you so happy too. Oh, I can't wait for Zahra and Lilibet to meet. Our own little family is growing so beautifully."

Frederick shook his head with his grin, slowly stepping down to help her onto the boat. "I hope it continues to grow and perhaps provides me with at least one son to fit within all of these ladies of mine."

Ladies of mine. Oh, the way he said it brewed with such tenderness. She nearly kissed his cheek, no matter if the other guests for Laraby's party filed on behind them.

"Anything from Elliott?"

He shook his head. "Nothing more than his last note to say they'd arrived safely in England." Her expression must have given away her disappointment because he leaned close. "Do not worry. I feel certain he'll have quite a story to tell us once he has the chance."

"A romance, I hope." She wiggled her brows. "My favorite."

"I have no doubt about that." He raised a paper in hand. "There's a telegram for Jack as well. Once I get you to a chair, I'll deliver it to him, but in the meantime"—he gave her the telegram from the inspector—"you can read this one and start planning all the ways you'll introduce Zahra to Eng—"

Someone bumped into Grace from behind.

"Pardon me, miss." A slender young man, blond hair and matching mustache, skimmed past them, his attire marking him as some sort of serviceman. He tipped his hat to Frederick. "Gov'nor."

He offered a flash of striking green eyes and a tip of his lips before slipping past them to make his way toward Laraby, who had moved to the very front of the boat.

"I'll tell you about my letter from Lillias when you return and all the delights of her upcoming motherhood." Grace nodded as she took a seat.

"So she's adjusted to life as a banker's wife, has she?"

Grace grinned at Frederick's gentle teasing. "As much as she is able, I believe. At least Tony lavishes her with adoration enough to curb her need for the finest fashions of the day."

He didn't attempt to control his smile before touching the tip of his beige hat as he went into a slight bow, held her gaze for a moment longer, and then turned to seek out Jack.

Oh dear, he was the loveliest man in the entire world. She followed him with her gaze, appreciating his easy stride and the way his white shirt and beige pants fit him so well. She sighed. Marriage was such a lovely idea.

"To have a woman look at me the way you look at your Lord Astley. . ." Paul—did she even know his last name?—took the seat next to Grace, the one meant for Frederick, and edged so close she caught the faint scent of port on his breath. His gaze met hers before trailing down her in a most uncomfortable sort of way.

He may have been surveying her fashion choices for the day, which were always rather uncertain, but Grace didn't think so. Glances of clothing admiration or ridicule left her feeling very different than the look on Paul's face.

She leaned back a little and pushed on a smile. "Well, I do hope you find one someday, Mr. Paul."

"They're not so easy to find, but I'm glad I have *your* good wishes." His voice took a more intimate turn, his focused attention heating her cheeks for some reason.

Her eyes popped wide. Was Paul a possible Henry Crawford from Austen's lesser-loved *Mansfield Park*? And was he trying to woo a married woman? Surely not.

The man was handsome in a boyish sort of way, and his expression seemed to hold a perpetual look of mischief. Was it a result of having been raised in the circus too? Laraby certainly carried himself with levity and playfulness, though he'd never spoken to Grace in this sort of way.

"You know, as an orphan, the one thing my heart has been searching for my whole life is love."

Ordinarily, such a statement would have tugged at her heart, and it still did to some extent, but the way he said it shone with deceptiveness. She decided to stir up her inner Fanny Price and distract the man from his own naughtiness.

"I've read about orphans being left in various places, and since you seem so keen to talk about your experience, I'm terribly curious to know more." His smile faded into a look of surprise, so she kept talking. "I do hope you weren't raised like poor Pip in Dickens' *Great Expectations*. His sister was horrible to him."

"I. . .I can't say," he muttered, his eyes narrowing with what she supposed was a look of confusion.

Poor man. Was he as little a reader as Laraby? Well, hopefully the circus was the catalyst to ignite their imaginations, since reading evidently didn't.

"I do hope the people who brought you up were kind to you. Other orphans haven't had it so good. Take Oliver Twist, for example. He was put into the workhouse." She nodded, but his eyes only narrowed more. "Imagine that sort of horribleness."

He blinked a few times in quick succession.

"Did you have some mysterious trinket left behind from your mother?"

His jaw slacked, and she felt much less uncomfortable. She understood *this* expression.

He gave a shake of his head. "No. . .no, nothing."

Hmm, well, she supposed not every orphan had a romantic or tragic history.

"And your name? Did you come with that, or did the people who adopted you give it to you?"

His brows crashed together, eyeing her as if he was trying to sort something out. "A note had the name Paul on it. So I was called Paul. My circus family gave me Hopewell."

"Well, at least you have something from your mother." Her smile spread. "And maybe even you have her eyes, because they are a lovely shade of green. What sort of skill did you do in the circus? I don't believe flirting is considered a showstopper."

He drew in a deep breath and gave his head a little shake. "I did trapeze with Jo—" He coughed. "Laraby."

Ah, so the new name hadn't quite made it into habit just yet. Then she paused, an idea moving through her. Or she succeeded in distracting him so well, he'd given away unintended information. She almost smiled. Now that was a very detective sort of thing to do. She didn't always think herself clever, but for that moment, she sat up just a bit taller at the idea of her own cleverness, unintended as it had been.

"How amazing. You must be very secure about your eternal future to risk death so often."

For some strange reason, he looked down and began fidgeting with his shirt sleeves.

"Were you glad to leave it? The circus?"

His gaze came back up to hers, and his features hardened into a frown. "At first." He looked away, and she followed his attention to where Laraby, Miss Benetti, and a group of four others sat talking. What was that about? His attention shifted back to her along with a less confident smile. "It's Italy. How can I not be glad?"

"It is a beautiful place, but it's also the City of Masks." She raised a brow, attempting to keep her expression from displaying her cleverness. "With a long and glorious history of people hiding within plain sight."

Paul's gaze sharpened on her for a second before his smile partially resurfaced. "Well, my lady, we are getting ready to showcase a mystery for Mrs. Reynolds and her brother, so no one wishes to guess the ending too quickly."

"Of course not. And as long as it all remains fun and games, then I am happy to join in the masquerade." Oh, she was getting the hang of these verbal illusions and suggestions.

"Then you're bound to enjoy Laraby's house party," he added, moving to stand, his smile not reaching his eyes. "We're circus men. We're always here for the fun and games." He doffed his hat before slipping away to the other side of the boat.

Her face still blazed a bit too hot from the idea of a man openly flirting with a very married woman. And how dare he imagine she'd accept his overtures?

She pressed a palm to her cheek, reliving the interaction. She'd never been the object of men's attention very much because most of them found Lillias more to their liking, so her only real experience at romance of any kind was either fictional or with Frederick.

But Paul Hopewell. . .

She drew in a breath. No wonder she'd felt so uncomfortable. He was certainly hiding something. Could he be one of the lost grandchildren of Accardi? The age would fit.

She narrowed her eyes at his retreating frame. Paul Hopewell moved right to the top of her suspect list.

With a huff, she shook her head. No, no! One of the important rules in detective business is to not allow one's emotions to cloud one's judgment. And she could add morally gray to the characteristics of Mr. Hopewell, which could certainly fit an art thief or murderer.

Rascal.

Jasmine Benetti sat in one of the wicker chairs near Mr. Laraby, a long rose gown wrapping around her lovely body. *Beautiful* should not be a reason to add someone to a suspect list, but having access to the art gallery certainly could, along with developing a deep interest in art, particularly the time period of *The Juliets*, and being an employee of the gallery.

Grace frowned. Miss Benetti, however, was Laraby's fiancée, so why on earth would she steal artwork from him that she'd eventually possess when she married the man? And if she was a protector of such artwork, why would she wish to steal it from a relatively safe place like a guarded gallery?

Her attention moved to an older couple seated near Miss Benetti and Laraby. The lady must be the author Dolores Reynolds and the man—her husband? Or brother? The house party revolved around Mrs. Reynolds' research and inspiration for her newest novel, or at least that's what Laraby had said. But what if she and her husband were really the thieves and were using this book research as a ploy to get into the house of the last known *Juliets*? The angle in which the gentleman sat highlighted an excellent streak of white running along the temple of his black hair. His wife boasted a head of tight brown curls bunched up on her head and topped with some sort of massive feather flittering in the breeze. Her exuberant laugh assaulted the air with as much potency as her perfume, and when she spoke, her voice rose well above the hum of the steam engine.

Well, Grace had always thought authors were probably rather odd sorts of people because they spent a great deal of time in their own heads with hundreds of characters and possibilities that only they knew about. Why had she imagined authors to be more inclined to hover on the periphery of social circles, sending mysterious glances or looking off in dazed sorts of ways, instead of regaling the room with perfume and volume?

Beside the couple sat another man. Younger. Likely *he* was Mrs. Reynolds' brother, the movie producer. She couldn't recall his name. But what if he wasn't really a movie producer at all? He had one of those faces that didn't give away his age. Midtwenties?

Early thirties? She concealed a gasp behind her gloved hand. Near the same age as the lost grandson of Accardi!

"Sorting out suspects, are we, Lady Astley?"

She raised her gaze to find Jack Miracle standing nearby.

"Making a mental list, if you must know, Jack." She gestured for him to take the seat Paul had recently vacated, as Frederick slid into the chair to her other side. Ah, between her darling and her favorite real-life detective. This had to be one of the safest places on the boat. "That is, after I distracted Mr. Paul Hopewell from his shameless flirting."

"Mr. Hopewell? Laraby's friend, Paul?" Frederick shifted beside her, and she turned to him. "What did he do?"

"Nothing worth your valiant protection, but it was highly uncomfortable, so I distracted him with questions he didn't seem prepared to answer."

Frederick's attention shot to the man as he engaged in a conversation with the blond valet or footman. Whoever he was.

"Excellent use of diversion, my lady," Jack added.

"I'm not certain, but I feel as though Mr. Hopewell is not too happy to be in Italy, Jack." She removed her notepad from her valise and made a note of the thought under the heading "Paul Hopewell, the flirt."

"I've sensed a bit of tension between him and Laraby but can't quite put my finger on the problem," Jack stated, then crooked his grin. "Placing all of these people in a remote villa together, no matter the size, may induce a great many unveilings as we move forward."

"And what is the name of the younger man along with Mr. and Mrs. Reynolds?" Grace asked. "Is that the movie producer?"

"Indeed." He waved toward Frederick. "I was just informing Frederick about him. A Mr. Harry Finch. I can't help think I've met him before, but I've no memory of being introduced to a movie producer, let alone a Canadian one. He'd worked in the past with the Hepworth Company, one of the leading film studios in Britain, but now he has, purportedly, successfully started his own film studio. Eager to make a name for himself, I'd wager."

"What a perfect group of suspects." Her lips split wide. "Who's to say they're not all a part of some farce to confuse us?" She raised a brow. "We are among circus performers and artists."

She could almost feel Frederick's grin at her side as Jack's smile broadened. "Indeed, so anything is possible, my lady."

"Will you ever call me Grace instead of Lady Astley or 'my lady?'"

"I'm not certain I can make such a leap yet." His eyes danced. "Though your husband has finally succeeded in convincing me to throw propriety to the wind in his case."

"Good. I should be next." Grace nodded. "We are friends and, at present, coworkers."

"Or coconspirators." He narrowed his eyes and wiggled his brows. "But I do feel we are getting ready to begin a different sort of game with much higher stakes than I prefer, especially with the two of you involved."

"Jack, we've joined of our own accord," Frederick interjected, placing his hand over Grace's. "We both have. Whatever comes of it, we'll accept our own consequences, so no more of this worry about us."

"Exactly. It will only distract you from clues and suspicions." She pulled at her gloves and scanned the boat again. "Do you feel the thief is among us or waiting in the shadows of the villa?"

"Either is possible." Jack's expression sobered. "Whoever is after the paintings wants all of them, and the only two left to take are those at Laraby's villa. All the others have ended up in the hands of mysterious persons who no one can seem to locate. So if the thief, or thieves as the case may be, is not aboard this water taxi with us, then they mean to come to the island by some other way." He gestured toward a paper in his hand. "This telegram from one of my colleagues confirmed that the last *Juliet's* owner died by drowning."

Grace flung her gaze back to Jack, her hand moving to her throat, and a vision of Hamlet's dear Ophelia popped to mind. "Not the best news to hear while one travels aboard a water taxi toward an island home."

"She is an excellent swimmer though, Jack."

"I never realized how handy that certain skill would be while married to an earl." Grace sent a smile to Frederick. "I'd always suspected abilities like sewing or charming the room would prove more appreciated." She turned back to Jack. "So you can imagine how glad I am to be married to Frederick instead of some stuffy earl who has great designs on making me a very British lady."

Jack's laugh burst out, and he glanced at Frederick. "I must say, my lady, you did fair well with your pairing. I know quite a few earls who would have been horrified at a pistol-wielding, knife-throwing, mystery-loving bride."

"Every man should know the limits of his constitution," Frederick added, and Grace shot him a mock glare. He smiled. "And I must say, those same earls would have missed out on the benefits and surprises of such a woman."

"Who only hopes to improve under her dear husband's generous tutelage." Grace placed her hand over Frederick's and turned back to Jack, lowering her voice. "Did you know, he's going to teach me cane fighting?"

Jack's smile spread so wide, Grace's automatically responded.

"Well, I should like to witness that."

"Private lessons, Jack." Frederick's own lips tipped. "Sorry, old boy."

"But I'm afraid I've gotten us off our topic." Grace turned back to Jack. "This most recent death, the drowning, how long ago did it occur?"

"Only a month." Jack rubbed his jaw and looked out over the waves. "Which makes me feel as if our mastermind collected all the other pieces before coming back to the central location of the paintings."

"Someone wants the treasure," Frederick added. "Whatever the treasure is."

A wonderful thrill traveled up Grace's arms, which had nothing to do with the mid-April breeze. Looking for Egyptian antiquities was one thing, but an actual treasure hunt? How many times had she daydreamed about such an opportunity? Her daydreams usually included her being captured by pirates, but at any rate, it was treasure hunting. And she didn't care a wink about the treasure, but the hunt. . .

"Careful there, my lady, that you don't romanticize this too much." Jack's pale gaze took a sober turn. "These thieves are not the storybook sort. They may very well be murderers. It's fortunate no one was killed at the gallery or in the stealing of Laraby's first painting."

Grace frowned. Was Jack clairvoyant too? Or perhaps her facial expressions were easier to read than she thought. Oh dear, as a detective, she needed to work on hiding her feelings.

"Speaking of the gallery, when Grace and I made our investigation. . ." Frederick swallowed as if something was caught in his throat.

Why did he always have trouble saying that word?

"We noticed the back doors had been tampered with but not broken. It was as if the thieves wished to make the robbery look like a break-in without actually damaging the locks."

"But we wondered why they would do something like that," Grace offered. "I mean, if you had a key, why would you even bother with damaging a door? To merely try and trick us?"

"As I thought. Someone on the inside is involved. Whether they were the masterminds of the heist or merely the conduit to allow the true criminals inside, we don't know as yet." He pulled himself up to sit straighter and drew in a breath. "Well, someone wants *The Juliets*, and it seems they're willing to do anything to get them. The best place to catch a mouse is in the place where the cheese is set."

A tapping sound from the front of the boat kept Grace from having to respond to Jack and admit her obviousness. Mr. Laraby stood near the front with Paul at one side and Miss Benetti at the other. The light-haired footman stood off to the corner, head down, as if waiting for his next assignment.

"Welcome all," Laraby announced, waving his hand as if to encompass the crowd.

His voice held the ring of a showman. The smile on his face proved the look of a mischief-maker. Was it possible that the man who had hired a detective had created his own crime?

"I've gathered all of you for my house party because I believe each of you has an investment in me." He sent a smile to Miss Benetti. "Or my art." He waved toward the Reynoldses. "Or in saving both me and my art." He raised a brow in Grace, Frederick, and Jack's direction, which inspired a laugh from some of the others in the crowd. "Which I hope won't find me in need of saving any more than usual, but I'd rather have some good brains about in the instance my island becomes another victim to a thief. I hope all of you will have the opportunity to become good friends over the next few days while you enjoy the best my villa has to offer." He turned and raised his arm as if showcasing something.

And so he was.

In the closing distance rose a mound of lush, foliage-filled earth, rocky ledges on all sides. And poised on the edge of one of the cliffs, as if painted on the spot for any viewer's pleasure, stood a glistening white. . .villa?

It was nothing like any of the villas Grace had seen so far. This edifice stretched in various directions with a flat, window-lined front, but a tower on either side, each with a pointed top.

An Italian castle of sorts.

"Welcome to Isola di Sogni."

Grace turned to look at Frederick, his gaze meeting hers with a raised brow. A look at the empty horizon on all sides told her one thing.

If a murderer wanted to search for a treasure without the bother of police or doctors, an isolated island villa would be the perfect spot.

Chapter 9

Isolation.

The mixed scents of honey and some unfamiliar flora wafting toward them in the open carriage failed to lighten the weight of that realization.

Frederick looked to Jack, who sat across from him, and then to Grace at his side—her words about the island being the perfect place for a murder taking on more foreboding than he cared to speculate. But they were here now. In the thick of it.

His gaze met Jack's, somehow reading the same intention in his friend's expression that he held in his own heart.

Resolve.

They were out to protect one another, and if Frederick knew Jack at all, it meant Grace first.

"Eyes and ears," Jack said, tapping a finger to his temple. "And communicate anything you notice, no matter how seemingly insignificant."

"Should we meet tonight in our room perhaps?" Frederick offered. "After dinner? I have a feeling we'll have a better knowledge of some of the other guests and staff by then and can make a plan."

He felt Grace's stare. Over the course of the few days they'd started this. . .investigation, she'd been sending him the most distracting and, at times, highly enticing looks of adoration. She may not even realize how alluring some of those small smiles and hooded glances were, but his pulse knew. And so did his continually surprised imagination.

An imagination that had been stifled until her.

A new type of energy pulsed through him. Or perhaps, a resurrected one he'd thought lost beneath all the hurt and rejection of his earlier life.

"Very good. After dinner then." Jack tapped the top of the cane he held by his knee. "I feel as though Laraby will certainly make our time here an adventure."

As if on cue, their carriage came to a stop in front of the house's grand entry, and the two sets of double doors burst open in synchrony. Six servants, donned in black and white, emerged from each door carrying trays and lining up on opposite sides of the entry stairs.

"Like I said," Jack continued, "I think we should prepare ourselves for quite the performance."

Laraby met them at the bottom of the entry stairs, his smile as broad as ever. Frederick had always been rather suspicious of showmen. Perhaps he'd met too many a swindler, and it had curbed his trust, but something about a man going to such extravagance to impress left him with a sour feeling. It was one thing to wish for your home to be presented admirably; it was another to dazzle for the mere purpose of gaining attention.

"Each of my servants carries a platter with one of your names on it. Pay solid attention to that particular servant, for he or she will be assigned to you. Their goal is to fulfill whatever needs you may have, give you direction as needed, and ensure that Isola di Signo becomes an exciting home away from home for you."

"If he proposes to make things more exciting than Havensbrooke, then we are in for an adventure," Grace whispered, and Frederick wasn't certain whether to grimace or grin.

"When you enter the house, follow your servant to your rooms," Laraby continued, as a rather tall, gruff-looking man with dark hair and even darker countenance moved to stand just behind Laraby to the man's left. In almost complete contrast to the man, a woman with brilliantly blond hair and pale skin took her post at Laraby's right. She wore spectacles and an unassuming soft green day suit, giving her the odd appearance of a schoolmistress.

A very young school mistress.

"My butler, Mr. Zappa, is also at your service. He runs the staff like clockwork, as you British say." Laraby laughed and gestured to the woman. "And this is my secretary, Lydia Whitby. She runs me."

Again he laughed, but Miss Whitby's expression did not share in his amusement.

"I'm certain you all would like to freshen up and rest before dinner, but before I leave you to your leisure, I must alert you to two things." His gaze moved toward Frederick, Grace, and Jack. "I am pleased to have Detective Jack Miracle and his team, Lord and Lady Astley, joining us for our little party. They are investigating the case of the stolen *Juliets*." He nodded to them as if in amused appreciation and turned back to the crowd. "And despite my very best attempts to persuade her to leave, Madame Accardi, our resident ghost, has refused to move, so if she should trouble you with an appearance or two, simply stay out of her way. She's not the confrontational sort, but she appears to enjoy a little haunt now and then, and her visits have only increased since the robberies, so I think she may be a bit unhappy at the current goings-on."

"Perfect, simply perfect," Mrs. Reynolds announced, applauding, her smile wide as she swept a glance over the group.

"Well, it's a very good thing we have someone who specializes in ghost hunts, as I understand," Jack murmured, his lips failing to keep a grin in place.

Grace's face flushed, and she smiled. "I did prove rather adept at my last one."

"Then I bow to your knowledge on such cases as ghosts, my lady." Jack chuckled and tipped his hat. "Until dinner."

He walked on ahead of them, finding a man bearing a tray with his name. Frederick drew Grace forward toward a young woman who appeared somewhat nervous.

"You are Lord and Lady Astley?" Her accent proved native, her voice soft.

"Yes," Frederick answered. "And you are?"

"Martina, Signore, Signora." She offered a small curtsy.

"What a lovely name," Grace added, causing the woman to send a fleeting look to Grace before dipping her head in acceptance.

"I am at your service. Allow me to show you to your apartment."

With that, she turned and led the way through the doors.

Grace squeezed close to Frederick's arm as the daylight disappeared behind them. "Did you notice the butler?"

He shifted his attention from the massive, two-story entry room with a balcony surrounding them from the second floor. A stained-glass mural poised in the dome of the ceiling of the room, sunlight making the color shine in brilliance on them below. "Um. . .the butler. Yes."

"He had very shifty eyes," she whispered, "and a scar over one eye. Did you see it?"

"I didn't notice the scar."

"And he looked at us as if he didn't like one thing he saw. Very unlike Mr. Brandon back home."

Their Havensbrooke butler could certainly present as unwelcoming, but never in a ruthless sense. *Stalwart* might prove the better word, but nothing menacing. Except when someone disrupted his place settings on the table. He could become rather intimidating then. Frederick wrangled his smile. "I suppose that makes Mr. Zappa suspect?"

"He's the butler," she stated and offered him a pointed look. "Butlers should always be suspect. It's a popular fictional theme in mystery novels, you know."

Frederick gave a slight nod, taking in the path they followed to their rooms. East side, from what he could tell.

"I just thought we ought to keep those sorts of things in mind," Grace added, one of her ginger brows raised.

A vast display of landscape paintings lined one side of the stairway.

"Those are lovely," Grace gasped, distracted from their conversation, although Frederick doubted the moment would last for long.

"Yes," Martina added, casting another furtive glance to them. "It is my understanding that those were gifts from Accardi's friends across the world. Masterpieces in their own right."

"Oh yes." Grace's feet faltered as she stared. "What do you think of them, Lord Astley? You would know better than me."

"You know paintings?" Martina's quiet voice took on a little more volume, and her lips slipped into the tiniest smile.

"A little." He paused, appreciating the use of light and carefully placed color to draw the eye to specific points on each of the works. "But these are remarkable."

"Do you have a favorite, Martina?" Grace turned to the woman, whose smile broadened a little more.

"I have always liked the one of the castle ruins in the field of flowers." She gestured to the painting to their right. "It feels like. . .peace."

Grace sighed. Frederick studied the girl's young face. Until Grace came into his life, he'd not spent a great deal of thought on his servants, much to his shame. He'd built a friendship with Elliott and respected Brandon, but truly getting to know them? Not the way Grace made certain to find out about them, great and small.

What sort of hurt turned this girl's thoughts toward finding peace?

A clock somewhere in the house struck the hour, and Martina's eyes popped wide. "Oh, I must help with dinner preparations." She gestured toward a door to their left and opened it into a lovely suite. "I shall return soon to see if I may be of assistance."

She bowed her head and disappeared down the hallway.

"As to our previous conversation, my dear Lord Astley"—Grace turned to him, removing her gloves as he closed the door behind them—"do not underestimate the power of fiction, particularly in relation to butlers. Most plots come from somewhere very real."

"Even ghosts?"

Her eyes narrowed into a powerless glare even as her smile tipped. "You tease me again, but I'll have you know that the best ghost hunters are the ones who believe in them just enough to try and guess what they may do next." She stepped close to him and slipped her arms around his waist. "Oh my darling Frederick, not only are we on a remote island, but there's a dangerous-looking butler, an unsolved robbery, a treasure, and now a ghost. I really am living a fairy-tale romance."

His chuckle broke free. Fairy tales seemed to apply only to their private time together. Many of the other scenes were beginning to resemble more of a gothic novel. "Well, darling, I think we should be much more on our guard like Sherlock rather than fanciful like the fairy tales." He sighed, offered a prayer, and gave her a quick kiss. "I believe our very lives may count on it."

"When you're finished, would you mind helping me with my dress?" Grace called from her dressing room to the next, where Frederick readied for dinner. They'd become a bit accustomed to not having the assistance of a lady's maid or valet, relying on each other to assist with buttons or ties.

It all had been rather quaint and romantic, except for those not so flattering instances when Grace became entrapped in a corset or entangled in a crookedly buttoned blouse.

Otherwise, the shared space and freedom proved delightful—though she missed Elliott immensely.

His last telegram only mentioned that Amelia was spending time getting to know her grandfather and the new life in which she'd found herself. His subtle statement, "I plan to stay on for a few more weeks to ensure she is sufficiently settled," spoke of his kindness toward her but nothing else.

No mention of budding romance. Or secret elopements. Or a furious patriarch who refused the union of a valet and a reformed thief. Grace supposed they both were reformed thieves.

But Elliott never seemed the sort to divulge such details, should they exist.

She imagined Frederick missed Elliott, though he wouldn't say. They'd known each other a long time. She paused as she twisted another strand of hair up into a pin. Did Elliott know that Frederick used to paint?

"I'm surprised I never knew you liked to paint. I meant to mention it to you after we visited the gallery, but then we learned of the murders from Jack and I got distracted," Grace called toward Frederick's room. "I feel as though that's something I should have known about you within the first month of our marriage."

"I haven't painted in a very long time," he responded, out of sight. "I'm not certain an old hobby should find its way easily into regular conversations."

She paused on the thought. But she'd learned the nickname his grandmother called him, the name of his childhood pets, his imaginary friend who'd been a goose, his least favorite uncle's dramatic aversion to turnips, and Frederick's secret love of pineapples.

Did things like that come up in regular conversations? She'd always found they did when she was involved.

She frowned. Is that why Lillias always tried to get her to stick with talking about the weather and the state of their gardens?

"But what a lovely hobby." She pinned up another strand of hair. "And oil paints, which take a great deal of patience, I understand."

"Well, if I was feeling impatient, I'd use watercolor." He entered the room, buttoning the sleeve of his shirt. His bowtie hung undone around his neck, his shirt unbuttoned at the neck.

There was something wonderful about knowing him in such an intimate way.

"You used watercolor too? See, these are little details wives should know about their husbands. Right up there with your favorite book or childhood memory." She smiled her welcome. "Though I know the answer to the memories part because you love talking about the summer visits you'd take to Scotland with your grandparents when you were a child. Wasn't it to visit your grandmother's ancestral home or something like that?"

He began working on his bowtie. "It was."

"Did you know my great-grandfather was Scottish? He came to America because of some conflict involving Jacobites and battles that my great-grandfather's father had gotten in the middle of. Father says there is some sort of ancestral home of ours there too. My mother's people."

"Do you recall what area of Scotland?"

"No, but I can write to Father and ask." Grace focused on Frederick's fingers as he made quick work of the tie. She attempted to sort out how it was done, but every time she'd tried, she'd knotted the thing into something almost impossible to untangle.

He drew close, his grin crooked in a rather dastardly way, and then nudged her to turn around. She complied and immediately felt the slow pressure of his fingers as they worked the tiny buttons on the back of her gown. The familiar tingle of his closeness, his touch, traveled from his fingertips up her exposed back to her neck, trailing delicious warmth along with it.

"This gown is new?" His low voice ignited another round of delightful tingles.

"Your cousin helped me choose it in Cairo, but considering all the chaos that happened while we were there, I never had the opportunity to wear it. Do you like it?"

"Very much." The way he scraped out the words sent heat branching from her chest, up her neck, and into her face, bringing a shallowness of breath.

She turned. "Well, you always look so dashing and delicious, I do hope I can at least compliment you."

His grin tipped. "Dashing and delicious, is it?"

Her pulse increased with expectation. "Come now, that cannot be the first time you've been accused of being tall, dark, and handsome, can it? Surely not!" She gestured toward him. "You look as though you walked directly out of a description in a novel."

He drew close, his gaze roaming over her face with such intensity, she nearly grabbed him by his newly tied bowtie and kissed him.

"Hero or villain?"

She raised her playful brow. "Depends on my mood and what shade of brown your eyes are at the time."

His palm slipped around her waist. "There are different shades of dark brown to my eyes?"

"Oh yes, like right now you look quite villainous in your expression."

"Perhaps I feel quite villainous."

Her breath caught as he tugged her so close, she thought he would kiss her. Instead, he caressed her jaw, then neck with his thumb, a sweet hum slipping from her lips. Oh, if they didn't have dinner in a quarter of an hour, he'd undo all the progress they'd just made on their attire. He slipped his lips over her cheek to her ear and whispered, "Turn back around. I haven't finished with your fastenings."

He gently nudged her back around. His gaze met hers in the mirror, and he trailed his finger against her skin to the next button.

With slow motion, he leaned forward and placed a kiss between her shoulder blades.

Her quick intake of breath appeared to fuel further exploration as he prolonged the kiss all the way to the base of her neck before he drew it to an unsatisfying close. She didn't move. Barely breathed.

"Oh, that. . .was"—she trembled out the words on a breath— "lovely." She sighed and opened her eyes to meet his gaze in the mirror. "Now I won't be able to have one sensible conversation at dinner because I will be daydreaming about how wonderful it will be for you to finish what you so deviously started before dinner." She forced a frown. "Very villainous."

"No, my beautiful darling. It's like a promise." He turned her around to face him. "We can pick up where we left off as soon as we return to our room."

He took a long taste of her ready lips.

"Assuming neither one of us is attacked by a ghost," she whispered against his mouth. "Or nabbed by the butler."

He chuckled against her lips. "Well, with an inducement like you on my mind, I'll be doubly on my guard to keep you free of both so we can continue with a thorough dessert."

"And I plan to keep you safe too." She leaned back slightly, searching his handsome face. "I've even made sure to hide my knife in my bodice, just in case."

Some of the heat dwindled from his eyes for a moment before his grin resurfaced. "I have high hopes you'll not need to use it and I can safely remove it for you later."

Chapter 10

"Blast it all, Laraby." Jack's voice boomed from a room nearby, just as Frederick and Grace had made it to the bottom of the stairs. "Do you want to save your paintings or not?"

"We're merely showcasing the reason Mrs. Reynolds and her brother are here." Laraby's voice carried down the hall. "Setting the stage for Mrs. Reynolds' novel, helping her visualize the possibilities. The painting will be guarded the entire time."

Frederick sent a look to Grace, and they both increased their steps to the door's threshold to find three men in the room. Jack, Mr. Hopewell, and Laraby.

"Ah, perhaps one of you can talk some sense into the man." Jack waved a hand toward Laraby before placing both palms on his hips. "He means to display one of *The Juliets* in the room while we dine as a way to encourage a grand revealing of the thieves."

"Aren't you afraid someone will steal it, Mr. Laraby?" Grace voiced the question on Frederick's mind.

"In a crowded room?" Laraby laughed, dusting at the sleeves of his dinner suit as if her suggestion was similarly insignificant. "If so, then we'll catch our thieves red-handed. Otherwise, we can watch how all the guests respond and make our deductions." He shook his head, donning a smile Frederick was beginning to dislike.

"Really, Jack. You should have thought of this idea."

"We're not dealing with an amateur," came Jack's quick response. "These thieves have succeeded in stealing all seven of the other *Juliets*. If we are to set out bait, we will do so in a very controlled manner. Not some spontaneous ruse of the moment."

"I've already told Mr. and Mrs. Reynolds I plan to display it." He shrugged. "My favorite of the paintings is still carefully hidden away, but it can't hurt to give my esteemed guests a little view of the real thing, especially with all the drama in the paintings' history."

"Laraby."

"She can use it as research. The actual paintings, in all their glory, will be much more inspiring than a tiny black-and-white photograph." His tone took on a desperate sort of edge. "I will win her over. Be sure of it."

"And I tell you that you are making an elemental mistake."

"Paul means to guard the painting the whole night." Laraby waved toward his friend. "And look at him. He's taller than all of us and just as broad as you or Lord Astley. And if the two of you are on your guard, what is there to fear?"

"We should not be placed in additional danger when the history of these paintings is already fraught with it." Jack folded his arms across his chest. "I will reiterate, Mr. Laraby—"

"It's settled, Jack." Laraby turned to leave the room. "I am the master of this villa and footing your bill, so why should you worry about what I do with my things? If I can take the opportunity to get a bit of notoriety too, the better for it. Your job is to see which guests start salivating over this lovely *Juliet* and then nab them."

"I will not be held responsible if you lose another precious painting, Mr. Laraby," Jack called after the arrogant man, who didn't look back as he exited the room. "Idiot," Jack muttered. "I've a mind to give up on the whole investigation."

"There's no point in trying to reason with him, Miracle."

Paul paused as he began to place a sheet over the painting nearby. "He's always been the stubborn sort. Add money to it and he's nigh impossible."

"Which only deepens my conviction to leave before his stupidity puts me or my colleagues in danger." Jack groaned and stepped forward, Frederick on his heels, to get a closer look at the art.

The painting drew him in, somehow, as beautiful art had always done. He'd loved this particular mode of expression his entire life. His grandmother had been an amateur painter, and her appreciation for the beauty influenced Frederick. Of course, the past few years, he'd lived in a fog of guilt and rejection, the joys of such beauties lost to him, but living with and being loved by Grace had begun to revive the man he once was. Being reminded of God's love for him had somehow opened a closed door in his heart, reawakening the dreamer of his youth and reintroducing the joy and freedom in being loved well.

Framed in gold, the painting's rich colors and Romantic period style took up more space than the actual size. Dramatic. A play of shadow and light. The artist's intricate care shown in the facial expressions down to the fur on the gray cat sitting beneath a small table in the background. This particular piece showcased a party: Shadows of people of all shapes and sizes created a backdrop to the highlighted pair in the foreground. A young woman, hair spun up in braids and ribbons, wore a pale blue gown of an older fashion, her eyes almost alive. She stood at one end of the room. Reflected on the other side was a young man, his expression one of complete bewilderment. The two stood frozen in the frame, gazes locked.

"Fascinating, isn't it?" Paul queried, leaving the covering back for their inspection. "It's entitled *Love at First Sight*."

"When Romeo sees Juliet for the first time?" Grace sighed, stepping close. "What a wonderful beginning to such a sad story. They look so real they could step right out of the painting."

"It's truly a remarkable piece." Frederick looked up. "Are the others in the same style?"

"As far as I know." Paul tipped his head. "I'm not much for art, myself, but Laraby's other piece, the one that was stolen, held the same look as does his favorite. The balcony scene."

"This appears to be much more of a Romantic style than that of Accardi's actual time period. I was expecting Impressionism, but he could have joined in the later styles of the Pre-Raphae—" He stopped.

Paul raised a brow. Jack did as well. Grace's eyes grew wide before her smile spread in complete appreciation of his assessment.

Heat crept into Frederick's face at the sudden attention. "My grandmother was a great lover of the Romantic style."

"Isn't that perfect." Grace's eyes brightened. Her definition of romantic, in this sense, and his were likely not the same thing.

"Perhaps your appreciation will come in handy in figuring out the message to a secret treasure." Paul shook his head. "I'm all for the easy way to riches."

A gong sounded through the house.

"We've been brought on to find the missing *Juliets*, Mr. Hopewell, not decipher a possible hoax," Jack countered, gesturing with his chin toward the door. "There is the dinner gong. I suggest we prepare ourselves for more theatrics to come." He sighed. "And usually I'm a great proponent of the stage."

The stage was gloriously set.

Just as Jack had suggested.

Grace glanced around the long table situated in a dining room as immaculate as the rest of the villa. The house glimmered with gilded everything, either still in celebration of the Victorian era's love for embellishment or simply part of Mr. Laraby's exhibition of wealth.

Mr. Hopewell stood guard at the entrance of the room with the *Juliet* poised on an easel to the man's left, and in truth, with his sober expression and in his dark suit, he did create an imposing presence. Mr. Zappa stood by a serving table on the opposite side of the guests, poised for service, his expression as impassable as ever.

One by one, the cast of Laraby's party made their way past the masterpiece, each showing various levels of appreciation. Nothing to overtly point to thieves or murderers that Grace could tell, but a few, including Mr. Reynolds, gave the piece considerable attention.

Of course Jack had mentioned Mr. Reynolds was an art collector himself, which only deepened Grace's suspicion about him.

On the opposite side of the room stood a wall of glass doors that opened out onto a veranda overlooking the sea. Mr. Hopewell remarked that Laraby had locked all the doors to ensure no one entered via the veranda and directed all guests through the main dining room entrance.

Frederick sat across from Grace, with Mrs. Reynolds to one side and Mr. Reynolds to the other.

To Grace's right sat. . .Miss Whitby?

Because the woman was Laraby's assistant, Grace hadn't expected her to dine with them, but she approved of the choice. Besides, the only way to sort out suspects was to engage in conversations and observations. If the possible suspects were hidden away, it made observation and conversations much more difficult.

Though Miss Whitby had reportedly been in the circus with Laraby and Mr. Hopewell, she didn't look very circusy in her simple yellow evening frock. With her hair pulled up in a tight and refined halo of curls and her spectacles in place, she looked the part of an elegant, bookish lady. Grace paused. What did a bookish lady look like really? Grace didn't have spectacles and rarely wore yellow, and she was very bookish.

The woman possessed the greenest eyes Grace had ever seen, made all the more noticeable when framed by her glasses. Truly remarkable. Nearly distracting. Perhaps that was the circus part of Miss Whitby coming out. Through her eyes.

Grace paused. And the woman looked strangely familiar. Had Grace seen their circus performance in the States?

"I don't believe we've met properly." Grace offered a smile to Miss Whitby.

"No, Lady Astley, but I have already heard a great deal about you from Mr. Laraby." Miss Whitby offered a pleasant smile with an impish sort of look tagged onto her expression. Yes, it must be the eyes.

"Oh, I can't imagine what his account might convey, but I hope it was pleasant." She took a drink.

"Laraby has a tendency toward exaggeration, but in this case, I believe he may have hit the mark."

"Well, I've not heard *anything* about you except that you are quite the manager of Mr. Laraby's finances and you were part of the circus."

Her smile fell. "When he listens to my advice, then perhaps I do him good, but he's prone to follow his own conscience, which rarely bodes well."

"He does become rather fixed on an idea, doesn't he?" Grace stared down at her soup, a concoction of white liquid with some sort of. . .spinach?

"Quite infuriatingly so."

"What did you do in the circus?"

Her gaze moved back to Grace's face, all humor fleeing her expression despite her smile. "My stepfather was an illusionist. My mother and I were his assistants, so I learned to do a great many things."

"An illusionist?" Grace attempted to control the excitement in her voice. "I imagine there were many interesting things about such a life. Did you learn to make things disappear?"

"Yes." Miss Whitby's smile fell.

"Oh, I'm sorry. I didn't mean to bring up bad memories."

Miss Whitby drew in a breath and gave her head a little shake. "It is not you. Forgive me. But I'm afraid my stepfather preferred I make other people's things disappear and never return."

The implication melted into comprehension. "Oh, you mean he made you steal?"

"He wasn't the nicest of men, I'm afraid, and as he regaled the crowds with his magic, I would take cash or jewelry from the patrons." She shook her head. "I'm not proud of it and thankful to be away from *him*, though I loved the community of the circus." She shrugged a shoulder of her simple gown. "And I did learn resilience, which is an excellent life skill, isn't it?"

Grace studied the woman, unable to shake her familiarity. "Resilience is an excellent skill. I would think you learned creativity, as well. And you must be very trustworthy for Laraby to have you keep his finances, so those are good qualities too."

"Trustworthy? Even with my past, you'd think that?" Her eyes brightened a little. "I do appreciate the insight, Lady Astley. In Laraby's world, of late, I've felt more of a fixture than a friend, so it is refreshing to look on the positive side." Her smile brightened. "I'm usually more fun-loving, so you'll have to forgive my momentary melancholy."

"We all experience it at times," Grace offered, remembering her first few weeks at Havensbrooke. "But I find reminding myself of who I truly am and how much I am truly loved helps a great deal in moments like that. No human is worthy of defining us, are they? The only one who truly has the power and the insight is of much higher wisdom and power than humans."

"That does change things, doesn't it?" She stared at Grace with those intriguing eyes. "I think I'm going to like your fresh perspective, Lady Astley."

Miss Whitby couldn't have been much older than Grace. Perhaps a few years?

"You may call me Grace, if you'd like."

"Grace? Hmm. . ." Her golden brows rose behind her spectacles. "Lydia," she offered. "I've never heard of a female detective. I was quite surprised when Jack mentioned you on the ferry. I think it's high time to add females to the sleuthing business. We have particular sets of skills that would benefit an investigation, if you ask me."

"I agree and am happy to have the opportunity to learn and grow under Detective Miracle's tutelage." Then she replayed Lydia's words. Ferry? Lydia hadn't been on the ferry. Again, the familiarity proved almost unnerving. Green eyes. Blond hair. A strange realization dawned. No, it couldn't be.

"I don't recall seeing a blond-haired, green-eyed *woman* on the ferry this morning."

"Oh, I did give myself away, didn't I?" Lydia's eyes widened, and her smile took a Cheshire-cat tilt. "The fact you even noticed and remembered me says something for your observation skills."

"But"—Grace gave her head a little shake—"you were dressed as a footman?"

"I've always been good with disguises." Lydia leaned close, her eyes brimming with contained laughter. "Illusionist," she stated, as if that explained everything.

"But why a footman on the ferry?"

"Laraby wanted a few extra eyes and ears to look for possible thieves among us." She shook her golden head. "Or to hear the latest gossip, since he's so concerned about such things now that he's among the upper crust." She rolled her eyes to show her thoughts on the matter. "People are always freer with their words when an invisible servant is nearby. So I was strongly encouraged to provide my brand of services, if you will." One golden brow rose. "Being invisible."

How clever of her and well done too! Grace had attempted disguises on several occasions, but none of them worked out very well. She presumed it was because of her inability to hide her hair, but now that she thought about it, the problem may have rested more with her inability to maintain character without giggling.

Her attention moved the length of the table to where Laraby sat at the head. "It doesn't sound as if you are as friendly with him as you once were."

"You could certainly say that." A puff of air came from Lydia, a humorless laugh. "Money changes people, I suppose. And since he's gotten his sights set on these *Juliets*, he's become obsessed about the mysterious treasure, which is likely as invisible as anything I could make disappear." Her smile took a downward turn. "Once he started moving among the artist circles, he met Miss Benetti, who took no time at all in making him fall desperately in love with her."

Miss Benetti sat to Laraby's right, her purple gown shimmering in the light. She and Laraby seemed engaged in a pleasant and intimate conversation from the look of delight on their faces. Could Miss Benetti have used her beauty and womanly wiles, as the books call it, to capture Laraby's affections in order to steal his paintings?

Very clever, indeed.

Grace turned back to Lydia. "You don't seem to like her very much."

"I do nothing to hide my suspicion of her. What working-class woman wouldn't wish to catch a millionaire?" She shrugged. "But at this point, I've washed my hands of Jo—Laraby's choices."

A high-pitched laugh pulled Grace's attention to Mrs. Reynolds, who wore some sort of stylish golden turban over her brown hair. Large blue earrings dangled from each ear and matched the hues of her gown. She didn't look anything like what Grace had envisioned authors to look. No pen behind her ear. No ink smudges on her fingers. And she seemed to speak too much to be incredibly observant of others.

If Grace could locate one of Mrs. Reynolds' books, she felt she could make a much more accurate assessment of her. Of course, not all books were for everyone, but with the amount of mysteries Grace had read, she felt fairly qualified to judge a fictional mystery with some knowledge.

"If you'll excuse me a moment, Lady—Grace," Lydia corrected, "I must speak to Laraby about the evening plans."

She stood from her place and walked away. Grace looked up to find Frederick watching her from across the table, a few seats up from Mr. Finch. He tilted his chin in question and raised his glass as if in toast to her. She'd felt his attention most of the meal, sending tender glances her way on occasion—except for the one time she'd shot a slippery boiled potato across the room. Her dear husband's expression had held a more shocked look, but not as shocked as it used to be. Lucky for the potato, one of the footmen caught it in midair.

Frederick sat beside Mr. Reynolds and no doubt had been gathering his own bits of information. She offered him a smile and went to raise her glass in response when the lights suddenly flickered.

Laraby stood from his place at the head of the table on the side of the sea. "What?"

And then the lights vanished completely. A woman screamed. A man groaned. Glass crashed.

"What is going on?" came a voice from across the table. Mr.

Reynolds, perhaps?

A few silhouettes rose from their seated positions, and a strange glow swelled from Grace's left. The hairs on the back of her neck stood eerily to attention.

In the entryway of the dining room, a pale light shone from the darkness of the windowless space. Something like a thin vapor ascended and swirled over the threshold.

"Is there a fire?" a woman called.

As if in answer, from out of the smoke appeared a woman.

The image of a woman.

Grace's throat tightened.

A *ghost* of a woman.

And unlike Grace's previous ghost experiences, this specter presented exactly the way she'd always imagined. Otherworldly, lonely, and completely transparent.

Chapter 11

Frederick had never seen anything like it.

As the last remnants of evening waned from the windows on one side of the dining room, a pale glow of light pulled everyone's attention to the hallway just outside the room's entrance. A wisp of smoke. A flash of light. And from out of the shadows and fog beyond the doorway came a figure in a pale gown.

A woman, though her features were unclear. Her dark hair fell loose about her shoulders, and one of her hands gestured to the left as if grasping something from the air.

"She came!" Laraby exclaimed, thin light drifting in from the windows behind him outlined his silhouette as he stood. "I knew the painting would bring her."

A woman's quiet cry pierced another few seconds of silence and then the ghost turned toward the table, pointing her finger at the crowd. Another gasp. A murmured exclamation, and someone—was it Paul—rushed toward the specter.

Paul made it to the threshold of the doorway, when the ghost redirected her pointing finger toward him. The man jolted to a stop as if seized by some invisible force. He reached for his throat, ushering up a noise like a man gasping for breath.

Frederick pushed to a stand. Paul grappled as if some invisible hand was squeezing the life out of him. Just as Frederick started forward, a shadow rushed from the right, tackling Paul to the ground.

The ghost quivered, raised her arms heavenward, and disappeared, leaving a smoky glow behind, before another flash of light shattered the shadows.

All went dark.

Something clattered to the floor to Frederick's right.

"Are we going to die?" came a woman's voice.

Was it Miss Benetti?

"No, not right now at any rate," came Grace's quick reply. "I imagine the ghost has already done her work, and if any of us are bound to die, it will have to wait for later."

The woman's whimpered response followed.

Well, for all her imaginings, Frederick was incredibly grateful Grace had such a practical head on her shoulders. Especially in times of ghosts or life-threatening dangers.

"George, Milo," Laraby called from somewhere in the room, his words likely directed toward the servants. "Find the lanterns."

As if insulted by such a request, the electric lights flickered back to life, brightening the room with such brilliance, it took a moment for Frederick to blink the view into clarity.

"Mr. Hopewell may need a doctor." Jack bent over the man, likely the figure Frederick had seen rush from the right. Frederick joined him. "He has what appears to be a wound on his head."

"What?" Laraby rushed forward followed by Frederick. "But. . .but no one was supposed to get hurt."

"Do you have the foreknowledge to predict a ghost's behavior, Mr. Laraby?" Jack ground out the question. "Another circus gift of yours?"

"It's all for fun." Laraby blanched, whispering, clearly grappling for a response. "I never supposed anyone would really—"

"I imagine no one was supposed to steal your painting either?"

came Jack's curt response.

All eyes moved to the spot where the painting had stood. The easel lay on the floor void of any *Juliet*.

"The painting?" Mr. Reynolds surged forward, his attention roaming the room. "What. . .but. . .this is preposterous. How—"

"A surprise we would not be dealing with if Mr. Laraby had heeded my warnings."

"Right now, I think our focus should be on the injured man." This from Miss Whitby, whose face looked almost ashen, her golden hair a bit unruly. She dropped to the floor beside Jack. "It's not as if a ghost could really hurt him, is it?" She raised her gaze to Laraby. "Did you see?"

Something Frederick couldn't quite place passed between the two before he turned back to the unconscious man. "I—I don't know what happened."

"Don't you?" Jack countered, pulling back Mr. Hopewell's collar.

"*The Juliets* are masterpieces." Reynolds stepped closer. "Of course they're important."

"And this is a man's *life*," Miss Whitby countered and turned toward Jack. "Is he in real danger, Detective?"

Jack didn't immediately answer. For some reason, he seemed frozen in place as he stared over at Miss Whitby. He cleared his throat. "Not that I can tell. His breathing is consistent and not shallow, but he's taken a bump to the head." He gave his own head a little shake and looked back at Frederick. "First things first. A doctor."

Frederick took the cue from Jack and stood, turning toward Laraby. "Do you have a telephone to ring the mainland?"

Laraby blinked over at him, his hand running absently through his hair. "Um. . .yes, a telephone." He cleared his throat and gestured absently toward the left, his gaze fastening on Paul's still body. "There's one in the hall," he stated,

As if Frederick would know who to call.

"Your fiancée is Italian," Jack groaned, sending Frederick a look as if to communicate how annoyed he was at the rest of the group's lack of usefulness. Evidently, whatever had shaken the man wasn't a problem anymore. "She will know who to phone. Send her."

"I refuse to go into the hallway alone when we have just witnessed the visitation of a spirit, and evidently a spirit with designs to harm us." The woman, donned in a slender gown of purple, shook her head. "I saw what the *lo spettro* did to Paul. Who is to say she is not waiting to hurt someone else?"

Jack murmured something unintelligible, but Frederick thought he caught the word ridiculous among the syllables. Evidently, the response almost sparked Miss Whitby's grin, if the sudden tilt of her lips gave a clue.

Frederick moved his attention between the two and tossed the distraction away.

"Fine." Laraby moved to Miss Benetti's side, his palm to her back as he softened his voice. "I'll send Zappa with you."

"We need to search the grounds for anyone who may be trying to escape with your painting. The most logical conclusion is that they'd try to run." Jack stood. "Have two of your men move Mr. Hopewell to a room where he will be more comfortable. Those same men are then on guard in the house."

"You don't plan to leave us, do you, Detective?" This from Miss Benetti, who stood at the doorway with Mr. Zappa. "How can you think we are safe after such a spectacle?"

"Spectacle, indeed," Jack ground out the response. "I doubt the ghost"—he exaggerated the word—"has any designs on anyone else tonight."

"I must agree with Jasmine, Detective." Mrs. Reynolds stepped forward, her palm against her chest. "I have a great appreciation for suspense, but we've already witnessed one man wounded by this"—she waved one hand in the hair—"apparition, and if you hadn't intervened, Mr. Hopewell could possibly have died."

"I hate to place a wet blanket over such an excellent display of drama." Grace offered a most comforting smile. "As an avid student of ghosts, I agree with Detective Miracle. For the present, our ghost has done her work."

All eyes moved to his wife, and Frederick tilted his head to study her. What was she going to say next? He narrowed his eyes in contemplation. This seemed to be a constant question in his mind about his lovely bride.

Jack's brows rose. Laraby's eyes widened, but Grace merely raised her chin in a way to show she was quite proud of herself and stepped toward the dining room doorway.

"An avid student of ghosts?" Mrs. Reynolds tilted her head, staring at Grace as if she'd grown a horn from her forehead.

"Copious amounts of reading on the subject, as well as a real ghost hunt or two, does prepare one more readily than not." Grace nodded. "And I must say it isn't a usual occurrence for smoke to accompany the visit of ghosts, as far as my research is concerned, which begs the question, why did the smoke appear and how did it get there?"

"Who cares if there was smoke?" This from Mr. Reynolds, who moved to stand by his wife's side, his body poised tall in excellent dramatic display. "A ghost attacked someone. Didn't you see it?"

"We saw what we were meant to see. It was really fantastically done, don't you think?"

"And Paul's wounds are highly superficial," Frederick added, the realization dawning. "A hit to the head enough to cause unconsciousness but not break the skin or create a depression." So whatever wound he'd been given wasn't serious or meant to kill. "It would have been fairly easy for someone to attack him from behind while the rest of us were focused on the ghost."

Grace rewarded him with a smile. "I've seen a ghost like that appear in a few other places. The first time, of course, is always the most memorable, so I understand your high emotions."

Frederick exchanged a look with Jack, the latter donning a slow, growing smile. His wife found the most uncanny times to be brilliant.

"But it makes perfect sense, doesn't it?" Grace stepped toward the dining room threshold, gesturing toward the empty easel on the floor. "If I were going to steal a painting in plain sight, I'd choose a distraction to assist me, wouldn't you?"

"Are you telling me there wasn't a *real* ghost?" This from Mrs. Reynolds, who finally seemed to be catching up with the conversation. To her credit, she appeared more curious than incredulous.

"I highly doubt it, don't you Jack?"

The detective moved from his place beside Paul, who was slowly being raised on a makeshift cot by two of the male servants. "It does seem terribly convenient, my lady."

"And I've never read of a ghost stealing a painting before." Grace nodded, slowly starting toward the hallway with Frederick on her heels. "Slashing it, perhaps, or taking up residence in the frame, but not making one disappear."

"Which means we have been sufficiently distracted so that our thieves have gotten away with the painting." Jack moved to the doorway. "Now we must make wise use of our time. Finch? Reynolds? Do you mean to remain inside?"

"Well, I'm not too certain," came Mr. Reynolds' grumbled response.

"Go on, Donald." Mrs. Reynolds released an exhausted sigh. "I have no need of you in here."

Mr. Reynolds didn't so much as grimace at his wife's dismissive tones.

"I have no intention of going through the dark in search of

some thieves," Finch announced, standing taller.

"Very well," Frederick offered, holding the man's gaze. "You can remain inside to keep the ladies safe from a revisit of our specter."

Mr. Finch's face paled. "This is ridiculous," he growled. "But if you are in such need of extra hands, then I will stay near Miracle."

As Jack directed the men, including a few willing servants, Frederick pulled Grace aside.

"You'll stay inside, won't you?"

"Of course." She blinked those azure eyes up at him. "There's much more to investigate in here than out there."

His stomach tightened, and he pinched his lips closed. Perhaps, *he* should remain inside to protect the ladies.

"Don't worry. I'll be very cautious." She nodded, as if the added movement would assuage his concern. "And as you'll recall, I did bring my knife."

Frederick had barely left her presence before Grace turned her full attention to the hallway outside the dining room. She'd only seen such a wonderful display of ghostliness on stage or when Grandfather purchased his own Magic Lantern, but she had a fairly solid idea of how the apparition appeared.

The smoke was truly just an extra benefit.

"What are you doing over here?" Mrs. Reynolds emerged from the dining room, her long blue gown trailing behind her. "Aren't you concerned to be off on your own, Lady Astley?"

Grace offered a smile, a little distracted by the woman's indulgence of purple eye powder, though purple had an amazing effect on hazel eyes.

"As I said, I think the theatrics may be over for this evening."

Mrs. Reynolds scanned the hall. "And what do you plan to do now?" For an author of mysteries, the woman really ought to be the one coming up with those sorts of solutions.

"Looking for a few clues as to the creator of our ghost."

"You. . .you think you can actually uncover who created the ghost?" This from Lydia Whitby, who studied Grace with those piercing green eyes.

"Well, since I don't really believe in ghosts and have had a grandfather who adored experimenting with theatrical lighting, I have a general idea of how one might appear." She shrugged a shoulder. "I am a detective after all."

Miss Whitby's smile fell. Served the woman right for dressing up as a boy on the ferry just to spy on perfectly decent people. Though Grace had to admit the idea held a little fun.

"May I join you?" Mrs. Reynolds' eyes brightened, or perhaps it was the effect of the eye shadow. She stepped closer. "I've never encountered a female detective before, and I feel this could bode very well for my newest novel."

Grace preened a little at the idea of not only being referred to as a detective but possibly inspiring a book character. Another dream to come true? Oh, it seemed much too generous of God! Detective, fictional inspiration, and romantically attached to the most wonderful man as they traveled the world solving mysteries? She almost sighed but thought that might give away too much of her fanciful nature.

And as a detective, she needed to appear a little more. . .composed?

"It would be helpful to have another set of eyes and ears, Mrs. Reynolds."

"Please, call me Dolores, won't you?" She offered her gloved hand. "I know we are to become excellent friends."

The woman was probably closer to Frederick's age, likely older, with eyes even older still.

"Call me Grace." Grace took the woman's hand. "Friends are certainly a benefit in life, especially in life-threatening moments."

Mrs. Reynolds' smile stilled on her face before she seemed to recover. "Yes."

"I would love to join you in your little hunt for clues." Miss Whitby smoothed her palms together. "But I'm rather more concerned for the welfare of Mr. Hopewell than the pretension of a ghost hunt. If you'll excuse me."

Grace followed the woman with her gaze as she left the room. Her blond hair had come loose from its rather tight coiffeur from earlier. Perhaps she had unruly curls like Grace.

And she'd been much more playful and jovial at the table earlier. But now? Well, she seemed. . .angry? Of course, she was upset about the painting's disappearance, but something seemed odd in her sudden change of demeanor. Could it be her concern for Mr. Hopewell?

"So what do you glean from our current situation, apart from a distraction to steal the *Juliet*?"

Grace pulled her attention back to the woman. Dolores' soft accent gave off a comforting sound. Gentle, in contrast to her vibrant appearance, and curled with tones Grace couldn't quite place. Some English, maybe? But not quite all.

Grace began walking about the periphery of the hall, reimagining the ghost's placement. "A trick of mirrors and light, I'd guess." A haze from the smoke still hovered in the air. "And there should be a pot of some sort nearby. The thieves would need glycerin and water to create such smoke as we saw, so they'd need a large container in which to mix the solution."

"How remarkable." Dolores followed, tugging a notebook and tiny pencil from her pocket. "Smoke and mirrors truly do come into play."

Grace appreciated a good note taker. The fact that Dolores was taking notes on what *Grace* said just made things all the more delightful.

A ceramic pot used for a large indoor plant of some sort proved the culprit. Not only did the scent of smoke still cling to the area around it, but a small bit of residue also waited at the bottom of the pot. She wondered if the thieves had planned a better cleanup job but were thwarted by Paul's interruption.

"I'd imagine they'd created a Pepper's ghost, which means there should be a sheet of. . ." She tapped what looked to be the space within an empty doorway. "Glass for the reflection."

"What do you mean?" Dolores moved to Grace's side, taking in the sheet of glass wedged into the bottom half of the open doorway. "Some sort of reflection off this created the ghost?"

"Yes. My grandfather loved making them." She studied the direction the glass was angled. "One time he terrified the gardener to such an extent, the man quit the next day. Needless to say, Grandfather didn't create any more Pepper's ghosts for the staff, but if you were family, you always got one for your birthday. My sister, Lillias, hated the tradition, but I always assumed that's where I developed my fascination for ghosts. One time, he even produced a ghost dog. I think that was his favorite."

Dolores' eyes grew wider, and she barked out a laugh. "Your grandfather sounds as if he was a rather unique man."

"Oh yes. He was born in the mountains near where I grew up and became rather rich through hard work and. . .creativity." Grace didn't think sharing some of her grandfather's more nefarious endeavors would bode well for the current situation. "I do so hope I am able to do half the things he did in his long life. Everything except sea bathing in his"—she cleared her throat—"well, less than he ought to have worn." Grace kneeled down to examine the glass, the angle fixed to such a degree its trajectory pointed toward a narrow door on the other side of the hallway. A narrow, poorly lit hallway. Perfect. Much less obvious and would allow a quick, shadowy getaway for possible thieves. "I think we may have our spot." She marched to the closet door. The slight opening only showed darkness.

Grace drew in a deep breath and carefully placed her palm over her chest so that her fingers would have quick access to her dagger.

"What are you doing?" Dolores whispered behind Grace.

"Don't worry." Grace took another step. "If I'm right, the thieves are gone."

"And if you're wrong?"

"We'll be forced to fight them."

"We?" Dolores squeaked just as Grace kicked the door open to reveal a small closet.

An empty small closet, except for a crumpled bunch of cloth on the floor and a dark wig.

Grace reached down and gathered up the cloth, shaking it out to reveal an old-fashioned gown.

"That. . .that is what the ghost was wearing." Dolores' voice shook. "But now there isn't a body to go with it."

Grace held up the gown in one hand and the wig in the other. "I highly doubt there is a ghost roaming the halls dressed in what my grandfather wore to sea bathe. And do you really believe a ghost needs a wig?" Grace spun around and peered down the narrow hall. A cool breeze, tinted with sea, rushed from the direction. "Let's see where this leads."

"Are most female detectives as curious as you?"

Grace turned to the woman, blinking. "I don't know a great number of female detectives in real life, only in fiction, but most of them must possess some curiosity to be good at their jobs, I should think." Grace dipped her head toward Dolores. "Much like an author."

Dolores blinked. "Oh yes. Of course."

The hallway grew darker, colder, with rooms closed off on either side. A sense of emptiness cloaked the chilled air, rooms left too long without the warmth of life. Grace swallowed against the thought. She was incredibly good at talking herself into near-hysteria.

They came to a door, open wide, that led out to a stone balcony stretching over endless sea.

"This must be how the thieves escaped," Grace suggested, peering out into the darkness. This side of the house was poised near the edge of a rocky cliff that dropped hundreds of feet down to the sea. For some reason, thoughts of Dracula climbing up the cliffs to his mysterious castle came to mind. But this place was much too beautiful and white to be the home of a vampiric sort of villain, of course.

"How?" Dolores questioned, peering past Grace to look over the balcony's ledge. "It's a sheer drop!"

The question didn't help the Dracula thoughts, but Grace made sure to keep her facial expression poised. She stepped out onto the balcony, which stretched the length of the house on this side, easily leading to doors or windows through which the thieves could have gone.

A shiver trembled up Grace's neck. Yes, it was.

"Likely they found a way back inside from the veranda." Grace gestured toward the length of the porch. She drew in a breath and turned around. "Which means, our thieves may never have left the house at all."

"They're still inside?" Dolores' eyes grew wide again, her voice dropping. "With us?"

"Wouldn't that make the plot even better for a story? All the suspects closed up together?"

"I suppose so." Dolores drew in a shaky breath and attempted a smile, glancing behind her toward the dark hallway. "But I must say I prefer my intrigue in fiction."

"It is usually much safer there," Grace muttered, giving the veranda another look. Most of the doors to reenter the house led along to her left. Which rooms waited there? And were the thieves still hiding among those rooms? Or had they returned to the party as if nothing were amiss? And if they had returned to the party, they must have stored the painting somewhere.

"We should probably let the men know what we've found." Grace stepped back into the house, Dolores on her heels.

"A very good idea."

For a mystery writer, the woman didn't seem to think very clearly on matters like thieves and dangers. Of course, Grace had imagined much worse scenarios than this, which likely helped her keep a clear mind. At least in this scenario, there were no sea monsters. That particular one always made her feel quite prickly on the inside.

Dolores started down the hall with Grace trailing behind. But the thieves couldn't have gotten very far carrying a painting that size. So they may have needed to stash their prize somewhere to come back for it later and left the outside door open as a ruse.

Grace stopped. One door stood the slightest bit ajar, and the faintest light from windows landed on a bookshelf.

Dolores looked back at her. "Are you all right?"

Grace flashed a glance to her and then back to the door. "Yes, I'm going to check on a hunch."

Dolores followed her attention to the door. "A hunch?"

"Please, go ahead, Dolores." Grace ushered her forward. "The men need to know what we found. I'll join you shortly."

She hoped.

"And I don't want to waste our window of opportunity, as you well know. The longer the time between the crime and the apprehension, the more difficult the mystery has a tendency to become."

"But. . .you don't want to go alone, do you?" The woman peered from Grace back to the door. "In there? It doesn't seem like a very safe place."

"Oh, don't worry. I've been in much scarier places than that." Grace smiled to reassure her. "I fell into a freshly dug grave once. It's surprising how far a fall that really is. It's one of the first times I realized the value of ropes."

The woman's lower lip dropped by slow degrees.

"But that was nothing as terrifying as getting stuck inside a sinking barrel in a river. If you've never been stuck in a sinking barrel, don't wish for it."

Dolores pressed her fist to her chest. "Good heavens."

The poor woman looked horrified. Perhaps Grace had gone too far. How could she reassure her?

"But don't worry." Grace waved toward the room. "I shall only take a peek. It's always a good idea to look for clues while we can. Besides, this room has books. If I'm trapped for some reason, at least I'll have something to read."

Dolores' eyes narrowed for the briefest moment, as if she wasn't quite certain what to say next.

"And you can tell the others where I am."

Dolores' smile resurfaced in a strange, frozen sort of way, and she dashed off, her gown flowing behind her in elegant waves.

Grace drew in a breath and looked both ways down the hallway before she reached into her bodice and pulled out her little dagger. She didn't really expect to need it, but the feel of the metal in her hand boosted her confidence a bit.

In fact, she felt very sleuthish.

With a nudge of her foot, the door creaked open to reveal a study of some sort. Pale sunset gold slipped between half-closed curtains, bathing the untouched space in soft light. The room reminded her so much of her first view of the east wing in Havensbrooke when she'd arrived in England. A slight chill skittered up her arms. And that place had introduced consecutive opportunities for adventures since.

Grace didn't notice a switch for electric lights, but since the rest of the villa boasted such, there had to be one somewhere.

A sheen of dust-covered furnishings of an older fashion scattered across the room, but the most beautiful sight were the rows of abundantly stocked bookshelves. How a room like this remained untouched, Grace couldn't fathom. She pulled her gaze from the shelves, feeling a bit lonely for those unloved books, and scanned the room with what light the fading horizon provided.

Nothing seemed out of place.

A door to Grace's left, likely a servants' door from the way it blended into the wall, stood slightly ajar. With a look toward the hallway, Grace tiptoed to the hidden door. It opened into another room, which appeared even more vacant and unused than the first.

And darker.

Grace moved to one of the windows and pulled back the heavy curtain enough to douse the room with a little light. Dust puffed from the movement, inciting a few coughs and stinging her eyes.

She wiped at the ready tears and blinked the room into better view.

A rocking horse stood forlorn in one corner. Two high-backs waited by a blackened fireplace. A few dolls poised on a settee stared back at her with lifeless eyes. She stepped away from them fairly quickly. How could something as pleasant as a doll take on a very different appearance in a shadowed, empty room?

At one corner of the room stood a magnificent wardrobe and beside it a beautiful carved trunk. A table stood in the center of the room, almost as if beckoning a passerby to stop and appreciate its offerings.

Grace obeyed, drawing close and squinting into the hazy shadows. A row of framed photos lined the table. One of a little girl on a bicycle. Another of a boy and a dog. A larger one with six people. An older man and woman, a younger couple, and two children. Tingles shot over Grace's scalp and neck as she peered closer, gently taking the latter photo up in her hands.

Were these the Accardis? Her attention fell to the children. Were those the lost grandchildren?

Suddenly, a creak sounded behind Grace.

Before she could turn, a hand covered her mouth, cloaking her attempt at a scream. She fought against thick, strong arms, tightening so much, she dropped her knife. One elbow landed with enough force to loosen the man's hold for a second, but before Grace could take a step, she was captured again. She struggled as he lifted her off the ground, taking advantage of her long skirts to wrap them like a mummy against her legs so that her flailing kicks failed to help her at all.

The man threw her down. Pain shot up her back and temporarily stole her breath. Within a second of landing, some sort of lid closed down upon her and doused her world into darkness.

Chapter 12

The last of daylight flickered on the horizon, molten behind the aqua sea. The view deserved a longer perusal, and if Frederick had actually been on his honeymoon, perhaps he could have afforded the view its due. As it was, he'd been cheerfully hoodwinked into another mystery by his darling wife and their detective friend.

So instead of sunset dinners with the promise of a rewarding evening alone with his wife, he walked through the gardens of an island villa searching for the dastardly thieves, or ghost, who'd stolen a millionaire's beloved painting. He sighed. Truth be told, something in him craved this sort of adventure. Whether it was Grace's influence or the resurrection of his younger self, he wasn't certain.

He glanced over at Jack, who walked beside him, pistol in hand.

Was it truly possible to be like Jack? An aristocrat who put his life in danger on a regular basis and solved mysteries on the side?

And Grace? Was it possible to enjoy these adventures with her for as long as they could before their family began to grow? Assuming they lived long enough to grow a family.

He shook his head to the dimming skyline. Well, he was in the thick of it now, and there was no going back. So for good or ill, he'd embrace the experience like the reluctant sleuth Grace, and evidently Jack, believed he was.

"I'm almost full up of Mr. Laraby," Jack murmured as they kept in step together. "Reckless, arrogant."

Frederick glanced back to find Laraby following far enough to have not heard Jack's remarks.

"I can't blame you." Frederick kept his voice low. "I can't make out whether Laraby is truly a victim or part of the problem."

Jack slowed his pace as they moved through a tiered garden near the back corner of the villa. As the sunset gold hit the white facade, it nearly made the house glow into the darkening evening.

"And how many of these characters are in it with him?" Jack shook his head, carefully slipping around a long hedgerow.

Several men followed behind them, including Laraby, Mr. Reynolds, and two servants. Zappa and Finch had taken some other men around the other side of the house to a second access point to the Grand Canal.

They'd walked a good half hour along the front of the house all the way down to the dock, and then around the side of the house without one hint of any mischief, unless one considered excessive complaining and swearing a mischief. At which point, Mr. Reynolds could certainly be arrested and convicted on both charges.

"There must be more than one person in it all. To get into the gallery and then take the painting in such a short amount of time? That alone required at least two people."

"Yes," Jack agreed, moving around another hedge. "And this ghost business tonight certainly took more than one. Someone had to man the specter as another took the painting." Jack drew in a breath as if reaching his limit of the situation. "I've secured a meeting with Laraby in the morning after breakfast so we can view all the photos of the paintings. We need an idea of what they look like so we will have a better idea of what we're searching for."

"And if someone is stealing them to puzzle out whatever code there is to the treasure, perhaps we can locate the thieves by locating the treasure."

"If there even is a treasure. Lore and murders have no end of mysteries to compound them, leaving a great many people wasting time and resources to come up with nothing." Jack took another turn and slid to a sudden stop. His arm flew out to brace against Frederick's chest. "Careful, old bean. Looks as though the setting is as dramatic as the actors."

Without warning or barrier, the ground gave way to a sharp cliff. The edge curved around the back of the house, where a veranda jutted out over the perilous drop. It was as remarkable a sight as it was startling. And the veranda must have been created in order to take advantage of both the breathtaking sea view and the staggering experience.

But those taking an evening stroll need watch their step.

"What are you thinking, man?" Jack's voice burst through the sound of the ocean waves hundreds of feet below as Laraby caught up to them. "Don't you need a barrier or warning to this drop for your own safety, let alone the safety of your guests?"

Laraby peered over the edge and grimaced. "I hadn't noticed this one." He gave a shrug. "I've only had the house a few months. You can't expect me to have renovated my living quarters, hosted tremendous parties, and searched out all the dangers within that time, now can you?"

Jack's expression told much more than he spoke.

"I'd say you need to hire better servants, Laraby." This from Reynolds, who stood poised on the edge of the cliff staring back at the house. "It looks as though someone has left one of your doors wide open to allow the evening chill inside. Irresponsible, that."

Everyone followed Reynolds' gaze. A set of double doors was situated near the center of the veranda, and one of the doors gaped open into the shadows of the house.

"How odd."

"It's not a common occurrence?" Something in Jack's voice

drew Frederick's attention back to the detective.

"I don't use those rooms." Laraby turned up the collar of his suit jacket, the evening breeze blowing cool. "They're the former families' rooms, untouched since the whole murder happened." Laraby's lips tilted into a grin. "The last owners would charge a fee to tour the rooms, and I had plans to do the same, now that most of my renovations on other parts of the house are complete."

"The visitation of a ghost would likely assist in your costs?" Frederick asked.

Frederick thought he caught a slight hesitation, a brief widening of Laraby's eyes, before the man responded. "That may have been the plan before I had a ghost make off with my property tonight."

"Well, I assure you, Dolores found the entire event captivating. She's a lover of all things dramatic." Mr. Reynolds patted his waistcoat. "It's why she married me, after all. Theater and all that."

"Theater?" Frederick stared at the man. "I thought you were an art collector?"

Mr. Reynolds wrestled with his expression, finally landing on a laugh. "As you know, there's no money in theater, so I took up my second love, and here we are." He chuckled again and moved his attention to Laraby. "I feel certain she'll put the whole experience in one of her books."

"One would think you're as interested in the drama of disappearing paintings as Mrs. Reynolds, Laraby." Jack shot Laraby a severe look.

"I didn't hire you to make me a suspect." Laraby gestured toward the house. "I hired you to find my paintings."

"Then perhaps next time you should heed my warnings." Jack released a long sigh and gave another glance to the surroundings. "Is there any other way off the veranda?"

"Other than rappelling?" Mr. Reynolds laughed.

Laraby shook his head. "No, anyone must go back inside to

find an outlet."

Jack's gaze flashed to Frederick's.

Which meant, if the thieves used that door to attempt escape, they would have had to return inside. . .with the ladies.

"We need to return to the house," Jack said, starting at a brisk pace.

Frederick attempted to temper his pulse. No use in raising alarm where there may not be any. Best-case scenario was the thieves blended back into their occupations in the house as either guests or servants or escaped via another door. Worst case. . . Frederick quickened his pace. He didn't want to consider worst case, especially with the unwelcome possibilities blinking through his head, mostly involving Grace and her knife and a very evil man.

"Laraby, I would suggest you encourage all your guests to lock their bedroom doors tonight, just to ensure their safety." Jack tossed the words back to Laraby.

"Surely you can't be serious, Miracle." The man's shoulders tightened. "Clearly the ghost is a hoax, and the thieves already have gotten what they wanted."

"There's another painting yet to be found, isn't there?" This from Mr. Reynolds, who worked hard to keep his rather significant self caught up with the rest of them.

"No one will find that one without me." Laraby raised a brow, his smile proving much too self-assured for their situation. "It's in a very secret spot, and I mean to keep it there, especially with thieves inside my own house."

Could Laraby truly have no idea of the thieves? Frederick examined the man. Or was this all as much a facade as Laraby's name?

Martina, the young maid, met them as they entered, her gaze scanning the group as if looking for someone. "Mr. Laraby?"

"Yes, Martina."

"The doctor is on his way." She dipped her head. "I phoned

because Miss Benetti was not up to the task."

"Is she all right?" Laraby bypassed the young woman and entered the foyer, Martina trailing behind.

"She's in the sitting room, sir, with Mrs. Reynolds. She was quite distraught after you left the house. I feel certain your presence will calm her."

"Of course." Laraby dashed off.

"Sir, should I have tea brought in?" she called after him.

Laraby paused only a moment. "I think we all may need something a bit stronger than tea." He disappeared down the hallway.

A sudden weight pressed in on Frederick's chest. "Are the other ladies in the sitting room as well?"

"No, sir, but as I understand it, Miss Whitby replaced me at Mr. Hopewell's side." Her eyes brightened. "He has recovered consciousness, and Mr. Hopewell believes his injuries are not severe."

"That's excellent news." Frederick's throat tightened for some reason he couldn't quite define.

"I have not seen Lady Astley, sir."

Frederick exchanged a look with Jack, and they both made their way to the sitting room. Mrs. Reynolds and Miss Benetti sat on the couch together in quiet conversation, the elder apparently comforting the younger.

"Oh, it is good you've returned, Mr. Laraby." Mrs. Reynolds stood and allowed Laraby to replace her at Miss Benetti's side. "Were you able to find anything?"

"Nothing." Laraby sighed, taking Miss Benetti into his arms. "There, there, dear girl. It's all right. Just a little game is all."

"A game?" She sniffled against him. "You saw the ghost and poor Paul." Her voice broke, and she buried her face in Laraby's shoulder. "*È orribile.*"

"Now, none of that," Laraby cooed. "Our chaps here are going to prove the ghost a fake, and I can assure you Paul will be right as rain. Especially with Lydia at the helm."

"Lydia." The woman's voice darkened. "She does not like me. Maybe she is the one who wishes to frighten me away from you."

Jack rolled his gaze to the ceiling.

"Oh, she's just protective, that's all." Laraby patted Jasmine's shoulder and offered his audience an apologetic grin. "As I told you, Lydia has a way of managing everything, you see? Except, well, she didn't have a hand in this romance of yours and mine, so I'm afraid she's a bit unwelcoming."

As if called by Laraby's words, Lydia stumbled into the room, her hand pressed against her head. She braced herself against the doorframe, but even that didn't seem enough, and she started to crumble. Jack, the nearest, rushed forward and caught her before she hit the ground.

"What on earth?" Laraby shot up from his seat, nearly sending Miss Benetti to the floor.

Lydia looked up at Jack, removing her hand from her head to take hold of his arm. A thin trail of blood smeared over her skin. Frederick moved to assist in steadying her.

"What happened to you?" Jack asked, searching her face, his voice bereft of his ever-present sarcasm.

"I. . .I was walking down the hallway to take a glass of wine to Paul, and I heard someone running at me from behind." Her face grew paler as she spoke. "When I turned to note the person, the lights in the hallway were switched off."

"Mamma mia," Miss Benetti gasped. "Daniel, we cannot stay here. It is not safe."

"Who was it, Miss Whitby?" Jack guided her to a nearby couch.

"I couldn't see in the dark." She locked eyes with Jack. "I feel certain it was a man, from the size and shape of his silhouette. He crashed into me, the force knocking me forward, and left me behind."

Jack lowered himself to the couch and took a seat beside her, tugging his handkerchief from his jacket.

"I'll go see to it, Jack." Laraby started for the hall and sent a glance to Zappa as the butler walked through the door. "Come with me, Zappa. We must investigate."

Zappa's usual impassive expression quivered with a hint of confusion, but without question, he followed Laraby from the room.

Mr. Finch entered, dusting off his jacket before taking in the room. "What's going on here?"

"I. . .I really am all right," she whispered to Jack, taking the proffered handkerchief and pressing it to her head. "And would have been fine had my head not hit one of the wall sconces when the man pushed by."

"Regardless, that is two people who have been injured in one night." Jack removed his arm from around her and rested her back against the couch, his tones uncharacteristically soft. "We not only have a thief among us, but someone who will harm others to get to the paintings. I'm afraid that makes the game a bit more serious, doesn't it?"

Lydia stared back at him, something unreadable passing over her expression. Concern? Fear? She looked away, and Jack stood from his place, wiping his palm against the side of his jacket as he rose. "I advise all of us to turn in for the evening and reconvene in the morning to discuss how to proceed. We can do nothing more this evening, and I strongly suggest we lock our bedroom doors."

"Have any of you seen Lady Astley?" Frederick voiced the gnawing concern he'd felt since walking in the villa and hearing from Martina that she hadn't seen Grace. Failing to find her in the sitting room and then having Grace not appear after the commotion about Miss Whitby didn't bode well.

"She's not here?" Lydia looked toward Mrs. Reynolds. "She went searching for clues along with Mrs. Reynolds over a half hour ago."

Frederick turned toward Mrs. Reynolds. "Where?"

"Oh dear, I'd quite forgotten about her since finding Miss Benetti so distraught here in the drawing room." Mrs. Reynolds stood, her fist to her chest. "Surely she's come back by now."

"Where did she go?" Frederick didn't curb the edge in his voice.

The woman's eyes grew wide. "The back hallway. To the left. She. . .she found an open door and thought the painting might have—"

Frederick turned and nearly ran in the direction Mrs. Reynolds gestured, a prayer on his lips and Jack on his heels.

Grace pressed her palms against the sides of her prison, the darkness closing in on her like the sand in the trap in Egypt. Her throat squeezed with sudden panic, her breath growing shallow. She could almost feel the weight of the sand promising to steal her air as it had in the sand trap. Her pulse thrummed in quick succession. Doom. Death. Darkness.

She gripped at the neck of her blouse, pulling it loose, as if that would help. She couldn't catch her breath.

"Oh, God, help me," she whispered.

Just the sound of her prayer in the dark shook her spinning thoughts. She grabbed at the logic. What had her grandfather told her? When anxieties arise, check your thoughts against God's list. She focused on her breathing. In and out. She searched her memory. What was the list? From one of the little books in the Bible. Short. The sort she could read without getting lost.

A phrase filtered through the panic.

Whatever is true?

She drew in another breath. True.

What *was* true about right here and now?

She was not in the sand trap. She was in a trunk. And the

trunk had air coming through the little keyhole, so for the time being, she was not suffocating.

So basically she was physically well, just trapped.

What was another one?

Whatever is lovely.

Right. Yes, lovely.

Frederick came to mind. His smile. His tenderness. His strength. Then she thought of God's goodness to her and His love. Even if she ended up dying inside this trunk, which seemed highly unlikely, she'd be with Him.

She frowned. Were dying thoughts still considered lovely?

Whatever is admirable or excellent.

Well, it would be excellent to get out of here. She nodded, her breaths coming more regularly. Her pulse slowing.

She smiled. Yes. She might very well be able to get out. After all, she'd learned a thing or two about picking locks since the last time she'd been trapped inside a trunk.

Her hair had already loosened enough to make finding two hairpins an easy feat. Armed with her pins and a newfound focus, she turned her body in a rather uncomfortable direction so that she had better access to the keyhole. True, she'd not experienced picking a great many locks. Once the gardener had shown her a few tricks, assisted by Elliott, she'd succeeded in unlocking six out of seven doors at their English estate of Havensbrooke. Thankfully, dear Brandon, the faithful and generous-hearted butler, had heard her knocking from the other side of a locked closet and rescued her from the seventh door. He proceeded to bolster her wavering confidence by informing her that the closet's lock had been broken for over a decade.

But she'd not practiced on a great many trunks. She'd have to remedy that when they returned to England.

Wardrobes would prove somewhat similar, she supposed. And

she'd practiced on plenty of those.

She'd just gotten the pins into a promising position when the sound of footsteps clipped against the floor nearby. Maybe in the room next door? She paused her movement, listening. Was her assailant coming back to finish the job?

"Grace?"

Her fingers paused. Oh, she knew that voice.

"Frederick?"

The footsteps stopped. Could he hear her? She reluctantly removed her pins from the lock and placed her lips to the keyhole. "I'm in the trunk."

A few seconds later, the footsteps stopped near her. "Grace?"

"Before you ask, I did not get myself trapped in this trunk by myself." The top flew open to reveal her darling husband and Detective Jack, who was holding a lantern. "I was thrown in."

Without a word, Frederick pulled her up into his arms. "Good heavens, woman, what were you doing in these unused rooms?"

Though his words sounded frustrated, his tone took more of a desperate turn, and she rested her head against his chest to offer him a moment to compose himself. After all, she'd had the privacy of a trunk to compose herself, and he had an audience of two.

"What do you mean by thrown in, my lady?"

She raised her face from one of the most comfortable positions in the world and peered over Frederick's shoulder to Jack. "Well, when I noticed the opened door to the veranda, I thought the thieves may have returned into the house and thought to store the painting somewhere while they made plans for another means of escape." She pulled back from Frederick and looked around the room. Even in lantern light, the dolls looked creepy. Maybe even more so. She looked at Frederick.

"But I noticed some photographs." She turned toward the table in the center of the room. Where there had been at least six framed photographs, only two remained. One of the gardens of the villa, and one of the back of a woman with a dog at her side. "He took them."

"What?" Frederick moved along with her. "Who took what?"

"There were at least six photos here." She gestured toward the table. "And I'm certain one of them was of the Accardi family. There was an older couple, a younger couple, and two children, a boy and girl. Just like the story."

"So the man who attacked you took those photographs?" Jack moved close to the table, examining the space around it.

"It's a mercy he didn't do worse," Frederick muttered, his palm resting at the small of her back. "I know you are quite capable, Grace, but traveling into darkened rooms with thieves on the loose is not the wisest of choices. We are not in Havensbrooke."

"Harm can happen anywhere, my dear Frederick, when one has a mind toward deviousness." She sighed. "You were kidnapped in broad daylight out the front door."

Jack raised his brows, perfectly aware of the unexpected man-napping of her dear husband just before Christmas. She looked around the room, the slightest tinge of discomfort in her chest. "But you are right. I didn't use wisdom, did I?" She shook her head, disappointed in herself. "I must become better at thinking before acting. And of course there were the books."

"Books?" Frederick's brow crinkled with his confusion.

She gestured with her hand toward the other room. "I saw those lonely books in the next room through the open door as I was walking down the hallway. Books should never be a lure. Well, of course they should lure readers into adventures, but not in such a literal way."

"Do you think you would be able to identify the people you saw in the photo if you saw them again?"

Grace turned to Jack. "I'm not certain. It was rather dark, but

I could try."

He nodded and started for the hall. "I think we should return to your room, discuss our findings of the day, and make a plan for tomorrow. As long as you are feeling up to it, my lady?"

Grace looked to Frederick, the worry lines around his eyes more pronounced in the shadowy space. "Are you?"

A ghost of a smile lit his face. "As long as you promise to remain within sight for the rest of the evening, I'll be fine."

She took his proffered arm and leaned close as they followed Jack from the room. "And I think I could benefit from those cane fighting lessons, Frederick. I know there must be a technique for protecting oneself when attacked from behind."

He didn't immediately answer. His body stiffened, his feet paused, and then he continued on. "We'll have a lesson first thing in the morning before breakfast. What do you say to that?"

"Perfect."

Chapter 13

"No wonder I responded as I did to Miss Whitby." Jack stood from the seat he'd occupied in Frederick and Grace's room. "I noticed her in her disguise as a footman on the ferry, but of course, I saw her as a footman. It's difficult to forget eyes like those."

He murmured the last part of the phrase and then seemed to realize his audience. He sat to attention. "It's my job to notice everyone." He tapped his temple. "Be observant, of course."

"Of course," Grace nodded, something in Jack's tone almost triggering a laugh. But why? It was true, Miss Whitby had unusually green eyes, but the way Jack noticed them, well, Grace wasn't quite certain why it made her want to smile. After all, Miss Whitby had as much likelihood of being one of the thieves as anyone else on the island, maybe even more so with the access she had to Laraby's belongings.

"I didn't realize there was an additional footman on the ferry." Frederick pushed a hand through his hair, sending it in wonderful, confused disarray.

"We're aristocrats, Frederick." Jack grinned. "We're trained not to notice servants, remember?"

"But you noticed, Jack."

He raised a brow and shoved his hands into his pockets. "I

am a detective, my lady. I'm paid to notice."

Perhaps that was part of Jack's mild discombobulation, Grace mused.

"From our dinner conversation, Miss Whitby has an incredibly interesting history. Not just as an illusionist's assistant, but also as a thief. Evidently, her father forced her to dress as a boy and steal from patrons in the crowd until she grew old enough to escape his beatings."

Jack winced. Frederick lowered his head with a slow shake.

"How horrible to have such a father!" Grace continued, the same heat rising back into her face she'd felt when Miss Whitby shared a little of her history. "And if he was worth anything as an illusionist, you think he could do the stealing himself."

"But that does give Miss Whitby the skills to create the ghost," Frederick offered.

"And the skills to steal the paintings?" Jack paced the carpet in front of one of the windows of their room. "Though I don't think she has access to the gallery and certainly isn't the person who attacked you, my lady."

"No, I'm certain a man attacked me." Grace tapped her chin, attempting to remember any specific details about her attacker, but apart from his sex, nothing came to mind.

"And she was attacked herself," Jack added.

"But she could have faked such an attack, couldn't she?" Frederick offered. "To distract us, like the ghost? Give time for her partner in crime to escape with the painting?"

"Or hide it somewhere?"

"Pretending?" Jack looked between the two of them, his frown deepening. "Could Paul have done the same?" Jack moved toward them, drawing two handkerchiefs from his pocket. "One of these I used on Paul's head wound, the other on Miss Whitby's."

When he opened the handkerchiefs, both held a red stain,

but two very different colors of red. Jack raised one to his nose, sniffing it, then the other. His gaze shot to Frederick and Grace. "One of these is tomato sauce."

"Tomato sauce?" Grace laughed out the words.

"Which one went with whom?" Frederick leaned close, Grace at his side, examining the handkerchiefs.

"I don't know." Jack released a frustrated breath. "I wasn't thinking of tending fake wounds when I offered my handkerchiefs."

"So either Lydia or Paul was pretending to be wounded?" Grace asked, looking from the handkerchiefs back to Jack. What an idea! And clever.

"What do we know about Miss Whitby's attack?" Frederick offered. "Reynolds and Laraby were with us outside, so they couldn't have attacked Grace or Lydia. And if we confirm what time the other men were gone, we may be able to narrow down our list of suspects."

"Mr. Hopewell was convalescing." Grace paused and turned back to Jack. "Mr. Zappa? Mr. Finch? Or one of the other servants?"

"Possible. They were both supposedly searching the rest of the grounds." Jack started pacing. "And if the history of the stolen paintings tells us anything, it's that there is more than one person involved."

"And one is a woman," Grace offered.

"And they're willing to kill for the paintings." Frederick's comment sobered the discussion even more.

"Here's what I think we should do," Jack suggested. "I'm going to take a ferry back to the mainland in the morning to send a few messages to my constituents in England. What can we learn about Mr. and Mrs. Reynolds or about Laraby's former life? Is Mr. Finch truly making movies?"

"Would you ask your men to research any of the books by Dolores Reynolds?" Grace gave a shrug at Jack's curious stare.

"It may be my imagination or poorly placed expectations, but for some reason she doesn't strike me as a mystery-writing sort of person."

"And what sort is that?" Jack did very little to hide his amusement. "Rope swinging? Pistol wielding? Knives in the bodice sort?"

The fact that Jack's teasing almost brought out Frederick's smile made the slight goading worth the heat climbing into Grace's cheeks. He'd been terribly somber since finding her in a trunk, which was hardly surprising. "Very funny." She grinned. "But more along the lines of not thinking in a mystery way or even an imaginary one." She sighed. "Even though I am prone to like her a great deal, something seems a little off. I can't explain it. However, she did refer to me as a detective."

"As well you are." Jack sent Frederick a grin. "Both of you. And will only prove more so the further into this case we go."

"Do you want Grace and me to meet with Laraby over the photos tomorrow in your stead?" Frederick nestled a gentle hand on Grace's arm, a sweet touch of his nearness and her inclusion. "Remember, we'd hoped to review the photographs of *The Juliets* he possesses."

"Ah yes." Jack drew in a breath and made his way to their bedroom door. "Ten o'clock. That way we can kill two birds with one stone, so to speak. Will that work for you?"

Frederick looked to Grace, and her smile must have secured his answer.

"Good, we have an early appointment in the morning." Frederick's lips twitched ever so slightly, giving Grace a hint to their "appointment"—the cane fighting lessons. "Then we plan to meet with him."

"I'll alert Laraby to my plans and then catch you up over lunch." Jack reached for the door, stepping out into the hallway.

"See you then."

"And do lock your door." Jack tapped the door. "No reason to invite trouble."

A cry peeled into the silence. A familiar cry.

Frederick hadn't been able to sleep anyway. His mind still roiled with the day's activities and Grace's attack. Thoughts of her being hurt or of him losing her rifled through him like knives against his heart. It was his job to protect her.

Grace thrashed in the blanket as if struggling with some unseen enemy.

Or the weight of the invisible sand pressing down on her and stealing her breath. He offered a prayer to heaven and moved toward her.

Still she fought. Struggled. There was nothing he could do to take the fear away. "Grace, darling."

A whimper emerged from her lips. Her face was damp with tears. His hand went to her shoulder, gently smoothing over her gown. "Grace, wake up."

She shivered, and he took it as a sign to draw her into his arms. The nightmares happened every night at first. Starting a week after the events in Cairo, but each time it was the same dream. Sand rushing in, covering her, stealing her breath.

Gratefully, the nightmares had gone from every night to every few nights. A good indication of the natural healing process, but the terror still haunted her face. Her eyes.

"It's all right," he murmured against her hair, and she shivered again but pressed into him. Waking. "I'm here."

Her cry grew softer until it came to a stop, and she drew back. "I'm so sorry to keep waking you, my dear Frederick."

"It could be much worse, darling." He brushed back her hair from her damp face. "I knew a soldier once who had multiple nightmares every night with little relief. And yours have become less frequent."

"But. . .but why won't they go away entirely? I. . .I'm sure I have enough faith for it."

"It may be less about the power of your faith and more about the consequences of someone else's sin paired with your humanity." The lingering memory of pulling her still form from a sandpit quaked through him, but he calmed himself with a steady breath. "Your body is remembering the physical experience and will take time to catch up with your mind, I think."

"But we are in the middle of our first investigation." Her bottom lip trembled, those eyes watery and wide. "How can you trust me to learn cane fighting if I can't overcome a nightmare? I need to be brave. I need *you* to believe I'm brave."

He trailed his palms down her arms, and with one hand he reached for a handkerchief while the other kept hold of her hand. "Were you afraid when you first left your home to come live across the ocean in a house you'd never seen with people you didn't know?"

Her gaze searched his in the moonlight. She tilted her head, the tremors of breath slowly subsiding. "Yes, but only a little. At first."

"And were you afraid when you went on your first ghost hunt alone at Havensbrooke?" He pressed the handkerchief into one of her palms.

Her smile shifted ever so slightly as she wiped at her eyes. "I was a bit excited too. Ghost hunts can be rather thrilling."

"Perhaps I should choose a different example." He raised his gaze to the ceiling, searching for a better option. After all, his wife excelled in areas no other woman of his acquaintance would dare dream. Like ghost hunts. "Running after Amelia in Egypt and attempting to save her from a fire? Were you afraid then?"

She pulled in a shaking breath and gave a slight nod.

"But you went after her anyway?"

Her attention darted to him.

"You've taught me so much about strength of heart and faith despite circumstances." His hand brushed an errant tear from her cheek. "You've also taught me a great deal about courage."

"Courage? Me?" She sniffled. "Even now?"

"Even now." He nodded. "Because courage isn't about being fearless. It's about choosing to do something when we are afraid." His fingers stopped on her chin. "Even ghost hunts. Or chasing after a madwoman who'd kidnapped your husband."

"Man-napped, you mean," she whispered, her smile growing.

"Or saving a woman from a fire." He sighed. "Sometimes the bigger the fear, the greater the courage. And I would add, as you've so often reminded me from almost our first encounter, you, me. . .*we* are never alone."

She pressed a palm against his chest, her gaze so gentle, so loving, it nearly crippled his weakened defenses to tears. "God is with us."

He nodded at her whispered phrase.

"And when you feel your courage is small, He is quite capable to lend you some of His." He touched her cheek again. "Remember that, darling. These nightmares will run their course, but life will bring other things, maybe even on our newest adventure, for which we will need courage." He spoke the words to his own heart. The idea of having almost lost her in a sand trap tore at him. Kept him up. He may not experience visible nightmares, but the terror gripping him at the idea of losing her burned as palpable as any dream. "And when we are weak, He is strong." Frederick fought against the next words, battling with his own selfishness, his own fear. "And you are His." Ultimately and eternally.

Grace Percy wasn't Frederick's but was held in hands much

more capable than his own. It was almost like God was forcing Frederick to this realization at every turn—from the "case" to the daily possibilities of danger to the continual reminders of His presence. Frederick's pretense of control proved only that, a pretense as unstable as his hold had been on stopping his brother's death or earning his mother's love or keeping Grace from falling into the sandpit. So the real question was to whom his heart would bow. Ultimately, he needed to choose Christ over and over again. "God will take care of you wherever you go, even if you must bear these nightmares for a season."

Her smile spread wide, oblivious to his inner turmoil, his realization. His submission to a higher love than his own.

"You're right. No matter what. He's holding us on this side of eternity or the next." She leaned her head against his chest. "Though I am overwhelmed with joy at the idea of heaven and Jesus and a brilliant, beautiful place, I do hope I get to enjoy this side of eternity for just a little while longer. Not only do I experience your wonderful love, but I would hate to miss cane fighting lessons from my very roguish husband."

He released the tension in his shoulders as he breathed a sigh over her hair.

"And I would hate to miss our very first official case together." She snuggled closer. "I really can't imagine a more perfect honeymoon than this."

Frederick looked heavenward, offering a prayer for wisdom and strength. . .and adding a little chuckle of thanksgiving at the end.

Chapter 14

"I have the perfect parasol for this, Frederick." Grace disappeared beside the bed, barely able to contain her delight. Cane fighting! What an exciting opportunity.

And taught by her very own hero. She nearly sighed as she pulled a box from beneath the bed and opened it, bringing the long accessory with her as she stood.

Frederick stood, grin crooked and arms folded across his chest, his expression much more relaxed than it had been the night before. He'd held a distance or sadness she couldn't define, but not this morning. Whatever worry had crinkled his brow and deepened his frown last night left with the dawn, and sweet light softened his features.

What had caused the change? The ease?

When they'd prayed together after her nightmare? Had something happened then? He'd sounded so sincere, his voice even trembling at one point.

She tucked the thought away for later and raised her unassuming weapon for his perusal.

"Isn't it beautiful?"

He took her offering and gave it a proper and rather impressive review. "Where did you purchase this?"

"When we were in Rome." The pride in her voice inspired her smile. "I suppose with their extensive history of weaponry, they would think strategically, even about parasols. Some of the shops had the very best assortment of things, and when I saw a variety of unique parasols, and I considered how my parasol had come in handy in the past, I chose strategically."

"It's certainly heavier than your others."

"The hook is pointy at the end." She gestured toward the curved handle, myriad possibilities dancing through her mind. "That has to be useful, doesn't it? Especially in self-defense."

He raised a brow, a gleam in his eyes. "Perhaps not for your hand health."

A laugh burst from her at his gentle teasing. "What would I care for hand health every once in a while when a pointy hook could save a life?"

"How can I argue with such a magnanimous and strategic line of reasoning?"

She rocked up on tiptoe and kissed his cheek. "So where do we begin?"

He drew in a deep breath and placed the parasol back in her hand. "We start with the fundamentals. Because you will likely not be as strong as your assailants, you will need to be smarter." He winked. "Which shouldn't be a problem."

"I adore it when you wink at me." Heat rushed into her cheeks. "I feel as though it's a little window into a part of your heart that very few people get to see."

He slipped his hand to her waist and drew her forward, capturing her mouth with a lingering kiss. He rested his forehead against hers and narrowed his eyes.

"We only have an hour before breakfast, so no more lovely distractions, darling."

It seemed almost criminal that his kisses could distract her enough from the idea of cane fighting that she nearly dropped the parasol and dove into his arms with every intent of keeping him engaged in a very different yet still physical way.

Loving him proved such a wonderful and surprising distraction from even the most interesting things.

"All right, first things first." He took up his cane from the bed and held it out to her. "The grip for cane fighting is different than a usual hold."

"Do you mean when they twirl the cane around to knock people in the head?"

His eyes widened followed by his grin. "Ah, I see you've been doing some reading." He chuckled. "That is a more advanced skill, which we can learn eventually, but today we'll stick with the basics."

"Besides, there are too many breakable things in here, aren't there?" She offered a helpless shrug.

"Probably not the best start." He grinned again and lowered his grip from the hook of his cane to the neck. "This hold gives you more control and power."

Grace copied him with her parasol.

"As soon as you realize someone is on the attack, you should move your hand to this position on your cane. . .er. . .parasol, if you can."

She nodded, attention focused on his movements.

"So let's say, heaven forbid, someone goes to grab your neck." He reached his hand out toward her. "Bring your parasol around to the bend of their arm." He guided her hands so that the parasol hit horizontally between his wrist and elbow. "Then take the other end of the parasol with your other hand. Two hands will give much more pressure down on the bend of his arm. It's a weak spot and will either break his hold or bring them lower to counteract the unexpected pressure."

"Then I can raise my boot and catch him in a very vulnerable spot to ensure I have time to flee."

Frederick's brows rose before he cleared his throat. "Yes. . .yes that would certainly work."

"I've imagined all sorts of ways to escape being captured after my very real life situations in Cairo."

"I feel certain you have." His grin broadened. "Now, if the assailant attempts a two-handed grab of your throat, you can either bring the parasol down across both of his elbow bends or jab the end of your parasol into his stomach or chest with all your might." He waved in the direction of his torso. "If my hands are on your throat, then I am unprotected here."

"And the very hard end of the parasol could prove extremely painful in the right spot."

"Painful enough to give you a chance to escape." He gently tapped the spot on her arm between her elbow and wrist. "It's important to remember that if you hit someone's arm with solid force here, there is a good chance you could crack his bone. It's a vulnerable spot."

"Oh! So while he's distracted by the pain in his arm"—she drew her parasol up from his arm toward his face and neck—"I could give him a good hit in the chin or windpipe."

"You're rather ruthless at this, darling." A breath of a laugh burst from him. "I'm tempted to return us to your pistols."

"But there are times when the report of a pistol will cause too much noise, and since beatings with canes are more likely to cause internal wounds, there will be less blood to clean up afterward."

"Which is what everyone is concerned about when fighting to stay alive." He winked again, inciting her smile. "The mess."

"I believe your sense of humor is getting better the longer we're married." She waved her parasol at him. "I don't recall you being so free with your teasing a few months ago."

"Perhaps you inspire all sorts of hidden characteristics to come to light after lying dormant for too long."

She paused to study him. The idea of his loveless childhood and the hurtful way his parents had treated him ached like a sore in her chest for him. "I do hope the good will outweigh how very troublesome I am."

"Grace." The gentle reprimand in his voice paused her movements. "We are both troublesome in our different ways. I've realized how much I struggle to control things and. . .well, even you. Part of the desire is a good one, to be your protector."

"I do like that part."

His expression softened. "Navigating between protection and treating you as a child is where my struggle lies, I believe. You're not a child, clearly." His gaze trailed down her with an appreciative look. "You are a beautiful and intelligent woman, and despite your age, you are quite capable of many more things than any lady of my acquaintance, but you are still very young."

"And you have life experience that I don't. I want you to guide me in those things, and I dearly wish to become more thoughtful and less impulsive." She smiled. "Perhaps it's a very good match because I get to be *your* teacher in matters of heart and hope and in finding your joy again, and you get to be my teacher in things such as etiquette and protocol and self-defense."

He searched her face in a way that made her warm all over. "It is a very good match."

She shook off the desire to linger in his lovely admiration and raised her parasol. "So, what do I do if I am attacked from behind like last night?"

Frederick's smile slid right off his face. "Yes, well." He took her by the shoulders and turned her away from him, then he wrapped his arms around her shoulders in a tight sort of hug. "Like this?"

"Yes. Exactly."

He buried his nose into her neck. "I love the way your hair

smells." His lips warmed her neck, and she leaned back into him, asking for more. "And the taste of your skin."

"I much prefer your sort of assault, my lord." She tilted her head to the side, giving him better access to more skin.

He drew in a deep breath, as if rallying to the task, and gave her hair a lingering kiss. "I hate the idea of you feeling at his mercy, so if there are other ways I can teach you to protect yourself, especially if we are bound to engage in these adventures on a regular basis, then I will"—he paused, forcing a swallow—"happily do so."

She turned just the slightest bit so that she could see him. "I'm afraid I've started us on a path that will be difficult to squelch, my dear Frederick. Especially now, with Jack diverting our path a little." She kissed his lips. "But I am so glad we can have these adventures together and rely on each other. As you said last night, our heavenly protector holds us both in hands much more capable than ours."

He nodded, his gaze roaming her face before he smiled. "Indeed, He does." He straightened and nudged her back around. "Now, let us get on with our training before we run out of time." He tightened his hold on her to make it more secure, his cheek near her ear. "Thank heaven, your attacker didn't hold you by the neck in this position, but this same initial response would work for that too. Do you have a firm grip on your parasol?"

She tightened her hold on the handle. "Yes."

"Notice how your arms are still free from the elbows to your fingers, even if I hold you like this."

She looked down, his arms gripped around her upper arms. She wiggled her parasol. "I see."

"You have several attack options, but here is the first in hopes of loosening your attacker's hold on you and gaining some control in the situation." He squeezed a little tighter. "The pointed hook on your parasol will be particularly beneficial in this case." He adjusted his hold a little. "Use your free hand to cover one of mine so that you gauge where my arms are, and then drop your full weight so that it puts me off balance a little."

She did as directed. Frederick held his stance, but the sudden impact shook him. "Good. Although you aren't a very difficult person to lift as it is, this is an unexpected move for your attacker to contend with. Now drive the parasol hook between my hands and your chest and jerk downward while at the same time pushing your derriere back to break the hold."

She obeyed, being careful not to thrust the pointed hook too painfully against his arms, but it was good to know that the hook would certainly cause a great deal of discomfort if she pushed it hard enough to break loose for real.

He stumbled back, releasing his grip on her, and she turned to face him, parasol pointed toward his chest.

"Now you are in a position of some control, which means your first course of action, if you cannot run, is to defend yourself." He rested his palms on his hips, his shirt sleeves rolled up to the elbows. His grin edged crooked. "I'm not certain smiling with such welcome provokes the desired response from your opponent."

She spun the parasol around and hooked his waistcoat, pulling him forward. "I suppose it depends on the opponent, my lord."

"How long have you been secretly practicing spinning that rather impressive parasol?" His palms warmed her hips as his gaze warmed the rest of her.

"Since the first day I purchased it." She shrugged rather helplessly, sliding the parasol to her side. "But apart from the spinning and an occasional wallop here and there, I didn't know how else I could use it defensively until you so wonderfully showed me."

Her adoration must have shown on her face, because Frederick raised a brow. "You shouldn't look at me that way, darling." He tugged her closer. "If you wish to finish this lesson and make it to breakfast at all."

"If seeing those photographs wasn't so important to this case, I would be very tempted to forgo breakfast to reward you for your excellent teaching skills."

His jaw tightened, gaze darkening in that wonderful way that incited her pulse. "Tempting." The word rumbled with delicious danger.

"But I promise to make up for your patience and fortitude tonight." She stepped back and twirled her parasol, sending him what she hoped was a flirtatious grin. "Thoroughly."

He brought her back against him and lowered his mouth to capture hers, letting her know he understood the definition of thoroughly quite well. Perfectly, even.

The door to Laraby's office stood slightly ajar as Frederick approached, Grace by his side. The sound of raised voices reached them before Frederick could knock.

"It's time to stop all of this, John."

Frederick tugged Grace out of the way of the door, raising a finger to his lips in silent warning.

John? Ah, Laraby's real name. John Walker.

"There has to be another way for you to get what you need besides this."

Was that woman's voice Lydia Whitby?

"This is the start, don't you see?" Laraby replied. "Visibility will bring people, and that's how to move in the right direction. I will not be a failure."

"You may walk directly into becoming much more than a failure if you keep up this ruse," Miss Whitby returned, a hardened edge in her voice. "We never planned on someone getting hurt, John. The ghost was only supposed to keep Mrs. Reynolds' and

Mr. Finch's interest for another day or two. But people were hurt last night. Paul? Lady Astley? Me?"

Grace's gaze flew to his, her thoughts likely turning the same direction as his. The ghost *had* been planned by Laraby as a show for Mrs. Reynolds and her brother, a way to impress them into using the villa for movie and book inspiration. It would certainly bring visibility, but why? Why did Laraby want visibility, unless it was for the mere desire to be seen? And what else had he planned in all this? The disappearance of the painting?

Was he truly so shallow? Desperate?

And Lydia's response. Her concern appeared genuine. Could she have been the one who had truly been attacked while Paul pretended?

"I am sorry you got the brunt of someone running away, but who's to say it wasn't some servant who'd gotten caught philandering with one of the upper class? Dolores doesn't even share the same room with her new husband, and a man has certain needs, you know."

Grace blinked up at Frederick, her eyes growing even wider. He had heard Mr. and Mrs. Reynolds were newly married, a little longer than he and Grace, and the last thing he wished to do was sleep apart from her, even if she unintentionally kicked him in the side on occasion.

"You're not taking this seriously, John. A problem you've had for much too long. That's why your finances are in shambles."

"I'm trying to fix that right now." He huffed and then sighed. "Besides, Paul is going to be fine. The doctor said he likely stumbled in the dark and hit his head." Laraby chuckled. "And you know how Paul is. He doesn't have the strongest constitution. I should have listened to you about the painting, though. I shouldn't have put it on display."

"You've not listened to me in months," came Lydia's sharp reply.

"Perhaps if you did, you wouldn't be in this mess from the start. You follow that woman's whims like a thoughtless child, buying her whatever she wants—"

"You're just jealous."

"Jealous?"

"That I chose her instead of you."

"Oh, John." A sound like a humorless laugh emerged from the room. "Perhaps once I would have been jealous, but that was before money replaced the man I used to know. I've gotten my share of living with men who find bills and coins more important than people."

"Leave then."

Silence filled the moment. "Don't say things you don't mean, John Walker. If not for me, you'd be on much shakier ground than you are right now. Tread carefully with the people who have stood by you."

Grace's gaze asked myriad questions that would have to wait until later to sort because the sound of footsteps approaching had Frederick stepping toward the door and giving a resounding knock.

Hushed tones followed before Lydia opened the door. Her expression gave nothing away, except for a slight sheen in her green eyes. The pale aqua of her day dress likely made them look even greener—and brought out the slight red-rimmed look too. "Ah, Lord and Lady Astley, good morning."

"Good morning, Miss Whitby." Frederick dipped his head.

"How are you feeling this morning, Lady Astley?" Lydia dipped her chin with a smile.

"Grace, if you remember, Lydia." His wife offered one of her brightest smiles, which appeared to cause a reflection in Miss Whitby's face. "And I am much improved. How about you?"

Lydia raised a palm to the plaster on her forehead. "Better, thank you. Mr. Laraby is ready for you." She stepped back, gesturing for them to follow. "Hopefully, you can shed some light on his little mystery hiding in the paintings, though I must warn you, he's had several painting enthusiasts have a go, and they've not gotten any closer to uncovering this obscure treasure."

"Don't discourage them, Lydia." Laraby stepped forward, dressed leisurely in beige slacks and white button-up. "Perhaps a few pairs of less-trained eyes will make all the difference."

The study took advantage of the morning light with a view from three large windows overlooking the nearest gardens and the sea beyond. A massive desk perched beneath one of the windows with one side apparently connected to a bookshelf. Soft blue chairs and a matching couch dotted stone floors covered with colorful rugs, giving off an airy feel that was nothing like the rooms Frederick had found Grace in the night before. This was modern. New.

"I've laid them out—the seven of them here, only missing two." Laraby walked toward a circular table in the center of the room. "You'll have the best lighting to view the set."

Frederick and Grace stepped to the table, large black and whites of various paintings laid out in rows. "Lydia put them in order of the scenes from the play."

Lydia straightened her glasses, her face growing pink. "As best I could remember. It's been a few years since I've read Shakespeare."

"Yes." Grace leaned close. "This one of the three young men talking together. Is that of Benvolio and Mercutio trying to convince Romeo to attend the Capulet ball?"

Lydia nodded.

"And here's the one most recently stolen," Frederick added. "Of Romeo and Juliet at the ball."

"Of course, the balcony scene," Grace sighed. "I would love to see the original in glorious romantic color."

"It is quite fascinating," Laraby said. "It's the only one left in my possession and my favorite of the three I'd possessed. My grandfather's favorite as well."

"Then the marriage with Friar Laurence," Frederick interjected, following beside Grace. "The consummation of the marriage, I presume." Frederick waved to the next one, though the figures were tastefully covered, there was no doubt of their shared intentions.

"The one of Romeo fighting and killing Tybalt is missing." Laraby waved toward the photos. "But I've never seen it. Jasmine mentioned it in her studies, as well as the one of Romeo's banishment from Verona." He shrugged. "I really don't know much about the story except through these paintings."

"According to what previous art collectors have said," Lydia offered, "Juliet is somehow featured in every one of the paintings, thus the reason why the collection is referred to as *The Juliets*, but no one has sorted out which paintings are the special three that hold the treasure's secrets."

"So Accardi must have had a fascination with the ill-fated heroine." Grace reached into her pocket and withdrew a magnifying glass.

He pinched his eyes closed for a moment. Why was he surprised? Of course she brought a magnifying glass.

Miss Whitby and Laraby didn't recover from their surprise quite as quickly as Frederick.

"Oh, and here is the death scene." Grace pressed a fist to her chest as she leaned closer, magnifying glass raised. "I imagine it's terribly gripping in real life. Look at Juliet's grief as she presses the knife to her heart to stop the pain of her lost love forever."

Miss Whitby tilted her head and examined Grace, a hint of amusement twinkling to life in her expression.

"But I've never really liked this story." Grace straightened, surveying the room as if nothing were amiss. "The two were children, and they'd only known each other two weeks. It seems like both of them were a bit high on spirit and low on logic, don't you think?"

Miss Whitby snickered behind her hand. Laraby stared, his brow crinkled in confusion. Frederick's grin took a subtle turn as he looked to Laraby. If nothing else, his wife disarmed people's pretense. . .usually unintentionally, which proved an excellent "sleuthing skill," as she would say.

"What have previous professionals uncovered about the paintings, Mr. Laraby?"

Laraby pulled his gaze from Grace back to Frederick. "Nothing to help solve the puzzle. They've studied how light was portrayed to see if there was some sort of pattern. Carefully reviewed the stones in the walls of each house, and even taken a detailed look at the seams in the characters' garments to no avail."

"Any hints at all?" His darling wife's brow puckered, and he wondered if she felt this puzzle may be beyond either one of them. "From any of the experts?"

"Or perhaps the history?"

"I can't think of anything," Laraby answered. "No more than what I've already told you."

Frederick scanned over the photos as Grace moved from one to the next with her magnifying glass at the ready, completely oblivious to the entertainment she offered for Miss Whitby. It sounded as if the woman could do with a bit of lightheartedness.

"How did you come to meet Mr. and Mrs. Reynolds, Mr. Laraby?"

"Not in any spectacular way." Laraby shrugged a shoulder, leaning back against the desk. "Jasmine had met the couple as they toured the gallery, and when they mentioned their interest to Jasmine, well, she shared it with me and thought I'd get some fun out of it."

"And some financial remuneration," Miss Whitby added.

"Nothing wrong with a little fun and funds, is there?" He laughed. "But Mrs. Reynolds has offered to pay me a handsome sum to allow her to use the villa as inspiration for her new novel while her husband tours the art galleries in Venice, so I didn't see a loss in it all. Her brother's profession as a film producer just made the situation even better, especially if we catch his eye as a place to turn Mrs. Reynolds' book into an actual film."

"It all sounds very exciting." Grace looked up, one eye enlarged from the magnifying glass.

And remarkably convenient. Miss Benetti "meeting" Mr. and Mrs. Reynolds at the gallery, and it turning into all of this?

"Indeed." Laraby smiled and moved toward the door. "I have a grand dinner planned for tonight, so there's a great deal to do in preparation. I mean to keep our guests happy so they'll stay as long as possible." He waved toward the table. "Those photos are copies for you and Detective Miracle. You're free to take them with you."

Without another word, he exited the room. Lydia Whitby stayed, assisting Grace in collecting the photos.

"How long have Laraby's finances been in trouble, Miss Whitby?"

Her gaze shot to Frederick and her face paled. "I. . .I don't what you mean, Lord Astley."

"We're here to help him," Grace said, gently taking the photos from Miss Whitby's hands. "Any information you have that might assist us will only be for his good in the long run."

Miss Whitby searched Grace's face and then Frederick's and opened her mouth to reply when the study door burst open to reveal Jack.

"I need to speak with the two of you at once." His attention fell on Miss Whitby, and he came to an immediate halt. "Excuse me, Miss Whitby. I need a private conversation with the Astleys, if you will."

Her gaze flickered back to Frederick and Grace before returning to Jack. "Of course, Detective."

What would she have told them if Jack's entrance had been

delayed a few moments? What did she know?

Jack nodded toward Miss Whitby as she left the room, and he turned to Frederick and Grace, the intensity in his eyes somehow clenching Frederick's stomach. "I'm sorry to cause you alarm." Jack stepped forward, lowering his voice as he did. "But I'm afraid our enigma just got a great deal murkier."

"What is it?" Grace asked. "Is someone else hurt?"

"Dead, actually."

"What?" Frederick straightened. "What do you mean? Who?"

"Dolores Reynolds."

"Oh no, Jack!"

"That's not the worst of it." Jack drew in a deep breath and leveled Frederick with a look before turning to Grace. "According to my contacts, mystery author Dolores Reynolds has been dead for over a year."

Grace gasped.

"And she had in her possession one of *The Juliets*."

Chapter 15

"What?" Frederick stepped forward with Grace on his heels.

Had she heard Jack correctly? The mystery author Mrs. Reynolds who had just joined her in a little sleuthing adventure last night was in fact dead? Grace gave her head a shake. That meant, of course, the Mrs. Reynolds from last night wasn't dead. She blinked back to Jack, trying to understand.

"According to my sources, mystery writer Mrs. Dolores Reynolds died almost a year ago as the result of a robbery."

"A robbery?" Frederick repeated.

"Stabbed the woman in her sleep, just like in one of her novels."

"Oh, how horrible." Grace sat down in a nearby chair.

"Since she was more of an English writer, her name and works haven't become known in Italy." Jack shook his head. "So her identity wouldn't be as familiar."

"Which means our false Mrs. Reynolds could assume her identity without any real trouble."

"Then Mr. Reynolds and Finch are involved in the business too." Frederick shook his head. "It's much too convenient for her to find a man with the last name of Reynolds who would go along with the author ploy if he didn't have some inkling as to what was going on."

"He did mention he was an actor last night, if you remember."
Jack tapped his chin.

"Well, that would make sense about not sharing a room, wouldn't it?" Grace murmured, a little relieved at the thought.

"They'd fit the previous profiles, wouldn't they, Jack?" Frederick stepped forward, his head tilted, his gaze intense, and his profile every bit the view of a dashing and young detective.

A little thrill shot through Grace at the idea and nearly distracted her from her continued review of the photographs. She excelled at ciphers, likely because she'd been practicing both solving and creating them since she was about ten years old.

Maybe younger, if she included the time she notched sticks to create a code to her treehouse. She frowned. And then forgot the code.

"According to accounts of the previous thefts and murders, there is at least one man who played the part of a manservant and one woman who played the part of a female servant. Mr. and Mrs. Reynolds *could* fit the mark," Frederick continued.

"But how would they have gained access to the gallery and exacted that particular theft with such ingenuity?"

"Could Miss Benetti be a part of it too?" Grace offered.

"Possibly." Jack shoved his hands in his pockets and leaned back on the desk as Laraby had done. "And how much is Laraby involved, if at all?"

"Should we confront Mrs. Reynolds before anything else happens?"

Jack looked from the photos in Grace's hand back to Frederick. "I'm afraid if we do, we may lose out on finding all the culprits *and* the paintings. There's no assurance that Mrs. Reynolds, or whoever she is, is the mastermind behind it all." He began to pace, rubbing his chin. "No, I think the best course of action is to spend the next day attempting to locate additional clues now that we know a little more clearly what we're up against."

To think Mrs. Fake Reynolds was pretending all along and likely even pretending to find Grace's sleuthing skills impressive. The idea created a pinch in Grace's chest. What a nasty sort of thing to do! She probably didn't think there was any merit in Grace being a detective. Laughing at her behind her back.

How rude!

"Another thing I've learned from my contacts is that none of *The Juliets* have reappeared for sale."

"So it's less likely someone is looking for remuneration." Frederick relaxed in a chair and folded his hands in front of him in a very detective sort of way. "Art dealers are notorious for finding the perfect buyers for special selections like *The Juliets* and equally known for spreading the news when they have purchased one."

"Precisely, which means our thieves mean to keep the paintings close."

Close? Grace placed her magnifying glass on the table. "Then it's possible the paintings are in Venice?"

"Or in this very house."

Grace looked at Frederick, who only raised a brow.

"Which gives me a plan." Jack crossed the room to stand near them. "Any idea where all our characters are at the moment?"

The sudden change in topic paused Grace's response.

"When we came toward the study, Miss Benetti and Paul were swimming in the pool," Frederick offered. "Grace and I saw them out the window as we walked down the hall."

"Mr. and Mrs. Reynolds"—Grace sighed—"or whoever they really are, were in the garden with Mr. Finch. And Laraby had just left the meeting with us to prepare for some surprise at dinner."

Jack groaned. "If he is unveiling his final *Juliet*, I may string the man up myself."

"It appears to be his most prized painting, so I'm not certain he'd risk it." The sarcasm lacing Frederick's words inspired Grace's smile.

"Don't hang your hat on that one, old bean." Jack shook his head. "Pride and arrogance lead to all sorts of feats of incompetence."

"Speaking of Laraby and possible incompetence. . ." Frederick stood and approached Jack, his voice lowering. "Grace and I overheard a conversation between Miss Whitby and Laraby earlier today." Frederick relayed the basics of the conversation, ending by saying, "It sounds as if our millionaire isn't as rich as he wants the world to believe."

"Desperate and arrogant. An atrocious combination." Jack reached into his jacket pocket and pulled out a thick envelope. "But my contacts confirmed as much, I'm afraid. Before leaving England, I'd left a few specific requests with my housekeeper." Jack grinned. "She's incredibly efficient, and I feel if she weren't hovering around the ripe old age of sixty, she'd make an excellent sleuth in her own right." He opened the envelope. "At any rate, I left her with a few things to research for me, and her letter arrived today."

Without further comment, he opened one of the sheets from the envelope and handed it to them. Grace peered at the paper Frederick took. An old news clipping. A photo of two children took up the front page with the heading in Italian. Grace looked up at Frederick.

"'Where are the lost Accardi children?'" he read.

Grace examined the photo. "Those are the children I saw in the photo. I'm sure of it."

"I'm not surprised at all. And I don't believe our thieves are random art collectors." He dipped his chin. "I'm afraid we're dealing with people closely associated with the true story behind these paintings, and either they're in it for the treasure or for family retribution." His brow darkened. "Or both."

"Which could lead to desperation," Frederick said.

"Or self-righteousness and revenge, a combination that rivals arrogance and desperation, I'm afraid. Especially if they have any wits about them." Jack ran a palm over his chin. "We must be on guard." He gestured toward the photos. "Any help from those?"

"We've not had much time to look." Grace placed her magnifying glass back in her bag. "I do wish I had the originals to study. The photocopy is only in black and white and so tiny."

Yes," Jack murmured to himself, his brows close together. "I wonder. . ."

"What are you thinking?"

His gaze rose to Frederick. "Those old rooms. I wonder if there may be more to discover in them than just countesses trapped in trunks."

Grace shot a look at Frederick and back to Jack. "Like more photos or history about the family?"

"Anything that would help us understand these children better may be of use to us. I have an idea." Jack stood and rested his hands on his waist. "I'm going to take a quick inventory of all our players and perhaps get a bit of breakfast. What do you say to reconvening in about an hour? That will give you both some time to review the photos and the papers I brought." His pale gaze moved between them. "And then I'm going to take the Reynoldses and Mr. Finch on an extended walk in the gardens to help me look for clues." His lips tipped ever so slightly. "I plan to keep them occupied out of the house for a good hour or so."

Frederick seemed to share Jack's thoughts, because his lips tipped in the same crooked way. Grace replayed Jack's words and then gasped. "Oh, do you mean you want us to investigate the rooms where I was attacked?"

"If the grandchildren of Accardi or anyone else associated with Accardi's story is behind any of this, then I think those rooms may be the perfect place for a more thorough investigation."

"If only the prints were a little larger," Grace muttered, leaning as close to the photos as she could get, her magnifying glass the only thing creating distance between her face and the photos.

Frederick shifted between the photos and the information Jack had brought. In addition to reviewing the news clipping about the Accardi grandchildren, he read an article announcing the mysterious death of author Dolores Reynolds and a rather detailed accounting of her small estate in the hamlet of Ashover.

News articles following the consecutive robberies and mysterious deaths were included, a connection unseen before, now growing clearer. The thieves had been ingenious, creating a patchwork of crimes no one thought to connect to one single set of paintings from Venice.

"Do you realize there are bookshelves in two of the paintings?" Grace stood, holding a photo to the light. "No, wait, in three of them. The balcony scene has one in the background too. I've been trying to read the spines but can't make out any letters in such small photos."

"Perhaps they're not meant to have readable spines." Frederick skimmed over an article with a series of photos of the author's estate, staff, and some interviews.

"Why put them there, then?" She looked over at him. "It seems a terrible tease for a reader to see a bookshelf full of books and not be able to identify a single one."

"For as avid a reader as you are, darling, I'm certain it feels anticlimactic."

She looked up at him, one eye enlarged by the magnifying glass. "You never know when the tiniest detail of letters leads to a clue." She pulled the glass away. "There are quite a few novels where messages were hidden in plain sight through letters and words, you know."

"You are right. I remember reading about such a set of messages too."

"Archie Sutherland's book *The Red Letter Rhyme*?" She looked skyward in thought. "Or *Cryptic March*." Her eyes grew wide. "In that one, the message was left in obituaries. Marvelously devious, if you ask me."

He raised his gaze to her, attempting to sort out how and why someone would leave clues in obituaries. Clever, but also disturbing. He happily ignored the delight in Grace's voice about the idea, for his peace of mind, if nothing else. "I've not read the latter of those."

"Well, it was very good." She nodded. "But you are also right. It may only be my hopeful imaginings. And perhaps painters think very differently than readers." She returned to the photos. "If I were going to hide a secret message, I'd certainly choose something with words or books or both."

His grin tipped as he returned to the paper, attention catching on one of the photos. Or rather, *someone* in the photo. He leaned closer, examining the man's face. "Grace, would you bring your magnifying glass here a moment?"

Grace rounded the table where *The Juliet* photos lay strewn for her perusal and gave Frederick her glass, scanning the print before him as she did. "What is it?"

He placed the magnifying glass to his eye and peered closer, the faces in the crowd clearer. His attention stopped on one man, half-hidden behind a woman, but looking directly at the camera. His skin went cold.

"Who does this look like to you?" He handed the glass back to Grace, and she took his place over the paper.

"Oh!" she gasped. "Frederick, is that Mr. Finch?"

"I thought the same."

"So it's true. Mr. Finch must be a part of it all." She sat down next to him. "He was at the *real* Dolores Reynolds' home near the time of her murder."

"And standing with other household staff." Frederick scanned the faces in the crowd, but none of them looked familiar, though the woman near Finch had her back to the camera. Curls? Miss Whitby, Mrs. Reynolds, and Miss Benetti all had curls.

"That's terribly convenient." Grace raised a brow, her intelligent eyes alight. "I'd wager his name is not Mr. Finch either." She sighed. "This whole case has been a series of things or people not being what or who they're supposed to be. Mr. Laraby isn't Mr. Laraby. Mrs. Reynolds isn't Mrs. Reynolds. And who is to say who Mr. Finch is?"

"But this certainly places a connection between Mr. Finch and our Mrs. Reynolds." He stood and walked to the window. Their room overlooked the back loggia, which led to a series of exquisite gardens, some walled, some not. This villa could not have been more beautifully situated as a home. . .nor more perfectly placed for a mystery. "Who are they? How are they connected to Accardi? Mrs. Reynolds and Mr. Finch are too old to be the lost grandchildren."

"Could it be as simple as treasure hunters?" Grace walked over to stand beside him. "The couple could have just learned about the treasure and decided to take it for themselves."

"That's true." Frederick looked down at her. "But to be so ruthless in their thievery? All of this murder?"

"In books it can be something as simple as greed." Grace returned her attention to the window. "But I do wonder if it's something more. This has certainly been a series of crimes for over a year."

Just then, Jack appeared out on the loggia with Mr. and Mrs. Reynolds and Mr. Finch along with him. Somehow, in his persuasive way, he'd convinced them to join him, just as he'd said. Was that the hint that Frederick and Grace should start their search?

As if in answer to Grace's unvoiced question, Jack looked up at their bedroom window and doffed his hat before returning his attention to the other three.

Frederick took Grace's hand and searched her face. "Are you ready?"

"Without a doubt."

The rooms appeared less daunting and eerie in daylight, though an unusual chill still lingered in the air of the untouched rooms.

Frederick knew the sensation all too well. Even now, after months of reentering the rooms in his estate of Havensbrooke, and with the new plans of renovation in process, the space still held an unsettled air about it. The feelings lessened each time he entered and, with Grace's innovative and joyful mind at work to re-create the rooms once used by his elder brother, the apartment would soon be transformed for his and Grace's own.

Making new memories there—brighter ones—helped. And would continue to banish the shadows of his past. As his wife and God's grace continued to do little by little in his life.

But Laraby meant to keep these dusty rooms as they were at the time of the Accardis, and somehow the idea produced a ghostlike aura to the space. The light streaming through the large windows revealed the dust-covered bookshelves and faded furnishings. Shadows lurked in corners untouched by the midday sun.

"Should we begin in the room where I was attacked?"

He pulled his gaze from a painting on the wall to look at Grace, who held her parasol clenched in both hands. He tapped one of her fists. "Are you going to start carrying this around everywhere you go?"

"Well, not everywhere." Her brows shot high. "I mean, not

to meals or swimming, but when one plans to visit a possibly dangerous place, one should always carry a means of defense. I happen to have three."

"Three?" He choked out a laugh.

"Yes." Her lips crooked just a bit. "My parasol, my knife." She pressed a palm to her chest in reference to the placement of said weapon. "And you."

He gave a curt nod. "And hopefully you won't require use of any of them for the time it takes us to search these rooms."

"Well, I always require *your* presence." Her smile spread with the twinkle in her eyes. "You're my favorite of the three."

His grin shot wide. "Glad to know where I rate, darling."

The room with the trunk and dolls revealed nothing more than old toys and musty smells. Two adjoining rooms showed an expansive suite with a bedroom and sitting area. Nearest the veranda, the room with the most windows showcased what must have once been Accardi's studio. A half-finished painting waited as if on display for the artist himself to return any moment. Brushes and easels dotted haphazard spots throughout the room. A child's doll lay in one corner as if it had just been discarded, but for the layer of dust coating its features.

"I thought for certain we'd find something here." Grace sighed as they made their way back through the rooms, stopping in the final room with the wall of bookshelves.

"I would have liked to give Jack something else to go on." Frederick rubbed the back of his neck and scanned the room. "This entire case is a tangle of false information."

Grace walked over to the bookshelf, giving rapt attention to the rows of spines and stories. "It seems a pity to leave these poor books untouched, doesn't it?" Her fingers trailed along the dusty rows. "All in Italian, I suppose."

Frederick moved closer, examining the shelves. Classics. Art books. Architecture. Mostly in Italian.

"Oh, Frederick, there's a copy of *Romeo and Juliet*." Grace reached for a slim book at the edge of the middle shelf. "At least I can read names in Italian." Her fingers hooked the top of the book. "It's stuck."

A sudden awareness whooshed through Frederick. "What?"

With another tug, a strange click sounded from the bookshelf, and by some special mechanics, the bookshelf slowly opened from the wall. Frederick rushed to shield Grace from anything emerging from the dark unknown.

On the other side of the shelf, hidden within a small room, stood a simple table, and hanging on all the walls, in chronological order to the story, hung eight of the nine *Juliets*.

"Frederick," Grace whispered, sending him a wide-eyed look.

"I see." He took her hand and stepped with her into the room, taking a match from his pocket to light the lantern situated on the table.

The glow illuminated the space, bringing out the colors of the paintings surrounding them. How long had the paintings been here? And if Mrs. Reynolds and Mr. Finch were the ones behind the robberies, how did they manage to get the paintings here when they had just arrived only yesterday like Frederick and Grace?

Was someone else, part of the original party, another accomplice? Miss Benetti, who would have easy access to the house due to her relationship with Laraby? Paul, for the same reason? Miss Whitby?

A map spread out on the table, and Frederick paused to examine it. The paper curled at the corners with age, and everything about it suggested it had been hand-drawn by someone with artistic talent. Isola di Signo marked the top of the map in beautiful black curls. The map detailed the entire island. From the carefully drawn villa to the dock, the ornate gardens—complete with their

Roman god statues and intricate gazebos—to the plethora of cliffs throughout the island. Even the caves along the cliff's edge were marked with special names like *cuore di pietra*, "Heart of Stone," and *posatoio di passero*, "Sparrow's Roost." One featured the rather uncreative name *grotta dei pirati* or "Pirate's Cave."

"Frederick." Grace's voice pulled him from his examination. She stood next to the painting of the ball, the one the "ghost" had taken. "I knew if we had a better view of the paintings, we'd make out something more. The bookshelf in the back of this one has real letters on the spines of the books. They're not creating any word I can read, but on each spine at least one letter is recognizable."

He left the map and moved to her side, peering at the easily overlooked bookshelf situated in the background of the painting. Just as Grace had said, of the books shown on the shelf, one letter on each of the spines was readable but not overly noticeable unless one was looking. Of course, Grace's unique interest drew her attention to just the right thing.

He pieced the letters together, but they didn't make any word he knew.

"Is it Italian?"

He looked again, attempting to rework the letters into something recognizable, and then. . . "Grace, I believe it's a phrase but backward." He stepped closer. If he reworked the letters. . . "Yes. *Ai piedi degli dei*. 'At the feet of the gods.' "

"At the feet of the gods?" Grace squinted up at him. "What does that mean?"

Before he could answer, the sound of a click came from behind them.

Frederick's blood went cold. He knew that sound.

A revolver.

"Well, well, what do we have here?"

He turned, slowly pushing Grace behind him.

Out of the shadows and around the entrance to the hidden room stepped Miss Lydia Whitby, revolver poised in her hand.

Chapter 16

Grace froze in place, her mind hiccupping against the idea that Lydia Whitby could be the villain of this story. The spectacle-wearing secretary, friend, and former thieving illusionist who held something over Laraby's head didn't make sense.

Grace's shoulders deflated. Well, if she described Lydia that way in her mind, then Lydia's villainy made much more sense than how she'd gotten Mr. Smallwood wrong in Egypt. And since Grace hadn't ascertained Lydia's reading interests yet, perhaps the idea of being wrong wouldn't feel so disappointing.

Mr. Smallwood had completely tricked her with a dedicated love for Dickens!

She sighed. What sort of sleuth was she going to be if she kept guessing wrong about people so often?

Frederick stepped in front of Grace like the dashing hero he was. "There's no need for that, Miss Whitby."

With a little crook to her grin, Lydia lowered her weapon and slipped it back into the pocket of her skirt. "I'd think after all that's happened so far, Lord Astley, you would encourage everyone to be on their guard, especially the detectives." She stepped into the room, her gaze roaming the walls. Her smile slipped from her lips. "The paintings." She looked over at Frederick and Grace and then back to the walls. "They're here?"

"So you're not going to shoot us?"

"Shoot *you*?" Lydia pulled her attention from the paintings and stared at Grace. "Why would I shoot the pitiful few people on this island I can trust? Goodness, no. But if you'd been a host of other people, I may have shot you without one hesitation."

"Do you suspect someone in particular?"

Her attention switched to Frederick, the power of her emerald gaze almost disarming. "I'll not pretend, Lord Astley. I grew up in a world of pretention and know how to play the game, but it's done nothing but wound me my entire life. No. I'll have no more of it." She raised a brow. "There's quite enough of pretense going on in this villa already, don't you think?" She stepped forward, scanning the little room.

"How did you know we were here?" Frederick asked, relaxing his stance but keeping his guarded position. "You overheard us in Laraby's study?"

Oh, Frederick was terribly good at this sort of guessing—all he needed was the opportunity to try out his skills.

"I said I was *done* with pretense. Not intelligence." She shrugged a shoulder. "I plan to keep on my guard, but I can't trust Laraby to keep up his. Paul isn't much better, I'm afraid. Both of them have been relatively worthless since Jasmine came on the scene."

"What do you mean?" Grace asked, following Miss Whitby to the other painting with a bookshelf in the background. The one where Romeo and Juliet consummate their marriage. Another bookshelf waited in the shadows of the painting of Juliet's bedroom, but there weren't as many books on this one as in the ball painting.

"She's the type who garners the attention of men." Lydia looked away and shook her head. "The sort who constantly *needs* rescuing."

Grace looked from Lydia to Frederick, a little unsure of what she meant. Of course Grace needed a good rescue now and again, but she'd done her fair share of rescuing too. Was she the same type of woman Lydia described?

Something told her not.

But after being stuck in a trunk for a while the day before, perhaps she wasn't the most accurate source for measuring herself.

"Who would have accessed these rooms over the past few months?" Frederick asked, stepping aside for Grace to draw closer into the conversation.

"You think it's someone who has been in the house?" Lydia's eyes sharpened. "I hadn't considered. . ." She looked down at the map and back to him. "Any of us, though these rooms weren't frequented by me or Paul or Laraby, to my knowledge. Laraby hoped to put some energy into these spaces once he finished his renovations to our main living areas, and Paul usually follows whatever Laraby is doing."

"The servants?" Grace offered.

"I suppose they'd have as easy access as anyone." Lydia's brows crashed together. "I helped hire most of them. Locals. All with solid references from what I could tell."

Grace's mind went through a list of the people in the house. The only servants she'd had any semblance of interaction with were Mr. Zappa, Martina, and another maid named Leanna, who Grace had accidentally frightened while practicing her cane fighting moves in the hallway. Could any of them have helped Mr. and Mrs. Reynolds and Mr. Finch get into the gallery?

"What do you plan to do about the paintings?"

"Keep them untouched until we can discuss the findings with Jack." Frederick stepped toward her. "Can we trust you to keep this a secret as well?"

Her gaze roamed back over the paintings, pausing on the one of the ball. Some flicker of concern crossed her countenance before she returned her attention to Frederick. "You can trust me. Any new information about a possible treasure or anything to give reason why someone would take them?"

"We were just beginning to explore when you found us," Grace said, moving back to the paintings with Lydia at her side.

Grace made mental inventory of the stand-out letters in the bookshelf to review with Frederick later. Lydia didn't need to know their more recent discovery. At least not yet. Though Grace was inclined to trust someone with such a sincere and quick response, she'd learned the hard way how much trust needed to be earned. Especially in the middle of mysteries—and with this crazy cast of characters who weren't all they seemed to be. Though she wished to trust quickly, God had also given her a mind with which to exercise wisdom as well.

In the large paintings, the colors brought out the words within the bookshelf, now that she knew what to look for: A-r-e-s-s-a-p.

She turned them around in her mind. What was that? *Passera?* And how did it relate to the feet of the gods?

"Do you think the treasure could be real?" Lydia peered closely at the painting of Juliet meeting with Friar Laurence. "It seems much too fantastic to believe."

Frederick sent a look to Grace and smiled at Lydia. "It would certainly be an excellent reason for someone to cause all this trouble for Laraby."

"The paintings are worth a great deal of money on their own, though." Lydia looked around the small room again. "And as a complete set, I can't imagine how much someone would pay for them."

Certainly a point Grace hadn't fully considered. Would an art collector or thief have designs to collect them all to sell the whole set? Mr. Reynolds was purportedly an art dealer, and if his wife, the false Mrs. Reynolds, was helping him, that would make sense, wouldn't it?

"You seem surprised to see the painting of the ball here." Frederick's statement drew a quick look from Miss Whitby.

She held his gaze a moment and released a sigh. "Laraby had planned the entire ghost-and-painting fiasco to impress Mrs. Reynolds, though I can't understand why. A fiction writer should be able to make up her own ideas without having a man re-create something to place in a book."

"You created the ghost, didn't you, Lydia?" Grace asked. "A trick learned from your history as illusionist's assistant?"

"You two are clever, aren't you?" A small smile flickered on her lips. "I didn't want to do it from the start, but Laraby holds the purse straps, and until I can save enough to leave on my own, I'm inclined to follow his requests. Besides, he usually doesn't ask for anything outrageous, just silly or slightly dangerous. And he used to be much more of a friend instead of a taskmaster." Her smile fell, her gaze growing distant. "But money can be its own taskmaster to change people."

"You don't think he's had anything to do with the stolen paintings, do you?" Grace asked. "In order to sell them himself?"

One of her brows rose. "It's not a bad idea, but if he was behind it all, I'd know. I'm the one who keeps up with almost all the finances and travel."

"So that's what your argument with Laraby was about earlier?" Lydia looked up at Frederick, her frown deepening. Frederick raised a brow to match Miss Whitby's. "We know how to eavesdrop as well."

Instead of the frustration Grace had expected, Lydia's smile took a slow turn. "Ah, turnabout is fair play then, I suppose. And I think with all these shared secrets, you should call me Lydia like your wife, Lord Astley." Her smile flashed wide. "Miss Whitby always makes me feel much older than I am." At Frederick's silence, her smile faded. "Right. Well, John. . .um. . . ." She shook her head. "I suppose you know his history, as well?"

PEPPER BASHAM

"Yes." Grace moved to stand beside Frederick. "And fairly early on in all of this too."

"When he first went to live with his grandfather, he handled the sudden affluence well. He was careful. Smart. And I took advantage of the willingness of his grandfather's secretary to teach me. Over time, John's grandfather allowed me to join in on some of the financial discussions because he'd seen my skills. It was the first time I'd ever felt so seen and competent. When his secretary resigned due to the needs of her older parents, John's grandfather gave me the position, and I continued to learn." The glow in her eyes faded. "After John's grandfather died, with John's newfound freedom to spend at will, purchase what he wanted, and become whatever he wanted, he changed." Deep lines creased her brow with her frown. "He hired me as his secretary, though at first we shared the responsibility as friends. But then John started surrounding himself with people who were more interested in his money than him, and the attention and ease of pleasure went to his head."

"So he spent at will."

"He did many things at will." She nodded, pressing her fingers into her forehead with a sigh. "And Paul and I, despite trying to give good advice, were ignored and sometimes ridiculed because of our lack of wealth and connections. We truly became servants to him instead of the friends we once were. His finances were already in poor shape when he decided to purchase this island and start courting Jasmine."

"Yet you've stayed with him." The hurt on Lydia's face pricked at Grace's heart. The previous conversation she and Frederick had overheard came to mind. Perhaps Lydia had loved him romantically once, but she'd certainly cared for him as a longtime friend. And now to be passed over? Ridiculed even? Grace couldn't fathom turning on the people who'd cared the longest and best.

"Of course"—Lydia released a humorless laugh—"neither

Paul nor I had money when we left the circus, and despite John's treatment of me, I've learned so much about finances and trade and how to be independent. Information like that is valuable for a woman in this day and age who desires independence over marriage." Her lips pressed tight, determination creasing her brow. "I haven't the resources to leave yet. But one day I will. And I'll choose my own future. But until then, I'll bear the brunt of his snobbery and look forward to the day when I can leave him to manage his own affairs, as tangled and desperate as they are. And to pay the debts he has no interest in discussing."

Grace caught Frederick's look and wondered at his thoughts. Did he believe Lydia's tale? Or was he wondering if she spun a story to turn attention away from her possible hand in the middle of all this? Grace frowned. Trying to sort out the good versus the bad was a tricky thing and not nearly as easy as in books.

Now that Lydia knew where the paintings were, would she steal them herself and disappear?

A scream rang out from a distant place. A woman's scream.

"What on earth has happened now?" Lydia moaned and ran from the secret room.

Grace exchanged a glance with Frederick before following Lydia, and Frederick pushed the bookshelf door closed behind them. Another scream followed from the direction of the back loggia. Frederick took Grace's hand in his and increased his pace.

The scene on the loggia was bedlam. Mr. Reynolds stood by his wife, both pale and staring toward the veranda of the house. Mr. Finch stood poised on the edge of the veranda, looking back at the people on the loggia, his expression as stricken as that of the Reynoldses. Paul waited next to him, his head in his hands. Poor Martina stood, teapot poised in hand, her dark eyes as wide as saucers. And Mr. Zappa held a hysterical Jasmine in his arms, her face buried in his shoulder. The man didn't appear to mind her nearness as much as he ought. Mr. Brandon would have been utterly discombobulated if Grace had started weeping on the poor man's shoulder. He was the best of men but not demonstrative in affection at all.

"What on earth happened?" Frederick asked the crowd.

"He's gone," Jasmine sobbed. "The horrible man ruined everything for us."

"Ruined everything?" Grace repeated, trying to make sense of the scene.

"This house is mad," Mr. Reynolds murmured, pushing a palm through his hair and looking down at his wife. "I'm not sure what you hope to find is worth staying here another night."

What they hope to find? A treasure, perhaps?

"I ask again, what's happened?"

"What's happened?" Jack stepped from beside Mr. Finch on the veranda, his voice raised enough to be heard across the small space between the separation of the loggia and the corner of the veranda. "It seems that Mr. Laraby decided to jump from the veranda."

"What?" Lydia gasped. "But. . .but. . .he can't survive."

"No," came Jack's short response. "He can't."

"He wouldn't have killed himself," Jasmine moaned. "No. He had made me promises. We were to be married."

"We saw it." An edge hardened Mrs. Reynolds words. "From the corner of the loggia here. We heard a call, like a cry, and then. . ." She blinked. "Mr. Laraby's body came into view as it tumbled over the railing."

"You're certain it was him?" Frederick asked.

"Yes," Mr. Reynolds countered. "He looked back at us when he stood up on the railing. Looked back just before he—" The man's voice broke off, and he shook his head. "Madness. Just like the entire curse surrounding this place."

"Laraby jumped off the veranda?" Grace moved to the edge

of the loggia and glanced down, nothing but rocky coastline and crashing surf within her view.

"He was pushed. He was looking back at us to seek help," Jasmine screamed, her dark gaze scanning the crowd and finally landing on Lydia. "Someone here must have wanted him dead."

Frederick kept hold of Grace's hand and pulled her back into the house. He'd feared something darker and more dangerous would happen next, especially in the middle of all the secrets of the people in this villa, but murder?

He walked down the hall toward the veranda to find Mr. Finch still staring over the edge in a state of shock and Jack pacing the length of the space like a prowling lion. What clues did the man see? Was he thinking murder or suicide? Could Laraby have chosen to end his life because of his debts? Had he discovered Mr. and Mrs. Reynolds' secret, and had they silenced him?

Frederick approached Jack with Grace just behind him. "Any ideas?"

"Do you mean whether it's suicide or murder?" Jack raised a brow, his stare growing more intense. "Well, the Reynoldses and Mr. Finch were with *me*."

Which meant their current suspects had an alibi.

"And Miss Whitby was with us"—Frederick stared back as intently, lowering his voice—"searching the rooms."

Jack's attention shifted to Miss Whitby, who stood by the veranda, staring over the edge, the wind blowing so hard it sent her blond hair loose from its pins much like Grace's. Jack moved along the veranda, his palm smoothing along the railing, his gaze shifting from the floor to the cliff and back.

"Mr. Zappa," Jack called toward the loggia. "Hand Miss Benetti over to"—he waved his hand—"someone else and phone the police, won't you?"

"I'll go see to her, Detective." Paul cleared his throat, averting his gaze. "Laraby would want that." He gave the cliff drop another look and left the veranda.

Mr. Finch shook his head and followed Paul.

Did Paul know something? Or could he have grown tired of Laraby's lording over him and taken out his anger on the man?

"He wouldn't have killed himself." Lydia stepped forward.

"No?" Jack countered. "Why not?"

"He's not brave enough. Not really." She narrowed her eyes, refusing to break contact with Jack. "Swinging from a trapeze is one thing. Tossing oneself off a ledge is another."

The slightest twitch crooked Jack's mouth. "No, I don't think he's brave enough either."

"Then who killed him?" Grace looked up at them. "Who else was on the veranda with him?"

"I was standing on the loggia with the Reynoldses and Finch. Miss Benetti was having tea there and had invited us to join her." Jack studied the railing again. "One can only see a small part of the veranda from the loggia." Jack stared over the space, his gaze roving, likely taking notice, problem-solving. "I had just started to walk inside to look for you when I heard Miss Benetti scream. I only saw his body fall. Nothing else."

"And no one else?" Frederick asked.

Jack shook his head. "Not from where I was standing. The corner of the house blocked my view."

Grace walked over to the doorway to the house. "Someone could easily have tucked themselves out of sight of the loggia by standing here. In fact, they could have been anywhere on the veranda with Laraby and not been seen from the loggia."

"Let's interview everyone and see what their stories reveal." Jack rested his palms on his waist. "Something doesn't feel right about this at all, but I can't quite put my finger on why."

"Who do you want us to interview?" Frederick asked.

"I believe with Miss Benetti's opinions, you and Lady Astley should speak to Miss Benetti, Mr. Hopewell, and Mr. Zappa. If Miss Whitby is amenable, since she seems to be an uninvited part of our investigation, she can accompany me to question the Reynoldses, Mr. Finch, and that little maid."

"Martina," Grace provided.

"Yes."

"I may just come in handy, Detective, invited or not." Lydia lifted her chin. "You can learn a great deal about escapes and ruffians and the impossible from being in the circus."

Jack's brows rose. "Then I hope your unique set of experiences comes in very. . .handy, as you say, Miss Whitby." He looked to Grace and Frederick. "I've learned not to underestimate the ingenuity of Americans. Isn't that right, Frederick?"

"It's certainly a perspective to change, Jack." Frederick pressed a palm to Grace's back. "And once we've completed our interviews, we need to speak to you about what we've discovered. Lydia knows about it as well."

Jack shifted his attention from Frederick to Lydia and nodded. "Very well. Let's meet back here on the veranda in an hour. Will that suit?"

Frederick looked down at his pocket watch before giving Jack a nod. "In an hour."

Paul had replaced Mr. Zappa as Miss Benetti's comforter by the time Frederick and Grace entered the sitting room. The way Paul held her with such familiarity piqued Frederick's disquiet. Paul hadn't been a possible suspect from the start, but men did a great many horrible things out of jealousy or desire. Could it be that Paul had wanted Miss Benetti for himself and found a way to remove Laraby from the scene permanently? After all, he'd possibly faked his wounds last night and clearly proved unaffected by a bump to the head today.

And what if the paintings and Mr. Laraby's death were not connected at all? In Egypt, he and Grace had made the mistake of attempting to connect all the crimes to the same possible motives and suspects, but what if this mystery proved similar in that there were distinct crimes and motives?

When questioned about their whereabouts, Miss Benetti confirmed she was having tea on the veranda and that Paul had just left the veranda to fetch Daniel to join her.

"He hadn't been gone more than a minute or two," Miss Benetti clarified. "I'd not seen Daniel all morning because he said he had business to attend to and we could spend our time together over tea." Her voice shook, and she brought her handkerchief to her face. "I was waiting for him."

"I don't know what happened, truly." Paul shook his head. "He had everything. He couldn't have wanted to end his life."

"And we were to be married in only a few months." Jasmine broke into a wail and returned her face to Paul's shoulder.

Mr. Zappa confirmed that he'd phoned the police and had witnesses who placed him coming from the kitchens at the time of Laraby's fall.

"Do you think he truly ended his own life?" Grace asked Frederick as they returned to the veranda. "It doesn't seem to fit him, does it?"

"No, and I'm inclined to believe Miss Whitby's assessment of him."

"But if everyone has a solid alibi, then who else could it be?"

Frederick paused and looked down at her. "I can only come up with two possibilities. One, someone is covering for the real murderer by providing an alibi."

"Yes." Grace's eyes widened as she stared up at him. "I've

thought of that."

"Or there's another thief among us whom we haven't accounted for."

"Or a disgruntled servant?" she asked and shivered. "Someone hiding in plain sight who has been waiting for the opportunity to take out their anger?"

"I don't know." He gestured with his chin toward the door. "But if the potential murderer was after the last *Juliet*, they wouldn't have killed the only person who knows where that painting is."

Grace nodded. "You're right."

Frederick's mind ciphered through the information, attempting to make sense of it. "Come on. Let's find out what Jack and Miss Whitby discovered."

But all their suspects had proper alibis as well. Nothing pointed to foul play along the veranda. Nothing hinted that there was a struggle.

"And I told Detective Miracle about the secret room." Lydia leaned back against the railing, arms crossed. "But I couldn't divulge what you learned about any hidden treasure, since you wouldn't share your thoughts on the matter."

Grace's bottom lip dropped at Lydia's accurate implication.

"A discovery that confirms some of my deductions." Jack sighed. "Someone believes there truly is a treasure. It's the only thing that makes sense. Miss Whitby's idea about someone selling the entire collection is noteworthy, but then why would they collect all the paintings here instead of somewhere safer?"

"Unless they needed the paintings together here to solve the puzzle," Grace finished.

"Precisely." Jack released a long breath and returned to the veranda railing, tapping it as he stood. "Despite the legend of the treasure, only an elite few would have known the location of the secret room."

"Which could have been servants," Frederick offered, meeting

Jack's gaze. "Or family members."

"Family members?" Lydia straightened. "You're referring to the missing grandchildren?" She leaned back again, shaking her head. "A real treasure and two orphans returning to get their inheritance? There's a story."

"And a powerful motive," Frederick added. "If the intention is securing a family inheritance, then the long-term planning of all the crimes would make sense. The criminals weren't in a hurry. They wanted to ensure a careful and deliberate plan." Frederick took a slow turn toward her, shaking his head. "But why kill Laraby? It doesn't fit at all."

"Hello." Jack drew out the word, and he kneeled closer to the railing. "What is this?"

Frederick, Grace, and Lydia moved closer. Jack's fingers traced a spot on the railing. At first, Frederick didn't notice anything, but after closer examination, a groove within the stone railing came to light as if something had been. . .tied there?

He dropped to his knees and reached into his inside jacket pocket to pull out a set of tweezers. With careful hands, he picked up something from the shadows of the railing and came back to a stand. In the light, the small strands within the tweezer became clear. Fibers? Were those rope fibers?

"Interesting development, wouldn't you say, Miss Whitby?"

Lydia looked up at Jack, back to the groove, then to the fibers, her expression moving from confusion to surprise, then realization. "No, he wouldn't have done that."

"Done what?" Grace reached out to touch the groove, but Frederick's attention went to Jack. Something in his friend's look darkened.

"I believe, my friends, we've been tricked by our host for the last time."

Chapter 17

"I didn't know about this." Lydia fisted her fingers and turned toward the veranda door. "It wouldn't have happened if *I'd* known about it. Ghosts are one thing. Pretending to die is quite another."

Grace blinked and looked over at Frederick. Jack had already begun to follow the woman, and with a rather large sigh, Frederick turned in the same direction, offering his hand for Grace to come along. But what was happening?

Pretend to die?

Grace played through the evidence on the veranda. Something clicked in her brain. Trapeze artists. Games. Did Lydia and Jack suppose Mr. Laraby had faked his own death by propelling himself off the veranda?

Grace looked back over her shoulder at the veranda. She wasn't certain whether to be horrified or indescribably impressed.

"There's only one place he'd choose to hide. It allows him to hear all the activity going on in the sitting room without being observed." Lydia continued her march down the hallway, then made a sharp turn to the left.

Pushing through a narrow doorway, they entered Laraby's study from the opposite wall that Frederick and Grace had taken that morning. With a slight hitch in her step, Lydia moved across the room toward a large marble fireplace.

"I made a promise not to reveal this place to anyone." She sighed and reached for a sconce on the wall. "John had it built during the renovations of the house. But since he's done something as foolish as fake his own death, I think all promises are off."

With a small turn of the sconce, a panel beside the fireplace loosened to reveal a hidden door. Grace barely held in a gasp, but from Frederick's quick glance in her direction, he may have heard it. She wasn't certain if she'd convinced him to make her a secret entrance into the reading room he'd designed for her in the east wing at Havensbrooke, but she'd certainly made excellent arguments for it.

And discovering not one but two secret entrances in the villa hopefully gave him a few more ideas of how delightful such benign secrets could be.

The panel revealed a narrow and dark hall, barely large enough for Frederick and Jack to fit their rather impressive shoulders. An equally narrow stair rose into a small, sun-soaked room. Windows braced the room on two sides, a food- and drink-laden side table lined one wall, and in an armchair by one of the windows sat Daniel Laraby, very much alive.

"What?" He shot up from his seat, his attention falling with a narrowed-eyed glare on Lydia. "You led them here? You promised. You're the only one I trusted with this secret."

"They sorted out your ridiculous scheme, John." Lydia waved toward Jack. "He's a detective after all."

"But. . .but now they'll know where *she* is." He turned back behind him, and poised in a shadowed part of the room on another table stood the final *Juliet*. The balcony scene.

Grace shifted a step toward it, her focus zooming in on a shadowed bookshelf nearly hidden among the translucent curtains of Juliet's room in the background. Another bookshelf. The final clue to the treasure?

"They're not the ones you need to worry about stealing your precious painting, John," Lydia shot back. "There's a *real* criminal in this villa stealing art pieces, and you decide to go off and play this game? What were you thinking?"

"Mrs. Reynolds is paying for a mystery, Lydia. I must give her what she wants. Make her stay longer."

Jack stepped forward. "Paying you?"

Laraby shook his head. "She and her husband are paying to stay here. A considerable amount. The longer she stays, the more she pays. It's that simple." He ran a hand through his hair. "If she's a mystery writer, she'll want a mystery. And I doubt the old tale of the Accardi murders is enough to keep her. But if I can give her more reasons to stay longer, then the better for me."

"If you hadn't spent money like it was water in the ocean, you wouldn't even be in this predicament," Lydia growled and turned away from him. "Of all the things to do, John. A pretend ghost is one thing. But a pretend death?"

"People are genuinely distraught at the thought of your death, Mr. Laraby. Your fiancée being one of them." Frederick's voice pulsed low with his frustration. "Real deaths have occurred at the hands of the people seeking *The Juliets*. Real murders. This is not the time for more charades."

"I'm not responsible for those murders," Laraby shot back, crossing his arms and pouting like a petulant child. "I must see to my own welfare by whatever means I can."

Grace's bottom lip dropped. The lack of awareness of the situation, the selfishness—the complete absence of care and carefulness proved baffling.

"Ah, an excellent notion, Mr. Laraby." Jack sent the man a scathing look before turning from the room. "I shall take your exceptional advice as my own. For the welfare of *myself* and *my* associates, I withdraw from this case. I will send my bill to you to add to your growing debts." He tipped his hat, a humorless smile in place. "You can hire someone else to play your game, but I am finished."

With that, Jack turned toward the stairway, catching Frederick and Grace's eye as he did. "There's nothing more I care to see related to this villa or Mr. Laraby."

"Wait." Laraby ran after them. "Not all of it was a game. I swear."

Jack kept walking without a turn in Laraby's direction. He appealed to Frederick next. "The paintings at the gallery and my *Juliets were* stolen. Except for the balcony scene." He waved toward the painting in the room, teasing Grace's curiosity back to life with a fury. "My other two were taken by some thief."

"Have you ever heard the tale of the boy who cried wolf, Mr. Laraby?" Frederick raised a brow and followed Jack down the stairs.

"Blast that Jack Miracle. I wish he'd never come," Laraby cursed under his breath, causing Grace to pause her steps.

"Why on earth *did* you ask for Jack to investigate these paintings, Mr. Laraby? If you wanted a ruse, you could have gotten someone cheaper and more local than a known English detective."

"He came highly recommended," Laraby groaned.

"Recommended? By whom?"

Laraby blinked up at her. "I. . .I can't remember. Jasmine? Someone. At any rate, he clearly knows more than I expected now that he's found *me* out." He returned his gaze to hers, searching her face, his expression open, honest. "But someone is stealing the paintings. And it has to be someone in the villa. Don't you see? Paul was supposed to pretend to steal the Capulet ball painting when the ghost arrived at dinner. But the painting truly was taken by someone else in the dark."

An image of the painting in the secret room flashed to Grace's mind. Should they reveal the secret room to Laraby before leaving?

Help him retrieve what was his? Grace's attention flashed down the stairs. "Why didn't you tell us of your pretense with the ghost? If you'd been honest from the beginning, it would certainly benefit you now."

Laraby looked back at Lydia. "Lydia tried to convince me to tell you everything, but I. . .well, I wanted to keep Mrs. Reynolds and her brother interested, and I thought if news got out that I'd made up the ghost, they wouldn't stay for more. Besides, it was all a lark. Nothing serious."

Grace sighed. Mr. Laraby was still such a boy in a man's body. Though he was likely only a few years older than she, he acted much younger—or at least he chose to use his creativity and passions in a very unwise way. "I'm afraid you'll have to find someone else to help you locate your paintings and save the museum's because I believe you've tricked Jack for the last time."

Even stating it brought about a frown. She'd just solved the painting puzzle and had to leave before she had the chance to see if the clues revealed a real treasure. Her shoulders slumped. This was much worse than having to wait to finish the last chapter of an excellent book.

Grace started down the stairs when Lydia's voice called her back. "I. . .I remember. Mr. Zappa. He was the one who recommended Jack. Evidently, a fellow servant had heard of Jack when he worked in service in England and recommended the detective when John's first painting went missing."

"Any idea who the servant was? A name?"

Lydia tilted her head, studying Grace a moment. "No, he only mentioned the man came from a house in northern England. Cumbria, perhaps?"

Cumbria? Grace knew the name but had never visited the purportedly beautiful part of England. Who lived there? Why did the connection of Mr. Zappa and some unnamed manservant with

Jack feel. . .unusual? Contrived?

Cumbria? Had one of the crimes been at a house in Cumbria?

She shook off the tingle and continued her descent down the stairs and back into Laraby's study. The little panel door slid closed behind her exit, but as she reached the study door, Laraby and Lydia both emerged from the panel following her.

"You'll tell Jack, won't you?" Laraby's voice rose in desperation. "Show him I'm trying. See if the news may change his mind?"

"I can't vouch for that, Mr. Laraby. Detective Miracle is quite done with your games."

Grace had barely made it into the foyer when a loud commotion of voices brought her to the sitting room. Three policemen and an inspector stood in heated conversation with Jack, Frederick, and Mr. Finch. Jasmine sat on the couch, pale, tears still evident on her shocked face. Paul stood nearby, his expression matching Jasmine's.

"He faked his death?" Mr. Reynolds shouted toward the other men. "What sort of place is this?"

"I've sent my servant to pack up my things," Jack announced. "And we will leave on the ferry once it arrives. I'm afraid if we stay any longer, we'll become part of some other mischief, and this time it may not prove as correctable or benign."

"Benign?" Jasmine released a sob. "I have been tricked, possibly used for my knowledge at the galleria." She dabbed at her eyes. "What if he was the thief all along and I've somehow helped him commit these crimes against Accardi?"

As if drawn by Jasmine's cries, Laraby swept into the room and approached the weeping woman. "Jasmine, I've no hand in the stolen paintings."

"How can I believe you?" She shrank back from him. "First a ghost that isn't real. Then a death that isn't real." Her eyes widened. "And now I learn from Mr. Reynolds that your name is not real either."

Laraby looked over at Mr. Reynolds, who looked like a child whose hand had been caught in the cookie jar. Grace frowned. So that's what she'd looked like so many times.

And how did Mr. Reynolds know about Laraby's true identity?

"How did you know that, Mr. Reynolds?" Mrs. Reynolds stood from the couch, her gaze intent on her husband. "Mr. Laraby is not Mr. Laraby?"

Mr. Reynolds' face flushed. "Why, you know exactly—"

"I'm afraid I can't stay here one more night." Mrs. Reynolds turned away from her husband, her blue gown shawl whisking about her shoulders as she moved toward the grand stairs. "I shall take the detective's cue and go along with the ferry as well." She paused as Mr. Zappa, who appeared out of nowhere, met her at the bottom of the stairs.

"Ah, Mr. Zappa, please assist me with my things. Mr. Reynolds, Mr. Finch, and I plan to leave as soon as the ferry arrives."

"This is ridiculous, everyone." Laraby raised his palms as if to calm the emotions with a wave of his hands. "I offer my sincerest apologies and promise to answer all questions in due course, even as we enjoy an expansive meal together this evening. Cook has assured me that it will be an excellent offering of some of Venice's best—"

"Find someone else to swindle, Mr. Laraby." Mr. Finch raised his chin and walked past. "Or whoever you are."

"Jack, we need to speak with you before we leave." Grace joined Frederick and Jack in the foyer as they moved toward the stairs. "To share what we've discovered."

"Very well, let's meet in your rooms." He swept the room with a gaze. "I can't explain it, but I feel as though the sooner we leave this island, the better."

Frederick looked back over the railing of the ferry as Isola di Signo grew more distant.

The sooner they arrived back on the mainland, the sooner he could relax. Frederick had grown increasingly concerned about Jack and Grace's safety the more surprises unfolded with the day, and Laraby's unpredictable behavior only made things worse.

At Jack's direction, Frederick remained on the open deck of the ferry with Grace, keeping watch as Jack spoke with the inspector inside the enclosed portion of the ferry. Hopefully, with additional brawn and brains aware of the fake Mrs. Reynolds and the secret room of paintings, Frederick's disquiet would ease. It would take the Reynoldses and Finch a few hours to leave the city, which would allow the police ample time to retain the trio and pursue whatever legal course proved necessary.

But the fact that Mr. and Mrs. Reynolds, Mr. Finch, and Jasmine were all aboard the large ferry with Frederick, Grace, and Jack put a kink in the theory that one of them was the mastermind behind the stolen *Juliets*. Why would they leave the paintings behind if they were either planning to sell them or use them to search for the refutable treasure?

Who else could the possible culprit be? One of the existing servants? And why the fake identities if Mr. and Mrs. Reynolds had no hand in all of this?

Heat fled Frederick's face. Lydia Whitby?

No, surely she wasn't responsible. His thoughts filtered through evidence. She certainly had access to both the villa and the paintings. Had been present at the death of Laraby's grandfather. But the other deaths?

And what about Paul? They already knew he wasn't honest about his head wound. What else had he been hiding?

"I wish I'd been able to get close enough to the final *Juliet* to read the clues on the book spines," Grace said as she stood at his side at the railing. Their current ferry stretched long, with half of it enclosed and the other half open to the elements, a slight sprinkling of rain. "I was able to read the second one while we were in the secret room though."

He raised a brow in welcome for her to finish.

"There weren't as many visible books on that shelf, so I think it only showed one word. *Passera.*"

"Passera?" Frederick repeated. "Sparrow?"

"Sparrow? Oh, it is a pretty word in both English and Italian." She returned to the topic at hand. "So we have the phrase 'at the feet of the gods' and the word *sparrow* as our clues." Her brows pinched. "How could those go together?"

"I'm afraid we won't be the ones finding out." He fisted the railing, the sea breeze blowing soft mist against his face. The rain came gently from a pale gray sky. An unexpected pinch swelled in his chest. Something about leaving this mystery unfinished didn't sit well with him. No, he had been reluctant to dive into Jack's case from the beginning, but now, as they'd joined the thick of it, the idea of not supplying answers bothered him.

There were too many unfinished things.

The paintings, a treasure, the Accardi murders, the map, Mrs. Reynolds' true identity. . . His list paused. The map?

"Grace, do you remember the map in the secret room?"

Those azure eyes of hers sharpened. "I remember seeing it, but I must admit I was more focused on the clues in the paintings."

"For which I'm grateful. While I reviewed the map, you were making excellent progress with the paintings. Otherwise, we wouldn't have gotten as far as we have since we were interrupted."

"Was there something on the map that caught your attention?"

"Yes, actually." He rubbed a hand over his chin. "I didn't see anything about the feet of the gods, but there was a point marked as Sparrow's Roost."

"Do you think the clues were points on the map, then?" Her eyes widened. "But that would be perfect, wouldn't it?"

"It doesn't seem to matter much now, since we're not likely to return to work for Mr. Laraby, but it does make me wonder."

"Very sleuth-like wondering." She grinned and wrapped her arm through his. "And highly attractive to my mind."

His lips broke into a smile, and he sighed into her touch, his gaze dropping to her smile. "I suppose things could have ended much worse, but at the very least, we can return to the delights of our honeymoon trip."

"I don't suppose that's very bad." The twinkle in her eyes hinted to her growing gift of sarcasm. "But I do hope Jack tells the inspector about all the connected deaths. At the very least, that should bring some resolution for the families of those victims."

"Indeed, I believe that is his plan."

"Good." She looked back toward the disappearing island, likely trying to solve the rest of the mystery as far as imagination and clues could take her. "That will be some sort of good ending to this story, but don't you think we should share the possible connection about the map with Jack?"

"He's speaking to the inspector on the other side of the ferry." Frederick looked down the length of the ferry, unable to get a good view of the people in the enclosed portion. Mr. and Mrs. Reynolds sat inside with Mr. Finch, so Jack would likely keep his remarks carefully placed if they were within earshot.

"Is he telling the inspector about the paintings? Where to find them?"

"I believe so. But we can share about the map once we reach—"

A scream broke into his words followed by the sound of a large splash. Frederick and Grace rushed in the direction of the sound, at the juncture of where the boat switched from being open to closed.

"Help! I—I can't. . . ."

Frederick ran to the opposite railing and peered over.

"Oh my goodness!" Grace gasped at his side. "It's Miss Benetti. She's fallen in."

Flailing in the water, the weight of her water-soaked gown likely pulling her under, Miss Benetti coughed and cried.

"We have to help her." Grace started reaching for her shirtwaist, and Frederick stopped her hand.

"I'm going in, but alert the captain to slow the ferry."

Grace nodded and dashed away as Frederick removed his jacket.

"Help me!" She thrashed, going under the water again.

Frederick tossed his hat to the side, followed by his shoes, and used one of the gaps between the railings from which to dive. The cold water rushed over him, shocking him to the alert. He surfaced, but she wasn't anywhere to be seen. Bubbles erupted in a spot nearby.

Frederick went back under the waves. Clear as glass, he quickly made out the position of Miss Benetti from the bright blue of her gown.

He surfaced a few feet from her as she sank beneath the waves again.

"What is going on?" someone called from above. Frederick spared a glance to see Mr. Finch leaning over the railing. "I say, Lord Astley, do you need assistance?"

Frederick took hold of Miss Benetti's waist and pulled her to the surface. "Steady there." He kept his voice calm. "I've got you."

With another whimper and a few coughs, she relaxed against him, allowing him to guide her body through the water. Frederick turned his attention to the ferry. "Is there a ladder or something to help us board?"

The mainland emerged in front of them, nearing. Good.

"I have it," Grace called, returning in his view with a bundle in her arms.

"Get Finch to help steady the ladder."

Grace shook her head. "He's not here any longer, but the driver is on his way to help."

Hadn't Finch just been at the railing? Where had he gone?

With a little assistance from the ferryman, Grace secured the rope ladder over the edge.

Seconds, probably, minutes passed as Frederick brought the woman forward, the ladder became more secure, and finally they were able to touch rope.

"Here now, Miss Benetti." Frederick guided her cold, quivering fingers to the ladder. "Grasp here."

She shivered before fisting the rope in her hands and ever so slowly making her way back onto the ferry. Frederick followed suit, greeted at the top with a dry towel from his bride.

"Whatever happened?" Grace turned to Miss Benetti. "Surely you didn't jump because of your despair about Mr. Laraby, did you? There are much nobler reasons to die than for him."

Miss Benetti stared at Grace a moment, her porcelain brow crinkling before her expression cleared. "No, I did not jump. I was pushed."

Frederick met Grace's gaze. Pushed? By whom?

And why?

"Who pushed you?" Grace asked, rubbing the towel against the woman's arms.

"I do not know." The woman's chin wobbled, and she shook her head. "I came out to view the mainland as it appeared. I always do this because the city is such a beautiful place for my heart. A comfort with all that has happened." Her breaths shook with her voice. "And. . .and then as I leaned against the railing, someone came behind and pushed me over."

"You didn't see anyone?" Frederick stepped forward, searching her face. "Hear them? Anything?"

She shook her head, her dark hair unraveling into ebony tendrils around her face. Something about her at that moment triggered a memory or. . .a slight sense of familiarity. But how? Dark hair? Dark eyes? A childlike face?

"We need to tell Jack." Frederick turned to Grace. "I can't believe he isn't out here after such a commotion." Frederick started toward the enclosed side of the ferry. "We can incorporate the police more fully now that we are on the mainland."

But as they entered the enclosed portion of the ferry, they found the inspector on the ground at the opposite exit door. Frederick ran to him, searching for life. A consistent thrumming of a pulse brought a breath of relief.

Grace kneeled at his side. "Is he. . . ?"

"No, he's alive." Frederick examined the man. Blood mingled with the inspector's dark hair. "Someone must have attacked him."

"That's a mercy." Grace stood, looking around the inside of the ferry. "Where is everyone?"

The inside of the ferry was completely empty except for Frederick, Miss Benetti, and Grace. No sign of Jack, Mr. and Mrs. Reynolds, or Mr. Finch anywhere.

No one.

Frederick pushed to a stand, scanning the inside of the ferry, and rushed out, racing to the railing and looking back the way they'd come.

The tiniest hint of a motorboat in the distance was the only clue of anyone leaving their area. Frederick stared down at the water, the waves moving in slow, gentle undulations, nothing like the present pace of his heart.

Where was Jack?

And why would he disappear?

His gaze flicked back to the way the motorboat disappeared.

And who had driven the boat to meet the ferry?

Someone other than the Reynoldses and Finch was involved in this mystery, but who?

Chapter 18

Jack was missing.

The Reynoldses and Mr. Finch were missing.

Inspector Verga had been attacked, and Miss Benetti appeared to know nothing about any subterfuge at all.

What on earth was happening?

Grace stared out the window of their hotel, the sunset hues across the Grand Canal bowing to the deep purples of evening. Frederick had gone with the police to search the lagoon for any sign of Jack but to no avail.

The police had taken charge of Miss Benetti in order to question her and escort her to her home.

Frederick had left a half hour ago to secure transportation back to the island in the morning to look for Jack, and despite their desire to return immediately to the island, searching at night would prove less effective and much more dangerous, especially with murderers and possible man-nappers on the loose.

There was no doubt about murderers and man-nappers now. Because where Jack was concerned, one of the two was the only conclusion. Grace pressed her fist to her chest. She prayed for a man-napping over the alternative.

How had the Reynoldses and Mr. Finch managed to get away

with a man-napping right under their eyes? They would have heard the scuffle and motorboat, wouldn't they?

She drew in a breath. Not if they couldn't hear over the sound of Miss Benetti's screams when she'd fallen into the lagoon. Grace turned back to the room, all their evidence strewn across the nearby table. Someone had pushed Miss Benetti over the edge of the ferry to create a distraction in order to attack the inspector and man-nap Jack Miracle.

Heat fled her face. Unless they'd killed Jack and pushed him over into the canal after incapacitating the inspector. Grace's pulse took an upswing at the thought. She'd lost people to death before. She knew the pain of it. Her grandfather had been the hardest one of recent memory. But Jack?

No! Pushing the consideration from her mind, she approached the table, her gaze taking in what paper evidence they had. The photos of the paintings, the news clippings, and some notes she'd taken from their interviews and Jack's information. Could the murderers associated with the paintings be the same people who had stolen them from the gallery and Laraby? And which people? If the reported people in service were young, then could it have been Mrs. Reynolds?

She needed to sort things out.

Sitting at the table, she took out her notepad and pen.
What do we know?

1. Mrs. Reynolds is not Mrs. Reynolds.

She stared up at the ceiling. But then who is she? An art collector, as she confessed her husband to be? A former servant of the house?

2. Mr. Finch is likely not Mr. Finch, *and* he'd been on the scene of one of the *Juliet* murders. Which one?

Grace pulled out the article about Mrs. Chambers in Cumbria and reviewed it.

Mrs. Chambers. Now why was her name familiar? Something about Jack? Grace's eyes shot wide. Mrs. Chambers had been Jack's neighbor! Which meant Mr. Finch probably *knew* Jack and had made the recommendation to Zappa. But why recommend Jack? What could anyone possibly want from him? And why would *Finch*, a possible criminal, recommend Jack?

Grace shook her head and returned to her list.

3. Almost all the paintings were in a secret room in the villa, which means whoever stole the paintings knew the villa well enough to find the secret room. That suggests that the thieves have a much more personal connection to the paintings than being mere art collectors. Former servants? Friends? The lost grandchildren?

The only people close to the Accardi grandchildren's ages were Lydia and Paul. Perhaps Laraby, but he had a lineage with his grandfather, so he wouldn't fit. Lydia and Paul had known Laraby most of their lives, so it wasn't likely they were long-lost children, was it? Maybe Paul?

4. Who had access to the villa's secret room and could have been present to steal the painting when the ghost appeared? Anyone at or near the dining room.

She drew in a breath. Even if Jack was off being man-napped, she could use his methods like she'd done, somewhat successfully, in Egypt.

The MAP method. Method, ability, and purpose.

She scanned over the papers. Perhaps she should start with purpose. Who would have a reason to steal the paintings? Art enthusiasts, of course. Money seekers, especially with a reputed treasure. And children who not only had their family taken from them but their inheritance as well.

Method? Well, taking into account all the ways the individuals died, the murderers used various methods. Poison, early heart attack, pushing down stairs, drowning, and so on. And with the accounts of the people involved, the whole affair would require more than one person, as Jack and Frederick had thought. A man, for one, who could have passed as a footman and a woman to pass as a maid. Could Mrs. Reynolds have been the woman who pretended to be a maid? She wasn't old, but she certainly was not as young as the person described in the articles. The same could be said for Mr. Reynolds or Mr. Finch. The articles described a "young" man. How young was young?

She would describe Laraby, Paul, Jasmine, and Lydia as young. All a little older than she was, she'd guess. Some of Laraby's servants were young as well. Martina and Mr. Zappa along with a few others, and they all had service experience, at least currently.

But Laraby didn't seem to have any previous connections to Italy and had been acting much too carelessly to be the thief. Paul's history was ambiguous. Jasmine was Italian, so her connections were rather strong, and Lydia's mother was reportedly French, which is where the lost children were last seen with their governess, according to one of the articles.

Grace's attention fell on the news article with Mr. Finch. It was much too convenient for Mr. Finch to be one of the "staff" and appear in Italy where the final paintings were, not to mention his connection to Jack. So Mr. Finch must be involved somehow, but he was too old to be one of the lost children. Had he been one of the staff for Accardi fifteen years ago? That would allow him to have intimate knowledge of the house. That moved him directly into "ability" on the MAP method.

With the secret room and the murder histories, someone would have to either have been in or known about service in order to take jobs as maids and footmen in the houses where the murders took place. Who of their suspects had ever been in service? Besides current servants, such as Martina and Mr. Zappa, Grace didn't know, and since most people were pretending to be people they weren't, she really had no idea.

Her attention fell on one of the news headlines, one in English from Jack's resources: "Where Are the Accardi Children?"

She leaned closer and skimmed over the information. Ten and eight years old. The only remaining family of painter Luca Accardi. Last seen with their governess. Suspected to be in France.

She paused. Last seen with their governess?

Grace reread the last few sentences. French-Italian governess Beatrice Russo remained with the children through the devastating loss of their mother and grandmother. Only a few days after the double funeral, Accardi disappeared in pursuit of his son-in-law, leaving the two children at the villa. When Accardi and his son-in-law both turned up dead a month after the murders, presumably from a murder-suicide at the son-in-law's hands, police secured the villa and all of Accardi's assets.

But the governess and children had disappeared.

As Grace rifled through page after page, her gaze finally landed on a small photo of the villa and staff soon after the double murder. The children stood in the distance on the front steps of the villa next to what seemed to be Accardi to one side and a woman on the other, the black-and-white photo showing unclear faces.

Those children! The young girl's face, even though blurred, kept drawing Grace's attention back. What was it about her that seemed familiar? Large, dark eyes. Pale, innocent face.

Jasmine? Grace shook her head. No, not quite.

Grace pulled out her magnifying glass and peered close. How scared the children must have been! To lose everyone.

Except their governess.

Grace moved the magnifying glass to the woman. Grace had experienced her fair share of governesses. At one point, she thought to stop counting. And governesses held varied positions in fiction. From Jane Eyre's diligence to the devious Lucy Graham in *Lady Audley's Secret* to Emma's loving Miss Taylor or—Grace shivered—Henry James' unnamed governess in *Turning of the Screw*. Grace wasn't certain what sort of governess the Accardi children had from the undefined looks of the woman, but she didn't appear very old.

And her facial features reminded her of someone.

Grace squinted into the magnifying glass. Darker hair, from the looks of it. Not terribly tall. The shadow of the magnifying glass fell over the governess' head as Grace moved the glass around, and the shadow gave the woman's hair a larger look.

Grace blinked. If her hair had been curly. . .

Her fingers tightened on the magnifying glass handle. Perhaps add some unnatural eye shadow?

A lump started growing in Grace's throat as a chill started from her shoulders and skittered up her neck.

The Accardi governess would look a whole lot like the fake Mrs. Dolores Reynolds.

Pain throbbed through Jack's head, and he attempted to sift through thick thoughts to rise to consciousness.

Having experienced similar moments in his history as a detective, one thing he knew from the start. *Don't open your eyes too quickly unless the sound of gunfire is nearby.* Otherwise, it was best to pretend unconsciousness as one gathers one's wits and makes an assessment of his surroundings.

He pushed beyond the pain, grasping for clarity.

What was his last memory? Thoughts swirled through blackness.

He'd been on the ferry back to the mainland. Who had he been speaking to? Inspector Verga? Yes, they were discussing what had been found at the villa, including the paintings and Jack's own thoughts about who might be behind the robberies and murders. Someone struck Inspector Verga from behind, and before Jack could turn to defend himself, all went black.

He stifled a groan. How could he have committed such an amateurish blunder? He'd let his guard down while in an enclosed space with people who were likely part of this entire *Juliet* heist. His brain sifted through possibilities. Frederick and Grace had been outside, as he'd instructed them, in order to keep watch for anyone who may try to board or leave their ferry. Had they been hurt too?

His stomach swirled with a mixture of nausea and concern. Hopefully, they escaped a similar or worse fate.

He delved back into his murky memory. Who had been on the ferry with him? Had Mr. Finch been inside? He'd seemed to move in and out rather suspiciously. And Mr. and Mrs. Reynolds—they'd looked to be in a very intimate conversation in the back corner of the ferry.

An argument, perhaps? He had high doubts they were really married, even if they were arguing.

A movement at his back had him holding his breath, and he took inventory of his senses. He was sitting in what felt like a chair and not a sturdy one at that. His arms were bound behind him, and despite the hard chair back, his shoulders also abutted something else. Softer. The scent of sea and. . .lavender wavered in and out of his recognition.

Where on earth was he?

Without moving any other muscles, he slowly opened his eyes.

Faint light glowed from a lantern to his left, barely filling the vast space. Was he inside some sort of tower? Or cellar?

The room looked solid and cylindrical, without a window in sight. He breathed in a deep breath. Sea? Earth? Was he underground?

"Oh good. You're finally awake."

The female voice came from behind him, and the soft material at his back moved as she spoke. When he turned his head, a wealth of golden hair greeted him. Lavender and golden hair? His stomach tightened. Lydia Whitby?

"What. . .what is going on?" Was that his voice? He'd moved beyond his youthful voice well over a decade ago. Why had it suddenly returned?

"You're the detective. Haven't you worked it out?" came her quick reply. "We've been kidnapped."

He attempted to turn to take a better look at her, but his bonds wouldn't allow it, and the throbbing in his head didn't help. "Are you hurt?"

Quiet greeted his question before she answered. "They used chloroform on me, which means I have a nasty headache and have almost expelled my breakfast three times."

He winced.

"But otherwise, I am fine." She drew in a breath. "I wasn't conscious when they brought you in, but when I awoke, two people were in the room, talking. I'm sure they thought I was still unconscious."

Ah, smart woman. She already knew some solid sleuthing techniques. Did she have a history of kidnapping? Awaking from being knocked unconscious? And how was she so familiar with chloroform?

"I overheard them speaking about you and a ransom, so I put two and two together and assumed you were the person with whom I am temporarily shackled." The chair shook behind him, and her fingers hit his.

Ransom? And shackled together? His clearing head started digesting the information and the situation. Back-to-back in rickety chairs. He looked down. Tied by rope.

The questions about Miss Whitby's curious past would

have to wait.

"Do you mean to tell me, as an illusionist, you couldn't slip out of these ropes?"

A burst of air left her. Was it a laugh? Exasperation? "Special ropes and special knots are used, my dear detective, so I'm afraid you'll have to wait for another opportunity for me to be *your* rescuer."

He grinned and was particularly glad she couldn't see it. Verbal sparring with a woman didn't happen often for him, and the fun sort proved even rarer. A pleasant warmth branched through his chest, and his smile fell.

Attraction? He gave his head a shake. He didn't need to think of anyone in a romantic way with his sordid history, especially some American illusionist and possible thief. Heaven knew, his last romantic relationship had ended in shambles, with his heart more scarred than he imagined it could ever be.

A wife was supposed to be faithful. Remain. Yet, as soon as Jack's father lost his title, his wife left him for a titled man, filed for a divorce, and disappeared from his life in every way except memory.

"Why would whoever took us think they could hold you for ransom? A detective?" Her voice edged with humor. "Is business that good?"

"I don't know that it's ever been *that* good." Despite himself, his grin flared again. "Let's just say I have family I haven't offended beyond rescue."

This time she clearly chuckled, and the ache in his chest lessened just a little.

"And why are you shackled with me, Miss Whitby? A ransom also? Perhaps from Laraby?"

"With what money?" she scoffed. "No, I'm not quite certain why I'm here, but based on what I've learned today, I think it's because I'm the only other person besides John who knows where the final *Juliet* is. Well, except you and the Astleys, but our assailants didn't know that little detail."

"Could you make out anything from their voices?"

"If I was to hazard a few guesses, I'd say one was the infamous Mrs. Reynolds, though her accent became decidedly more French than she'd displayed for us. I think my English accent is better than hers."

"Is it?"

"I will not prove it, especially at the current moment, though I feel the acoustics in this place would make for excellent reverberation." She shifted again, sending another whiff of her hair in his direction. "Two others in the conversation were men. One may have been Mr. Finch, but the other? I'm not certain. Italian, though."

Italian? Did they have someone helping them who had remained behind the scenes? A native?

"So whoever has taken us needs you alive in case Laraby doesn't give them the information they want?"

"It's my only deduction, Detective. That happens to be your expertise over mine." Her hands jerked against his, shaking both their chairs. "But I'd rather not wait around to find out if Laraby told them or not, because the ending for me, in particular, won't be very happy. I don't have any rich relatives to buy my rescue."

Who would have known about his status? Or his relatives? What had Frederick and Grace just told them before they boarded the ferry? Mr. Finch had been in some photos at Mrs. Chambers' house after her death?

If that was the case, then Mr. Finch would have known of Jack's connections. And was likely the one who recommended Laraby call on Jack for the investigation.

A back-up plan in case the treasure fell through?

How clever.

He looked around the room again, the surroundings almost like a cellar. Tall stone walls on every side.

"Miss Whitby, I—"

"Lydia, won't you? I think since we're nearly holding hands as it is, Detective, we should be on a first-name basis."

Blast. There went his smile again.

Oh, he liked her. Too much. From the first time he took her in his arms after someone pushed past her in the hallway. Those eyes? The intelligence in her eyes?

He frowned. Hearts proved helpful in pumping blood through the body but not in staving a man's desire for love.

And what a relief that Miss. . .Lydia didn't break out into hysterics about their current situation. She kept her wits too. The world could do with a few more women like her.

He cleared his throat. "Our captors must have been in a hurry or else they would have checked my pockets. As it is, we are rather fortunate. My pocket knife is still safely housed in the right pocket of my trousers."

"Ah, so we can either deduce that our captors were in a hurry or not so clever. I prefer the latter for our sakes, don't you?" She shifted again, her hair tickling the back of his neck. "But I don't see how you can reach the knife and become the hero of the moment, Detective."

"You'll not call me Jack?"

She hesitated. "For some reason, Detective suits you better, but I'll think about it some more. In the meantime, while we wait for the inevitable, what about this daring rescue you're planning?"

"I believe, my dear Miss Whitby, you are going to have to prove the rescuer. Not me."

More silence. "How hard did they hit your head? I worked in the circus, not in performing miracles, though at the moment, I could usher up enough faith to try."

"I think we are a bit more likely to experience a practical miracle, if I may." He curbed his laugh. "Since my hands are tied behind my back, I have no way of reaching my knife, but perhaps *you* can."

"Me? Your knife?" She moved, almost as if she straightened. "You think?"

"I'm not certain, but you have a better chance than I do. And since they didn't tie our feet, I can raise my knees to see if it will help slide the knife closer to the entrance of the pocket." It was a very good thing she couldn't see him at the moment, because attempting to get his knees up while his hands were tied proved rather ridiculous.

Clever woman that she was, however, she took his cue.

Her left hand began moving at his back, then to his hip. Every fiber of his body became suddenly aware of her touch, so he pinched his eyes closed and focused on shifting his right hip closer toward her.

"Well, I certainly think you should call me Lydia now."

His body stiffened against a laugh. "Keep to the task at hand, my dear Miss Whitby."

"Ah, Miss Whitby, is it?" Her fingers pressed at the opening of his pocket.

"Under the circumstances, it seemed a proper boundary."

"How very gentlemanly of you, my dear detective." Her body shook with what he supposed was a laugh. "I can almost reach it." She ground out the words, her body likely tensed to the painful point and possibly as contorted as his own.

Her fingers slid deeper into his pocket, tickling the juncture of his hip and leg. He pinched his lips as tight as his eyes to keep from laughing or shifting away from her.

"I got it, Jack." The pressure on his hip disappeared. "Now, let me see if I can open it."

His muscles relaxed. "I believe I can help with that part." With their two pairs of hands moving over the knife, teamwork resulted in an open blade.

"You do realize that neither of us can see where I'm cutting, so I could possibly slice right through your hands." Her fingers prodded over his.

"I'll just have to take that chance, Miss Whitby."

"Hmm." She paused. "If you'll let out a yelp, that may be a good clue."

"I don't yelp, Miss Whitby." His grin spread wide. "Not even for you."

"No special favors for your fellow captive, huh?" Her movements stopped and restarted. "At least now I have an additional goal to rescuing us."

Jack thanked God once again that Miss Whitby couldn't see his expression.

In only a few minutes, she shifted. "Got it," she announced, and the ropes started shaking at his wrists until they loosened. Jack pushed the rope off his chest and turned to find Lydia standing, her pale blue dress stained and torn in various places and her hair completely undone about her shoulders.

He looked away and dusted at his jacket. "Excellent rescue."

"I call that mutual rescuing." She offered his knife back to him, her green eyes glittering.

He pulled his gaze from hers and immediately noticed a scrape across her forehead. "You *were* hurt." He gestured, and she raised a palm to her head.

"What do the heroes in books say, Detective?" Her grin crooked, and his chest tightened. "It's a mere flesh wound?"

His gaze lingered on her for a second longer, and he gave the room another look just to get his eyes off her face. She had a small nose to match her small chin, and sandwiched in the middle were a pair of perfect lips. He silenced a groan. Where on earth did that thought come from?

"Are we in a cellar?"

"I'm not sure, but I'd prove much more helpful if I could locate my glasses."

He turned back to her. "You dropped them?"

"I woke up without them." She frowned, scanning the shadowy floor.

The light glittered off something in the corner, and Jack reached down to retrieve them. From the dim view, he made out a few scratches.

"I'm afraid they're not as pristine as they once were." He offered them to her.

She raised them up toward the light and frowned. "Better than nothing, I suppose. At least they'll be more helpful than my natural eyes."

She placed them back on her little nose, their frames drawing his attention back to her eyes. A mesmerizing sort of green. She studied the space. "The cellar in the villa looks nothing like this. All white stone?"

"But there is the scent of sea and earth, suggesting we are somewhere underground near the coast." How did a woman manage to make even tangled hair attractive? Very unhelpful of her. Especially for *his* peace of mind.

Oblivious to his perusal, she stepped toward a column on the far side of the small room and disappeared around the other side of the pillar. "Well, well, what do we have here, Detective?"

Jack joined her on the other side of the pillar. A stone spiral staircase led down into darkness. "Down isn't my preference, but out is." He stepped back into their confined room, taking inventory of any other options. "I believe this is our only alternative, so perhaps we should take advantage of it?" He took the lantern off the hook on the wall. "What do you say, Miss Whitby?"

"As opposed to waiting around for our rather unwelcome hosts?" She offered a smile and started down the stairs. He followed close, holding the lantern aloft to shine before her.

"I just wanted you to know that I didn't have anything to do with the stolen paintings."

Her confession echoed up through the stairwell.

"I didn't want you supposing that since I am responsible for our ghost, I had some other, what would you English say, dodgy plans?"

"Dodgy? Yes." His smile spread again, and his gaze, despite himself, fell on the way her loose hair spilled down her back. He cleared his tightening throat again. "Though I don't suppose creating ghosts is of vital importance to managing Mr. Laraby's finances."

She paused on the step and looked up at him, the lantern light haloing her face. "I've always been good with planning and numbers." She continued the walk, the stairs ending in a narrow corridor. "But when the late Mr. Walker took me in hand to teach me about his business, he seemed to recognize my gift for managing things. Overcoming problems." She chuckled. "I suppose it's a little like solving mysteries and crimes, except less. . .life-threatening."

The sentence lodged in his mind somewhere, and he wasn't certain why. "Except for now, of course."

"I think this situation is unique for most secretaries, don't you?"

"Perhaps, but I know very few secretaries who were former circus performers, so you may prove a breed apart, Miss Whitby."

"Of that, Detective, I am certain."

He adjusted his hold on the lantern, keeping his other palm against the earthen wall. "I hate to disappoint you, but I only suspected you for a short period of the investigation."

"How very disappointing." The smile in her response inspired his own. "Dressing up as a footman and then creating a ghost wasn't proof enough of my villainy?"

A small glint of daylight shone in front of them, ushering forward the sound of—the sea?

"I am not in doubt of your *ability* to be villainous, Miss Whitby, but I do doubt your heart to be villainous."

Lydia turned back toward him, studying him before resuming her descent. "Or I am a very good actress who is leading you to your doom, which would be very villainous of me."

"If you are this good of an actress, Miss Whitby, and did not slice my wrists when you had the chance, then my doom is deserved."

Her footsteps faltered for a second before she continued. "I was incredibly tempted to hear your yelp, Detective."

The path turned again, and the light before them suddenly opened up to reveal a spectacular site. They stepped out onto a rocky outcropping with waves rushing up to crash against their perch. Mists from the water salted the air around them, but the most spectacular view surrounded them. They'd stepped out into a massive cavern with towering cave openings on three sides. The fourth side revealed open water.

The mouth of one cave resembled a massive oak. The next had the faint look of a heart. And the third was a double cave with a large rock jutting out between the two openings like the head of a bird. Each cave entrance nearly touched the water's edge, and a boat poised right outside the double cave.

"Where are we?"

Before he could answer, someone called out not far from them. Jack pulled Lydia back against him and into the tunnel they'd just left. She pressed close for the briefest moment, sheltered by him, her body fitted quite perfectly against his chest. It had been so long since he'd held a woman this close, and something about the woman in question being Miss Whitby rattled his nicely controlled emotions.

He liked her. More than he ought.

"Who was that?"

He looked down at her face, pushing through his brain to find an answer. "I believe, Miss Whitby, those would be the people looking for Accardi's treasure."

Chapter 19

The lagoon offered no clues to Jack's whereabouts as Grace and Frederick headed toward the island. No sign of him in the murky water, thank God. So Frederick chose to view the lack of evidence in a hopeful light. Perhaps Jack hadn't been killed and tossed overboard. But where on earth could he be, and why would he disappear?

With Inspector Verga rendered unconscious, all evidence pointed to Jack being taken. But why? What could the thieves or murderers want with Jack alive?

Grace's discovery that the governess bore a striking resemblance to Mrs. Reynolds started a series of possibilities that began to click the mystery into place. If Mrs. Reynolds was the former governess and if she was the one who had had the children all this time, then she would know about the secret room. She'd also likely know about the puzzle in the paintings, but whether she knew the cipher or not was yet to be seen.

From what Frederick gathered in the articles, the children had lost everything, so wouldn't it make sense for them to want to find a way to lay claim to their grandfather's treasure—*their* inheritance? But to cause such death in their wake? And if Mrs. Reynolds was the governess, which of their suspects would end up being the lost granddaughter and grandson?

"It might be Martina," Grace suggested, looking out toward the island as it slowly grew closer. The house towered above them from its cliffside perch, the gardens slowly coming into view along the right. "It's often the unassuming ones that make the best murderesses in fiction."

"Both Miss Whitby and Miss Benetti fit the part as well." Frederick gripped the railing, his thoughts sifting for something, anything to give them more clues. To prepare them. "Not to mention a few of the other staff."

"But we left Miss Benetti in Venice with her mother. Wouldn't she have disappeared with the rest of the suspects?"

Frederick nodded his agreement. "True."

"And what of the grandson?" Grace tapped her gloved finger against her chin. "Paul? If he truly was an orphan, the scenario and age could fit."

"But unless Laraby and Miss Whitby are both part of the mystery, they would have called Paul out on his lies." The dock of the island came into view.

Frederick glanced behind him, placing his palm over the revolver at his waist. Inspector Verga had promised to send policemen once they did a final sweep of the waters around the place where Jack had vanished. "If this case is about the grandchildren, which it appears to be, then they've planned this for years. At least two years, when the first paintings were stolen."

"And they'll have no qualms with killing us." Grace's gaze met his. "They'll be desperate to fulfill their long-awaited plans." Despite the foreboding in her words, her lips quivered into a tiny smile. "This all sounds very much like a novel, my dear Frederick. I know it's very real and dangerous and we'll possibly die, but don't you feel the tiniest thrill in it all?"

"I feel certain there would be a much bigger thrill"—his arm came around her waist and pulled her to him—"if I wasn't terrified at something horrible happening to you."

She rested her head against his shoulder, squeezing him close. "God knows we've come back to find our friend, but we also have the real opportunity to bring an end to a very long string of wrongs. And God is the great wrong breaker, so He would certainly support our desire." She looked up at him, her beloved gaze grazing his face. "There's something you've taught me in the middle of all my nightmares. Or I suppose, God taught me through you."

His throat tightened. "And what is that?"

"When you spoke about God holding us no matter where we are." Her brow pinched then released, as if giving the thought over. "That means in life *and* death. Both of them. That we're held each step of the way from this world to the next by a loving Father. And His hold is not uncertain."

He nodded, accepting the realization again and again. Reminding his heart of it over and over. Not for himself but for this darling gift God had given him in his wife. It was a truth Frederick had to repeat so his head would remind his heart to trust and so the trust could move into peace. "All the days ordained for you were written in His book before one came to be."

Grace's eyes lit. "Is that poetry?"

"Yes, but specifically a paraphrase from a psalm. One I just read yesterday, and the verse stood out to me."

"The book part?" Her eyes deepened with the spread of her smile as she teased him from his worry.

"As strange as it is to me now, when before I've been so angry at the brokenness of my life, I find comfort in the knowledge that each day we are here is not a random act of life but a deliberate plan on God's part to work in us and through us. To serve and trust and love Him."

"And then, when we have fulfilled all the plans *He* has written for our lives here, He takes us home." A glossy sheen covered Grace's eyes, but her smile never faded. "His book must be a wonderful read, because all the endings for His children are going to be happy ones."

His grin tipped. "I feel certain it is one of the very best endings of all books in the world."

"Or beginnings, if we think about it."

He brushed a kiss against her cheek, the island now in full view. "He's written your days and mine, darling Grace. And even if He must pull my worry about you from my fisted hands, I must trust you to *His* story for your life."

"And I you." She leaned close, searching his face. "But I have every faith God has a few chapters still written for us here on this earth, my dear Lord Astley. You are due an heir, and I'm far too impulsive to be fit for heaven just yet."

He chuckled, and even as the ache around his heart grew, he gave her a quick kiss when the ferry pulled into the dock.

"Be on your guard," he murmured against her hair before releasing her and walking to disembark. Frederick paid the ferryman an additional sum to keep him docked on the island for the rest of the day. At least, they'd know a ride to the mainland would be prepared for them as soon as they'd have need.

A carriage took them up the long drive and deposited them at the front door, just like it had a few days before when they'd first arrived. But much had changed since then. Dangerously changed.

No one greeted them at the door, which wasn't uncommon with Laraby's relaxed lifestyle. It wouldn't surprise Frederick if the man gave a house key to his guests and let them arrive or leave as they liked, but as soon as they entered the grand foyer, the uneasiness in his stomach magnified exponentially.

"It's a rather different feeling being here when the house is relatively empty," Grace whispered, her pale blue day dress complementing the pristine white-and-gold surroundings. She held her dangerous parasol in one hand, her satchel slung over her shoulder. Ah yes. She'd come prepared for danger.

He sighed and released another hold on his pretense of control.

"Let's try Laraby's study first." Frederick held out his arm to her. "At least then we can enlist his help in trying to find Jack."

They made their way to the second floor, not a soul meeting them along the corridors. Even their steps sounded too loud for the cavernous silence. Had Laraby dismissed his servants? Were they all below stairs?

Laraby's study door stood ajar. Frederick eased Grace behind him with one hand and placed his hand on his revolver with the other as they approached the threshold of the room.

"Laraby?" Frederick's voice sounded too loud in the silence.

No response came from the room.

Frederick nudged the door wider with his shoe. The hinges creaked with the widening door, revealing an empty room.

"Frederick." His whispered name sounded tense on Grace's lips. "Is. . .is someone at the desk?"

Frederick's attention shifted back to the desk by the window, focusing on the occupied desk chair. Someone sat slumped against the desk, nothing but a sandy mane of hair visible to identify the occupant. Grace's arm tightened around his as they neared the unmoving man.

"Laraby?" Frederick repeated.

Grace left Frederick's side and rounded the desk, placing a palm to Laraby's shoulder. "Mr. Laraby? Are you well?"

The body slumped to the side, and Laraby's head turned toward them, revealing wide unseeing eyes and a knife protruding from the man's neck. Grace gasped and stepped back. "We're too late for him." She moved back to touch the unfortunate man's face, and Frederick wondered at his wife's actions.

"He's still slightly warm, Frederick." She looked up at him. "He can't have been dead long."

For a second, he stared at his bride and replayed her actions. He should feel somewhat concerned at the ease with which she not only responded to a dead body but also made assessments. But of course, what she hadn't learned from her rich fictional world, the real world may have provided, especially with the help of her intrepid grandfather—and the bizarre events of their first four months of marriage.

"Which means whoever killed him may still be close."

"He was writing something." She tugged the paper from the desk and frowned down at it. "In fiction, the letters usually trail off into indistinguishable drivel, but his penmanship and content seem perfectly intact for a man getting ready to be murdered. Look."

It took a moment longer to digest Grace's words paired with her rather nonchalant demeanor, but he took the paper. The letter wasn't addressed to anyone but was written in familiar style.

You won't believe it, but the legend is real. There is a code in the paintings that leads to some treasure left by Accardi to his grandchildren. I overheard two of the servants talking about it only an hour ago. Evidently, they hadn't discovered the third clue but had enough to go on for a search to start. I mean to join them secretly. If there's a treasure to be found on my property, it could solve all my financial troubles. I would have told you in person, but I can't seem to find you.

It sounds as if the servants are headed to the caves now. I mean to find Paul and take him with me.

What a look you'll have on your face when you read this!

"Two servants?" Frederick looked up at Grace.

She shrugged. "You know my immediate answer to any

potentially dangerous servant."

He almost smiled at her wide-eyed response. "The butler?"

"I'm only saying that he's chosen quite regularly in fiction for a reason." She raised a finger as if making a point. "And he was nowhere to be seen when we entered."

"But Mr. Laraby's expectations of his servants were more relaxed than we're used to in England, darling." He placed the paper back on the desk. "However, Mr. Zappa would have more access to information and people than most in the villa."

"And servants are known for being invisible, so he could sneak around well if not better than I when we visited my grandmother's house." Grace visibly shivered. "Her hearing was supernatural."

Frederick decided not to ask for clarification on this grand-mother or the reason for Grace's sneaking. "None of the evidence has pointed to Zappa so far, but at the moment, anyone is suspect."

"Then it sounds as if we need to find the treasure in order to solve the mystery." Her grin brimmed. "That sentence was positively delightful to say aloud."

"And I have a feeling if we find the treasure, we'll find Jack."

"You think?" Her smile faded into a frown. "Alive?"

"I hope." Frederick gave the room another look, and this time something caught his attention. He moved toward it. "Grace, it's the final painting." The oil sat poised on a table, papers scattered beneath it as if someone left in a hurry. And the map they'd seen in the secret room lay to one side. "Wasn't this displayed in Laraby's secret room?"

"Someone's brought it here?" She followed, reaching into her satchel as she neared. "Either Laraby or the criminals." She drew out her magnifying glass and leaned near the painting. "Yes, this one has the letters too." She turned to look up at him, the magnifying glass still directed over one eye. "Our third clue, Frederick."

He'd already gotten a pen to give to her in anticipation of the last cipher. She lowered the magnifying glass and thanked him with one of her disarming smiles. "Look how well we're starting to understand one another. It's as if we were made for this very adventure together."

Despite the gut-wrenching idea of more "adventures" such as these with her, he knew there was nowhere else he'd rather be. Even if it meant. . .this.

"Oh, this is a rather long one." She began placing letters on one of the loose papers on the table.

He leaned close, reading as she wrote and then reversing the letters. *Sotto l'ala sinistra della pietra.*

"Under the left wing of the stone." He reread it. "Stones are everywhere here and have no wings."

"But what if we move things around," she breathed, her voice shaking with excitement. "What do we have so far? Beneath the feet of the gods, sparrow, and under the left wing of the stone. . ."

His mind made the calculations. "An easy switch would make a sentence." He completed. "Under the left wing of the stone sparrow."

"But what does it mean?"

Frederick's attention moved over the papers to land on the map. Hadn't he seen something on the map about a sparrow? He took the parchment and placed it out on the table, finding his mark. "Sparrow's Roost. Here."

"And the left wing?" She moved her finger over the spot.

"I don't know, but everything points to this."

She nodded, looking over the papers and map. "They left all of their papers here within easy access to anyone. It seems rather careless with such secrets. Why would they do that?"

"Because they don't mean to return." His gaze met hers. "And if they've found everything they want, they won't need any captives or witnesses."

Her eyes widened. "You mean, you think they may have Jack as a captive."

"There's a reason they took him and didn't leave him dead or wounded like the inspector. There has to be." Frederick stepped back and looked toward the windows, the garden, and the cliff edge just beyond. "I'm going to take the path to the caves to see if I can find Jack."

"Excellent." She gripped her parasol and started for the door, but he caught her by the arm.

"I need you to stay here. Find a servant who can phone the police. If Jack returns to the villa, one of us needs to be ready to share what we've uncovered." He sent another look to Laraby's body and swallowed through his tightening voice. "Though you may be safer with me."

"We need police help, I believe, especially if Jack is in even more danger than we are." She nodded. "If you'll leave a note with the Italian translation of how to ask for help to call the police, I'll go to the kitchens and see who I can find. "

He hesitated, searching her face. "Perhaps I should wait."

"Frederick, we've already lost an entire night without Jack. If these people are reckless and desperate enough to leave the precious paintings behind, then if Jack is still alive, he won't be for long." She took his hand in hers. "You *have* to go."

"Grace." The word pressed low, almost a plea. God, help him.

"Just don't try anything too dangerous unless you know it could help Jack." She studied his face, a smile almost surfacing. "And come back to me."

"Promise me." He squeezed her hand. "No unnecessary danger."

"Unless it can help Jack."

He held her gaze, tilting his head to show his displeasure at the thought of her taking extra risks.

"You're going to have to trust that I'll be all right, just as I'm going to have to trust God to take care of you." Her gaze bore into his. "Either way, Frederick, ultimately we will be all right."

Grace wished she'd gone with Frederick as soon as he left her at the bottom of the stairs. The large villa swelled into cavernous silence around her. Thankfully, she'd found the cook, who, after Grace had almost attacked her with her parasol—and then apologized profusely—agreed to phone the police.

As Grace topped the servants' stairs to the main part of the house again, a strange sound drew her attention toward the hallway that led to the Accardi rooms. Grace looked down the hall, shadow and light making a strange chessboard across the carpet to the veranda door. The sound came again. A thumping noise.

Then she heard a muffled call, like a cry for help.

She pinched the parasol tight, her breathing becoming shallow. It could be a trap, but that didn't make any sense if all the players had gone to the caves. She moved a step toward the hall. Women had a longstanding history, though mostly covertly, of being spies and detectives. Grace swallowed through her tight throat and took another step. Kate Warne helped the Pinkertons save President Lincoln, and hadn't Grace read a few years ago about a female detective in Chicago by the name of Strayer? She took another step. And London's own Maude West, the mistress of disguise. Or Isabelle Goodwin, New York's very first female detective.

Those were real women. Not fictional ones. Actual detectives.

Likely they'd been placed in dangerous positions and had to make a choice between what seemed logical and what might end up killing them.

The thumping continued, and the muffled voice began to take shape as having a male timbre.

Could it be Jack? She increased her pace, her parasol in one hand and her fingers at her chest, ready to secure her knife. The sounds intensified as she stepped into the room with the bookshelf and hidden closet. Soft sunlight filtered through light clouds to illuminate the room in a gray hue.

She paused, listening into the sudden silence. Where should she look next? A glance behind her proved she was still alone—except for whoever was making the noises. An anticipatory chill worked its way up her spine. Unless Signora Accardi had decided to come back and take vengeance on all the people who were doing very unkind things in her lovely house.

Grace squeezed her eyes closed. There were no such things as ghosts.

She nodded. But if there were, Signora Accardi would certainly approve of Grace trying to stop murderers, since she had died so horribly at the hands of one.

Another thump nearly sent Grace yelping like a frightened puppy. The sound came from the adjoining room, the one where she'd been assaulted. She peered into the room to find it empty, yet the thumping continued.

Maybe Signora Accardi *had* returned, though in most stories, ghosts made themselves visible, else the author would never be able to describe them so well.

"Jack?" Grace whispered because addressing Signora Accardi just seemed to go against everything she truly believed. Not what she pretended to believe, however.

A sudden burst of muffled cries responded. She could make them out. "Help. I'm in here."

The calls came from the back corner of the room, from the exact chest in which she'd been deposited by her attacker. Rushing forward, Grace drew a hairpin from her head. "Just a moment."

The muffling paused before the sound of sobbing followed. "Please, get me out. Please."

An American? And a male? Grace shook her head. What American would be stuck in a chest in the Accardi family's old rooms? She thought for certain she'd be the only one. Or maybe this particular attacker didn't like Americans.

The lock clicked, and the chest lid flew wide to reveal a rather sweaty, sobbing, and badly beaten Paul Hopewell.

"What on earth happened to you?" She offered her hand and pulled him from the chest.

He moaned as he accepted her assistance. One of his eyes was purple and swollen closed. Dried blood patched a corner of his mouth, and a nasty-looking bluish knot was developing on one side of his forehead. He wrapped his free arm around his chest, wincing as he stepped from the crate and then nearly falling to the floor.

"I. . .I think I have some broken ribs."

Grace wrapped her arm around his back and led him, limping, to a nearby chair. "Who did this to you?"

He groaned as he relaxed down into the chair, his one good eye swirling with tears. "I didn't know. I swear it. I didn't."

She pulled a handkerchief from her bag and started dabbing at the blood on his face. "What do you mean? Do you know where Jack is?"

"You have to believe me. I only did it for the money." He looked at her, his already pale face blanching even more. "Well, I mean, I thought she really cared for me, and so I had this romantic notion I'd get the money and the girl in the end."

"I don't understand."

"She caught my eye from the first day, and when she asked me to help them steal the paintings, I thought. . ." His jaw tensed. "I thought Daniel had made a mess of his finances and treated me and Lydia like we were slaves to him because he'd raised us out of our circus life to his rich world, but living with him was worse than the circus. He lorded his money over us. I. . .I wanted out of it all. She offered a chance, or so I thought."

"Well, we know you didn't get hurt when you *supposedly* were hit in the head at dinner."

"No." He shook his head, his frown deepening. "I was told to create a diversion."

"And what else?"

He lowered his gaze. "Keep Miss Benetti occupied and provide any information from Laraby about the last paintings that I could."

"And you did all that?" She offered him the handkerchief.

"I did." He hung his head. "To my shame, I did. I should have known they weren't to be trusted."

"Who?" Grace leaned forward. "Miss Benetti? The Reynoldses?"

"No, I mean, I don't know about the Reynoldses. They were odd ones." His brow wrinkled. "And Miss Benetti, well, I think she must have been as much a pawn in all this as I was. I was instructed to get close to her so I could steal her keys to the gallery."

So Jasmine wasn't a part of any of this? Had she been pushed off the ferry to create a diversion so that Mr. and Mrs. Reynolds could disappear with Jack?

"But I told them I wouldn't hurt anyone. Even when they wanted me to help them kidnap the detective. I didn't know they had plans to hurt people."

"They kidnapped Jack?" Grace grabbed his arm. "Where is he?"

"I—I don't know." Paul shook his head. "They said something about how they'd always planned to use him for ransom if they didn't find the treasure. And then, when I found out they'd taken him yesterday, all Lucia told me was that he had been placed in a safe place with the gods."

"Lucia?" With a head wound, perhaps Paul hadn't gotten the names right.

"Lucia." He sighed. "But she'd been in disguise as a servant in the house."

"The lost granddaughter?" Grace whispered, the previous chill now sweeping up her neck to her scalp. Everything began to come together in Grace's mind. The dark eyes. The innocent face. "Martina?"

He nodded. "I didn't mean for anything bad to happen, but after last night, when I wouldn't help with Jack, well, her brother dragged me into this room and just started beating me." His voice tightened, almost a cry. "He would probably have killed me if Martina hadn't shown up. I—I don't think she wanted me dead."

"Just locked in a trunk until who knows when?" Grace rose. "We need to get you to a doctor. Do you think you can walk as far as the sitting room?"

"I think so." With Grace's help, he stood. "Just rather slowly."

"Paul, who is this brother?"

A sound like a caught kitten escaped the man's throat, and Grace looked up at him, but he wasn't focused on her. She followed his wide-eyed expression across the room.

In the doorway, knife in hand and scowl in place, stood the rather menacing figure of Mr. Zappa, the butler.

And the first thing Grace thought, as her heart began pounding in her ears and she tightened her grip on her parasol, was that her beloved fiction proved right yet again.

The butler was responsible after all!

Chapter 20

"Who is it?"

Lydia Whitby's nearness kept muddling Jack's thinking, likely from her scent. And maybe those confounded eyes of hers. It had nothing to do with the fact he'd just been tied back-to-back with her and she'd proven impressively resourceful with a plan. . .and a knife.

He stepped back. "I have a few people in mind but didn't have a chance to see the author of that voice. A man, certainly."

She nodded, studying his face. "So how do you propose moving forward?"

"Exactly that." He gestured toward the caves. "Forward."

"Without a weapon or a plan?" She raised a golden brow. "Is this how you usually operate, Detective?"

Despite every ounce of his common sense yammering for distance, his grin took flight all on its own, carrying away his good intentions with it. "I find, Miss Whitby, that my plans rarely go as planned, and I've had to make do without a weapon before. Though"—he gave his brows a shake—"I do still have my knife."

She surveyed him, taking her time, her gaze roaming from the tip of his head to the toes of his rather scuffed shoes. Heat rose into his face. Clearly not from her thorough perusal. Likely from the unseemly scuffs.

He stood up a bit taller and patted down his unruly hair.

She opened her mouth to say something, and a noise in the tunnel from which they'd come pulled his attention in that direction. Someone was coming and quickly. He tugged her against him again and spun around the edge of the rock facing, hoping the crevice in which he'd drawn them proved enough to keep them hidden.

Heaven help him, he liked her fit against him much too well for his own good. Blast the woman! It was likely nothing more than a long-held abstinence from any romantic ventures, but his brain seemed to push back against that very rational argument.

A figure ran past, smaller than any of the men he'd expected. He peered around the rock to see a young woman making her way along the lagoon's edge to the double cave.

Lydia gasped, and he immediately covered her mouth with his palm, meeting her gaze and giving his head a small shake. A fire lit in her eyes but then dimmed, those large emerald orbs staring back at him as if searching for something he didn't have to give.

Or did he? Her lips warmed his palm, her body pressed against his, and for the first time in two years, he had the undeniable urge to replace his hand with his lips.

He'd been so certain that particular part of his heart had been annihilated beyond repair after his wife's ultimate betrayal and desertion. That the desire for romance and lifelong partnership had been squelched into nothingness by her thorough bashing of every tender affection he held toward attraction and commitment. But here and now, in an incredibly inconvenient place and time, he discovered his heart was quite prepared to fall readily for a pair of green eyes, golden locks, and a fiery personality.

Emotions were terribly troublesome things.

"I beg your pardon," he whispered, sliding his hand from her mouth.

She stared at him a moment longer in silence and then looked away. "That was Martina, the maid." Her whisper came faltering.

He followed her gaze, the idea of the young woman's involvement not fitting into his predictions at all. He'd suspected Jasmine. She seemed the high-strung sort. At one point, he'd even thought Lydia to be the culprit. She'd certainly proven fiery and intelligent enough for the blame.

But the quiet, unassuming Martina? "I would wager that is not her real name any more than she is truly a maid."

Lydia's attention swung back to him, imploring.

"I believe Martina is none other than Lucia Bartoli, Luca Accardi's granddaughter."

"The lost granddaughter?" She turned back toward the disappearing form. "Then she's after the treasure?"

"And I'm afraid she and whoever is helping her have been the instigators in a string of murders across Europe. All associated with gaining *The Juliets* in order to find this reputed treasure." He realized he still held her close and instantly let go of her. "Now if you'll find a way up to the villa and bring help, that would be an excellent use of your time."

"And leave all the adventure hunting to you?" She caught his arm as he made to move toward the cave. "That's not very gentlemanly of you at all, Detective."

He stared hard at her. Was she serious? "Miss Whitby, this is no circus game."

"Don't underestimate what a woman can learn in the circus, Detective." Her smile fell. "Nor what she can survive." She blinked and drew in a breath, as if regaining her focus. "By the time I go for help, you'll either have lost your villains or be dead. You can't expect me to miss out on that sort of fun now that I'm in the thick of it, can you?"

He raised a brow, every bit of doubt urging him to turn her

back toward the surface. Yet how on earth could he ever get her to comply?

"Don't waste time thinking up another excuse to get me out of your way." She nudged him forward. "Two heads are better than one anyway."

"Depends on the internal makeup of those two heads, I should think," he shot back, rolling his gaze heavenward and praying she'd change her mind.

"True, so it's even better that I'm coming along."

He glared over his shoulder only to be met with her grin, and somehow the power of that twinkle in her eyes started an infernal smile of his own. She was horrible for him. He wasn't supposed to be thinking of whatever this was while trying to stop murderers. With a groan, he turned back toward the caves, Lydia on his heels.

Voices rose from the entrance. Arguing.

"Did you notice the tide is rising?" Lydia whispered behind him.

He looked down at the cave entrance. Sure enough, the water appeared to be farther up on the rocks at the entrance. Well, they just needed to get in, locate the culprits, and without drawing attention to themselves, follow the villains out when they left. At least in this case, since he had no weapons or ability to capture the thieves, he'd be able to describe them to the police.

The cave split in two at the entrance, and Jack paused to listen. The voices bounced off the walls, not giving clarity as to their exact direction.

"Left?" He turned enough to see her in his periphery. Why was he asking her opinion? She wasn't his partner. She wasn't even in any sort of detective work. She was an illusionist-turned-secretary, for heaven's sake.

"I think so too."

Her assurance bolstered his confidence in a way working solo rarely did.

"Stay close," he whispered back to her.

"How else will I keep you safe if I don't?" came her immediate response.

He ground a chuckle into submission.

"I heard that," she whispered. "But I can't sort out whether it was a laugh or a scoff."

He refused to abate her curiosity. American charm rarely tempted him. . .but she did. "Are you always this cavalier, or does the attitude rise to the surface in life-threatening situations alone?"

"The company might have something to do with it."

"Ah, dashing and intelligent men sharpen your tongue and wit?" He took another step forward, remaining carefully behind the jutted stones along the path.

"Or put me on my guard."

He looked back at her, catching a flicker of caution in her eyes before her expression turned playful again. The caution he understood to his soul.

"No reason to keep the mood as dark as the circumstances," she continued, her lips crooking a little.

"Exactly." He steadied his gaze on hers, looking for further meaning behind her expression, her words. "Sober-minded but lighthearted it is, then."

A glint lit her eyes and somehow ignited an unused spark in his chest.

"Excellent life motto, Detective."

He pulled his gaze from hers, his jaw tightening. God, help him! He needed to focus on the task at hand, not the woman so near.

They drew closer to the voices, all the while Lydia keeping close to his back. The sounds took shape, their conversation coming in partial Italian and English. Jack knew enough Italian to get the gist of the conversation and peered around the edge of the rock to find Mrs. Reynolds removing something from an old chest—the type of old chest Jack had envisioned when he was a lad and pretended to be a pirate. Mr. Finch stood nearby, assisting Mrs. Reynolds.

He blinked. Was this real?

From the lantern light on either side of the chest, he made out glittering coins. Gold. They were removing gold coins from a chest like something from *Treasure Island*. The chest wasn't particularly large but full and brimming with wealth enough to see the three of them rich for the rest of their lives.

They were placing the coins into smaller cloth bags, likely to lessen the weight for carrying. How Accardi had gotten so many coins, Jack had no idea. Family inheritance? The right connections? Accardi's own machinations? But such coins would prove the best sort of thing to store in such a damp place.

"I don't understand why you had him killed." Martina...er...Lucia stood nearby, watching the couple work. "He did nothing wrong, just like the ones before."

"Laraby was a loose end, Lucia," Mrs. Reynolds responded, turning her back as she continued shoveling the coins into bags. "Don't allow your soft heart to steal more of your inheritance than time already has."

Laraby? Jack looked over at Lydia, whose brow pinched. She shook her head and looked up at him, eyes growing glossy as she did. They may not have been close the past year, but he had still been her friend. A dear friend once.

He placed a palm on her arm, showing comfort he could not voice in the moment. The fact they'd killed Laraby didn't surprise him much, but it meant the masterminds behind all this were getting either sloppy or desperate. Maybe both. He pulled his knife from his pocket and turned back to the conversation at hand.

"You have killed so much that it doesn't matter to you anymore. My grandfather would have grieved over what we've done to gain this."

"Grieved?" Mrs. Reynolds turned on Lucia, her gaze alight, her face flushed. "I saw grief in his face. I saw hatred in his eyes when he came home to find two of his loves dead. And he made me promise, promise upon my soul, to make sure you and your brother would be taken care of. That you would claim your inheritance. And I will do it. My soul will be free."

"What about their souls?"

The woman almost hissed at the younger girl. "We will not have this argument again! Do you want to go back to living off crumbs when you were born in the Accardi family? I have brought you this far, to this moment, and I will not lead you astray."

This proved Mrs. Reynolds had to be the governess— Beatrice. He couldn't remember her last name. Mr. Finch and Mr. Reynolds were likely collected along the way for the promise of a piece of the treasure or had also been Accardi staff.

"Help us, Lucia," Mr. Finch ordered. "We haven't much time before the tide comes in."

Jack noticed the waves seeping up over the lip of the low-lying cave entrance and spilling into the passageway. Did the cave fill with water? How long did they have?

"Then we'll just return tomorrow," Lucia countered.

"The police are onto us, Lucia," Mrs. Reynolds said. "This may be our only opportunity."

Lucia slowly began helping them. With the trio so involved in their task, Jack wondered if he and Lydia had a chance to subdue them. Mrs. Reynolds and Mr. Finch appeared to be the real danger.

Jack turned back to Lydia to give her a clue as to his plan only to see Mr. Reynolds entering the cave, his pistol raised and aimed directly at them. Jack grabbed Lydia in his arms and turned his body to shield her, attempting to dodge the bullet's trajectory.

The gun fired. Pain sliced through Jack's side as he and Lydia slammed against the ground.

"It's that detective," Mr. Reynolds called to the others. "They've found us, but I winged him."

Lydia lay beneath him, her gaze dropping toward the direction of his wounded side then raising back to his face.

"No worries. I can finish them off. There's only two of them."

They had to do something. They were sitting ducks, and Jack wouldn't allow them to go down without a solid fight. What skills did he have at his disposal? What skills did Lydia possess?

"Two?" came Mrs. Reynolds' voice. "Who else?"

"My knife," Jack murmured, holding her gaze. "Do you know how to throw knives?"

She stiffened to attention, her gaze never leaving his. "Yes."

"Laraby's secretary. The blond lady."

Without another word, Lydia reached between them, her hand slipping back into his pocket and slowly removing the knife.

"On the count of three." He adjusted so his palm steadied his body and gave her space to open the knife.

"Finish them off, then," demanded Mr. Finch.

"One, two, three."

He rolled to the side, while Lydia rose to a sitting position and threw the knife. With expert precision, the blade struck the center of Mr. Reynolds' chest, shocking the man back a step, eyes wide. He looked down at the knife and back at Lydia before his knees gave way and he fell to the rocky floor, dropping his pistol as he did.

It slid just out of reach.

"Get him."

Another gunshot sounded close. Jack glanced back to see Lydia drop to the ground. Had she been hit?

No! He spun back toward their assailant only to come face-to-face with Mr. Finch, readied for another shot.

Mr. Zappa! Of course!

He was the lost Accardi grandson! No wonder the little boy in the photo had looked familiar to her.

"I didn't want to have to hurt you, Countess." Mr. Zappa's accent, now free to express itself, curled over his words. "I was only going to kill Laraby and Hopewell, but now you know too much."

Grace pinched her parasol close to her side, waiting to parry his attack with the knife. "You could always just put me in the chest like you did last time."

He grinned and moved to the right. She paralleled his movements. "But I do not think you would just let me kill Hopewell, would you?" His gaze gleamed, dark and dangerous. "And I want to kill him because he tries to convince my sister to stop our plan, and now she is doubtful. She wants to stay with you." Zappa's lips curled, and he spat on the floor, his focus on Paul. "But you will not have her."

"She has a good heart."

Mr. Zappa took another step forward.

Grace swallowed through her dry throat and grounded her body, feet steadied for an attack. She stood between Zappa and Paul because the latter was in no shape to fight, and even if he did have some ability left in him—Grace looked at him from her periphery—she doubted he'd use it for anything more than running away.

Well, hobbling away.

"If you move to the side, Lady Astley, I will let you live." Zappa raised a brow in challenge and took another step forward. "This was my last stop before I join the others, you see?"

"I doubt you will let me go regardless, Mr. Zappa"—she

frowned—"or whoever you are. So I'll stay where I am, thank you."

He stood taller, raising his chin. "I am Nico Bartoli, grandson of Luca Accardi, and this island is *my* rightful inheritance, not some house of games for your Americano." His gaze darkened, and with almost catlike speed, he lunged toward her.

Grace stepped to the side in time to miss the man's knife, and then, as Frederick had taught her, she brought her parasol down with two-handed strength upon Mr. Zappa. . .er. . .Bartoli's arm.

His knife jostled free from his hold, and Grace would have smiled at the fact her attack had actually worked if Mr. Bartoli hadn't spun around toward her with such speed. Without warning, the back of his hand made contact with her cheek. Pain shot through her face and blurred her vision.

A noise from Paul must have distracted Bartoli from an immediate attack because he turned toward the wounded man, giving Grace full access to his back. What had Frederick said about weak points? Back of the neck. Knees.

Bartoli must have supposed his hit had either caused Grace to back away or knocked her senseless enough for him to lower his guard, which certainly worked in her favor. Though, she had to admit, her face stung and a few tears may have shot into her eyes for a moment.

Paul cried out as the man approached, and Grace stifled an eye roll, the motion and annoyance removing all tears. If Paul had only taken advantage of Mr. Bartoli's distraction, he could have picked up the discarded knife. Clearly, he had not been reading self-defense books. Or at the very least detective fiction.

She took the parasol in hand like a baseball bat and with all her might slammed it into the back of the man's legs. Mr. Bartoli cried out and stumbled forward.

"Grab the knife, Mr. Hopewell," she called, but Paul only shielded his face with his arms and attempted to sink into the chair.

"I'm done with you," Mr. Bartoli growled, releasing a long string of Italian Grace was certain she didn't want to have translated. He lunged forward, bypassing her next hit with the end of her parasol, and grabbed her by the left arm, his fingers pinching tight.

She bit back a cry. He twisted hard, and her knees gave way. The very idea he'd resurrected her tears made her angry.

"I will have no mercy now, Signora." He loomed over her, his features distorted into almost monstrous proportions. He would kill her and then Mr. Hopewell. She had to respond accordingly.

With a quick move of her free hand, she brought the parasol up into his stomach, and as he buckled, she jabbed the end toward his face. The contact caused a horrible cracking sound, and Mr. Bartoli covered his nose with both hands.

The chest still stood open behind Paul, and an idea formed.

"Quick, Paul. Help me."

But Paul didn't move, and Grace thought about giving the man a good jab along with Mr. Bartoli. Turning the parasol around in her hand, she sent another hit into Mr. Bartoli's exposed middle with the wooden hook. He stumbled back a step toward the trunk, and with a little twist to her parasol, she caught him by the shirt.

As Bartoli stumbled, Paul seemed to catch on to the idea, because he gave Bartoli a solid shove, and the villain's calves hit the edge of the trunk, causing him to lose his balance. With a loud crash, he fell backward into the trunk. Grace rushed forward with Paul hobbling to her side, and despite Bartoli's struggles and with another hit from her parasol along his knees, the trunk lid clicked into place, locking him, quite unhappily, inside.

Grace sat down on top of the trunk and pressed her palm against her chest, her breath and pulse pounding at the same rate.

They'd gotten him.

And she wasn't dead.

Those were two excellent truths.

Though she did wish Frederick or Jack had been there to witness her use of self-defense with a parasol. She frowned. Well, Frederick probably wouldn't have enjoyed it very much in the moment, but he'd have been so proud afterward.

She felt certain Jack would have cheered.

Jack!

"Paul, what did you say about where Jack was? Do you remember?"

Paul pushed a shaking hand through his hair. "I. . .I'm not certain. Something about the gods."

Grace stood from the trunk and swept down to bring Mr. Bartoli's knife into her hands. Never let a possible weapon go wasted. That was another point in Jack's book.

"Are. . .are you going to just leave him there?" Paul looked over at the chest where Mr. Bartoli still released long strings of words Grace was pleased to say she didn't understand.

"Yes, except I'm going to put a lot of those books on top of the trunk in case Mr. Bartoli is trained in lock picking as well as murder." She moved to the next room and brought back a stack of books that she deposited on top of the trunk. "And then. . ."

She left the room and came back. "You're going to find a servant to tie up the trunk until the police arrive."

"What. . .what are you going to do?"

What was she going to do? Find Jack?

She went to retrieve more books, and as she started back, her gaze moved to the windows that lined the room. The garden bloomed with all colors of flowers, completely oblivious to all the trouble and darkness happening inside the house. And then she stopped. At the edge of the garden stood the statue of Jupiter and Juno in an embrace, the edifice Accardi had erected to symbolize protection for him and his family on his beautiful island.

Grace came to a stop. *At the feet of the gods?*

The statue had to be at least twenty feet around at the square base. And the base stood four feet at least. She rushed into the next room and placed another set of books on the trunk. "Paul, I have a feeling I know where Jack is." She moved to hold the man around the waist and support him as he walked. "If I help you to the sitting room, can you call a servant from there?"

She urged him forward while he muttered. "What?"

"And if Lord Astley arrives before me, please tell him that I've gone to the gods in the garden."

"The gods in the garden," he repeated with a squeak, staring at her as if she were mad.

Well, now that she thought about it, she'd rather be mad than a coward.

She paused and looked up at the man. "I really think you should spend more time reading."

Chapter 21

The path down the cliffside took too long and proved a more treacherous endeavor than Frederick imagined. Rocks jutted into the path, causing Frederick to edge around them with extra care so as not to fall down the cliffside to the sea.

As he neared the bottom and the rocks grew increasingly more hazardous from the ocean mist, he listened for any sound of voices, but the crashing waves drowned out other sounds. The path ended at the entrance of a crevice in the cliff wall. Frederick withdrew his pistol and stepped through the space. A few man-made steps moved down between the rocks, and then he stepped out into a large cavern with rock walls rising on almost every side. Various cave entrances embedded the walls, most of the lower entrances partially underwater. He stepped forward, keeping his body in the shadows as daylight spilled from above, glistening off the pool in the center of the caves. More water rushed in from the wall open to the sea, filling the area with each passing second.

A shot rang out from Frederick's right, followed by a woman's cry. Frederick dashed toward the sounds coming from one of the caves with a strange rock outcropping in the center. As he grew closer, the rock formation took the shape of a bird.

A burst of air released from him.

Sparrow.

Beneath the left wing of the rock sparrow.

If the bird was facing him, the wing would be on the right. And there, partially hidden near one of the rocks, was a small motorboat. Possibly the same one he'd seen leaving the ferry.

Which meant the people he was likely looking for were still here.

And in that cave.

With careful movements, he waded into the cool water, nearly waist deep. Dipping his head so that the water swelled to chest level, he entered the cave. The ground inclined, bringing the water to a few inches at his feet, but the waves promised more.

A water-covered path moved between various-sized rocks in the cave, leading the way toward raised voices. A woman's? Frederick slid as silently forward as possible, edging behind a boulder at the curve of the path.

When he peered around the rock, he froze. Jack lay on the ground, blood stains on his shirt, his body partially covered in water. Thankfully, he lay on somewhat elevated ground, or he'd likely be submerged. Miss Whitby sat at his side, attempting to block Jack's chest with her hand.

A man stood between Frederick and Jack, facing away and pointing a gun in Jack's direction.

"Victor," cried a woman from just beyond Jack. "Behind you."

The man turned, revealing the face of Mr. Finch. He fired a shot. Frederick dove behind the rock, the bullet ricocheting off the stones near Frederick's head.

"We have to get out of here," Mrs. Reynolds called in French. "We have no time for these distractions."

"I cannot understand your French, Beatrice," Finch barked back. "You know that. Ten years together and I still can't understand."

"We must get out of here," she repeated, enunciating each word in English. "The water is rising, and we haven't much time."

Good. Mr. Finch was distracted.

Frederick peered around the rock and fired. Mr. Finch cried out as the bullet struck his leg, and the man fired another shot back in Frederick's direction.

Suddenly, a woman's cry burst into the silence.

"Lord Astley," came Mrs. Reynolds' calm, cool voice, her French accent curling around his name.

A chill traveled up Frederick's spine as he peered back around the rock. Mrs. Reynolds stood in the path, her gaze fixed on him, a terrible smile on her face. In her arms, she held a bleeding Lydia Whitby with a revolver pressed to Lydia's temple.

"There is only one way out of this cave, and you are blocking our exit. We did not go through the last two years of planning to fail now." She tightened her hold, and Lydia winced.

Blood stained Lydia's right shoulder and one side of her head, but she continued to struggle.

"If your plans hadn't been so ruthless, Mrs. Reynolds, we may not be in this predicament. You left quite the trail of bodies."

"My name is Beatrice Russo, Lord Astley." Her smile lit, wicked. "We did what was necessary to obtain what we deserve." She raised a brow to him, pressing the gun more tightly against Lydia's head, causing her to cease her struggle. "And you are going to move away from the exit to allow us to pass, or I will dispatch your friend here, and Victor will finish with Detective Miracle."

Frederick glanced to the right, where Mr. Finch had raised Jack to a sitting position, gun pressed to the back of his head.

What else could he do?

He held Jack's gaze and lowered his pistol to his side.

"I thought you seemed the reasonable sort," Mrs. Reynolds—Russo—said. "In all honesty, Lord Astley, I've tired of this game and am quite ready for Victor and I to live the rest of our married lives somewhere far away from here." She kept her hold on Lydia and moved down the path. "Lucia, bring the *brouette*."

The girl attempted to move the wheelbarrow, but whatever weighed it down refused to budge.

Mrs. Russo groaned. "Victor."

Before Frederick could do anything, Victor hit Jack across the head with the pistol, sending his friend sprawling on the ground, face first in the water. Frederick rushed forward, but Mrs. Russo cocked the hammer of the pistol in her hand.

"Not so fast, my lord." She gestured with her chin to Victor. "One more step and poor Miss Whitby will take the same journey as Mr. Reynolds, or should I say Mr. Parker."

She gestured with her chin toward the lifeless body nearby, knife jutting from his chest.

Frederick slid to a stop as Victor took the wheelbarrow from the younger woman, who Frederick assumed was Lucia Bartoli. The young woman followed behind Victor, her head down like a lamb led by her captors. Mrs. Reynolds passed Frederick, dragging a wounded Lydia with her.

Lydia held Frederick's gaze, and then, just as Mrs. Reynolds made it past Frederick, Lydia brought her heel down on the other woman's foot.

The woman released her hold, and Lydia dove forward, shoving Frederick behind a boulder as a shot rang out.

They both landed with a splash into the rising water behind the rock.

"We've got to get to Jack," Lydia shouted, pushing up from Frederick's body.

Another shot ricocheted off the rock, and Lydia dropped back to the ground.

"We won't do any good for him by getting shot in the process." Frederick looked around the rock, noting Mrs. Russo's lowered position by the cave entrance, which was now very close to being fully blocked with water.

Mr. Russo and Miss Bartoli must have created a type of assembly line to remove the bags from the wheelbarrow to the boat, because all Frederick could see through the remaining cave entrance was Mr. Russo, chest deep in water, handing one bag after another up to Martina—Lucia—in the motorboat.

Mrs. Russo fired another shot, causing Frederick to draw his head back behind the rock. Her shots were biding time for them to load the gold, but each second proved detrimental to Jack.

"We have to do something," Lydia demanded.

Frederick scanned the area. A rock, large enough behind which to hide, stood to one side of Jack. If he could just make it there, perhaps he could pull Jack behind the rock with him. How many shots had Mrs. Russo fired already? Four?

"Do you know how to use a pistol?"

Lydia's gaze sharpened, and she looked down at the gun in Frederick's hand. "I. . .I have before."

"Mrs. Russo has two more shots left from her revolver before she will need to reload."

Lydia looked from Frederick to Jack, her expression coming alive. "I can run to Jack in the interval."

"I'd prefer you remain here, but keep Mrs. Russo distracted with your shots."

"I'm not certain about my aim."

"Your aim isn't what's important." He pushed the gun in her hand. "Your goal is to keep Mrs. Russo distracted while I run toward Jack."

"Well, if I hit her, it will just make me feel better," Lydia murmured, taking the gun.

For some reason, Frederick had a quick sense of gratitude that Lydia and Grace hadn't become friends just yet.

"Ready?"

She gave a curt nod and positioned the pistol, rising enough to begin firing. At Mrs. Russo's ready return, Frederick counted. *One. Two.*

Click.

Frederick took one look in Mrs. Russo's direction and ran toward Jack, grabbing him around the waist and pulling him behind the boulder with only a few seconds to spare before another shot fired toward him.

Frederick turned Jack on his side. He coughed but seemed no worse for the wear—as far as Frederick could tell. His chest pumped up and down in a reassuring way, but he didn't envy the headache Jack would have when he awakened.

Frederick pulled Jack up against the nearby boulder and out of the swelling water, attempting to keep them both upright.

Silence stilled the moment. Nothing except the sound of water coming into the cave.

Frederick leaned forward to look around the boulder only to find the entrance void of Mrs. Russo but filled with a rush of water coming into the cave. How much more water, Frederick had no idea. Enough to fill the cave?

Lydia stood from her spot, looking from the entrance to Frederick and then down at the water now rushing over her knees.

She pushed through the water toward him. "We have to get out of here."

Frederick glanced back toward the other end of the cave, but the cave ended in a large rock wall about fifty feet back. There were no openings above that he could see.

He sighed and gestured with his chin toward the closing cave entrance. "The only way out is through the mouth of the cave."

Lydia followed his attention and then looked back at him. Her eyes widened, and for the first time, a flash of fear quivered over her face. "Lord Astley." She drew in a breath. "I can't swim."

Secret doors were the most delightful discoveries.

Evidently, Signore Accardi had liked them too.

Grace pushed back a rather prickly bush at the base of the gods' statue, following the indentation she'd noticed just below Jupiter's feet. The first direction led to nothing of consequence. As Grace followed the second, it led behind a pair of prickly bushes, and hidden behind them stood a small wooden door barely four feet high.

Perhaps the experience was a little like she imagined Mary Lennox might have felt when she first discovered the door to the secret garden. Grace glanced around her, the ocean breeze wonderfully cool and the sun shining down on myriad plants and Roman-style decor. Well, the atmosphere was likely different.

Oh, Grace hoped she didn't have to locate a lost key too. Time was of the essence. If the villains found their treasure, they'd likely dispatch any loose ends. She took the ring handle and gave the door a budge. At first it didn't move, but with a little harder push, the door scratched against the stone floor and opened into. . .complete blackness. Apart from the frame on which the door set, Grace didn't even see a floor but a gaping emptiness downward.

Well, this wouldn't work at all.

With a little tilt, she peered down into the blackness. Was it some sort of trap? She pulled back. Had Jack been dropped into this pit?

That didn't make any sense at all!

She scanned the space around the outside of the door, and her attention caught on a little tuft of rope nestled behind one of the prickly bushes. After a few scratches and one or two unladylike comments about the bush, Grace drew out the item and realized it was a rope ladder. Upon further inspection, she discovered two impressive hooks at the base of the doorframe, from which the ladder must hang.

She looked back down into the darkness, the memory of falling into an undiscovered tomb rushing to mind. With a quick check to her satchel, confirming a candle and matches, and a prayer for strength and that the ladder actually reached the bottom of something less sinister than she imagined, she tossed the ladder down into the abyss.

Now, what to do with the parasol? If she hooked it over her arm, it would get caught in the ladder. On the strap of her satchel would prove the same trouble. Finally, she ended up hooking it on the back neck of her dress. Even if it bounced against her backside on the way down the ladder, at least she'd have it for any possible fights.

With a wobbly step and a firm grip on the hooks, she began her descent.

Rope ladders weren't her favorite.

Of course, she'd been on ladders before. Her grandfather allowed her to climb, swing, swim, build, and indulge in all sorts of other very "unladylike" things, but this gangly experience of a rope ladder was a first. She actually appreciated the dark for a whole new set of reasons. If Jack lay at the bottom of this pit, he'd appreciate not getting a view of her wrestling on the rope. *Unladylike* would be one of the nicer words he'd probably choose to describe the scene.

And it's a good thing Frederick wasn't here. He'd been a victim of her rope swinging once before, and she felt certain he'd rather not repeat the experience.

The worst part proved that only after two rungs and a wild twist, her precious parasol plummeted into the darkness and created a rather noisy clatter below.

Her shoulders drooped. Well, at least the hole had a bottom.

And since she didn't hear anyone groan from impact, she hadn't impaled poor Jack.

The small light from above still hovered in the distance like a rectangular moon when her feet finally felt something solid. She steadied herself, keeping hold of the ladder with one hand until she felt sure the ground wouldn't give way, and she reached into her satchel and withdrew a candle and matches.

Light flickered and then steadied, small within the vast dark space, but enough for Grace to make out the surroundings. Apparently, she'd come down into a tall room hidden inside the cliff. Two chairs stood in the center of the room, back to back, with ropes of various lengths scattered on the floor. She leaned down and took up a piece of the rope.

Cut?

Had someone been held here? Jack?

She looked back up the way she'd come. But there was no way for him to escape through the little door unless the ladder had been lowered, which seemed unlikely since she'd found it stowed at the top. She retrieved her parasol and stood, taking closer inventory of the room. The candlelight flickered against the stone walls, highlighting a curve in one end of the space.

Why she chose to approach quietly didn't make any sense, because anyone hiding in the darkness would have been alerted to her descent by the noise of the parasol, but she still felt the urge to toe-step toward the curve.

A stone stairway led downward, deeper into the cliff. She sighed. Well, the only way to find out if Jack escaped in this direction was to follow the steps. She looked back at the rope ladder. She'd much prefer steps to rope ladders. Speaking of ropes. . . Her attention fell on the tangle of ropes on the floor, with another ream lying at the back corner of the room.

It would be hard to keep hold of her parasol and the rope, but having a rope seemed like an excellent idea, especially after her previous experiences with villainesses and tombs.

The stairs led through a stone passage and finally spilled out into a cavernous place, with sunlight blinking down from an open space in the cliff-framed cove. A roaring sound pulled her attention to the right, where a motorboat waited with Martina, rather Lucia, inside. Mr. Finch was placing a bag in the boat, his body nearly neck deep in the water in front of a sliver of a cave opening. Gunfire erupted from nearby, and Grace slipped behind the nearest rock, peering around, but neither Lucia nor Mr. Finch appeared concerned. He handed her another bag, which seemed rather heavy, and she put it in the boat.

Suddenly, out of the cave opening, bobbing in the water, emerged Mrs. Reynolds—or as Grace now knew her, Beatrice Russo.

"One is wounded and unconscious. He won't be easy to move," she called over the motor as Mr. Finch assisted her into the motorboat. "We'll be long gone before they escape to follow us."

"If they are even able to get out before the tide fills the cave," came Mr. Finch's response.

Grace's attention flew to the cave entrance from which Mrs. Russo had just come. Water nearly covered the entrance.

Lucia asked a question in Italian, which Grace didn't fully comprehend, but she heard the name Nico.

"We will bring the boat around to the back of the villa," Mrs. Russo replied in English, evidently for Mr. Finch's benefit. "He knows to meet us there if anything goes amiss."

"Do not worry. Your brother knows what to do."

Grace breathed out a sigh. At least Grace knew *something* ahead of the villains. Nico Bartoli would not be meeting them. Her shoulders slumped. Well, she hoped not. Not unless he knew how to pick locks very quickly or Mr. Hopewell failed to fulfill his end of the plan.

The motorboat puttered away, barely staying above the waterline as it moved slowly out of the cavern into open water. Almost any water vehicle could catch their motorboat at that speed. Something weighed it down besides the people.

Had there truly been a treasure?

As the boat disappeared around the edge of the cliff, Grace ran forward, surveying the situation. Someone was wounded inside the cave, and she had a sneaking suspicion Jack was one of the people inside.

A Jules Verne *Nautilus* or diving suit would have come in handy. How thick was the cave wall? If she had to hold her breath to get underneath it, would she be able to make it to the other side?

Surely! She'd always been a good swimmer, and her grandfather had often told her she must have excellent lung capacity for the amount of time she could talk about books without stopping.

She lowered the rope to the ground and reluctantly released her parasol. She should also leave the satchel behind because swimming would prove difficult enough in her day dress. Wait. She paused in her movements to relinquish the rope. What if she created a connection between the outside of the cave and the inside? Then, if they had a wounded person, it would make getting out easier, wouldn't it? Sort of a guide to get from one side to the other while pulling an unconscious or wounded person?

She looked near the entrance, where a tooth-shaped stone jutted up from the rocky ground. With quick hands, she tied one end of the rope around the stone, securing it in such a way her grandfather would have been proud. Then, with a longing look to her parasol, she stepped down into the water.

Her shoes weren't meant for slippery rocks, because she immediately spilled down the slope and went fully under. The cool water rushed over her, snatching her breath, but she also caught sight of something underwater in her periphery. She resurfaced, took a breath, and went back under. The clearness of the water allowed for longer views than back home in America. Wreckage from boats of the past littered the bottom, with wooden slabs or small masts jutting up like knives and shards from the darkness below.

The scene held a fascinating mix of frightening and fascinating. Hadn't someone mentioned this area being a place for pirates? Were those wrecks from boats long ago?

She shook off her distraction and resurfaced. Taking a tighter hold on the rope, she swam toward the cave entrance.

Even now, only a few inches of unsubmerged opening showed at the cave's arch. Well, at least she could take one last breath before swimming forward in blind faith. It was a good thing God knew what was ahead, because she clearly didn't.

With a deep breath, she ducked below the small space of cave not yet covered. Below the surface and rocky cave ceiling, she swam, one arm pulling her through, the other holding to the rope. The latter trailed behind her, slowing her progress as she attempted to keep it from dropping low enough to become entangled with the wreckage below her feet.

The thinness of her tea dress likely kept from slowing her down even more, but trousers would have proved more suitable for swimming. She refused to take another look below her feet at the wreckage because for some reason it made her think of vengeful mermaids and sea ghosts. Instead, she focused ahead.

A soft glow rose above her—some sort of light source. She had to be getting close to the opening. The sound of voices blended through the water, and then she had the unnerving realization that she wasn't 100 percent certain who waited on the other side of the cave.

She faltered. Another detriment of her impulsiveness. But surely, if anyone was shooting at Mrs. Russo, it had to be someone who at least knew about her subterfuge. Besides, she didn't have enough air to turn around now.

The cave ceiling opened, and with a little trepidation, she surfaced far enough that only her head broke the water.

"The water is continuing to rise," came a woman's voice. American accent. Was that Lydia Whitby? "Do you think it fills this cave in full tide?"

Grace couldn't see over the lip of the rock in front of her, but she knew the man who gave a response.

"I'm not certain, but I fear we shouldn't wait to find out. The deeper we have to dive to fit beneath the cave entrance, the longer we must hold our breath."

Frederick.

"But I already told you," came the woman's reply, a hint of tension in her words, "I can't swim."

Grace grabbed the rock ledge with her swimming hand and pulled herself up enough to see over.

"Frederick," Grace called, attempting to get her elbow up on the ledge without slipping and losing her hold on the rope.

"Grace?" came his familiar voice.

Oh, how she loved her name on his lips, even if it had that sort of bewildered tone to it.

"I'm here." She slipped from her precarious perch back into the water.

When she resurfaced, Frederick stood staring down at her, his expression as bewildered as his voice. "Darling, what? How?" Evidently, he couldn't quite finish his sentences.

Grace wanted to think it was because she looked so fetching coming from the water like a beautiful mermaid. Or that he found her creative abilities rather breathtaking, brave, and appealing.

But in reality, she likely looked a fright, wearing a soaking tea dress and holding a rope, with her hair in wild red curls all around her pale face. *Dear me, I sounded like a sea ghost!*

"Would you take this, please?" She offered him the rope.

He tilted his head in a curious manner and took the rope in one hand and in the other took her hand. With a strong tug, he pulled her up and into his hold, his clothes much warmer and drier than hers. She nestled close to appreciate his warmth for a little longer. He didn't seem to mind for he tightened his hold.

"Lady Astley?" Lydia stumbled forward, her eyes wide. "You. . .you swam here?"

Grace pulled back, offering her darling husband a smile before turning to Lydia. "I saw Mrs. Russo, Mr. Finch, and Lucia leave in the boat. They talked about someone being wounded." Her gaze skimmed over the path to land on the very still face of Mr. Reynolds, a knife protruding from his chest. His body began to float a little from the influx of water.

Oh, poor Mr. Reynolds.

"Jack." Frederick nudged her forward and readied to lay down the rope.

"No, wait." She took the rope back in hand. "Don't let go of it. We need to tie it somewhere."

"What?" He searched her face, then looked down at the rope, a sudden light dawning in his eyes. "As a guide under the cave?" His grin split wide, and he leaned down and kissed her full on the mouth. "You're brilliant."

Well, perhaps brilliance overshadowed a sea ghost.

He took the rope back in hand and proceeded to tie it around another boulder nearby. "Miss Whitby can't swim, so this will certainly assist her as well as give us a bit of bearing while getting Jack across."

"Can't we just wait it out and see if the water stops?" Lydia looked from Grace to Frederick and back.

"I heard Mr. Finch mention that the cave fills with water." Grace looked over to see poor Jack propped against a rock, his head dipped to the right and blood on his forehead and shirt. "I don't know if we can trust what he says, but it would be worse to gamble with the fact and be wrong."

"We need to get Jack through as soon as we can because there's still a little patch of air at the cave arch, but it won't last long." Frederick moved toward Jack with Grace beside him. "Jack won't waken, so he can't hold his breath."

"It's closing quickly though, Frederick." She reached on one side of Jack as Frederick went to the other, both raising him up beneath his arms and moving to the water's edge. "He may still breathe in water."

"We'll have to take that chance." He looked at the ground, water now to midcalf. "Because if Mr. Finch is right, then this is likely only to get worse and take even longer to swim out."

Lydia rushed to help them with Jack and carefully, with Frederick getting into the water, they lowered Jack onto his back.

"I'll try to keep us near the roof of the cave as long as possible." His gaze met hers. "And pray we get through quickly enough."

"Be careful." Grace relinquished her hold on Jack, and the unconscious man floated on his back with his head resting on Frederick's shoulder. "There are heaps of wreckage just below the surface. Broken boats. A sharp mast for a small boat."

He studied her face and gave a nod, then looked back to Lydia. "Grace will get you through, Miss Whitby." His gaze found Grace's. "Take care, darling."

Something in his look, his unvoiced words, spilled added strength through her. She nodded to him as he pushed off, skimming the rope with his body to keep his direction straight as he swam backward.

Lydia's face was pale, her breathing shallow, but she raised her chin and focused her full attention on Grace. "What do I do?"

Yes, she like Lydia Whitby even more.

"We'll swim above water as long as we can, but there will be a point where you'll have to go under." Grace moved with her to the edge where the ground began a descent deeper into the water. "Keep hold of the rope all the way through, and it will get us both to the other side." She turned to Lydia. "The wall thickness isn't as bad as it could have been, so you shouldn't have any trouble holding your breath."

"I'm not worried about holding my breath." Lydia nodded, looking down at the water as if preparing for battle. "My step-father had gotten me up to six minutes underwater when trying to unfasten myself from chains. Unfortunately, he never taught me to swim."

Grace started to ask about Lydia's fascinating experience but decided the conversation should likely wait until a more convenient time. "You go on ahead of me, and I'll follow behind you to help if you need it."

Lydia started forward, her left hand holding to the rope and her right moving through the water.

"And if you push your free hand like this"—Grace threaded her hand through the water—"it will help you move a bit faster."

Lydia imitated her form, giving a little boost to her pace.

Grace looked up to find Jack and Frederick had vanished, the last bit of space beneath the opening gone. Her heart pulsed faster, a prayer repeating through her head. *Be with them, Lord.*

She focused her attention on the back of Lydia's golden head. "And help us too."

Grace gave space as Lydia moved forward, deeper until her feet no longer felt rock and she raised into swimming position.

"Okay, time to go under," Grace called ahead of her, and with that, Lydia disappeared beneath the water, her hair flaring about her as she did.

A moment later, Grace took a deep breath and followed.

Unlike an experienced swimmer, Lydia attempted to keep her body straight, her feet slicing back and forth as if walking. The frantic movements of her right hand caused bubbles to obscure Grace's view, or she might have caught the problem before it happened.

Lydia jerked to a stop. The bubbles cleared, and Grace met Lydia's wide-eyed look. Lydia shook her head and looked down. The spear-like mast jutting upward, with chains twisted around it, had somehow caught the bottom of Lydia's gown. Lydia gave her skirt a strong tug.

In response, the chains began unbraiding from their hold on the wood, slowly dropping deeper into the water. Lydia began sinking. The chains unwound further, pulling Lydia down even more.

Lydia's wide eyes found Grace's.

A sudden fear erupted in Grace's stomach—the same feeling she remembered from the sand crashing in on her. The same inner mantra shouting to her, "Don't breathe or you'll die."

She couldn't panic. She needed a clear head. With the same reminder as she'd told herself when locked in the chest, she began attempting to catch the wild thoughts, taming them with words of truth. Focusing on the matter at hand.

If she didn't do something, they both were going to die.

She turned and pressed her feet against the cave wall to propel herself downward.

The chains released another link. Lydia sank even more. Bubbles swelled from the moving chains, making it difficult for Grace to find exactly where Lydia's skirt stuck to the chains.

But she needed to find it soon.

Because neither one of them could hold their breath forever.

Chapter 22

Frederick pulled Jack from the water, the man's silence more concerning than anything else at the moment. They'd been underwater longer than Frederick had hoped.

He leaned over Jack's body, cheek against Jack's nose. A chill traveled up Frederick's neck.

Nothing.

Jack wasn't breathing.

With quick work, Frederick loosened Jack's collar, steadied his head, and drew from some of the newer training he'd learned when stationed in India. What new method had the doctor suggested for a drowning victim? Chest compressions?

Braiding his fingers together, he pressed into Jack's chest and released. He wasn't certain how many times to compress, but he completed a few and then went to the next step. Pumping the victim's arms.

He took Jack's arms and pumped them up and down in synchrony a few times before starting compressions again. On the third set of compressions, Jack started coughing up water. Frederick immediately turned Jack on his side, steadying him as Jack expelled water from his saturated lungs.

Frederick provided support for Jack as he continued to

cough—a good sign and certainly a much better prognosis than the alternative. He looked up toward the cave entrance, now completely submerged, anticipating his wife's and Miss Whitby's imminent appearance.

Giving Jack another pat on the back, Frederick studied the water. A sudden burst of bubbles surfaced but not a person. Steadying Jack against one of the rocks, Frederick stood in time to see Miss Whitby emerge, both her hands clinging to the rope.

He rushed into the water, meeting her.

"My. . .my gown became entwined in the wreckage," she puffed out the words. "She. . .she went—"

Frederick didn't wait for Miss Whitby to finish but dove into the water. Myriad horrible scenarios flashed through his mind in a second. Skewered by a jagged mast? Trapped in wreckage and sinking to the bottom of the cavern?

His eyes adjusted to the water in time to see a mass of pale blue moving upward.

Grace.

He followed, surfacing directly after her.

Her ginger hair covered part of her face as she coughed and attempted to swim toward the land. Frederick came up behind her, taking her by the arm and giving her some support, tension uncoiling from his shoulders with the feel of her alive and well beside him.

As soon as they both set their feet on dry ground, he turned her to face him, pushing her hair back from her face.

"Her. . .her dress became caught," Grace whispered, a small cough escaping her quivering lips.

"I know."

"I couldn't just leave her."

"No, of course not."

"I hate to say it, Frederick, but it's another situation in favor of women wearing—"

He caught her mouth with his, her cool lips surrendering to his need. It didn't matter if Miss Whitby watched from her spot beside Jack. Or if Jack roused to a front-row view of husband kissing wife. All that mattered was, despite the circumstances, God had given them one more day together.

"I say, it looks as if someone is celebrating." Jack's rasped words brought Frederick's attention around to see his friend sitting upright, eyes squinted, and a crooked smile on his lips. "Did we win?"

"We did, Jack." Frederick looked back down at Grace. "For what matters most, we definitely won."

Jack waited in the hotel's lounge, his trunk poised nearby, awaiting transport to the train then subsequent steamer back to England. His side thrummed with a residual ache and so did his head, but in all honesty, he'd survived worse.

He only wished he had a clearer memory of what had happened inside the cave. Flashes of scenes came to mind now and again, but he failed to catch them long enough for a clear sequence of events. What he *did* remember was Lydia Whitby's knife skills, Mr. Finch shooting him, and the real existence of treasure.

His thoughts poised on Lydia Whitby, followed by an unnerving knot in his throat.

After they'd returned to the villa to find Inspector Verga and his police arresting Mrs. Reynolds-Russo, Mr. Finch (who turned out to be her real husband, Mr. Victor Russo), and Lucia Bartoli, Lady Astley had shown them the way to Nico Bartoli. The man's fight had gone out of him, and he surrendered to the authorities quite humbly. Of course, spending a few hours cramped inside a trunk without promise of rescue could likely humble a great many people.

Mr. Finch, or Mr. Russo, as the case may be, proved to be one of the servants at the home of a neighbor of Jack's father, one of the *Juliet* victims. Only at Mrs. Chambers' house, he'd taken the name Mr. Anderson. It would make sense that Mr. Finch-Anderson-Russo knew of Jack's family ties and possible family members who would pay a solid ransom, should Jack ever need one.

Thankfully, a ransom hadn't been necessary because those particular family members would hold the magnanimous rescue over his head for the rest of his life and likely accrue interest for repayment.

As for the paintings, the police recovered them from the secret room, returning Signore Capello's to him, with plans to return others to their inheritors. The gold was placed in police custody to sort out next steps, but with such a treasure, the governing body would likely need to be called in for disbursement.

With Laraby dead, whatever remained from the sale of the villa and his remaining property would go directly to paying off his debts, and according to his most recent will, any proceeds would be split three ways between Paul, Lydia, and Jasmine.

Did that mean Lydia would become an independent woman? For her sake, he hoped so. From the bits and pieces he'd heard of her relationship with Laraby and life in the circus, the woman deserved freedom and—he cleared his throat—a good man to love her.

He adjusted his hat and drew in a breath. Of course, he *wasn't* that man.

With his past record, he hadn't the capacity to delve into another commitment, and despite his laissez-faire persona, he had never learned the skill of superficial romances. He was the sort who charged in whole heart and half a brain.

So it was quite clear he was *not* ready for romance.

Even a jot.

He had too many wounds still healing from his past to offer

a full heart to a woman.

But if he were to think in the romantic direction, Lydia Whitby would be the sort to turn his head.

Intelligent. A keen sense of humor. Brave. Clearheaded under pressure.

The fact she wielded a knife well should bode poorly, but he couldn't help admiring her even more.

He groaned back into the chair, breathing in the scent of salt and some baked goods wafting in on the breeze through the open windows. After three more days in Venice, working with the local police and confirming how the suspects fit into which robbery and which murder, it was time to go home.

The mastermind behind the plan had been the former governess, Mrs. Reynolds-Russo, but she'd pulled her husband into the scheme and, it seemed, had even nurtured the bitterness and desire for revenge in the two children. Evidently, Accardi had left a letter for her when he went off in search of his murderous son-in-law, detailing the way to note the clues to the treasure and hinting to the whereabouts of certain specifics that only a person closely connected to the family would have known.

Thus, the reason the treasure remained elusive and nearly fictional.

Mr. Reynolds, whose name actually was Mr. Parker, had been a friend of Mr. Finch-Russo's and was brought on for a slice of the treasure. Since Mr. Finch-Russo thought he and his wife would be easier to recognize if they traveled as husband and wife, having Reynolds play the part of the husband was meant to deter possible detection of the pair.

Smart. And somewhat confusing in hindsight.

Lucia Bartoli seemed the least involved of them all, so perhaps some good could come from the devastation of the Accardi family. In fact, none of the murders or thefts were placed at her feet, though she'd assisted in them.

The sudden scent of lavender brushed over the air, pulling Jack's attention from the open window to scan the room. Hadn't Lydia stayed at the villa to finalize everything with Paul?

Yet she materialized before him, stepping into the room dressed in a simple brown walking suit, her hair pinned back just like the first time he'd seen her. Even her spectacles presented themselves, perched on her perfectly small nose.

Her gaze found his from across the room, the faintest of smiles softening her entire expression. His heart responded quite naturally to her presence, but he ignored giving any translation to such a response.

He stifled a groan as he stood and met her halfway across the sunlit room.

"Detective?"

His grin crooked, and he tipped his head. "Miss Whitby?"

They stared at each other, neither speaking, but the air took on a thicker, sweeter quality.

Lydia looked away.

"I thought you would need to be at the villa for a while yet."

She looked back at him, her smile sad. "As Laraby's secretary, I already know his finances and what paltry funds will be available to us. I'll stay to assist in the rest of the investigation and settling his affairs, but then I mean to leave Italy."

He rubbed the back of his neck to keep from touching her arm in comfort. "You have nothing, then?"

Her brow pinched, and she offered a humorless chuckle. "I have what I've saved, which is a mercy. And at the end of it all, I'll have enough to get myself started somewhere new, so there's that, at least."

He shoved his hands in his pockets just to have something to do. Why on earth he felt so unnerved, he had no idea. It was a simple conversation. He engaged in them daily. Sometimes, to his dismay, hourly. "Where. . .where do you wish to go?"

Her gaze flashed back to his. "I don't know. Start over somewhere. I have excellent references from John's. . .um. . .Laraby's grandfather, so I suppose I could take up as a secretary for someone."

He stepped closer, watching how the light from the window shone off her golden hair. His chest constricted. Truly, if he was going to fall in love, she'd tempt him beyond reason. He needed to step back. Distance himself from her.

In all honesty, he barely knew the woman. A handful of conversations and a near-death experience did not mean entangled hearts.

And shouldn't.

And then, in complete rebellion to his thoughts, his mouth took control. "I have a proposal for you, Miss Whitby."

What was he doing?

Her eyes widened, the green depths glimmering in the sunlight as if she were asking the same question. "A. . .a proposal?"

"Yes." He cleared his throat. Stepping fully into his lunacy, the idea emerged with more solidity with each second. "A solid, thoughtful proposal for a woman with your. . .skills."

"With my skills?" She gave her head a solid shake. "Detective, I am not so desperate as to be in search of a husband—"

Husband? His face burst into flames. "Wait, please." He raised his palm. "Not that sort of proposal."

"What?" Her breathless response both tempted him and left him wary.

She'd have turned down marriage swiftly if his proposal had been in that vein. But why? He was a stable, somewhat intelligent, wealthy man with enough good humor to keep himself alive for a while yet. Quite marriageable, even if his romantic past didn't bode well, though at present he wasn't seeking matrimony. At all. Ridiculous notion, actually.

Her shocked expression drew him back to the point. Proposal. Yes. But what sort of proposal had he meant? The answer rose to the forefront of his mind as if it had been waiting in the far recesses of his head to be noticed.

"I'm in need of a secretary."

"A secretary?" Her eyes narrowed, her shoulders relaxing. "Are you?"

"But more than that"—the words tumbled forward before he caught them—"I'm looking for a partner."

"A partner?" she repeated, her voice a bit higher pitched than usual.

Well, he might as well commit at this point. After all, the more he thought about it, the more he liked the idea. Females could get into places men couldn't. They looked at information from a different and complementary angle. And he needed someone who could not only help keep him organized but join him in crime solving pursuits.

He steadied his attention on Lydia's rather lovely face.

Yes, a rather brillant idea, if he did say so himself.

Lydia Whitby was more partner material than secretary material to his mind.

"Well, to be honest, I've had the need for a partner for quite some time now but hesitated in truly considering the prospect because it would take a very particular sort of person to fit the bill, you see?"

Her eyes narrowed even more.

He swallowed through his dry throat. "I believe you would fit the bill."

"As your partner?" Her brow rose in challenge.

He nodded, working up the words. "Yes. You have the makings of an excellent detective, should you wish it."

She blinked, the suspicion in her eyes fading to a fairly fetching look of wonder. "Do I?"

"Indeed." He rallied to the challenge, to maintain her wonder. "You are intelligent, shrewd, quick-thinking, creative." He waved a hand toward her. "Disguises do come in handy now and again."

Her lips tipped ever so slightly, encouraging him.

"Your unique history as an illusionist should bring a great many benefits given the ability to disappear is an excellent skill for a detective."

Her smile brimmed a little more, somehow causing his chest to warm.

"And though I wouldn't wish you to be tried on a regular basis, you're rather handy with knives."

"And I'm a decent shot," she added, folding her arms across her chest. "Though I could use more practice."

He dipped his chin. "More hidden talents to prove my point."

"There aren't a great many female detectives in the world." She studied him with those enchanting eyes. "Aren't you concerned it might look bad for you?"

Her encouragement bolstered his confidence, and he relaxed. "I think you could only improve the looks of any place, Miss Whitby."

A slight flush deepened her cheeks and only made her more beautiful, and a wild tug-of-war between wanting her to accept and not wanting her to accept his proposal commenced within his chest.

Oh yes, Lydia Whitby could be the most dangerous sort of partner. . .to his heart. His smile edged crooked. But he did enjoy a little danger, didn't he?

"But in regards to there being very few female detectives, don't you think it's time for that to change?"

She didn't reply, only stared at him with those enchanting eyes of hers, made all the more enchanting by the gold rim of her spectacles—like a well-placed frame to draw attention to the masterpiece.

He released a breath and dipped his head. "Here is my card."

He reached into his jacket pocket and retrieved the card, offering it to her. "When you are ready to decide, just know you have opportunities." He held her gaze. "And friends, Miss Whitby."

She looked down at the card and then back to him. "Thank you, Jack." She raised the card in gesture. "Thank you for the proposal." Her smile flared and then softened, holding his gaze. "And for the friendship."

Grace sat on the veranda of their hotel room, book in her lap but her attention focused on the fading horizon. They'd only been in Venice a little over a week, and it seemed an entire lifetime had passed. So many amazing adventures, a new friend or two, but also an entire history of aching losses.

A father losing his wife and daughter.

Two children losing their family and inheritance.

Several people losing their lives.

A former governess losing her way.

Grace sighed back in the chair, a prayer forming in her mind for so many lost people. The bigness of the wounds settling deep, almost overwhelming her.

What could be done with such brokenness? She didn't have the ability to fully comprehend it, let alone make a difference.

In fiction the hurts may linger in memory for a few days or months but mostly end with the turn of a page; but here in real life, they twisted and stung for much longer, like her nightmares. And even though her nightmares still lingered in the shadows of her life, God had been so kind to lessen them in the light of His care and love.

And thus came the dichotomy of living in a broken world. Hurts and grace. Loss and hope.

The pain would still happen. People would still become lost. They would still wound others out of anger or hatred or selfishness. Revenge would still prove to uproot people's lives, but God had placed her and her darling husband in this very world at this very moment in this part of *His* story to bring hope.

Something in her spirit caught on the thought.

God only called her to touch those in her little part of the world in the everyday ways of bringing hope. And she and Frederick *had* made a difference. In saving Paul, Jack, Jasmine, Lydia, and maybe, in some way, Lucia Bartoli, the most sympathetic character of all the villains.

Perhaps with Grace and Frederick's testimony to what they'd witnessed, the two lost grandchildren would find some hope.

Something the world needed in a little more quantity.

Her smile tipped. She felt certain a great many people still needed her and Frederick's certain brand of hope, whether in a neighborly way or in helping solve their mysteries.

After all, she and Frederick were detectives now. Jack had said so.

As if summoned by her thoughts, her dashing husband stood on the threshold of the veranda, his grin so broad, she stood from her seat to greet him.

"You look rather pleased about something."

He attempted to temper his smile but failed, which made her grin grow even more. Oh how she loved all of him, but the few glimpses into his boyish joy delighted her beyond words.

"I hope you don't mind staying a few extra days in Venice."

"Why would I mind? Despite our recent harrowing adventures, it's a lovely city that we've barely seen."

"Quite right. And we should certainly take advantage of that." He nodded, moving close enough to settle his palm against her waist. "However, I just received word from Inspector Randolph that he is en route from Cairo to Venice with Zahra in tow, so we should see her day after tomorrow."

Their beautiful adopted daughter would be with them in two days?

"That's wonderful!" She brought her hands together in a laugh and rocked on tiptoe to kiss him. "Oh, won't she love seeing all this water and the buildings? I'm so happy she'll finally be with us."

"As am I."

Another way to bring hope to the world in a small way. Loving a child in need of a family.

Frederick led Grace inside their room to the couch. "And I have another letter that you will enjoy." He tugged an envelope from his jacket and offered it to her.

Her sister's familiar handwriting greeted her. "Oh, I am so glad! From her last letter, she spoke of how her little baby was growing and moving inside her." Grace looked up at him. "It must be such a remarkable experience. And to think, I will be an aunt within the next month."

"Perhaps we could plan a trip to see her in August or September." Frederick joined her on the couch. "That will give us time to adjust to Zahra being a part of the family and then solidify some more improvements to Havensbrooke and sort out whatever is going to happen with Elliott." He brushed a hand to her hair, subduing a rebel curl. "I know you'd love to see your father."

"Oh yes." Grace stared down at the envelope, a sudden rush of longing bringing fresh tears to her eyes. "He always seems well in his letters, but one can never trust him to be completely honest." Grace looked over at Frederick. "He's notorious for faking peace even to the detriment of his health or finances. Lillias says it's his southern American upbringing, but I do believe it's just part of who he is."

"Well, perhaps we can attempt a trip much sooner." He covered her hand with his. "For *your* peace of mind."

She smiled up at him, and he rewarded her with a tender kiss. Oh, how she loved him. The feeling pressed in her breast with such abundance, she wondered how her heart kept it all contained.

"You saw Jack off?"

Frederick nodded. "He plans to visit us at Havensbrooke when we return home." Frederick sighed and looked away. "I think he has some ideas of how to ensconce us in another one of his simple"—Frederick raised a brow—"investigations."

"And what do you think of that proposal?" She searched his face.

He squeezed her fingers. "I think if we have some sort of interest and talent to help people in this way, then, God help me, we ought to use it."

She chuckled. "I feel as though God has been growing your fortitude since marrying me, so you're likely more fit than most for such an occupation."

"Jack wanted me to give you this." He reached into his other jacket pocket, obviously ignoring her comment, and placed something in her hand.

She looked down to find a single gold coin.

"Jack knew you already had the necklace as a token of your Egyptian adventure, so he wished to contribute something to your Italian one. It's from the treasure."

She smoothed her fingers over the coin, the carving of some sort of building marking the front. "It's beautiful."

"I'm grateful to give it to you all alive and well." He brushed his fingers against her cheek. "And beautiful."

She pressed her cheek into his touch and closed her eyes, reveling in his affection, in their mutual safety. "What did you learn from the police?"

He relaxed back into the couch and rested one ankle against the opposite knee, the very picture of gentlemanly repose in his light brown suit slacks and white button-down. "Mr. and Mrs.

Russo—or Reynolds and Finch, as we knew them—appear to be the main instigators of the entire affair, so they are likely to receive the brunt of the justice. Zappa, I mean Nico Bartoli, is being charged with Laraby's death but has complied with all requests, which will be to his benefit."

"And Lucia?" The young woman's face settled in Grace's mind. So innocent in appearance.

"She's not been connected to any of the murders, so at the moment, she is seen as an accomplice only. There's a good chance the legal ramifications will be more lenient in her case, assuming she continues to comply with authorities. Jack's testimony regarding her sympathetic response to Laraby's death certainly helped her reputation among the police."

"And my account of how she saved Paul from her brother's fury?"

"Yes, as well as Paul's testimony."

"I think we can make a difference by helping people, Frederick." Grace leaned her head on his shoulder, her fingers sliding into his. "I know we haven't the power to change the world, but we can start in our little corner where God places us. To help right wrongs. Bring about justice and mercy. Sprinkle joy where it's needed."

She felt his smile more than saw it. "You certainly succeed in the latter." He sat up, turning to her and drawing her close. "I'm not saying I want to seek out similar opportunities as we've experienced over the past few weeks, but"—he drew in a breath, a glint in his eyes—"I think we should be *open* to opportunities if they arise."

"Exactly." She nodded. "As if God hand-delivered them to us. Like a present."

Something caught in his throat, his smile faltering for a second. "Your idea of gifts and mine are singularly different."

"But complementary, I'd say, just like we are." She kissed his wonderfully heroic chin. "You keep my feet grounded and I. . ."

She studied his face, searching for an answer.

"Lead me to an untimely though interesting potential death?"

She frowned, certainly not the sweet response she'd expected. "Interesting potential death?"

"Who can boast nearly dying in a collapsed Egyptian tomb or drowning in a cave of lost treasure?"

"Oh." Her bottom lip dropped. "Those are very interesting ways to potentially die."

He raised a brow, his lips tipping ever so slightly. "And you've completely disrupted my plans and peace of mind."

She narrowed her eyes at him and attempted to pull away, but he caught her hands, bringing them to his lips. "But you always provide an overwhelming amount of joy and strength to more than compensate."

"Well. . ." She gave an exaggerated sigh. "At least there's some way I'm benefiting your life instead of leading you to your most *interesting* death."

He chuckled as he cradled her face in his hands, smoothing his thumbs over her skin. "I love you, Grace. With all my heart. And whatever adventures life brings our way, I am a happy man to spend each and every one with you."

He pulled her to himself, his warm breath moving over her hair, igniting a thrill over her skin. Her body burrowed into him, reveling in his touch, in the safety of his arms. The thick scent of spice on his skin brought a heat with it, surrounding her with as much delicious closeness as his strong arms encompassing her.

His love and a lifetime of adventures?

She sighed and turned toward him for a kiss.

Oh yes! Bring them all.

Pepper Basham is an award-winning author who writes romance peppered with grace and humor. She is a native of the Blue Ridge Mountains, where her family has lived for generations. She's the mom of five kids; speech pathologist to about fifty more; lover of chocolate, jazz, and Jesus; and proud AlleyCat over at the award-winning Writer's Alley blog. Her debut historical romance novel, *The Thorn Bearer*, released in April 2015 and the second in February 2016. Her first contemporary romance debuted in April 2016.

You can connect with Pepper on her website at www.pepperdbasham.com, Facebook https://www.facebook.com/pages/Pepper-D-Basham, or Twitter at https://twitter.com/pepperbasham

A Freddie & Grace Mystery

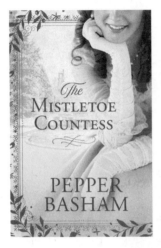

The Mistletoe Countess

When a reticent earl must marry an American heiress to save his fledgling estate, he never expects that a Christmas wedding to the wrong sister will result in a series of events that lead to a murder mystery, ghost hunt, and—the most frightening of all—the love of a lifetime. But happily-ever-after may be shorter than the newlyweds plan, when a thwarted widow has her sights set on the earl's inheritance at any cost. Packed with history, romance, mystery, and some good old-fashioned humor, *The Mistletoe Countess* offers holiday cheer and so much more.

Paperback / 978-1-64352-986-8

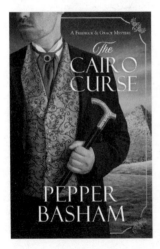

The Cairo Curse

Newlyweds Lord and Lady Astley have already experienced their fair share of suspense, but when a honeymoon trip takes a detour to the mystical land of Egypt, not even Grace with her fiction-loving mind is prepared for the dangers in store. From an assortment of untrustworthy adventure seekers to a newly discovered tomb with a murderous secret, Frederick and Grace must lean on each other to navigate their dangerous surroundings. As the suspects mount in an antiquities heist of ancient proportions, will Frederick and Grace's attempts to solve the mystery lead to another death among the sands?

Paperback / 978-1-63609-472-4

ALSO FROM PEPPER BASHAM

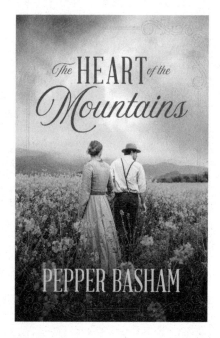

The Heart of the Mountains
To escape an arranged marriage, Cora Taylor runs away from her home in England to join her brother in the Blue Ridge Mountains of North Carolina, but not even her time as a nurse in the Great War prepares her for the hard landscape and even harder lives of the mountain people. With the help of Jeb McAdams, a quiet woodcarver, who carries his own battle scars, she fashions a place for herself among these unique people. But the past refuses to let go, and with dangers from within and without, can hearts bruised by war find healing within the wilds of the mountains?

Paperback / 978-1-63609-325-3